The Lord and the Gamekeeper

Also by Zinovy Zinik

The Mushroom Picker

ZINOVY ZINIK

The Lord and the Gamekeeper

a novel

translated from the Russian by

ALEX DE JONGE

HEINEMANN : LONDON

William Heinemann Ltd
Michelin House, 81 Fulham Road, London SW3 6RB
LONDON   MELBOURNE   AUCKLAND

First published 1991
Copyright © Zinovy Zinik 1991

A CIP catalogue record for this book
is held by the British Library
ISBN 0 434 89731 0

Phototypeset by Deltatype Ltd, Ellesmere Port
Printed in Great Britain by
St Edmundsbury Press, Bury St Edmunds, Suffolk

To my wife

You could tell at once that the author
wasn't human. He'd begin properly but
end up writing like a dog.

N. V. Gogol
Diary of a Madman

Asylum

'We are living in an age of theatrical poses and dramatic masks, which is why we insist on the need to be natural and sincere.'

'I think it has less to do with hypocrisy than with our attitude to insanity. We live in an age of vulgar sanity and like to think we're crazy.'

'On the contrary, I always thought we lived in a crazy age and supposed ourselves to be sane.'

'I think that the most telling sign of the times is the theory of relativity; whatever you say sounds more or less plausible, relatively speaking, and sometimes even true. That is particularly so concerning the plague,' said Dr Genoni in answer to the above exchange between three patients in his care – Felix, Victor and Silva. 'But, my dear friends,' he hastened to add, 'let me remind you why I have prompted you to this conversation on the subject of sanity and madness, hypocrisy and sincerity, complicity and innocence. You've been brought here on condition that, through an attempt to sort out and clarify your own Moscow past, you'd help me here in England to resolve the enigma of your liberator. Or is he your jailor? Let us not forget that we are here to find out who is our lord and who is our keeper.'

Silva casually tossed the birds a piece of walnut cake, on to the grass that the early morning fog had turned emerald green, mounted her horse and galloped off towards the big house, where Edmund (or was it actually Edward?) was recovering from a heart attack and was still unconscious. A goat moved rapidly in the direction of the piece of cake; a disciplined file of geese tried to get there first, hissing at some hens assiduously going about their business trailing behind a cock. The stallion, the first to reach the cake, gave a snort and galloped off along the edge of the meadow.

The countryside of Kent, 'the Garden of England', is

uneven, muddled and colourful, like its inhabitants. Here aristocrats live cheek by jowl with tribes of unemployed miners and their families, on the dole for three generations, while for centuries, together with the suburbs of London on the wrong side of the Thames, the country has provided a home for conspirators, dissenters, dissidents, terrorists and Satanists of varying degrees and persuasions. Since the time of Cromwell, the Reformation and the Great Plague, the very appearance of the countryside seems to have confirmed Kent's reputation as a hotbed for every kind of anarchist idea, religious schism, heresy, rebellion and plot against the monarchy, parliamentary democracy, the Protestant religion and all attempts to ban the sale of drink on Sundays. It was not just the county's exotic blend of rustic villages, and estates with parks and ornamental lakes which contrasted with the empty, neglected little towns, where plastered hovels and melancholy warehouses were surrounded by the massive tower blocks of the revolutionary Sixties: the spirit of the place is rife with cataclysm and upheaval, social conflict and the clash of opinions strongly held; the hilly woods and the wooded hills alternate with plains flat as the mind of a degenerate aristocrat, planted with hops and potatoes.

The English countryside has long been a part of civilization, long been an extension of the person and character of its inhabitants. Just such a resemblance was to be perceived in the somewhat happy-go-lucky and chaotic appearance of Edward's estate. Renowned for its Roman Catholic connections on the female side, and for the military traditions of its menfolk, the family was one of the richest in southern England. (Edward's ancestors, who had once owned munitions factories and been purveyors of pheasant to the royal table, had subsquently more than doubled their fortune by investing heavily in tinned dog food.) Although it had slippped a little in recent years, this aristocratic family still contrived to sustain appropriate relations with the yeomen and retainers who continued to live upon the lordly estates, and contribute a perfectly respectable yearly income in the form of rent and holiday lets. Thanks to the family's innate tolerance, decency and readiness to compromise, the lordly forests had remained intact throughout the turbulent and occasionally bloody history of the county; the pheasant shoot, which had been a feature of the estate for centuries, was, until very recently, considered one of the best in the area. The local gamekeepers were held in particularly high repute. They had served Lord Edward's family for generations, father to son, grandfather to grandson, uncle to nephew. This inclination towards the observance of tradition, together with the relaxed way in which tradition was observed, was reflected in a certain amusing disorder on the estate.

A certain casualness of both flora and fauna was most certainly to be perceived about the dense thickets growing in front of the former gamekeeper's cottage – where ivy, bindweed and rhododendrons seemed to hold great oaks and plane trees in an orgiastic embrace for their benefit only and that of the birds with their deafening twitter. Neither the current gamekeeper nor the foresters were allowed to clean up this disorderly mess, which was considered to be a kind of hunting preserve.

The wood separated the old gamekeeper's cottage from a three-storey building that looked like a country house, where the man who called himself Lord Edward was recovering from the heart attack which had so nearly proved fatal. In front of the old gamekeeper's cottage grew a massive specimen of the local flora, half tree and half bush, of the species that would, in Russia, be called flowering bird-cherry. Yet it was not upon that nostalgic oddity of English flora that Felix, one of the three Russian guests of the estate, rested his gaze that morning in the autumn of 1984. Who would have thought, just a few years before, that one day the three of them would be guests at the table of an English lord on his grand estate? As improbable as the fact of that meeting, it seemed to them, were the various routes these three former Muscovites had taken on their way to emigration: Felix, a person with theatrical ambitions, had managed to get to Jerusalem and from there he'd escaped to London via Verona; Victor, a professional dissident, ended up in London after being unceremoniously deposited in Vienna straight from a cell in Vladimir Prison; Silva, a Turner scholar from the Pushkin Museum, to her great surprise had benefited from family ties with certain patriotic members of a Scottish clan doomed to suffer prosperous exile in London, far from their Scottish homeland.

All three had settled down in England thanks to the efforts of their benefactor Lord Edward, whom none of them actually saw in person. Or did they? How typically Soviet their attitudes are, thought Dr Genoni, his lordship's personal physician. Having been brought here, to this luxurious asylum, to discuss the mysterious identity of their aristocratic benefactor and put together their shattered lives, these Soviet émigrés have instead became involved straight away in settling the ten-year-old personal accounts of their acrimonious Moscow past.

Three's a crowd

'When we discovered that cholera was approaching we all cried out in horror: the constitution is in danger! Without losing a moment we addressed representatives of all political parties in an attempt to ascertain their views on the subject and discover what measures they had taken to deal with our visitor from Asia.' As he finished reading the postcard Avestin had sent Victor on his birthday, Migulin, his spectacles as always shining with irony, crossed his legs and fidgeted, trying to adopt as dramatic a pose as possible, conducting with his right hand – his left held the postcard – and raising his eyebrows to lend emphasis to a particularly significant passage. Despite being a generation older than Felix and Silva, and despite his greying hair and haggard face, he created around himself an atmosphere of youthful agility; he was Felix's teacher of English as well as his guru in the theatre, but all this rhetorical gesticulation was quite unnecessary. The text of Avestin's home-made postcard (which consisted of cuttings from the illustrated supplement of a prerevolutionary newspaper, *Russia*, mounted on cardboard) in those hot Moscow days was so explicit and to the point that no commentaries were required.

To begin with, the newspaper was dated August 6 (old style), which was Victor's birthday. August 6 (old style) also marked the Festival of the Lord's Transfiguration, which is why they had decided, that fateful Moscow summer in the 1970s to celebrate Victor's thirtieth birthday in Felix's flat near Transfiguration Square. But the main thing was that Avestin's 'choleric' postcard had arrived at the height of a cholera epidemic, which had begun, as usual, by the Black Sea. Everyone believed that the *cordon sanitaire* around Moscow was contracting, the first indication thereof being the disappearance of salt, soap and yeast from the food shop. The intelligentsia kept their spirits up with jokes to the effect that the best defence against cholera and the plague was vodka. Vodka consumption that summer, the appalling heat notwithstanding, practically doubled. That in turn, doubled the intensity of the feverish, almost apocalyptic atmosphere of their gathering to celebrate Victor's thirtieth birthday. From the distance of ten years that birthday party looked like a last chance to preserve the dying spirit of the old Moscow, once happily ruled by keen jests, merry anecdotes, sharp repartee and humorous remarks most biting in its solemn gravity, and ready laughter that chased the stories told by the older generation of friends. Everything was done that day to feel the same. Only the closest friends were invited, almost relatives: Felix, of course, and the lady of the clan, Silva, and Avestin with Migulin, their gurus and teachers since university days. There used to be a beautiful symmetry even in the frequent confrontations between Avestin and Migulin, and Victor and Felix, respectively, as if contradictions in one's mind were reflected and echoed over generations. Silva was clearly looking forward to enjoying a bit of verbal fencing among old friends. But that symmetry in their relationships started to show itself in the wrong way: there was little chance that either Avestin or the celebrant himself, Victor, would show up. Avestin was incarcerated in a psychiatric hospital, and Victor's routes to his own birthday party were as complicated and tangled as they always had been. Both their chairs stood empty.

Felix and Silva, waiting for Victor, were sitting at the kitchen table by a window, peering out as if they were trying to find him amid the maze of high-rise buildings that could be seen looming out there like an endless caravan of camels against a horizon turned white from the heat. Who would ever have supposed, in those hot and oppressive Moscow days, that the metaphor of camels along a horizon would come to life for Felix once he got his Israeli visa? Who would have thought that the casual coincidences witnessed by the hero as a character would become narrative laws dictating the fate of the hero as a human being? Didn't Felix himself juxtapose the unjuxtaposable, by permitting causal coincidences to drive him into the jaws of fate?

The three of them had been sitting together in the tiny kitchen, muddled around a table as if pressed together by the oppressive heat outside and by dictatorship. Moscow in the

1970s was very much a guilt-ridden city. Those, like Victor, who would publicly expose the horrors of the past and falsity of the present were brutally suppressed. As a result, those like Felix, who managed to avoid a direct confrontation with the system, felt guilty because their stance could have been interpreted as a connivance with the authorities. This atmosphere of guilt by association, of shame and helplessness, pushed everyone into exile of one kind or another – to Siberia or to the West. Felix was still managing to stay put in his Moscow apartment.

Required to maintain a hundred-kilometre distance from the capital on completing his latest prison term, Victor apparently was unable to get through the *cordon sanitaire* to attend his own birthday party. Recently he had made two or three clandestine trips to Moscow, in contravention of his residence requirements. They'd decided to hold a quiet birthday party at Felix's because Victor used to stay at his flat. He obviously couldn't go home, that is to say to his father's flat in Beskudnikovo: his father had disowned him – which had brought on a heart attack – and would certainly have informed the police if Victor had turned up in Moscow illegally. Silva was staying in a communal apartment in the New Bird-Cherry neighbourhood – and that too was not an ideal place for an exiled dissident to hide out. After Lyudmila, Felix's ex-wife, had gone to Israel, the second room in Felix's flat, which used to be their bedroom, stayed unused. Felix felt it was contaminated. He was delighted when Victor and Silva needed somewhere to spend the night. But the chances of Victor turning up on that particular day were not good. What with the epidemic, Victor's chances of getting through to Moscow without the appropriate documents were slight.

As if replacing Victor on this solemn occasion, set on his favourite chair, was a splendid parcel from abroad, with foreign stamps, seals and postmarks covered with cryptic markings from felt-tip pens. This present from abroad, this cardboard box, clearly contained an abundance of mysterious delights quite inaccessible to ordinary Soviet citizens. Their inacessibility was currently being fiercely guarded by Kashtanka, Victor's bitch, still practically a puppy, who had moved into the flat with him. Ironically, they saw more of Kashtanka than they did of Victor – for then, as always, Victor was on the run.

Nothing special to look at, with a burn mark under her right eye, Kashtanka stood guard over the exotic offering from abroad with all the zealous solemnity of a novice; she was carrying out such duties for the first time ever. She sat by the chair without moving, looking around her like a senior doctor inspecting a hospital ward. As soon as anyone stretched out a hand to feel the parcel and try to convince themselves that there really was another world beyond the Iron Curtain, Kashtanka began to growl, show her teeth and nervously thump her ragged tail on the floor.

'Lenin, speaking on behalf of the Bolshevik Party, has issued the following statement,' Migulin said continuing to read from the ancient pamphlet devoted to the appearance in Russia of 'the visitor from Asia'. 'Everything is dependent upon the Mensheviks. If they are going to campaign on behalf of the cholera, we will be obliged to boycott it, and vice versa. For his part Martov, speaking on behalf of the Mensheviks, stated that everything depended upon the Bolsheviks. If they were going to boycott the cholera then the Mensheviks would have to campaign on its behalf with all their might, and vice versa. Prince Trubetskoy made the following statement: "I'm a pacifist and my ideal is peace and serenity. The most lasting peace and serenity are to be found in cemeteries. How is it possible that our party should view cholera as its enemy? On the contrary, we feel it is our party's leader.". . .'

The arrival of Avestin's postcard had been very timely. It was true that he, Victor's Italian professor at the university, was currently incarcerated, for his anti-Soviet Pirandellism, in the Ganushkin Hospital, close by the Sailor's Repose district. Here, in the repose of the psychiatric ward, they were stuffing him with insulin, which one might have supposed would have rendered him quite incapable of coherent thought. But all the same, Avestin had somehow managed to remember, and combine that birthday on August 6 with Transfiguration Square and cholera. Members of the Avestin–Migulin school had an astounding ability to mitigate horror with black humour, and thereby transform manic-depressive psychosis into splendid and triumphant theatre. A glass of vodka, a pair of spectacles, a ball point pen seemed to be dancing through the air, dancing on Migulin's words, as he sat comfortably at the kitchen table in front of a pile of notebooks, bits of paper and

8

cuttings. He shuffled them around like a conjurer and thanks to a series of impromptu quotations, the conversation became a kind of theatre to which the words were puppets, manipulated by Migulin the puppet master.

Only Migulin could have told Felix of Pushkin's dictum about the difference between plague (which was contagious) and cholera (which is carried in the air) and hence the pointlessness of quarantine. Of course cholera was immediately compared to the Soviet regime, which was also carried in the air, which was why 'It's pointless to divide the world into East and West, internal and external liberty,' said Felix, as if in answer to Lyudmila, whose latest letter from Israel had compared her departure from Moscow to the Jewish people's escape from Egyptian enslavement. He referred to a passage in Tacitus which stated that the Jews had quite simply been ejected from Egypt, since they were perpetually suffering from epidemics of leprosy, and Pharaoh, in his far-sighted wisdom, had tried to protect the local population from the lepers.

Migulin appeared to have prepared himself for this conversation in advance (or rather he had carefully orchestrated the whole affair), because he now produced an extract from a document pertaining to the plague of August 1654 (the Great Plague of London started somewhat later, and perhaps it was brought there from Moscow?), the time of the great schism. The conversation moved on naturally enough from the subject of the Times of Trouble to that of imposters; because there can be no great epidemics without great impostors. Besides, it should be recalled that the conversation was taking place by Transfiguration Square, the spot where Peter the Great staged his mock battles between the 'King of Poland' and 'the Russian potentate'. Both commanders, incidentally, bore the rank of generalissimo. And remember that legend had it that Peter himself was an impostor, who had been swapped with the real Tsar by foreigners when he was a child, so that a foreigner, one of them, was now upon the throne.

However, all these curious historic details had been inflicted on them in order to smuggle in a totally different idea, a different scenario. For the first time Felix heard Migulin tell the story of how, in the 1950s, he had tried, together with all his manuscripts, to get into the United States Embassy, to seek political asylum, by pretending to be a foreigner. To be specific,

9

he had pretended to be an Englishman (he'd known English all his life), who spoke fluent French and could make himself understood in German. Wasn't that why he'd been telling stories about impostors in the time of plague? Be that as it may, the policeman in the sentry-box outside the American Embassy (the old building, next to the Hotel National by Manège Square) behaved very politely and spoke in an exaggeratedly loud voice – which is how Russians speak to foreigners, as if they were deaf. While Migulin was correcting his grammatical mistakes the policeman got on the internal telephone. In his over-excited state of mind Migulin supposed he was telling the ambassador about the arrival of an important Englishman, with fluent French and some German. But shortly afterwards a black and far from ambassadorial limousine made its appearance, in order to pick Migulin up and whisk him off in an entirely different direction.

They'd have been delighted to knock his teeth out, but were hypnotized by the sounds of a foreign language. Even if his appearance, with his scruffy suit and socks with holes in, had something unmistakably Soviet about it, the magic sounds of a foreign tongue overcame those modest powers of deductive reasoning with which the local KGB men were endowed. The very fact that seemingly ordinary Soviet lips were contorted by various cryptic and devilish sounds (the ability to speak in a strange tongue is one of the signs of diabolic possession according to medieval books on exorcism) suggested that the peculiar gentleman who had fallen into their clutches was more likely than not to be a foreign spy. Let a higher authority sort things out.

In the car he was crammed between two well-fed lads from the KGB. When they went past the monument to Dzerzhinsky, one of them, smiling smugly in anticipation of a reward and promotion, said to the other: 'We've landed a big one this time,' meaning an important agent of imperialism. Migulin couldn't help giving a derisive sneer – which was a mistake. All it takes is a little sneer and you're caught: oh ho, he understands Russian, does he? No longer looking like the mysterious agent of a foreign power, it was as if a mask had slipped from Migulin's face to reveal the ordinary, wretched appearance of a member of the Soviet intelligentsia. The familiar physiognomy of the enemy within. The ironic grin of the saboteur. The two guards decided forthwith to deprive that grin of its toothiness. They beat him across his teeth, his ribs and his balls. And you might suppose that that was the end of the tale of the foreign impostor. But the tale was just beginning.

Migulin's interrogator at the Lubyanka came to the conclusion that, with his knowledge of three different languages, he must be one of theirs, that he was on special assignment and had been arrested outside the American Embassy by mistake. So they started feverishly digging through their agent records, checking names. The most amazing thing was the sheer inefficiency of the bureaucratic machinery. You'd have thought it would have been easy enough to decide whether or not you had a particular person on file. But it wasn't that simple. They gave Migulin the special treatment for a whole week, but once his identity was established they really let him have it. He soon discovered that when they break a rib it only hurts for a moment and then you pass out. The real pain comes later, when you come to with a bunch of broken ribs. But even without Migulin's broken ribs the authorities did not come out looking too good; the much-esteemed security forces had mistaken a crazy teacher of foreign languages for an important agent of a foreign power. So they came to a compromise. Instead of shooting Migulin they confined him to the Leningrad Psychiatric Prison Hospital, the scene of Migulin's historic meeting with Avestin.

Migulin transformed the bare and terrifyingly crude four walls of a prison psychiatric ward into something clownesque, farcical, fantastic, and yet heart-rending, like gypsy music that charms through its very phoneyness. It contained killers in white coats and lust-crazed nurses; there were mad geniuses adept in all the forbidden sciences who communicated their most precious secrets to secret mass-murderers. Some of the best minds in the country were there. The ward held geneticists, mathematicians and cybernetics experts, specialists in Cheyne-Stokes breathing (comrade Stalin's death rattle), and linguists of the Marr school (unlike Marr, Stalin believed that man thinks in words, and therefore anti-Soviet thoughts automatically constituted anti-Soviet propaganda). Avestin learnt Italian there with the help of a Latin professor.

'It's only now that people are protesting against the political use of force in psychiatry. They forget that in those days to get into a psychiatric ward, even a prison ward, meant survival. It meant you weren't going to die in the snow, weren't going to scratch at the frozen earth with broken nails, or break your back felling timber. Instead you'd spend all day in bed between clean sheets with three meals a day and regular exercise,' Migulin reflected.

Considering it from afar, in London, with his mind confused by jealousy and fear of death, it seemed to Felix that there was a reason why Migulin told his insane tales of life in the psychiatric hospital. As with all his stories, there was a hidden moral, a catch, a subtext, a sub-up-your-arse. He'd had good reason to talk about 'the use of psychiatry for political purposes'; he was obviously casting aspersions on Victor. In the sense that all his heroism was perhaps just politics; the use of psychiatry for political purposes. Just as the fact of mental sickness became a political act for Avestin. 'Someone who is sick in the head is sick at heart,' he used to say, meaning, as Migulin pointed out, that if you're not sick in the head you're never sick at heart and quite probably heartless. Avestin began to associate schizophrenia with dissent. To most people attending a compulsory meeting, any form of disobedience would be a sign of insanity. Schizophrenia also became a synonym for Soviet double-think; you say one thing, implying a second which hints at a third, while you act in a fourth and different way altogether. It was scarcely surprising that underground pamphlets and tapes were all full of romantic cant about nuts and loonies, fragmented consciousness and sick consciences. Moreover, the fact that Avestin was now undergoing forcible treatment in a psychiatric hospital, while Victor, his pupil and disciple, had been exiled on exactly the same grounds, made Migulin and Felix form a sort of party of opposition, sitting in a Moscow kitchen ironically curling their lip at Avestin's romantic conception of insanity.

In the eyes of Silva, who was squinting at them through a vodka glass from the other end of the table, they both began to blend together to form the single image of a two-headed talking monster, the embodiment of schizophrenic division. Silva noticed how promptly and willingly Felix served Migulin a drink, how he was asked to find, and found, a particular page in Migulin's notebook which he needed for the next quotation, how he helped him to snacks, moved a chair closer, acknowledged a witticism with an ever deferential smile, and approved a new paragraph with a nod of the head. Why was he being so obsequious? she wondered at first. But she finally realized that the impression of bustling obsequiousness derived from the almost mirror-like reflection and echoing of Felix's and Migulin's gestures, smiles, expressions and glances. In just such a way Victor had once seemed to be Avestin's double. All it needed in those days was for Victor and Felix to meet and start talking, and they seemed like dolls in the control of a ventriloquist, for all of a sudden it was as if Avestin and Migulin were in the room, with that perpetual antagonism of theirs that derived from knowing one another too well. Silva, somewhat absent-minded and affected by the vodka, was suddenly taken with the distinctly masculine idea that she wanted to experience this confrontational closeness physically, in all its corporeality, to reconcile or fuse them into a single being. Without realizing their own capacity for being copy-cats, each one reacted with indignant irritation to all the false and derivative notes they heard the other strike; they accused one another of being imitative and attacked each other's views with that degree of savagery which characterized the behaviour of their original role models.

As if bearing in mind this series of doubles and plagiarists, Migulin strung together a series of stories about the inmates of the psychiatric ward, who included, for example, a pretender to the Soviet throne who believed he was Stalin's son. This notwithstanding the fact that he had a perfectly ordinary father, which is why he despised his mother; because she had deceived his natural father and slept with Stalin. Migulin moved steadily towards the crowning story of the series: how Avestin put on a hospital production of his favourite Pirandello play about mad Henry IV. Not the English King but the German Emperor who went off to Canossa to stand barefoot in the snow and beseech the Pope to forgive him. More precisely the play was not about Henry IV, but about a madman who believed he was Henry. But then it emerged that Henry was not mad at all; he was pretending to be a madman who believed himself to be Henry IV in order to play a trick on his ex-lover, who had arranged for him to fall from his horse during a carnival masquerade, which made him lose his mind.

A play about a madman pretending to be mad, put on in an asylum and directed by someone declared mad by the authorities. It caused an uproar. Everyone took everything personally. It wasn't even a question of discovering a subtext: the text itself was pure subtext. How could it have been otherwise when a psychiatrist makes his entrance on stage and turns to an audience which contains a Soviet psychiatrist? The tension came to a head when the stage psychiatrist suggested that the pseudo-Henry might be cured by taking him back to that point in his life, that very moment in time, when he seemingly lost his mind. To that effect the psychiatrist proposed to substitute for the portrait of his former lover, the Countess Matilda, the living likeness of that portrait, in the form of her daughter, who was the spitting image of her mother as a young woman. When the hero, Henry, entered the throne-room she was supposed to step out of the portrait frame and 'enter' real life, thereby shocking the hero out of the 'frame' of his madness. The most remarkable thing, observed Migulin, was that the play was put on in the male section of the hospital. There was no one in the Soviet asylum who could play the countess, a deficiency which had nothing to do with politics. Consequently the parts of the countess and her daugher were played by a man, and the moment when the daughter steps out of the frame recalled the moment of confrontation with a witness during a KGB cross-examination. But it was only Avestin, Migulin and their friends, the ward's political prisoners, who grasped all these hints and echoes of the past. Not even the doctors themselves were able to grasp the full significance of the mad director's deep and pertinent allusions.

Felix followed Migulin's every word and gesture with open-mouthed enthusiasm. Here was a victim conferring forgiveness upon his torturers by dismissing the ordeal as nothing more than a stupid ludicrous farce. Just take the conclusion. After the play ended to roars of applause and they started to take the performers back to their various wards, it transpired that all the actors Avestin had cast in the role of the moral killers, assassins of the spirit, were all convicted murderers who had been confined to the psychiatric clinic after being medically certified insane. Talented actors to a man, one had killed Mummy and Daddy with an axe in the course of a childish tantrum, another had poisoned his wife, a third had strangled his children. They went out to take their bow, after which the handcuffs went back on and they were led away to a maximum security ward somewhere in the bowels of the clinic. The Gothic dualism, the two-tiered nature of this world, was amazing, where the top tier, heaven, held the political inmates, and the bottom tier, hell, contained psychotic criminals.

However, heaven and hell were simply the two sides of the same prison, one and indivisible; it was this schizophrenic separation into heaven and hell that made it possible to regard it as an asylum. Anyone who hadn't gone crazy there, who remembered everything yet survived, regained his liberty, was still able to talk about his experiences – anyone like that deserved a standing ovation. Felix contented himself with a round of silent applause. Kashtanka, no doubt sensing the excitement, started to bark enthusiastically. They all raised their glasses, only to find that the vodka had run out. Felix made a move towards Victor's parcel – suppose there was a bottle in there? – to be greeted by a growling snarling Kashtanka. He backed off and decided to run down and get some vodka from the neighbouring store. Anyway they were out of matches too.

It seemed to Felix that he'd been gone for no time at all. Maybe it was all the pushing and shouting in the liquor department that made him come back to the flat just as worked up as he'd been half an hour before when he'd left for the vodka. Nothing seemed to have changed about the kitchen or the view from its window. The only surprise was Kashtanka's deafening bark when he opened the door; he could never take that barking. Felix asked whether Victor had telephoned, as he started pouring the vodka in triumphant haste, looking forward to more of Migulin's conversation. But Migulin seemed different. It was as if the drink had got to him. He had grown morose, tired and flat. He tried to snap out of it, raised a glass, started to say something that made no sense at all, took his spectacles off and put them on again as if he were embarrassed.

There are two types of con-men: hams and genuine artists. Migulin suddenly started to behave like a cheap actor; he no longer delivered his lines in a lofty and exotic manner, but drawled them out without making any attempt to sound natural or convincing. Moreover it was clear that he hadn't shaved all day, and a grey stubble had appeared on his chin which looked like a false beard, a theatrical hairpiece that might stink of glue.

The magic wand of this production, the master of cere-monies' baton, had passed into the hands of Silva as if she had consumed all Migulin's verbal flare and transformed it into inner body heat. Strong and boyish as she was, built like a jockey and full of boyish mannerisms, she looked far younger than her contemporaries, Victor and Felix. She was sitting on the kitchen sofa, her legs tucked under her and her mouth half open as she panted in the heat, her damp hair stuck to her forehead. Felix couldn't help noticing her transformation from a sad pony at the end of its tether to a snorting, prancing, lively mare. He just couldn't take his eyes off her. Silva looked away, licked her lips, gave a fidget and tried to fill the pause by looking for matches on the kitchen table. Felix, pleased with himself for having done so well, patted his pocket and produced the box that he'd just bought in the store. She caught a sidelong glance from Migulin and turned away from her own cloud of cigarette smoke. Something had happened in this room while Felix was out.

Migulin's conversation and expression momentarily appeared to regain their earlier liveliness. The last story before the curtain came down was about matches in the psychiatric hospital. Smoking in the wards was of course forbidden. Matches were confiscated. The only way you could smoke was in secret, under the blankets (just in case a nurse looked in through the peep-hole), but to do so you needed to have matches hidden. Everyone hid their supply as best they could, but Avestin chose to pronounce that it was all nonsense, outlining his theory of concealment. It was based on the notion that man has no grasp of the obvious. 'But he better under-stands complexity,' according to Pasternak. Similarly we don't notice objects lying about in plain view. It sounded good. Avestin went to every bed, collected all the matches and put them in one big box which he placed upon a little table in the middle of the ward. It couldn't have been more conspicuous, all right? In came the nurse and surveyed the ward, straightened a blanket here, swept away some crumbs there. Then she went to the little table, picked up the box, shook it, realised it was full of matches, and with an incredulous shrug put it in her coat pocket. As she left she quite properly locked the door behind her. Everyone turned on Avestin, who was totally unpertubed. All that meant, he observed, was that the table in the middle of the ward was not the most obvious spot. Of course the most obvious spot in the ward was Avestin himself, yet henceforth no one gave him any matches: they lacked faith.

The evening sun filtered through the windows and shone in their eyes, which seemed to reflect its light like mirrors. Migulin looked at Felix as if not seeing him; his listener's eyes were just a looking-glass. Migulin's pupils grew dull, shrinking as if seen through the wrong end of a pair of binoculars. We don't notice the things before our very eyes. We don't see. He started saying his goodbyes; outside, the taxi he'd ordered sounded its horn.

It was hard to say why, with Migulin's departure, what looked like the end of the party suddenly began to feel like the start of a new life, feel like some kind of liberation – from Migulin's edifying and schoolmasterly presence perhaps? Or else it was just that it was now obvious that Victor wasn't going to turn up, and that the two of them were alone in this huge crowded white block of a ship, slipping on through the hot cholera-ridden night of Moscow, with neither rudder nor sail. What course were we to set? Wasn't it wonderful, the feeling that you had absolutely nothing to do with the world outside? Freedom from responsibility, freedom from guilt, wasn't that the point of those festivities in the time of cholera?

In any event, when Migulin had gone they both had one thing in mind. They both looked excitedly at the forbidden parcel with its fascinating foreign labels, and inscriptions in English. These, along with the stamps, labels, crossed-out addresses, made the parcel look like a piece of pop art, a museum exhibit guarded by Kashtanka. It had first been delivered to Victor's address in Beskudnikovo, but his father had refused to accept the offerings of foreign sorcerers and had forwarded it to Felix's address. Silva observed that if Victor ever found out that they'd run out of drink on his birthday, he'd be the first to tell them to open the parcel, whoever it might belong to. Kashtanka, however, evidently did not subscribe to this view, and started growling with considerable ferocity whenever anyone approached her charge. 'How does she know it's her owner's parcel? did he teach her to read or something?' said Silva and suggested they flip a coin to decide whether to open it or not. Kashtanka began thumping her tail joyously against the floor, either to signify her approval or to apologize for her recent outburst of aggression. They all three tried to catch the coin, Kashtanka leapt about barking excitedly, and their hands touched, palm to palm, hiding both heads and tails.

'Cheese. Don't tell me it's gone bad?' Felix muttered dejectedly, opening a metal can containing a yellowish cheese shot through with bluish veins. 'Idiot,' said Silva, breathing in the sharp, heady aroma. 'Of course it's not bad, this is genuine Roquefort.' But according to the label it wasn't Roquefort, but genuine English Stilton – the proper way to round off a Christmas dinner. Indeed, as an accompanying Christmas card made clear, the parcel was intended as a somewhat belated Christmas and New Year's present to Victor from the London branch of Amnesty International. It also announced that a certain Lord Edward proposed to visit Victor that winter (at this point the postcard became illegible, as if deliberately smudged by the censors). It would seem, however, that Milord never did put in an appearance. Either he got the address muddled or decided to postpone his trip for a year. But the citizens of Moscow were not much interested in lords in those days. Much more interesting was the fact that the Stilton was accompanied by a bottle of port. To their delight they saw that the black bottle was litre-sized. Highly excited, they grabbed the box and carried it, like a stolen treasure, from the kitchen, which had become something of a wreck, to Felix's room. Driven less by hunger than curiosity, they tried to get the cheese out with their fingers, but it was too soft and sticky. Silva fetched a spoon from the kitchen and they started to eat the cheese, feeding each other with the spoon and chasing it down with warming draughts of port.

'I don't know about the cheese, but at least the jeans won't have gone bad,' said Silva as she continued sorting the parcel. She started to try on the crumpled jeans, having casually removed her skirt without a thought for Felix's eyes wandering over her body. Her curly pubis seemed to thrust through the white semi-transparent panties. She could just get the jeans on but couldn't button them across her naked stomach. She took a wild swig of port from the bottle and dug into the parcel once again, removing a packet with something rattling inside. As she gave it a shake, it burst open and nuts spilt all over the floor. For some time now they hadn't even seen Chinese peanuts in Moscow, and filberts themselves were in short supply, but suddenly as if in Aladdin's cave precious stones scattered across the floor in the form of shining hazelnuts, bursting pistachios, porous almonds, together with something quite unknown in Moscow, finely shaped Brazil nuts and South American pecans that seemed waxed and polished to a high gloss. Felix and Silva, by now quite far gone, sat down on the floor in the midst of all these treasures, sorting through the various kinds of nut, pouring them from hand to hand, holding them up to the light, biting down on them like gold coins. Instead of a hammer they kept handing one another an old bronze inkstand in the form of a bust of Pushkin (his head, flung back in inspiration, constituting the lid). They picked them following a strict order, with no repetitions, first a filbert, then a Brazil, then a pecan, than an almond, then a hazelnut, never breaking the order. The Brazil nuts were hardest of all because of their rhomboid ribbing, and the hazelnuts shot out from under their blows like bullets. It was a risky, dangerous business; they could easily crush a finger. Every time they were about to strike they held their breath and exchanged a conspiratorial glance; each nut they cracked seemed to be a triumph for them both.

One kernel hit Silva right on her naked stomach. She shivered and straightened her back and Felix saw her breasts tighten under her blouse. She rummaged about inside her unbuttoned jeans and – from out of her panties? – produced the errant kernel. She lifted it to Felix's lips and inserted it. Slowly and deliberately, Felix started chewing the salty nut, afraid to move. He saw Silva swallow. She gazed at him fixedly. A smile came slowly to her lips, a smile of certain submission, watchful expectancy and greedy assent. The smile faded suddenly, leaving the lips a-quiver as if they had lost their place. In a single movement she grabbed him by the neck and, baring her chest, pressed his lips to the brown nutty nipple. Her lips were at his ear as if she were trying to whisper a great secret to him, one concealed in her increasingly rapid breathing, and the harder he sucked at her nipple the nearer he seemed to be getting to the secret; but when her breathing turned to groaning he forgot all about the secret which needed a solution, and if there were a solution it was not going to come by guessing the secret.

A shift took place; things started to duplicate themselves and slip away as they do when you have a fever, slip into the cholera-ridden night, into another place altogether, well to the east of reason. They ended up lying head to head under the table, and it seemed to him that they were in a darkened Persian tent – perhaps because the rough surface of his old Persian carpet was giving them rug burns? He gave a yelp when a broken piece of nutshell stuck in his thigh. It had happened once before, when he was a child with a high fever; he knew he was going terribly fast down a mountain on a sled, even though he was still tossing and turning his head on his mother's enormous pillow, his fingers clutching the warm quilted eiderdown. He cautiously opened his eyes a little, but was afraid to look at her in the semi-darkness, because with every moment, every repeated movement of her thighs, arms and lips, she was becoming someone else, someone unrecognizable and therefore frightening. She was doing what she had to do, biting her lip, like a bridle, as she carefully tried to pick up the rhythm of the gallop. He recognized neither her voice nor his own, and their sighs, cries and groans seemed to be coming from somewhere else, their own voices but distorted and rendered strange by distance. It was just that he had never heard her utter noises like that before, enunciated with a frenzied clarity of articulation. I love you. I you. Love you. Love uv, uv uv uv. You you you. On the other side of the door the dog began to scratch and growl, but neither of them paid any attention to the growling of the rejected third party. They became pitiless, as if possessed. She straddled him, raising him up with her, after her, and he began to slip away from himself as he joined together with his rider, who gradually, with every hoofbeat, turned into the horse as he became the rider. Her tail beat him across the face, her mane burned his thigh. Below the waist his body seemed to disappear, or rather flow into hers, and they became the monstrous two-backed beast. Once again he was able to recognize her, her nose, her lips, her eyes, her stomach, her breasts, her . . . her, as a part of himself which had come back to him through her. Through her he listened to the sound of his own heartbeat. And he was afraid he might lose her. The heartbeat shifted to a pulse, a knocking in his temple. Like someone knocking at a locked door. And his heart grated like the key in a lock. Someone was vainly trying to get into the flat.

The gallop came to a sudden halt. The riders were in a hurry. More precisely, they leapt out of the saddle. Silva jumped up, grabbing first her skirt, which was inside out, then the jeans, which she couldn't get on. Felix, pulling on his trousers and more or less buttoning his shirt with trembling fingers, made Silva move to the centre of the room, took a deep breath and stepped into the corridor. Kashtanka bounded down it, jumping up to greet her owner. Silva, her ear to the door, listened to the voices rumbling on the other side of the wall: '. . . you can't get a ticket without showing your passport. It's the cholera. I had to hitch. Where's Silva?' 'She went back to her place. Said she had to be up early tomorrow.' They went into the kitchen. A moment later Felix came into the room, a conspiratorial finger to his lips, grabbed the port bottle and went out again. Silva stared at him hard in the darkness. It wasn't easy to say how long she sat there, in a trance, with her ear glued to the wall separating her from the kitchen, trying to make out what Felix and Victor were talking about. About her? She was about to get up and go into the brightly lit kitchen when there was another, this time extremely loud, knock at the door. The noise made her take cover in a corner again. Kashtanka started barking a hoarse, poignant, protective kind of bark. Silva heard the sound of the door being unbolted again, the murmur of voices and footsteps down the corridor.

'Two comrades in plain clothes, a neighbour acting as witness and the divisional inspector. They're checking Victor's papers. Infringement of residence requirements,' Felix informed her in a rapid whisper through the half-open door. Silva tried to run down the corridor, but Felix grabbed her by the elbow and pulled her back. 'As if he didn't have enough to worry about without you. You're not here, you're at home. Stay put and keep quiet.' On the other side of the wall, fear was prowling; it could be sensed in one of the policemen's tread, the whispers of the witness, and the occasional dead-pan comments of the KGB man. They went into Victor's room. There was a noise of books falling on the floor, the sound of furniture being shifted about, the rustle of papers. A shout, the sound of a protest and silence once again. The passport with its proscription (denied the right to reside in the city of Moscow) was just the pretext for a renewed acquaintance to be followed by search, interrogation, arrest, and a new sentence. But this time she wouldn't be packing for him, wouldn't be kissing him before he set out. Fear prowled on the other side of the wall.

That very same fear that drove a Dostoevskian hero to keep walking down the darkened street, knowing that the girl he'd just walked past was just about to jump off a bridge. The fear of getting involved. At that moment the KGB man looked into the room.

When he opened the door, Silva was again sitting cross-legged on the sofa, with her stomach bare beneath her unbuttoned blouse and the jeans that wouldn't do up. The room reeked of cheese, port and sex. The KGB man inspected the room, and Silva, with a knowing leer, and clucked his tongue at her reprovingly. Felix, 'the iron Felix', came right in behind the KGB, looked round conspiratorially, and pushed the door tight shut behind him. 'You don't have a warrant to search my room, you've nothing on me yet, have you?' he said, trying to stay between Silva and the polite but insistent member of the security service. 'Not yet, but we will. Just give us time. Time. Ha! Ha!' the latter joked. At that moment footsteps sounded in the corridor; they were taking Victor out. Silva moved towards the door, but Felix got in her way. Then she rushed to the window like a suicide to get a glimpse, if not of the face, then at least of the back of the man she loved, who was being led away at dawn to a Black Maria.

'Where are you going? Sit!' the KGB man shouted like a dog handler, and Felix and Silva halted obediently in the middle of the room with faces white as bird-cherry. But the KGB man was really shouting at the dog. Flying through the window, Kashtanka smashed into the frame, hurting her ear, the frame came out and crashed to the floor, the glass shattering. Kashtanka dropped from the second storey, her limbs spread like an experienced parachutist. She landed on a flower bed and immediately ran, barking, to Victor. When the policeman stepped back and tried to block the way, she snarled and sank her teeth into his boot. The cursing policeman tried to kick her away and reached for his holster. Victor tore free, jumping over a series of garden fences and making off into the depths of the neighbourhood. The policeman, sent staggering by Victor, stumbled and fell on his back, then drew his gun, uttered his warning 'Stop or I'll fire' and discharged his revolver into the air. Sleepy heads emerged from neighhbouring windows as Victor yelled 'Run, Kashtanka, run' to the snarling bitch, and came to an obedient standstill in the middle of the yard. It seemed to Silva, who was still by the window, that a final glance he directed at the house caught her without registering who it was. Instinctively she jumped back from the window and covered her face with her hands.

'There'll be a case, all we need is a sentence.' The KGB man was playing with words as he closed the flat door behind him. In his wake, and saying not a word, Silva left on the first early-morning bus. Felix started wandering aimlessly about the flat, recalling what had happened, picking up bits of blue-veined cheese, which seemed like the rotting remains of some unlikely monster, that had been trampled into the carpet along with pieces of nut shell. He discovered a tuft of fur caught in the window-catch. He picked up the box of matches and gave it a shake or two, remembering Avestin's aphorism: we don't notice whatever is before our very eyes. There was clearly something that evening that he'd missed. He gave the box another shake and started to empty desk drawers and book-shelves of the ill-concealed typescripts and illicit literature that had accumulated since Victor and Silva had started using the flat. He put the pile of papers in the cast-iron kitchen basin and started setting light to it then, sheet by sheet, in an attempt to start an illicit bonfire. Dawn was beginning to break, and in the haze of another day of heat there loomed the silhouette of the bird-cherry tree by the filthy pond from which could be heard the chirping sounds of the emergent dawn chorus. Suddenly an unexpected puff of wind blew over the papers smouldering in the basin, and the black scraps, like specks of dust, started to float through the window. From the outside it looked as if the flat were on fire.

3

Asylum

Sitting at the little table on the lawn behind the house, Felix stared absent-mindedly at the fields, hills and valleys of Kent. Although the former gamekeeper's cottage behind him was as pretty as a picture, with a gingerbread red-tiled roof, its real fascination (no foundations, wooden floors laid directly on earth, an outside lavatory, and of course the total lack of hot water) lay in the fact that it closely resembled a village bath-house or a Russian holiday villa. That is no doubt why the guest sitting behind the house felt a certain nostalgic Russian holidaymaker's sense of enervation – as if all eternity were in front of them so that there was nothing to hurry for. Felix turned and looked towards the horizon, where hills jostled in disorderly rows, as if they were soaring up across the blue sphere of the autumn sky, casting shadows over one another, like a stage set along the wings of the valleys. The goat, lilac-coloured against the light of the midday sun, was finishing the cake. The hens, having accepted defeat after a series of aggressive moves from the geese, were having a delightful dust-bath in front of the cottage door, paying no attention to the barking dog who was enthusiastically pursuing a young donkey round the old oak tree.

'Let's go on about the plague,' said Victor, returning to Dr Genoni's remark about the relativity of reactions to the plague epidemic. 'Do you mean to say that whatever anyone says about the plague is true? So the plague always turns out to be what others want it to be, thereby satisfying all the demands that people may make of it?'

'The triumph of subjective idealism: things are what I think they are,' said Felix, not letting Dr Genoni get a word in. He ran a hand through his curly hair nervously tugging at it as if trying to cover his growing bald patch, the unwelcome evidence of his ageing. 'But this is also the age of subjective materialism triumphant: whatever we may conceive of materializes. Since we are thinking ceaselessly, the steadily expanding world of matter and materialized thought is beginning to put an ever-shrinking iron ring around the inconceivable and the inexplicable – God, in other words. God, driven steadily into an ever more confined space by the continuing encroachment of matter, will eventually explode – and that will be the end of the world.' He waved his hands frantically and then concluded with a flourish, smiling knowingly: 'The plague is God's way of disposing of muddled thinking, of excessive waste matter, the dead wood of creation.'

'Now I see why people in Russia like to discuss the plague so much: it provides them with an inexhaustible supply of interpretations,' said Dr Genoni. Let them talk. Let these Russians talk, he repeated to himself. The words are just a cover-up for the lack of action. After all, they were invited here to talk things out, to get it off their chest, to confess. But confess what? Lord Edward did not leave any instructions or directives on the matter. This type of talking is a Russian way of not talking about something really essential. Was there something in his manner of speech that betrayed his Italian ancestry? No, he didn't think so. While thinking, Dr Genoni absent-mindedly, but somewhat menacingly, rotated his heavy jaw in a measured movement as if testing the joints. Having finally caught the inquisitive eyes of his patients, he resumed his discourse with an affected agility. 'You Russians like to pile one metaphysical hypothesis on another, and then you prop the structure up with a third. This kind of feverish filling of an empty consciousness is doubtless to be explained by another kind of emptiness, the emptiness of daily life in the material world, and by the total lack of any kind of civilization.'

'It may be that there is no civilization in Russia, but on the other hand England clearly lacks any kind of ideology that binds everyone together,' said Felix, sardonically. 'That is why there are so many solitary crazies in England. Eccentrics they call them.'

'At least in England they don't put them in asylums,' said Silva.

She doesn't give a damn about what's happening to all the nutty and mentally screwed up people in this country, reflected Dr Genoni. Kicked out of the state hospitals, without care they are doomed to perish in the wildness of city life. Just like Felix, who can carry on in the same vein about Italy, even though he was there only a few weeks on his way to Britain after a short sojourn in Israel. All these countries are for them mere symbols, similes and substitutes for the things and thoughts they do not dare to express directly. They are afraid of something. The question is: of what? They use big subjects for small talk to cover their embarrassment.

'What's the point of putting their madmen in hospitals, when no one has anything to do with anybody else as it is? Everyone stays shut up in their own homes so you don't need asylums. As I understand it, there is nothing to choose in essence between a London pub and a psychiatric clinic,' said Felix. 'People here even have their own weather which depends on their particular point of view; there is no unity – just take a look!' He pointed a finger at the heavens.

There was a rainbow over the hills and plains of Kent, and above the rainbow, on a higher storey as it were, snowflakes tumbled. To the left an autumn downpour could be seen falling on to the fields from heavy autumnal clouds.

'Turner used to say that in England at any given moment you can see all four seasons,' said Silva.

'It's a typical case of split personality,' said Felix. 'Silva, you're the great Turner expert. Tell us about his double life, about how, as a member of the Royal Academy, he moved to a wretched attic room in Chelsea where he lived incognito. Tell us how he lived there with a captain's widow, the daughter of a cook, how they called him the admiral, and how no one had any idea, to the day he died, that he had an entirely different life, as a gentleman and academician.'

Dr Genoni registered Felix's incongruously aggressive tone. What did it mean?

4

A papal conspiracy

The so-called 'third wave' of emigrants from Russia has its hierarchy. It's almost a class matter. The privileged class of demonstrators and dissidents of the Sixties, exiled into the Slavic decadence of émigré Paris, was a source of envy to the Jewish intellectuals who became 'prisoners of Zion', having gone to Israel under false pretences simply in order to get out of the USSR, rather than as committed Zionists. Later the plebs of the emigration started to identify with the 'Americanists', the 'straight-shotters' (those who managed to go straight to America without a stopover in Israel), and, in comparison with the Odessites of New York's Brighton Beach, even the émigrés to Israel began to look like aristocrats; after all, there was Jerusalem, God, the War, the Great Idea. But then chaos set in. Russian intellectuals who had escaped on Israeli visas, thanks to their foreign and usually Jewish connections, wandered across the squares of Vienna and Rome, trying to acquire refugee status so that they could settle in Europe, whereas those who had been offered a place in Chicago endeavoured to secure one in New York and eventually ended up in Los Angeles – where they criticized America for its lack of culture and the absence of spiritual values and dreamt of moving to England (but never, under any circumstances, to Paris, where émigrés were packed tight as sardines!).

For Felix, the feeling that he had come to the wrong place on that August morning in 1983 began the moment he got out of the taxi with his suitcase on the deserted street behind Verona station. After the vulgarity of life in Israel, he had hoped to find a rustic wayside inn, an Italian taverna with Parmesan and macaroni. Instead he found himself looking at a concrete fence, and although the cast-iron gates were open, the asphalt alley with a disciplined lawn, the ferro-concrete building with its linoleum-covered floors, were all too reminiscent of a staff officers' academy, while the registration window resembled the entrance to a factory rather than a hotel for participants in a Russian summer school – Felix's destination.

There was no sign of any participants or administrators, just a sprinkler at work outside, scattering water, or poison perhaps, on the grass, while cicadas buzzed in the afternoon sun and a mowing machine was to be heard at the far end of the lawn. A young man walked steadily behind it, like a ploughboy in an old engraving, stripped to the waist, his back wet with sweat and blackened by the sun. He responded to the sound of English with a stare and a shake of the head, while the closest Felix could get to Italian was a rudiment of half-learnt French. In response to all attempts to obtain information about the 'seminaro Russo' the young man pressed the palms of his hands together and laid them against his cheek, while making a snoring sound to suggest sleep. It was siesta time.

Since arriving in Jerusalem from Moscow, he had come to associate the heat of the day with departure, with stations, with farewells and seeing people off, the end of relationships, escape from the past and fear of the future. He turned round and started back along the asphalt alley. Taking a deep breath to keep his spirits up, he knocked on the first heavy oak door he came to. Without waiting for an answer he gave it a push with his shoulder and the door opened wide.

His back to the window, behind a desk that looked like a gigantic carved wooden four-poster bed, there presided a man of imposing appearance. His face was crumpled with post-prandial sleep. It was clear that the repast had been accompanied by liquid refreshment, because his half-open eyes were looking in different directions. It even seemed to Felix that he was looking not at him but at the life-sized stuffed pheasant that sat on the right side of the desk. The eyes gradually focused on Felix, who had remained standing, with his suitcase, in the sunlight in the middle of the room. In the meantime the room came into focus for Felix. It was crammed with ecclesiastical paraphernalia, ritualistic religious rubbish and Catholic kitsch: several crucifixes where the victim's body could not be seen for grapevines and silver-plated leaves, faces of saints in the form of bas-reliefs made of refracting coloured plastic, half-naked Virgin Marys and entirely nude golden angels peering out of corners, hung with chains, censers, wreaths and beads that

28

shone in the sunset. Felix noticed a tonsure on the head of the fat giant behind the desk, and the fact that he was wearing a cassock, though admittedly it was worn over jeans. Who was he? A priest, a prelate, spiritual advisor to this mysterious establishment? Under his fixed gaze Felix started fidgeting like a thief or a foreign spy caught red-handed. His Israeli laissez-passer started to burn a hole in the left side of his chest.

For some time the prelate sat there without moving, peering at Felix with sleepy, fish-like eyes. Then he slowly rose, tottered, and with a solemn wave of his hand, as if he were sprinkling Felix with holy water, addressed him in English in curt and husky tones: 'Go, go, go!' he said, and crossed himself.

'Wait a moment, padre.' A rumbling baritone English voice made itself heard from the corner. 'Seminaro russo, per favore,' the invisible man explained to the priest, speaking Italian with a pronounced English accent. In the alcove of the bay-window, moving into a pool of light on the waxed wooden floor, there appeared a man built like a boxer, with a lumpy bald spot and bulldog jaw hanging over his bow-tie, hands in his pockets and wearing a beautifully cut three-piece suit. Felix's first impression of Dr Genoni was of a man far more sinister, powerful and self-possessed than Dr Genoni ever dreamed himself to be. 'Dr Genoni, Lord Edward's private secretary and personal physician,' he introduced himself, and his smile revealed a row of massive, snow-white teeth that shone bright as a salvo from a military firing-squad at a public execution. 'I shall see you later, right?' he said, and pressing a button on the desk he waved a hand at Felix as if he were a train in the process of departing.

'Right,' Felix repeated stupidly and also gave a wave of his hand as he backed towards the door. On the far side a silent servant was awaiting him, like a sentry, dressed, it is true, not in a cassock, but in blue workmen's overalls. The major-domo gestured to Felix to follow directly behind him down the corridor; a single step to one side would be taken as an attempt to escape.

'I had the feeling I was under arrest,' Felix said in a letter to Silva. They moved from one floor to the next, on stairs leading from gallery to gallery, with identical rows of doors that looked like the doors of prison cells. Not a breath of air reached Felix's cage, because the window looked out over the stifling inner courtyard. By hanging out of his window and leaning back across the sill it was just possible to see a little patch of blue. Sometimes a shutter opened slightly and he could make out the silhouette of another inmate – 'a reminder that our life on earth is no more than a spell in prison,' wrote Felix to Silva. The hall of residence for Catholic students had been built like a high-rise monastery, and thus was reminiscent of a high-rise prison. A prison of the spirit, while Russia was a prison of the people. Prison automatically made him think of Victor and Vladimir Prison, where Victor was frequently confined at particularly difficult times for 'bad behaviour'. As a matter of fact, Vladimir Prison used to be a monastery.

The sweat was running down his forehead in a warm thin trickle, like blood. Felix was afraid it would stain the paper, and that, heaven forbid Silva might mistake it for tears. 'Have you heard anything of Victor? The last I heard was from a Zionist who'd done time for trying to hijack an aircraft. He'd come across Victor in the camps and said that, whenever he could, Victor would go off to the recreational area where he'd take plasticine and model a medieval castle, complete with drawbridge, towers, a moat and all the accessories. A castle in prison; prison in a castle. A monkey in its cage making a sketch of the confining bars.

'I met the Zionist at Lyudmila's place in Bathsheba. I hadn't taken to my ex-wife's new home. She taught art at the high school there. Was it really worth travelling all that way for that? If she'd really wanted to drum Turner's techniques of chiaroscuro into the heads of the mentally deficient she should have stayed on as a guide at the Pushkin Museum!

'"And here is our Bathsheba," my ex-wife observed to me with that note of patriotic pride much favoured by the local population; any expression of doubt was held to question not so much the nobility of the place itself as that of the speaker who had elected to settle there. "What you mean is that this place used to be the biblical Bathsheba," I said. "That's it, Bathsheba," she insisted obstinately. This is the place where Isaac blessed Jacob as his first-born, confusing him with Esau. ("The voice is Jacob's voice but the hands are the hands of Esau," complained Isaac.) It's hardly surprising in a blinding light like that. You could lose your eyesight if you don't wear sunglasses.

'Your invitation to replace Avestin at the Verona summer

school came just in time to preserve my sanity – I don't know who to thank: you, for being so quick on the uptake, your lordly benefactor, who cares so much about the fate of the Russian language throughout the world, or the Soviet regime for not letting Avestin come to Italy? Although, strictly between ourselves, I am not sure how much longer I can stand it here either; the heat, the idiotic students, even the Soviet-speak – think of that particular tongue as the long arm of the Kremlin, anatomically interesting, wouldn't you say? – it's all got to me already. Whatever happens I have no intention of going back to Jerusalem. Have a word with your Lord Edward; if he can organize a whole Russian summer school in Italy, perhaps he could take me on as his secretary, interpreter, the director of his private theatre. The main thing is for me to get permission to stay in England. Where else could I go? They're going to kick me out of here the moment summer school is ended – Italy does not take in refugees, particularly ones with an Israeli laissez-passer.'

Like his English teacher, Migulin, Felix longed for the poets of the Lake District. This was alien territory, Avestin's territory. In Moscow, Avestin used to champion the delights of the Latino-Gallic temperament, so different from Anglo-Saxon phlegm, while the clear, light Italian language, with is cosmo-politan, easily grasped roots, contrasted with 'your unpro-nounceable English "tkhe" as Pushkin used to pronounce "the"'. In Moscow people were ready to listen to Avestin for hours as he explained the difference between café lungho and cappuccino, or spaghetti and pizza. He knew all about which hostels would give you a free bed for the night on your way, say, from Verona to Milan, and which ones threw in a free bowl of soup into the bargain. This was all part of a kind of instant Europe that had found its way into a Moscow kitchen by dint of quotations and scraps of information lifted furtively from briefly glimpsed, forbidden newspapers, picked up from contraband books smuggled in by foreigners; it was all a fiction invented by a reader's imagination, shaping a fantasy that had become a way of life for those who, amid clouds of Bulgarian tobacco in a smoky Moscow kitchen, sought to descry a different kind of reality, one that lay beyond all frontiers and restrictions, a reality founded in words, read in secret. (The Italian stream that Pushkin described as being nothing short of the river Hippocrene, flowing with milk and honey, was actually, according to Nabokov, nothing short of an open sewer.)

The unpleasantness in Verona took Felix back to Avestin's 'literature', but now, instead of being part of the audience, he was a protagonist, a hero even. But it was someone else's novel, someone else's drama. A tragi-comedy. More specifically it was a Pirandello play, called *Henry IV*, in a Russian translation, the textbook they were using in the summer school. The same Henry whose fall had made him lose his mind for a short time, only to regain his sanity and then decide to continue to pretend to be mad. Or perhaps he only imagined that he had regained his sanity and was just pretending to be mad, whereas in reality he was crazy and always had been, quite irrespective of his fall. Felix couldn't say how it all ended. The students didn't get beyond the first act, and he hadn't the slightest inclination to get to the end of this insanity wrapped in an insanity – if, that is, insanity has any ending. Felix always tried to avoid any kind of ending, happy or otherwise. The ending of insanity meant the beginning of responsibility – an unpleasant enough prospect, judging by the hero's example, and doubly so in such a grotesque translation.

An Italian play translated into Russian for the benefit of students at a Russian summer school in Italy – hence the choice of Pirandello as the course textbook. More specifically, Lord Edward got the bright idea because Avestin was the principal translator, interpreter and exponent of Pirandello. It was stunning how, in their fanatical, even hysterical reaction against the monotheistic ideology of Stalinism, the older generation insisted upon the relativity of all moral criteria and the fragmentation of consciousness. The grotesque translation made such paradoxes sound particularly cheap and pretentious. Because Pirandello's ideological correctness had always been subject to doubt, the Soviets banned Avestin's translation and refused him an exit visa. Felix was obliged either to use a samizdat copy with stunning gaps and typos, or the grotesque translation (what was the name, Schepkin, Kuprin?) in which, for example, the word 'dentist' was rendered as 'Dante scholar'.

He was summoned to an 'audience' with Lord Edward by letter (after Silva had assured him that they'd help him get set up in

London), with detailed directions to the lord's mansion in a medieval town near Milan. The train from Verona to Milan, hot as a shotgun barrel, proceeded at a snail's pace with endless halts which were as frustrating as waiting for the train had been in the first place. A sense of hallucinatory unreality increased as a funicular carried him up to the old town. The rectangular piazza within the walls of the citadel looked like a page torn out of a medieval history book. The sundial and the meridian marker he could see beneath the arches at the entrance to the cathedral did nothing to relieve the sense that he was lost in both time and space. In front of the cathedral in a corner of the square stood a statue of an honoured citizen of the town – Torquato Tasso, the author of *Jerusalem Delivered*, who went insane while serving a seven-year prison sentence in a dungeon in the castle of his former patron.

The clock in the cathedral belfry began to chime noon, and the chimes had not even died away before, as it were in echo, a second set of chimes rang out from the town hall, a minute later. It was as if they were providing Lord Edward with a two-fold announcement that Felix had arrived.

He had already heard about the lord in Moscow, in connection with parcels sent to political prisoners and their families. But here talk of his generosity was not confined to the fact that he had founded the Verona College for the Study of the Russian Language. Here they spoke of him with bated breath; he was a demi-god whose invisible presence illuminated every step taken by his followers and disciples along their life's path. It was true that Felix had not yet come across a single member of the college's staff who had actually met Lord Edward. However, they all knew the café in Verona where Lord Edward took his coffee and brioche (he never ate pheasant, and preferred potheen to grappa), the Scottish poets he read last thing at night (Felix had never heard of John Wilson). It seemed that every dog, every stone there knew all about Lord Edward. Whatever local landmark Felix might have been passing, someone was bound to stop and reminisce: 'A few years ago, when Lord Edward was here . . .'

When Felix finally entered the narrow little drawing room with its windows looking out over the city wall and the moat, he first made a nervous inspection of the faces, trying to determine which was Lord Edward. On a pair of sofas, four lugubrious gentlemen sat, glass in hand, scowling silently. Felix recognized only one of them: the same servant who had taken him up the prison stairs to his monk's cell, the day of his arrival in Verona. The others were no more impressive; they wore faded jeans and leather boots and sported beards. Moving to the window, Felix desperately tried to think of something to say, to break the uninterrupted silence. Instead the silence was broken by the chimes from the cathedral belfry, repeated, after a brief interval, by the clock from the town hall. Thereupon a waiter in the restaurant below, singing with operatic high seriousness, broke into the 'Toreador Song'.

'That aria should be banned! It's about bullfighting, isn't it, about the killing of innocent ruminants? I fear that Lord Edward won't care for such arias, no they won't do at all!' Dr Genoni had entered the room through the side door. His brisk chatter appeared suddenly, as if emerging straight from the wall. It was as faultless as his suit and bow-tie or his immaculately shaven chin. He turned and bowed to all and sundry and beckoned Felix to follow him into another room, holding the door for him. He seated him in an armchair and started to walk round and round him like a circus trainer.

'It's good that you are interested in theatre,' Dr Genoni observed, as if talking to himself. 'I liked your interpretation of Pirandello in the classroom – I mean in the sense that you associated psychiatry and theatre. Do you see? Have you noticed a unifying symptom in the behaviour of the mentally deficient, crazies, nuts, loonies . . .' – Dr Genoni checked his flow of synonyms – 'something peculiar about the external appearance of those who are internally abnormal? Let me give you a simple example: frighten someone, and immediately he'll start waving his hands about, trembling, his eyes wide with terror. His psychological state is reflected in his appearance. Elementary, is it not? Do you see what I am getting at? In our private psychiatric clinic (Lord Edward provided the funding for it a year or so ago), I have developed this idea into my drama therapy psychiatry. I stopped trying to discover the patient's phobias and fears. Instead I try to alter the external characteristics, right down to aspects of appearance and behaviour, and use those changes to reshape the inner state. A complete reversal.'

'By emigrating, for example?'

'For example,' agreed Genoni. 'Anyway, let's talk about all that when we meet again in England. Now I have to have a chat with the board of the Maltese Order,' and he jerked his thumb towards the adjacent room with the four lugubrious bearded gentlemen. 'I am afraid I didn't introduce you. I expect you've heard of the Order?'

'The Russian Emperor Paul I was a Knight of the Order of Malta, and, it would seem, went mad as a result, or so the story goes. It's a crusading order, isn't it? Formed to liberate Palestine from spitting camels and blasphemous Jews?' Felix's voice was charged with irony. He was trying to keep in mood with Dr Genoni, but that was proving increasingly difficult. Genoni's eyes shifted slightly as if he suspected Felix's sincerity. It was hard to say why this doctor assumed such eccentric posturings – because he affected the mad professor, or perhaps he was forced by somebody else to say things he believed were quite mad.

'I wasn't talking about blasphemous Jews or spitting camels, though Jews and camels, the animal world in general, are indeed relevant to the subject,' said Dr Genoni. 'I meant the Maltese Order of Gamekeepers. Malta, like Palestine, has practically no game. The woods are sparse, it's hot and there are nothing but exotic birds in the thickets, canaries, parrots, kiwis – as a matter of fact, I'm not good at birds. But people crave blood: killing is a part of their nature.

'When there are no wild boar, they shoot wild geese; when there are no geese, they take to killing first their neighbours and then one another. Malta and Palestine share the same problem: who are you going to shoot? In Palestine the Jewish–Palestinian conflict provides a release. So Lord Edward founded the Maltese Order of Gamekeepers. Lord Edward's estate sends scores, no, hundreds of pheasants – he always rears too many – to Malta and other countries with a similar problem, like Israel. They satisfy the local blood-lust while preserving the rare birds. In return the local gamekeepers send us Maltese hounds. And I can tell you, Malta has superb hounds. Our enterprise thwarts the work of the notorious International Convention of Game-keepers which has its centre in Eastern Germany. As usual Lord Edward has had to go away unexpectedly, so it's up to me to deal with the Order. Do you by any chance know the difference between a grouse and a quail?'

Felix shrugged.

'About your move to London.' Dr Genoni got to the point right away. 'Take a look at this pile of entry documents. This is for the Home Office, our Ministry of Internal Affairs, not for the passport people. Say one word too many there, and they'll suspect that you are not just a tourist but are planning to stay in England and take bread from the mouths of our unemployed natives, and then it will be bye-bye visa.'

'And what will be my duties and obligations as Lord Edward's secretary?'

'None at all really. I do all the secretarial work. As far as I know he wants you as a translator.'

'But I'm not a translator, I'm a drama scholar.'

It appeared that Lord Edward actually wanted a sort of 'theatrical translation' done. Something to do with Pushkin's *Little Tragedies*, which had not been translated into English. Consider for example 'The Feast held during an Epidemic'. Dr Genoni was clearly referring to 'Festivities at the Time of Plague', but Felix decided not to quibble. Besides, they promised him an English translator to assist his endeavours, a female translator to be more precise, and as the name Mary-Louise Wilson suggested, she was not English at all, but a pure-bred Scot, warned the doctor.

Leaving the house, Felix had snatched up a whole handful of hazelnuts from a basket by Dr Genoni's front door – doubtless an offering from the gamekeepers and foresters of the Maltese Order. With only a moment's hesitation, he went to the window, placed a nut between the window and the frame, and holding his breath to steady his hand, as if he were about to take a difficult shot, he slammed the window smartly down.

The window and its frame fitted together like a pair of well-made scissor blades. The nut whistled past his head like a bullet; it was his thumb that took the nut's intended place. Felix reacted quite fast: he managed to save the thumb itself, managed not to crush the bone, but the thumbnail shattered and broke in half. Rushing to the tap, he held the tumb under the icy stream for a long time and then stuck the nail together with a plaster. Regardless of the fact that he kept changing plasters, the blood continued to flow from under the nail; he didn't notice that his shirt was all stained and when he eventually landed at Heathrow and fumbled for his documents to have his visa stamped, he dripped blood on his Israeli laissez-passer.

36

5

Asylum

Towards noon the sun started to break through the fog, and trees began to emerge from the whitish morning haze, like photographic negatives. Next the horses came swimming up out of the mist, grazing around the oak tree, and then even the chickens abandoned their incognito. Betraying their anonymity with an anxious cackle, they went out into the meadow in single file, and waited, head on one side, to be fed the pieces of bread left over from breakfast.

'You make your arrival in England so complicated.' Victor turned to Felix, on the offensive now. 'Be honest. It wasn't ideological howls and camel spit that made you clear out of Jerusalem. It was Arab bullets.'

'To begin with, unlike you, I don't believe that fear is necessarily a bad thing,' replied Felix, mustering as much cool and academic sang-froid as he could. 'I don't believe that saving your own skin is an unworthy activity. I'd agree that changing your skin really is unworthy, and that may be the disgrace and tragedy of voluntary emigration. We just don't want to stay in our own skin.'

'Do me a favour and stop talking about "we"; you mean "you". It was you who didn't want to stay in your skin; I, as you know, was unceremoniously booted across the frontier,' Victor observed. Felix said nothing.

'Changing one's skin – permit me too to reply to Felix – was an activity which in no way demeaned our forefather Jacob.' Dr Genoni relished resuming his role of theoretician and stage director in this psychodrama. 'May I remind you that it was he who donned a goatskin so that he would resemble his hairy brother Esau to blind Isaac's touch. If you want to be blessed as the first-born you have to be prepared to disguise yourself a bit. And it's above all the sort of person who doesn't do anything in particular that goes in for disguises. Take Jacob. Jacob was a sort of intellectual and bookworm. He stayed home and didn't do much. But Esau had a respectable profession, he was a hunter. A pheasant hunter, or a gamekeeper. His father's gamekeeper, if you see what I mean.'

'Strictly speaking, it was Jacob's mother, not Jacob, who put the goatskin on him. It was her idea to play the first-born trick,' Felix interjected.

'I'm afraid you're taking this first-born thing too literally,' the doctor reprimanded him solemnly. 'But the Bible makes the point that you can only establish your spiritual primogeniture, that is to say arrive at an understanding of yourself, by donning another skin. That way you can see yourself from the outside for a moment, through someone else's eyes. I'll go further: you can only understand yourself when you become someone else. In your father's eyes. In the eyes of Isaac. When you become someone else under Western eyes. But no one is about to impose on you in this country; God has no middlemen here. No Migulins and no Avestins.' Dr Genoni smiled in self-congratulation. 'Frankly, I can't see why you don't admit that all your arguments about changing skin and the first-born pretensions are, in fact, related to your contentious emulation of your gurus, Migulin and Avestin. Isn't that so?'

6

On the Other Bank

It is practically impossible for an ordinary émigré to get into England. You need a special invitation, a personal letter of reference, you need to pass an exam at the BBC or be offered a chair at Oxford or Cambridge. The best and most unlikely way in is by means of an invitation from relatives, one which gives you 'residence', in other words the right to remain there indefinitely. Then you enter Albion as if at the invitation of Her Majesty Queen Elizabeth. Silva had been afforded that honour, as it were, gratis, for the simple reason that her family name was Lermontov, which meant that she was a member of the Scottish Clan MacLermont, and had relatives galore in the United Kingdom. And it should be noted that this all emerged unbeknownst to her; she didn't have to lift a finger. Lord Edward did it all – tracked down her distant relatives in Scotland, composed the invitation, and obtained a visa through the British Embassy in Moscow – while hoi polloi such as Felix were making the agonizing existential choice between Moscow and Jerusalem (Lyudmila had sent him an invitation from Israel) and were cooling their heels in queues at customs and passport offices. So Silva was greeted in London like one of the family, while Felix was neither an exile (the only kind of immigrant that the British respected) nor a foreign guest, let alone a tourist. Accordingly he kept having to make up excuses for his being in England. This obliged him to keep making up different answers to questions such as 'where are you from?', 'when did you leave, and why?' This in turn put him constantly on his guard and made him evasive with strangers: sometimes he resembled a hungry hunted vagabond.

Speaking volubly and with some difficulty (he had still to grow accustomed to the various kinds of London English), he proffered a variety of explanations and reflections about the nature and whereabouts of his roots (the British being of course great gardening experts), and gave his views on the Arab–Israeli conflict ('the Arabs and the Jews are stepbrothers, and you have to understand that as such no one can make peace between them!'), on the metaphysical aspects of Italian culture ('Italy epitomizes the view that the principle of perpetual repose gives birth to perpetual motion; beauty is repose, but with Italians beauty turns into a kind of madness'), or else, when seeing the New Year in as the guest of a Scottish household, he'd begin to hold forth on the way that one culture reflected another, Scotland and Russia for example. In each case their literatures looked beyond their frontiers, in Russia's case because of an authoritarian regime, in Scotland's because of domination by England.

People always listened to Felix attentively (he always considered this kind of polite and curious attention as a genuine dialogue, even though it was he who would do most of the talking – and in too loud a voice at that). And whenever anyone raised their glass they would ask: 'What's the Russian for cheers? Spasibo do zvidaniya?' It was a conversation that repeated itself more than once at Felix's first New Year's party in the British Isles. It was a Scottish party, after all, even if it was held in London. Glasses were being raised and emptied seemingly without interruption (accompanied by Felix's commentaries), and Felix was even beginning to feel that he was a brilliant conversationalist in the midst of this warm family of merrymakers, until he noticed that the conversation did not get beyond the subject of the different ways of raising and emptying glasses in Russia and Scotland. The tempo of the latter activity increased steadily, reaching its culmination after midnight, when they brought in an amber-coloured substance known as malt whisky in a silver bowl, and poured the amber liquid into silver cups with a silver ladle.

'Slangivar' rang out at midnight and an amateur group of Scots musicians, bagpipes, fifes and fiddles, struck up the band. The hostess, her husband, children, retinue and guests danced eightsome reels with a grandiose grace that was rivalled only by the graciousness of the hostess's grandiose form. Everything in the mansion seemed designed for giants, from the menu to the music. Silva was the only one to match the abandon of the entertainment, and soon the whole party was following her movements through the eightsome reel, clapping their hands and stamping their feet, the Scottish dance transformed into a Ukrainian one. Silva could get away with anything, because she was a member of the MacLermont clan, and even if her steps were not always strictly speaking in time or quite correct she was dancing our dance, thought Felix, before reeling at the implications. He was wrong. Silva was a Scot. She was in a Scots family. She was one of them. He was the outsider. And always would be. The fact that this Scots family in the English city of London felt themselves to be outsiders there, in just the way that Felix did in their midst, did not occur to him. In England they were émigrés too, hence the kilts, pipes and sporrans. As if, say, he, a Russian in England, had put on peasant bast-shoes, and started dancing kossak around a samovar. He had experienced the same sense of being an outsider many years ago in his own home. Silva was dancing there too, and he was watching her with the same feeling of jealousy and bitterness as he did now. For the first time in his life he realized then that certain prejudices and phobias would come to haunt you regardless of geography or politics.

On that fateful Moscow evening the émigré departing (for her 'historic motherland' – the customary expression used by applicants on forms requesting a permanent exit visa to settle in Israel) was Felix's ex-wife, Lyudmila. Felix was staying behind in Moscow, on principle, continuing, as he put it, 'to love his own fate despite himself'. The farewell parties held in their flat on Transfiguration Square were neither the best nor the worst. According to the unwritten law of the time these farewell functions started the moment a visa was granted and continued until the aircraft took off for another world. The remoteness of the West, of abroad, made the world beyond the frontier seem like an afterlife, so that the farewell parties were like wakes, thanks to the overpowering certainty that you would never meet again in the hereafter. This accounted for the way that totally unexpected faces from the past would turn up on these occasions – forgotten school friends, mysterious girlfriends, erstwhile and forgotten admirers and ex-lovers who had long since lost all power to attract.

On that occasion a hundred or so people, none of whom knew one another, were crammed into the flat, which had been cleared of its furniture. They crowded along the walls, glass in hand, forming groups or clustering around the last bottle of vodka to have been brought in. It was consumed on the spot, and since there were no more, each successive bottle seemed to be the last, and thus was consumed quickly and with an eager greed. As a result everyone got drunk rather quickly, and split up into little groups, which you could not break through without treading on people's feet. Everyone was shouting and interrupting everyone else, while no one was listening. Felix, who as the host was responsible for passing round the food and drink, frequently found himself forced into extremely embarrassing arguments. In the sitting room friends of Lyudmila's from her arts institute, who had clearly had the chance to spend time in the paradise of the West in their day, were heaping coals of abuse on absent friends, and on the countries they were no longer allowed to travel to, confusing forbidden territories with rejected friends.

'And as for the French, they'll pinch your bottom on a bus, and are quite happy to get very close indeed to you in public, but don't even think about being invited to their home. They even take their lovers to hotel rooms. With the English it's the other way round. The French live their private lives in public, the English do the opposite.' Passing by the sitting room on his way to the kitchen, Felix overheard a female voice prattling to her friend on the sofa.

'The French sit in cafés facing the street, side by side. They pay no attention to one another, they are there to see and be seen. An Englishman will go to a pub with his friend and pay no attention to his surroundings. Even the pub windows are made of opaque glass or hung with curtains. Sometimes there are no windows at all, just blank walls. Inner life there is like it is in Russia. An Englishman may be polite in public or solemn as an owl. But if he invites you home he'll treat you like a relation. I expect he explained all that properly, but let me tell you, after using French soap I can't go back to the Polish stuff!'

Felix never got the chance to hear the rest of this intoxicating discussion. A hand emerged from the flat's bathroom and pulled him firmly into that holy of holies of dissident conversation. Bathrooms in Moscow were the stage for the most clandestine goings-on. On this occasion they were reading an underground essay of Avestin's about Pirandello and the Soviet regime. Four people had crowded into the tiny bathroom and were handing sheets of typescript on to one another as they finished reading. The essay treated the history of the KGB and the trials as yet another play by Pirandello, in which the directors were the Soviet interrogators, the stage was the courtroom and the actors were the participants in the trial, with an audience made up of spectators when it was a show trial, and which took the form of a dress rehearsal if the trial happened to be closed to the public. Considered in those terms the entire country becomes a kind of KGB variant on the world of Pirandello, where more and more of the audience turn into actors, etc., etc. Nowadays all that anti-Soviet intellectual virtuosity sounds pretty contrived and banal; but then, in that plague-ridden Moscow summer, Avestin's essay was the talk of the town, but only the privileged were permitted to read it. In connection with a visit from some American senators, Moscow had been purged of its undesirable elements, and Avestin was one of the first to go. Already in Stalin's time in the early Fifties, after spending time in the psychiatric ward of a Leningrad prison, he was obliged to register at his local psychiatric clinic, which is why he was rapidly despatched, under police escort, to the Ganushkin Psychiatric Hospital, not far from Transfiguration Square, in the part of town known as Sailor's Repose.

At one end of the corridor there was crush caused by someone collecting signatures to a letter protesting at Avestin's forcible confinement in a mental hospital for political reasons (not the hospital but the act of forcible confinement). Of course it was Victor who had written the letter. And even though the burden of the petition was entirely predictable, no one as yet had seen the letter itself, because Victor was still polishing the final draft. Signatures were being collected on the basis of an agreement to protest in principle. Felix realized that there was only one corridor in the flat, and it was lined on both sides with guests holding glasses, like soldiers armed with staves, and he would have to run the gauntlet of a matter of principle: 'to sign or not to sign'.

'What you want to do,' continued a drawling and affected woman's voice from the sitting room, 'what you want to do is to empty the great man's chamber-pots, so that when he dies you inherit his books and papers and become the director of the museum. That's it, isn't it? Well, maybe not director, but at least the spiritual heir – yes, that's a great life for a woman. But how can you tell whether or not he's a great man? Apart from the fact that no one becomes great overnight, suppose you die suddenly emptying the chamber-pot, die before him, before he's become famous, so that you'll never know whether or not it was really worth devoting your life to him. In other words just any old great man who's due for recognition won't quite do, you need the kind of great man who's recognized already.'

As usual Victor made his appearance at the very end, when everyone was drunk and raucous. They talked a lot about Victor in those days, about his determination, his fearlessness, his refusal to compromise and his iron will. His appearance at Lyudmila's farewell party (it was curious that no one paid her any attention at all that evening, it was as if she had already left for Palestine) was a piece of dissident's luck; it was one of those rare periods when Victor was out of prison, and had not yet taken the next, always fateful, dangerous and defiant step, which, as usual, would lead to interrogation, search and seizure. Everyone pretended that his appearance at Felix and Lyudmila's was perfectly normal, and that nothing unusual was going on – celebrities drop in here every day. But Felix remembered his expression perfectly; to be exact, and like everyone else incidentally, he could not take his eyes off Victor, and watched his every move round the flat, and more or less unconsciously, without realizing it, he always found himself in the same room as him, close to the people crowding round him. He soon realized that it wasn't vanity or an urge to bask in reflected glory that made him follow Victor, it was pure unadulterated jealousy to do with Silva. Suddenly Victor drew back from the general conversation, or din to be more precise, and addressed Felix: 'Hey, old man, how about eating out of my hand?'

'What?' Felix really did not understand. It was camp slang most likely. 'Eat out of your hand? I don't know anything about prison literature. At the moment I'm translating some very different writers.' Like every expert on English theatre, Felix assumed that he would be very good at translating anything that he was interested in professionally. Every actor is a director at heart, while every director is convinced that a great actor is lost in him.

'A translation, from what into what?' asked Victor.

'A translator, I know the kind – he translates from shit into crap, that's the kind he is,' someone observed with a drunken giggle.

44

'I'm translating Thomas De Quincey,' Felix answered calmly and politely.

'Did you say Thomas Aquinsky? Or am I mixing him up with Torquemada and the Inquisition?' Victor looked around curiously, hardly expecting an answer.

'You're mixing him up all right.' Felix was relieved that a neutral subject for discussion had come up at last. 'Thomas De Quincey is the author of the book we call *The Opium Smoker*. The translation is wrong actually, because in those days opium was sold in tablet form, rather like a sugar-coated almond. That's why in the English version De Quincey is not a smoker but an eater.'

'How about a drink?' Victor emptied his glass and Felix realized what he meant by eating out of his hand. Victor was actually clutching all sorts of food, a salt cucumber, a radish, a slice of ham – all the plates had been emptied a long time ago.

'But as a drama scholar I'm not translating the opium stuff, I'm working on his reflections on the Knocking at the Gate scene in *Macbeth*.'

'And you're not afraid?' asked Victor, finally fixing his probing and piercing eyes on Felix.

'Afraid, what of? A knocking at the gate?' Felix laughed uneasily.

'I mean just sitting there and translating, you're not afraid?'

'What do you mean? Translating is not the world's most hazardous activity,' muttered Felix.

'Well, if you don't understand, there's nothing to be afraid of. See you,' said Victor, with that Moscow intonation which could mean that things were all right for the time being, though not for very long, but which could also be taken for an ordinary goodbye. Felix realized that he was already thinking like a foreigner, reflecting upon the literal and metaphorical significance of every word. It was only later that the penny dropped. It was frightening to study trivialities in a frightening world. That's what Victor had meant. But the hero's path was far simpler. Felix fancied that Victor was exploiting that selfsame heroic option which he, Felix, had so quickly rejected. He'd left, but Victor remained heroically behind, and thereby won Silva's heart.

Victor's 'See you' sounded more like a 'Farewell'. He turned in answer to someone calling him and moved to the far end of the room, rudely shouldering Felix aside. Felix stumbled and nearly fell, sent flying against the wall opposite. You remember, you remember it all, of course. The way you walked slowly across the room and spat something vicious at me. It was Silva who had popped through the doorway like a champagne cork, who hailed Victor, grabbed him and waltzed through the room with him. Felix felt his shoulder was on fire where Victor had hit him, as if it was his cheek which had just been slapped. He felt hot all of a sudden. Taking a look at Silva spinning round the room (she's going to throw up again – why does she have to dance all the time?), he started to leave. Leaving that life, loudly slamming the door behind him – which nobody appeared to notice.

He started to go down the stairs, stamping his feet, and was already leaving the apartment block when he heard Silva's voice shouting 'What's up, Felix?' and the sound of her footsteps behind him. He went out into the street to the bus-stop. She ran out after him, obviously feeling that she'd behaved badly and done something wrong (he remembered the way her eyes lit up when she looked at Victor, her half-open mouth and her silly grin, the lower lip jutting out, sagging almost, making her look like a helpless, hungry old man looking at his favourite dish). He suddenly lost control and started to scream at her, spit flying, hands waving, behaving like a drunken cuckold. 'You're crooked, you're a common little fool and you're crooked.' In total amazement she watched him leave, sitting inside the bus like some kind of reptile in a glass aquarium. It was only after a few stops that he realized that he'd run out of his own flat away from his own wife's farewell party.

It was as if the same bus transported him, as in a time-machine, from Transfiguration Square to Lewisham in South East London ten years later. Greenwich was just a stone's throw away. From the hilltop you could look out across the Thames at London, with St Paul's Cathedral on the horizon. If you made some minor allowances for factory chimneys and tower blocks the view was a re-creation of Turner's famous painting with the twin domes of Greenwich Hospital, now the Royal Naval College.

The zero meridian, a mere strip of brass rail set into the courtyard of Greenwich Observatory, divided up the territory, splitting off grand Blackheath with its private homes and mansions from vulgar proletarian Lewisham. Silva lived between the two. Like all new translators, Felix immediately gave vent to bewilderment and other thoughts with respect to the name Blackheath. Looking at the enormous grassy expanse of Blackheath, he refused to translate the place-name literally: Black Wood. You could not even call it a coppice. In the end he settled for a compromise, Black Wasteland. But all these translator's endeavours turned out to be pointless, since he soon reverted to the English version in a Russian transcription: Blekhit. It was not just the geography; everyday objects too lacked precise Russian equivalents. The best-known Soviet translators of English literature had never been to England, or had only been on a short visit, like visitors to a museum taking down a misspelt transcription of the guide's description of the exhibits. How could the landscape be translated into Russian if even its grass bore no relation to the word 'wasteland' and its associations; no docks, weeds or plantains? Besides, what did a double-decker bus have to do with a wasteland, moving across the green expanse like a ladybird – so that even the red postbox became its anthropological colleague? But his initial helpless attempts to cope with this linguistically untranslatable reality soon gave way to a sigh of relief; he finally found himself in a real world quite devoid of any insistently allusive quotations from the past. And that's what freedom really was.

'So where was your female relative? Why wasn't Mary-Louise invited to your relatives' party if you are all related?' asked Felix the next morning. He asked this question about his future collaborator on Pushkin's translation because he hoped to resume the habit of dissecting a party, gossiping about those who were present and guessing why others were absent, analysing the growing sense of alienation and signs of general disintegration, etc., etc. But Silva did not show any sign of encouraging such Moscow habits in her London existence. She had a purposeful air about her, fussing round the place as though in preparation for an outing. Instead of going into a lengthy and lazy discussion of the night before, she replied tartly to Felix's question that the MacLermonts of Blackheath had invited her, and Felix, to their New Year's party, not so much because they were related, or rather shared the same name, but because she was from Moscow, and hence a piece of local exotica, for whom all doors were open. Her 'cousin' Mary-Louise Wilson (the selfsame relation whose fictitious formal invitation got Silva into the country) was not so privileged, and was indeed something of a black sheep in the

MacLermont clan (her maternal grandmother had been a MacLermont). After seeing a bit of Silva soon after she arrived in Albion, Mary-Louise vanished for some time, although she lived quite near by, in Lewisham, earning her living as a shopgirl, a waitress, a hospital orderly and heaven knows what else. The subject of her Slavic studies and translations did not arise in the course of her conversations with Silva. Indeed, Silva was hard put to say why Lord Edward had chosen Mary-Louise Wilson to be Felix's consultant (should he encounter problems while translating Pushkin's 'Festivities at the Time of Plague').

Mary-Louise's name came up when the possibility of a phoney marriage was being discussed. Confirmation of Felix's status as Lord Edward's secretary and translator proved insufficient. The authorities were prepared to give him a residence extension if he were able to provide a document which could be stamped with such an extension. His Israeli laissez-passer expired in a month. He had to return to the Holy Land to renew it, and Felix had long since ceased to feel holy.

Silva had begun to suspect that it was not so much a matter of papers and stamps as Felix's attempt to invent some kind of hierarchy of émigré status, according to which he would, of course, be one degree lower than Silva – which gave him yet another excuse to play humiliated and insulted.

'Of course, lords don't stand in line to get me a British passport,' Felix could not resist observing. Remarks like these drove Silva crazy. Felix knew perfectly well that all Lord Edward had done to help Silva get into England was to unearth her more or less phoney relative Mary-Louise. Felix knew perfectly well that she had never actually met Lord Edward himself – she had only corresponded with him. She tried to explain to him that she had had to deal with exactly the same kind of bureaucratic red tape when her Soviet passport expired and she was eventually given British papers. He'd get them too, the authorities had no choice; he'd have an English identity card, and an English identity into the bargain.

'Why are you so obsessed with the idea of getting a stamp and having all the proper paperwork done? You're a passport patriot.' Silva was genuinely amazed.

'Of course, my patriotism is passport-based.' Felix nodded emphatically. 'A passport is like an oath of allegiance. What else do I have to swear to? All other manifestations of allegiance, fidelity and loyalty – such as God, sex and literature – I keep to myself, and I have no intention of declaring them at some customs and passport check of my personal relations with other people. I leave it to you Catholics to confess your secret little passions to those papal lackeys of yours with circumcised brains.'

'What on earth do you mean, circumcised brains?' Silva was already familiar with Felix's fits of preposterous rage. He used to spit most bizarre and venomous ideas into her face – just provoking a quarrel, the only purpose of which was to prove to her that he was always right and she was always wrong.

'You know those Catholic priests of yours with a tonsure on their heads, which makes them look like circumcised penises.' He was carrying on like a stubborn child.

'Since when have you been so anti-clerical?'

'Since when? Ever since that Pope of yours tried to have me sent back to Palestine.'

'What's the Pope got to do with it? You were in Verona, not Rome. Besides, what's all this about *my* Pope?'

'In the first place, the Catholic conspiracy reaches out all over the world, not just Italy, let alone Verona. Everything's caught up in the sticky web of papal conspiracy.' Felix was clearly enjoying the paranoid logic of his argument with Silva. 'As for you – you're a descendant of Scottish Catholics, are you not? Lermontov, MacLermont, eh? And you British Catholics have long been recognized by decent English folk as a bunch of Papist conspirators and plotters. You've been practising that hypocrisy of yours for centuries. The Old Deceiver and the Young Deceiver!'

'Pretender, not Deceiver. You can't even translate "pretender" properly, you confused two different meanings. Do stop trying to confuse me. I haven't been received into the Catholic faith yet, and the Pope of Rome is neither a father nor even an uncle to me. Even Mary-Louise Wilson herself is not exactly the closest of relatives.' She was fed up with his childish insults. What she had taken for his wounded pride was simply petty-mindedness and jealousy. 'You have just as much chance as I ever had of being allowed to live here permanently, being granted residence as they call it. Just find yourself a phoney wife – why not Mary-Louise – why not marry my relation for a short time? That way we'll all be related, and you will get the roots and soil you need for your passport patriotism. And she's a translator. Do you know what you have to do when you dream in a foreign language?'

'What?'

'Sleep with a translator.'

7

Asylum

The fog lifted. The weather cleared to the point that if you climbed on to the cottage roof you could see wooden structures above the Kent coalmines that looked just like concentration camp watchtowers. Felix gazed appreciatively at the cherry tree and the meadow, the horse, the goat and the chickens, sighed and went back to reading his translator's notes.

'Who would have thought that here in London, enjoying the dubious status of an Israeli displaced person, I'd have to translate Pushkin's "Festivities at the Time of Plague" into English? My legs wanted to go to a jazz club or a disco, my stomach craved Indian food, my eyes stared into the windows of Soho porn shops, but my conscience, which had sunk as low as it could get, kept me in the library for days on end. There were various ways of putting off doing the translation. Pretending that you are building up vocabulary for the future. The bookshelf was crammed with "plaguy" books; from Defoe and his *Journal of the Plague Year* to such bibliographical rarities as, say, a novel purchased in a junk shop on Lee High Road, S.E.13, entitled *Old Saint Paul's* by William Harrison Ainsworth (George Routledge and Sons Ltd, 1841), which the author, as he explained in the detailed introduction to his epic, based upon a tale told in a slim volume called *Preparation against the Plague, both of Soul and of Body*, which Harrison Ainsworth attributed to the pen of Daniel Defoe.

'Of course, the first thing that strikes you about Defoe is the detail, and the arithmetic of the plague years: how many died in May, how many in September. Much more interesting is the recurrence of certain themes in Defoe's work: nakedness, for example, a conscious involuntary striptease occasioned by the plague; the false prophets that wandered naked around London proclaiming the "destruction of Jerusalem"; the grave-diggers that robbed the dead then tossed them naked into the plague-pits; libertines in a state of total undress conducting orgies in the streets as they celebrated the plague. The theme of nakedness and the end of the world repeats itself so strikingly that it takes on a further, metaphysical significance. Nakedness as an attempt to revert to a prehistoric pre-civilized condition, to the innocence of Eden, identified with nakedness without a sense of shame. Biblical shame which has split into the Arab sense of disgrace and the Jewish sense of guilt.

'In those days they were not ashamed to touch on teleological topics and directly metaphysical themes in their writing. Witness the touching discussion between the narrator, Defoe, the believer in Divine Providence and predestination, with his brother, who was not unsympathetic to the notion of free will, as to whether or not they should flee the plague by doing their level best to cross the city walls, or else should stay and drink bad wine in its hellish alleys; moreover, for all they knew, the plague might still be rampant beyond the city walls, so why risk their lives trying to get across them? Even if the plague were not already rampant out there, anyone who had got across the city walls would be held to be so dangerous to others that he would be sent straight back – in which case was the game worth the candle?

'It would be three centuries before such dilemmas would be aired again, in Moscow at the time of the mass emigration: to leave or not to leave? The hard-and-fast teleological issue facing Defoe had become a metaphor for us. Who felt more guilty about being alive, those who escaped from prison leaving their comrades to their fate, or those who put up with prison? Who is the coward, the suicide or the one who clings to life? This is close to Pushkin's

> All that threatens to destroy
> Is a source of boundless joy
> To the mortal human heart –
> Life everlasting's pledge perhaps.

'What was Pushkin doing writing like that in 1830? What made him seek heady delight in "Arabian hurricane and in the exhalations of the plague"? "Time of the plague" certainly, fair enough, because cholera quarantine prevented him from leaving his estate at Boldino. But why "Festivities"? He had enjoyed the quarantine because the cholera relieved him of all responsibility for events in the outside world. There was no need to return to St Petersburg, to his fiancée, the bronze empress, the wooden emperor, to malicious gossip and the duel he would some day fight with d'Anthès. Wasn't this delight in his self-imposed confinement the source of "festivity"? Yet the actual quarantine was a piece of pure subterfuge, since the cholera, like Soviet censorship, was already in the atmosphere. In other words he recognized that he had fled from Petersburg to Boldino under completely false pretences. As he wrote:

> When people still believed that cholera, like plague, was transmitted by physical contact, quarantine was a necessary evil. But since they soon realized that cholera is in the atmosphere they should have put a stop to the quarantine at once.

'But to compare the atmosphere of mass denunciations and emigration to the plague is to confine oneself once and for all to the quarantine of a metaphor. For Daniel Defoe it's all literal: those who fled the plague-stricken City towards South London and crossed the Thames "were found starved to death in the woods and commons, that country being more open and more woody than any other part near London, especially near Norwood and the parishes of Camberwell, Dulwich and Lusum, where, it seems, no one durst relieve the poor distressed people for fear of infection". Lusum is, of course, the old name for Lewisham. More woody and more open, like the greensward of Blackheath. While for us, and for Pushkin, these were just exotic place-names, a romantic parody. Small wonder that Pushkin's "Festivities" bears the subtitle "From Wilson's tragedy The City of the Plague". Most probably one of Pushkin's parodic jokes, like his "Songs of the Western Slavs". Incidentally, I must remember to point out that the original manuscript of "Festivities at the Time of Plague" vanished, and was only rediscovered a century later, at the height of Stalin's terror. Perhaps he never did write "Festivities at the Time of Plague"? Who's Wilson? Why haven't we heard of him before? Who would have thought that Wilson would be a real name? I must ask my consultant Mary-Louise Wilson whether she is related to John Wilson, the putative author of "Festivities at the Time of Plague".'

8

The White Horse

The drunken New Year's party ended disastrously. He should have stayed away from Silva. He'd promised to give her up twenty times or more, but the drink made him think he could start all over again. He took her absent-minded air of distraction for a sultry gaze, the tired inclination of the shoulders for an inclination of an entirely different sort. When they got home it all turned out predictably. When Felix grew too insistent she simply slammed her door in his face, leaving him all alone on the drawing-room sofa. He stared at his own reflection in the darkened window, where the window-frame looked like prison bars, and hence foreshadowed Victor. Felix kept nodding off, and sleep came as a merciful relief to his feeling of rejection. He was awakened by the sound of bells. He thought he was back in Verona.

The bells of St Margaret's by the cemetery opposite were ringing. The bells of the church of All Saints on Blackheath were ringing. The bells of the chapel at the Catholic girls' boarding school were ringing just the other side of the fence, the bells of the sectarians, heretics, schismatics and dissidents of every stripe that inhabited the south bank of the Thames were ringing. Every church steeple seemed to be looking into the window of the flat, and filling it with the sound of bells. The view from the fourth storey window was confused. The back gardens of two-storey houses down below seemed to slant away like a stage set into the wings, screened by colossal chestnut trees in the foreground, so that there were four parts to the composition – the room, the window-frame, the trees, and the confused jumble of back gardens and roofs, with their magnolias, hawthorns and wild cherry trees. Between the various elements the watercolour curtains of winter air hung like screens, and on a clear day the words of a beer advertisement could be made out on a hoarding on the top of a high building in the distance: 'Take Courage'. Felix was on his way to meet Mary-Louise, the black sheep of Silva's clan, and a corrector of his still nonexistent translation into English of Pushkin's 'Festivities at the Time of Plague'. But there was something alluring about the sound of her name, Mary-Louise: a chance for a romance, a chance to get away from his obsession with Silva.

He had rung Mary-Louise the next day and she suggested they meet at the White Horse. Listening to her voice coming out of the crackling and hissing telephone receiver he could barely understand her carefully cultivated working-class accent.

As he went out of the alley he was greeted by the Russian birch tree (which was slightly damaged, like the conscience of the Russian intelligentsia) and the Jerusalem pine (from the kitchen window you could see a cedar of Lebanon – a trace of masculinity upon the lawn of the Catholic girls' school) and the rowan caught the eye with its frozen red berries – Tsvetaeva's symbol of homesickness. This symbolic confusion in the vegetation was compounded by the peculiar and unseasonal weather. The green seemed doubly unreal under the cobwebs of frost that shone so white that they were painful to look at. There was no snow that year, but the morning hoarfrost dusted the grass, like tinsel round a Christmas tree, creating a vision of childhood winter holidays. This confusion of seasons and times of year made one feel that time had come to a stop.

There was no one to be seen on the street. There was no wind either. It seemed that there was nothing there except his own body, which felt like an envelope enveloping nothing. He remembered the split thumbnail, which he had almost forgotten. Split down the middle, it had separated from the skin, and although the wound had healed, the loose nail often got caught and the pain it then caused was staggering. Silva had bought him a leather finger-stall at a chemist's, which looked like an enormous thimble with straps. When he put it on it looked like an eye-patch for a one-eyed pirate, and Silva immediately suggested that Felix was hiding a third eye on his thumb. This 'third eye' began to seem like something special to Felix, something like a spy's device, which separated Felix from this world and enabled him to peer anonymously at it from one side, without having to give an account of his conclusions to anybody. More than anything in the world he disliked definitive conclusions, and preferred anonymity, not so much because he was indecisive and lacked self-confidence, as because he was terrified of ever being caught red-handed.

Things in London only existed in so far as someone could testify to their existence. London was the irrefutable proof of the objectivity of the philosophy of subjective idealism ('The world only exists in so far as I think on it'). The city lay, as it were, spread on an open palm, open and visible to all, but the palm could not be clenched and the city grasped. It was not all of a piece, it had no centre, it was diffuse, scattered over a series of hills, in a score of villages existing in parallel to one another, through one another, like ghosts that live lives parallel to those of the earthly inhabitants that they have settled among. Turn a corner and you'll find a completely different life. He turned towards the greensward and mansions of Blackheath.

The White Horse was by a pond surrounded by trees, like a piece of an old landscape cut out of the canvas. With its Christmas holly wreath, its dog chasing ducks round the pond and the trickle of smoke from its chimney, it looked so stagily rustic that it seemed a pity to open the door, backstage so to speak, and shatter the illusion. But the door led you from the quiet of a still foyer to the tumultuous din of the stage. Chaotic movements were regulated by the hidden hands of the barmen, the directors of this production, controlling the customers by invisible threads. The theatre even had its intermission bell, hanging over the bar – three rings announced the last chance to order a drink before closing-time. The play was over.

When Felix went into this den of iniquity the play was in full swing. He inspected the whirling sea of faces in an attempt to guess which one of this motley crowd was Mary-Louise Wilson – Silva didn't even have a photo of her. The crowd round the bar consisted of bank clerks and salesmen who worked locally and who wore regulation prison-striped three-piece suits during the week. But it was the old age pensioners who were the regulars. They usually sat on their own, each in their favourite spot – with their cheap cloth caps, trilbies or artificial fur hats pulled down over their eyes, their nose buried in their pint, never letting go of their walking-stick – the personal side-arm of the old age pensioner, his knightly sword. They kept drinking beer steadily – one, two, three, four; just how many could their savings book, bladder and arthritic feet stand? Nevertheless they still proved able to stand up straight and walk the steady line towards the bar when they went to get another pint of bitter. Life ends the day you no longer have the strength to fetch yourself another. There are no waiters in this life, it's self-service only. The staff only make their entrance at the end, to see you out at closing-time.

Like a Russian queue the holiday crowd offered the appearance of community, and not just the appearance at that. Even the standoffish pensioners, old soldiers with red potato-noses, had crowded noisily together with their old lady-friends with their patent-leather handbags, patent-leather high heels, and their blue-rinse perms which made them look like sheep. They clapped their ancient gentlemen on their arthritic backs, 'Cheer up, love,' they'd say (all they ever called one another was 'darling', 'my love', 'ducks' and 'sweetheart') as they knocked back the next gin and tonic and started to sing 'We'll meet again, don't know where, don't know when . . .' in emulation of Vera Lynn, the English Claudia Shulzhenko and herself of Russian descent.

In one corner someone was playing pop songs on a keyboard, and when he took a break and went to the bar the jukebox took over, emitting the shattering sounds of heavy metal and reggae. Wandering, imperturbable, through the legs of this wild crowd, as if he were in another world, was an enormous dog. He clearly had no fear of being trodden on or being hit in the mouth. The warning 'Sorry no dogs' at the pub entrance seemed a little strange in view of this gigantic specimen who hung out here for days on end. Obviously one dog was enough. With his short greyish coat, his ornamental collar, the white blaze on his forehead and his colossal size, less a dog than a stocky well-fed mare, he was the only apparent reason why the pub should be called the White Horse. There was no doubt a good reason for the bar being decorated with bits, bridles and racing colours; perhaps its owner used to saddle his dog. The great beast's most striking feature was its flanks; they would quiver when he shifted from paw to paw as he went round the bar on a tour of inspection, graciously accepting donations from fawning customers. He would look into the billiard room, curl a nostril at the appalling music, rub up against the legs of the regulars. No doubt he protected nervous pensioners from the working-class yobs, and all and sundry from weirdos, outsiders and foreigners. Who was he really protecting the pub from?

'I suppose you think it's a dog?' A man with the face of a bulldog sitting on a bar-stool grabbed Felix by the sleeve. 'That's no dog – that, my good sir, is the pub owner's cock,' the drunk informed him, and laughed. 'Mine host's cock. Have you observed that mine host has no cock?'

'I haven't really got to know him yet,' replied Felix, making himself heard above the din. The man was one of those local drunks to whom one has to pay an obligatory respect, a kind of entrance fee to the establishment. 'I haven't been here long, I'm a stranger, from Moscow.'

'I'm a stranger too. I'm Irish. Have you heard of James Joyce? I have no respect for Joyce. He called Ireland a sow that eats its piglets. That won't do, my good sir! James Joyce lifted a whole novel from the Russian poet Lermontov. *Portrait of the Artist as a Young Dog* is simply *A Hero of Our Time*.'

'Lermontov had Scottish blood.' Felix decided to show off his knowledge.

'But Leopold Bloom was a Jew. Was he not, my good sir?'

Felix said nothing.

'Stream of consciousness. Big deal. Whose consciousness? Leopold Bloom's. Joyce wrote down whatever came into Bloom's head. That's all there is to it. Everyone knows the whole book is lifted from Homer's *Odyssey*. And who reads Homer? Bloom did. And Joyce just wrote his words down. How could he have had the time to read Homer when he was writing down other men's words the whole time? But Jews read a lot. Are you a Jew?'

'I've been to Palestine too. I was stationed there during the memorable time of the British Mandate,' said the man on his left without giving Felix the chance to answer, picking up on the word 'Jew'. It was odd that it had all started with the word 'Moscow'. Yet Felix seemed to recognize the greyish thinning hair with the scalp showing through, and the blue eyes, pale as a sky in the time of plague, watery from drink, the skin leathery from whisky, with a Dickensian touch of feverish colour on the cheeks, and the touch of grey in the whiskers, which made him resemble a Russian Academician of Pushkin's time. In place of the black double-breasted jacket of a Soviet sergeant-major in civvies, he wore a cheap checked tweed jacket of the kind favoured by British old soldiers. But he was still the same kind of retired old sweat you find in bars all over the world, ready to buttonhole you and tell the same old stories about the war. He took a worn wallet from his jacket pocket and removed a tattered yellowing photograph of an English soldier standing by a wall in the company of a dog of uncertain pedigree and colossal proportions.

'That's me in Palestine. That's my Palestine dog,' the old soldier explained, pointing to the photograph with a nicotine-stained finger. The fingernail had once been split, and now looked strangely lumpy. The photograph might as well have been taken in Lewisham. It bore no trace whatsoever of the mysterious Orient, no mosques, no camels, no pyramids, and as for the dog it was the spitting image of the massive creature wandering about the pub at that very moment. 'It's that dog's granny. I brought the pup back from Palestine, and the bitch whelped our Crab here. His time's coming too, soon enough,' and the old soldier stretched a hand out to the giant that went by the strange name of Crab and gave him a scratch. He sensed no irony in the account of the dog's origins. Like all those who had fought in the Second World War (probably this country's last decent generation), he viewed the world with a mixture of wonder and confusion, finding it hard to understand how, after all the horrors of the past, all the bloodbaths and atrocities, people still went on causing one another pain and humiliation. 'I can still talk, still talk Arabic. Arabic, yes. Shukran, Salaam-aleikum, aleikum-salaam,' he observed, enunciating awkwardly like a badly trained parrot. But he couldn't keep it up for long. He soon started to mumble incoherently, nodding his head and smiling radiantly at all and sundry.

The girl next to him saw that Felix was looking confused and explained that Charlie had emigrated to London from deepest Yorkshire, and that even she had difficulty understanding him first time round. Thank God Charlie, who was completely senile, repeated everything three times, so that by the third time you usually got it. Charlie, as an old age pensioner, worked as ticket clerk, manager and cleaner at a railway station in Kent. He had cataracts in both eyes and was practically blind, working by hearing and touch; you could say in point of fact that he didn't see the trains, or the tickets, although they had removed one cataract, but the other eye was still going blind, waiting its turn in the queue, and the longer 'that skinflint Maggie' stayed in power the longer the queue would become, and the less good Charlie would be at getting the point, or at recognizing old friends, with or without tickets.

She was accompanying her quick and mad ironical commentary with every possible gesticulation: she crossed her legs and fidgeted on her stool, conducting the cadences of her carefully worked accent with a cigarette in her left hand while in her right she was juggling a tumbler of whisky, raising her eyebrows to lend emphasis where appropriate. It flickered through Felix's mind that she might pass for a parody of Migulin, and the thought made him giggle uncontrollably. She was definitely a type far removed from Silva. Still, with her darting eye controlling the crowd around her, she was also a great lady in her own small world. Felix felt an immediate urge to belong to it.

'You don't recognize me, do you?' Mary-Louise Wilson (for it was she) remembered Felix, without yet knowing that it was Felix, from the time when she worked in the corner off-licence. 'You should have remembered me. Because of my nose. Can't you see?' she said, tapping her index finger against her nose. Felix immediately started telling her that her unusual nose was nothing to worry about. It was counterbalanced by a no less unusual chin. Mary-Louise gave Felix a tap on the knee and snorted with laughter, shaking her head as she listened to Felix's compliments. 'In point of fact,' Mary-Louise's face, with its powder, mascara and lavish application of rouge, lit by the lights round the bar and the spot-lamps, looked like Mr Punch, with a long hooked nose that seemed to join a long chin reaching forward and upward for ever. But in the clouds of cigarette smoke, amid the laughter and the music and with the aid of the third round of double scotches, something so clown-like, so theatrical, so exotic seemed to emerge from the peculiar proportions of that face, that you could no longer judge it by standards of beauty and ugliness – it just seemed strange and remarkably attractive.

It was hard to recognize the unkempt slut behind the counter in the off-licence, with her untidy hair, her crooked blouse and sleepy expression, in the girl on the bar-stool in the tiger-striped jacket, black leather skirt and tarty black fishnet stockings. He didn't recognize her because it never occurred to him to place people in London outside the circumstances in which he usually met them – sales clerks, dustmen, milkmen, bartenders all became unrecognizable when they were out of context. And as long as you weren't recognized, you could be ignored, as if you weren't really there.

The off-licence in question had closed, which was why Mary-Louise always looked in at the White Horse on her way home, where she drank Famous Grouse whisky in larger quantities than were consistent with the need for sobriety and the extent of her financial resources. Felix took the hint and ordered a round of double scotches. He enjoyed the conversation about the off-licence because it let him make believe he was part of local life, an insider, the kind of person who knows why they shut the off-licence on the corner between the dry-cleaners and the fish and chip shop. It was another fact of local life, and hence of life itself, and thanks to the closing of the shop Felix could feel he was fully part of it all. Rather the way that future lovers meet at a friend's funeral.

The shop shut because Bill, the owner, went bankrupt. He went bankrupt because he lived beyond his means and let his business go downhill. He kept horses in Kent, started going to Ramsgate casino and took to consuming staggering quantitites of Guinness and oysters in the restaurants of Whitstable. One day he simply vanished. And the shop was boarded up.

'How do you mean – vanished? Where did he go?' asked Felix.

'If I'd known then where he went to when he vanished I wouldn't have said he'd vanished. They looked for him in Ramsgate casino, and in the Whitstable oyster bars. But he'd vanished. Without a trace.' And Mary-Louise's romantic gesture as she pointed towards the wide blue yonder almost knocked Charlie's scotch over. The shop was boarded up and the roof had fallen in. Mary-Louise had passed it recently and it stank so strongly of dog that it was obvious that someone was staging dogfights there. There was a rumour that some Turks had bought the shop, the ones with the kebab place on the corner.

'The Turks used to rule Palestine. Before the Mandate. I had a dog there, Aleikum-salaam,' said Charlie the polyglot, thinking by association. Now, according to Charlie, the Turks had all moved from Palestine to Lewisham. Everyone was eating Turkish kebabs, and you couldn't find good old Yorkshire pudding anywhere. Charlie gulped the rest of his whisky and wiped a bead of sweat off his forehead.

'Charlie's eighty this year. He fought in three wars,' said Mary-Louise, giving Charlie a pat on the knee. She'd got to know him in Lewisham Hospital, right? In point of fact she'd been working as an orderly there. After Bill went bankrupt and the off-licence closed. But now she was working as a barmaid three days a week because that 'tight old bitch Maggie' paid hospital staff so little, and she was finishing a course for Russian guides and interpreters at South-East London Poly. She'd soon get her degree and wanted to work as a guide for the British Council, taking British tourists round Moscow, Leningrad and Samarkand. She was already working as a guide and interpreter for the Great Britain–USSR Friendship Society.

'The Jews hated the Arabs, the Arabs hated the Jews. And both the Jews and the Arabs hated us, the British, because the Jews thought we loved the Arabs, and the Arabs that we loved the Jews.' Charlie continued his reminiscences of Palestine. If it had been his brother who'd gone to Palestine and not him, he'd have found things much easier. His eyes were so bad he'd never have been able to tell the Jews and the Arabs apart. But with eyes like that the army doesn't want you. Which is why his brother spent the war years as a gamekeeper. On Lord Edward's estate.

'The Lord Edward?!' Felix asked in astonishment.

'Absolutely,' said Mary-Louise, who might well not have got round to the subject of Lord Edward had it not been for Charlie, his family's gamekeeping connections and his job as stationmaster hard by the lord's estates. Once again Felix sensed the hidden hand of Dr Genoni bringing them together. He started to pay careful attention to the backstairs gossip, although he shouldn't have been that surprised as he knew that Mary-Louise was a key figure in Lord Edward's strategy to bring Silva to England.

'It's the aristocrats and their governments that cause world wars,' said Mary-Louise. 'When they get bored with pheasant shooting they send ordinary people out to shoot one another.' But Charlie observed that being a gamekeeper could be more dangerous than being at the front. The year that Charlie was shipped out to Palestine, just before VE Day, his brother was accidentally killed during a pheasant shoot. Someone shot low and hit him right in the heart as he came out of a wood on to the meadow, beating the birds towards the guns.

'Perhaps he went the wrong way because of his eyesight?' Felix suggested.

'He knew the woods like the back of his hand, knew them blind. Besides, he was wearing spectacles,' said Charlie. They drank a toast to the gamekeeper in spectacles. Wearing a deerstalker like a two-faced Janus, he lies with a bloody chest-wound on the lush grass of the woodland glade. Around its edges proud birds strut, their heads rocking rhythmically like Chinese Buddhas. That is how he imagined the gamekeeping brother as he looked at Charlie's smooth forehead, red cheeks and whiskers, wreathed in cigarette smoke and sunlight, that afternoon in the noisy pub. Somehow he couldn't quite associate spectacles with this image of the dead gamekeeper stretched out on the grass.

'As I said, aristocrats get bored with shooting pheasants, in point of fact they start killing the working class instead, right? It was an aristocrat who shot your brother Charlie, right?' said Mary-Louise.

But Charlie was having nothing to do with revolutionary agitprop. Lord Edward's father died in the war. Moreover, it was just because an aristocrat shot him, said Charlie, that the lord had banned pheasant shooting on his estate. The pheasants had become something like a sacred bird; they were allowed to wander wherever they pleased like the arrogant peacocks of Palestine, and woe betide anyone who laid a finger on them! He knew whereof he spoke, because for the last thirty years he'd been stationmaster at the nearby station, and his nephew was the keeper on that crazy estate, and had gone a bit crazy himself in the process. He'd been made to raise the pheasants, feed them, protect them from stray dogs and wild animals, and then a bunch of foreigners would turn up and take them off to foreign parts. They said it was to develop the fauna and flora of wild desert lands such as Palestine. But it wasn't easy rearing pheasants: during the mating season the cocks try to lay each other's throats open – though you might say in point of fact that they had it made with ten hens apiece – you'd think they'd die of nervous prostration. Why send English pheasants to Palestine and Russian Jews to England? In the circumstances it was scarcely surprising that his nephew the gamekeeper had got himself sent to East Berlin for a gamekeepers' conference.

'What do they do there, shoot at targets on the Wall?' giggled Mary-Louise.

'The Jews in Jerusalem have their Wailing Wall, the Germans have the Berlin Wall. Besides, we all know that if people don't shoot pheasants they shoot one another instead.' Charlie was worried about his nephew. He'd nearly been killed by poachers. And the woods were full of foxes attracted by all the pheasants. There were too many to trap, so what were they to do, ship them all abroad? He was going to have to shoot them.

'The other day I saw a fox in our road,' said Felix. 'A real fox, reddish-brown actually, and nasty looking.'

'That was a dustbin fox. They live by scavenging, like rats, and they live in the catacombs,' said Charlie.

Felix didn't know what he was talking about. Not even Mary-Louise had heard of them. But Charlie said there'd been catacombs under the Heath since Roman times. There was even, he said, a tunnel leading from Blackheath to Buckingham Palace, and one to Dover too. It was in case an uprising should oblige the Royal Family to flee abroad. 'They say you can get into the catacombs from the cellars of this pub. But the proprietor won't let anyone in. He's a royalist. And his father before him, and his grandad, right back to Cromwell's time.'

'Who cares about the catacombs,' said Mary-Louise, agitated at the mention of the Royal Family and a people's uprising. 'I wouldn't stick my nose in them. All those underground passages are stiff with rats. After the war they walled all the rats of London up in the sewers. Just fancy how many there are now after forty years down there. There must be millions.'

'Billions, more likely,' said Charlie solemnly.

'And rats are restless creatures. One fine day, in point of fact, they'll gnaw their way through those cast-iron pipes, hatches and gratings, and will go straight up the royal catacombs to the open air, here on Blackheath. People just don't know what's going on underneath them.'

'Now I see why they don't bring the Underground this way,' said Felix. 'They're afraid to excavate, in case it lets the rats out, and spreads rabies and every other kind of plague. Let sleeping rats lie, eh?'

'There's things worse than rats buried here,' said Mary-Louise. 'Haven't you noticed how nothing grows around here? No trees or bushes, just grass. In point of fact no one plants anything, because they're afraid to dig, right? And why?' Mary-Louise moved closer to Felix and dropped her voice to a sinister whisper. 'Because three hundred years ago, at the time of the Great Plague, they brought the bodies here, from all over London, and buried them twelve hundred feet down. But people are still too scared to dig: just suppose a plague germ pops up! In point of fact your actual underground germ is asleep, right, but as soon as it hits the fresh air it wakes up and there you go. It starts gobbling up absolutely everything and we still don't know how to deal with it.'

All three lapsed into a thoughtful silence.

'So did they find the body?' Felix remembered to ask eventually.

'Whose body?'

'Bill's of course, the owner, of the off-licence, the one who disappeared?'

'It didn't come to that. He was declared a missing person, but they stopped looking for him after a while, and a year later a milkman recognized him living on our street, right? In a neighbour's house, right opposite his old shop. The milkman was just about to leave a bottle of milk on the front step when the door opened and out came Bill, bold as brass, to tell him they didn't need any milk tomorrow, thank you, because they were off to Kent for the weekend. He'd not been anywhere that whole year. Well, he'd been to his neighbour's house across the street, that's where, and no one had seen him for a year.'

'It's not as if you have much to do with your neighbours around here!' Felix observed with a wry smile. 'If you were to go by how much contact you people have with each other, you'd think there was some kind of epidemic here. Stay away, don't touch. It could never happen in Moscow.' Though actually something similar had happened to Silva's neighbour in her communal flat. Her husband apparently went off on a business trip, but all he did was go across the passage to a neighbour's room opposite, suitcase and all . . . Felix started to say, but had the good sense to refrain from telling yet another funny story about life in Moscow communal flats.

9

Asylum

The fog started to creep back again by lunchtime, as if in anticipation of evening, and the sun, low on the horizon, shone through the screen of trees like a lantern casting a cheap crimson glow over the trailing mist, the clumps of trees and the hindquarters of a white horse grazing in the meadow, and paying no attention to the dog that was barking at it in an effort to send it galloping off. Sometimes the sun would come out and you could see that high up in the clouds it was snowing, while in another part of the forest crocuses were out. When the sun shone through the window it lit up a miniature plasticine castle on the windowsill. One of its corner towers was in disrepair, as if it had been cut off by the fog, like one of the pithead structures visible on the horizon.

'We have gone too far, I think, into abstractions with all that metaphorical business of changing one's skin, the rights of the first-born, impostors and emigration,' said Dr Genoni with that nervous expression on his face that revealed his concern not so much for the mental health of his patients as for his professional reputation. He was clearly losing control of the discussion. 'We should try and make our conversation less Socratic, I'd suggest, and more personal. Try to be more concrete and intimate,' he added cautiously.

'How can I be more intimate,' replied Victor innocently, 'if Felix starts scowling at me the moment Silva is not around?'

'Who did you think I was? Some old fool? We're all equal here, are we? With our unique *ménage à trois*, are we?' exploded Felix, his voice hoarse with hostility. 'Silva and I sat there waiting for your triumphant returns to Moscow. You'd served one sentence, you were about to start another, and you had a martyr's bitter smile on your lips. Just who did you take me for, when you were gone, a eunuch taking care of your harem?'

'I didn't realize you were jealous.' Victor shrugged his

shoulders. 'And I really did think it was all over between you and Silva, had been for ages.'

'You of all people should know that once a criminal case is opened it's never closed.'

'Why do people who've never been inside, insist on talking about the Gulag to make their point?' Victor observed spitefully.

'My dear Felix, it seems to me that you embrace an erroneous view of the world as a place where punishment follows crime,' Dr Genoni interposed. 'Some crooks go to heaven, and some saints go to hell. God, as we know, is unpredictable.'

'God may be unpredictable but we crave repetition.' Felix turned gleefully to Victor, enjoying the scandalous nature of what he was saying. 'When you turned up in our London flat, I actually felt good about it, believe it or not, felt a surge of nostalgia. I lay on my back watching the moonlight on the ceiling and thought: here we go again, the old Moscow set-up. Here's young Victor back from prison for a while, fucking our Silva right through the night, I can hear her groans the other side of the wall. He's with her, I'm alone – just like before. You might think that I was jealous, but I wasn't. I was happy, because this echoing of the past created the illusion that the old order was back in place.'

'More like the old disorder,' Dr Genoni corrected him patronizingly. 'Everything back in the same old disorder – which you enjoyed, enjoyed a lot. Pray continue.'

'Memory is amoral. For us even the bitter aspects of the past, repeated in the present, contain a promise of sweetness and bliss. And in that sense I am not some kind of sick exception, a freak. I'm just an illustration of the rules of emigration – which apply regardless of what made someone emigrate from Russia. Do you love her?'

'Who? Silva or Russia? Do I love her, does she love me? And what's wrong with the fact that others reject you, consider you a pariah? Why d'you need the love of those who, as you rightly suspect, despise you?' Victor appeared to have regained his tough and sceptical self. 'I don't go in for emotional beatings, and I don't play the informer for a Soviet censor, writing lyrical letters to my friends.'

'As far as I know, you don't bother to write personal letters, period. You're not a human being at all, just a department of state,' Felix said sarcastically.

'So what? No, I don't write personal letters. I saw enough of those lovers of the epistolary art in the camps. Half blind and their eyes wet with tears, in a dark corner of the barracks, they sort through a bag containing ten years of correspondence with their loved ones on the outside. And later you get your wailing and your gnashing of teeth when someone takes their bag away because they're about to send them to a new camp at short notice. Is that the way you want me to be "true to the past"? Thanks, but no thanks. When your interrogator shows your woman, on the outside, a letter you're supposed to have written to your mistress, and when your faithful companion, the woman you love, after saying nothing for a month, suddenly breaks out in a jealous rage and starts spilling the beans, naming names, addresses, telephone numbers . . .'

'When did that happen? Who was it?' Felix was startled. 'It's obvious you're talking about something that actually happened. I'm afraid that here in England I've lost touch with the cryptic conspiratorial turn of Moscow conversation.'

'OK. If you insist. You remember the last time I was arrested before you left? The case against me featured a copy of Avestin's essay about Soviet Pirandellism as the chief anti-Soviet document. I was involved with samizdat at the time, and obviously I was the only one who knew the whereabouts of Avestin's original which we were retyping.'

'Obviously,' Felix and Dr Genoni agreed in unison.

'I'd hidden the manuscript in my father's country villa. All of a sudden there was a search, at dawn. The manuscript was confiscated. How did they summon up the nerve to search my father's place, eh?'

'What's so strange about that?' asked Felix in sincere amazement. 'What with our booze-ups there, from New Year's Eve to the festivities on the anniversary of the Revolution, we practially lived there. They were bound to start searching there at once.'

'And antagonize my father, with his Party connections? Particularly in those days? No, they had to have something more than our booze-ups to go on to warrant a search.' Victor shook his head. 'I think there's a very different explanation. The explanation is that Julia and I were typing copies of the *Gulag Chronicle* there, and we copied Avestin's piece at the same time.'

'I think I've heard of Julia. But what's she got to do with it?'

'You couldn't not have heard of her. One of the best samizdat typists in Moscow. But no one knew I was meeting her at my father's place. No one except Silva.'

'You don't say!' Felix muttered guardedly, as if he was anticipating a blow.

'Our Silva is a very jealous lady, which is hardly surprising with an operatic name like that. Silva!' Victor chuckled.

'Are you out of your mind? Are you trying to say she's an informer?' Felix noticed that Victor and Dr Genoni were eyeing him as if trying to gauge his emotional resilience. What if all these nasty suggestions about Silva were just lies designed to assess his ability to resist provocation, a test of loyalty to his close friends that he was about to fail dismally?

'I'm not trying to say anything. I'm just stating the facts,' replied Victor as if anticipating Felix's doubts. 'They showed her a bunch of letters I was supposed to have written to the typist. And Silva believed them. So then she was crazy with jealousy and all that, and went and told them where Julia and I used to meet. That's all there is to it.'

'That's all? And how d'you know all this? You were there when they were questioning her, were you? Or did they confront you with one another? What makes you so certain?' Felix jumped up and started pacing round the table.

'I'm not. But then I can't find any better explanation for my father's place being searched,' Victor replied, apparently resigned. 'Please. Sit down.'

'It seems to me that your ability, or lack of it, to find a better explanation simply reflects the limited nature of your powers of imagination.' Felix ignored Victor's plea to calm down. 'Anyway, I just don't understand how you could move in with someone, if you suspected them of something like that. And you have the gall to call me a freak and a moral pervert. Haven't you said anything at all to her, or even hinted?'

'To humiliate her all over again? When I was in Moscow I used to take calculated risks. I was never surprised by the way people changed when they were arrested. Her reaction under interrogation, when she was shown such "incriminating" material, taking into account the paranoid atmosphere of those years, her reaction was perfectly understandable. Anyone else would have done the same. Why should Silva be the exception?'

'Just because she is exceptional. Remember, we all thought we were exceptional in those days, the chosen ones. And nothing like what you say happened to Silva ever happened to you, nor could it.'

'I've got the feeling that you've got all excited, and are waiting for a whole series of confessions, self-reproach and exposures.' Victor's patience was seemingly running out. 'You'll get every Russian in London cranked up, just like you used to do in Moscow with your "Theatre for the Self"; somehow you always seemed to end up either in the audience or in the director's chair. I sometimes think that I courted arrest, went looking for confrontations with the authorities, just so as to be sent to prison and get away from your famous spiritual cosiness, everybody sitting round together, all seeing things the same way, with that stagey sense of being a tightly knit little community of "us". Isn't that what's making you so nostalgic now? I move in with Silva and it all comes back, that's it, isn't it, that creepy atmosphere of mutual spiritual trust!'

'Terrific!' Dr Genoni threw up his hands in delight. 'Te-rrific! Just what the doctor ordered, as Silva would say. At a stroke you've established a causal relationship between the KGB and sex. In the best traditions of melodrama. This makes for the magnificent misconception that it is, forgive the pun, those organs of yours that are responsible for all forms of sexual betrayal and adventure, those security organs, which are, of course, anything but a source of security. But I must disappoint you. There is no causal relationship. The misconception comes about, as it might in a play, by a careful juggling of times and events to give an illusion of simultaneity, which in turn is mistaken for a causal relationship. A man yawns and opens his mouth, a nightingale starts to sing in the bushes. We believe that the man sings like a nightingale.'

Far away in the bushes a pheasant could be heard calling, sounding like a woman in tears.

10

The Two Gentlemen of Verona

On August 6, 1984, Felix woke up in Silva's apartment, with the unexpected conviction (like a blue sky over London) that he was an Impostor. The actual word 'impostor' came later. He'd first thought of the word 'usurper' (closer, with its Latin root in English, to the Russian 'uzurpator'), which he'd come across in a dictionary, as the appropriate expression to convey his sense of being under false pretences. More precisely his sense of not belonging, accompanied by a vague sense of regret for the person he might have become but did not, because he'd ended up in the wrong place at the wrong time. The Moscow of those years was a city that you left. After leaving Moscow he should have remained in Jerusalem. Suddenly London seemed like a total mistake. He broke out into a light sweat. It felt as if it was all beginning, that it was all ahead of you. We bustled about, afraid of missing the train, dragging suitcases out to the doorway, with no time to sort out complicated relationships with old friends, interrupting our nearest and dearest in mid-sentence. We'd laugh nervously at nothing, clear our throats as if about to make an important speech, slap our comrades-in-arms on the back and keep looking nervously at our watches: friendship is all well and good, but the time has come, my friend, the time has come. The main thing was not to be late. And it was only when you caught a glimpse of your friend's sad expression that, for a moment, you realized that all this feverish bustle and enthusiastic impatience to get on with it were the kind associated with memorial services and funerals. We're leaving for an existence beyond the tomb, with a jaunty smile on our lips.

Leaving home of one's own free will, going abroad, departing, emigrating were always associated in Russia with the word 'rats'. Among those who were opposed to the idea of emigration were people who professed the opinion that anyone leaving

Russia for the West was to be considered a rat leaving a sinking ship. While those who left Russia compared militant opponents of emigration to rats huddling in a dark corner. It all depended not just on the opponents and advocates of emigration but on the historic moment, with its correspondingly varying versions of the quarrel between ratcatchers and ratophiles, Slavophiles and Westernizers. There were times when emigration was considered a heroic feat, an act of martyrdom in the name of liberty, light and the truth; there were also times when anyone leaving felt like a pariah, rejected, cast into outer darkness by a circle of friends who had unexpectedly decided to forget the West, preferring to dig deep and unearth their Eastern-Slavic roots and Tatar ancestors. But both times had come and gone; Felix left Moscow for ever at a moment when no one cared very much whether you stayed or went.

The past settled into a frame, like a landscape you see through a window – it became possible to contemplate it with a nostalgic smile. Even the clear chill of a London morning provided a form of climatic separation from the hothouse atmosphere of Moscow. This London existence, which was founded in illusion and artifice and was delightful in its anonymity and lack of responsibility, began manifestly to be broken up by the mighty torrent of stories and rumours pertaining to the inevitability of Victor's release. Victor was emerging from his own legend, coming back into autobiography and into Silva's life, and thereby putting Felix's émigré meditations back in the harsh setting of the Russian historical process. He returned Felix to the homeland which he had quite successfully contrived to forget. The telephone began to ring more and more often as journalists asked about key moments in Victor's career as a dissident, for details of his physical condition in confinement and the various ways in which he might be released. Silva was asked to do a broadcast or two, and the television even put on a Soviet 'show trial' which parodied and exposed Victor's first trumped-up 'case'. Increasingly Silva was attending various press conferences, public gatherings, private meetings and parties.

The more Felix was on his own, the more nervous he felt about his precarious situation in London, without a residence permit and without a job. Neither Lord Edward nor his doctor and secretary Genoni had put in an appearance, which in fact rather suited Felix for the time being, since he hadn't the first idea how to set about translating Pushkin's 'Festivities at the Time of Plague'. From time to time he would reread the 'Festivities' and make a note of various possible renderings of this or that word, of whole verses even, which he would follow up with a series of question marks, wondering yet again how he could have agreed to such a commission, only to set Pushkin aside once more. He could not bring himself to telephone his young lady by the name of Mary-Louise Wilson for help with the English translation, since he was afraid of exposing the modest extent of his talent as a translator. Every day he wandered about the room, Pushkin in hand, waiting for lunch (or a telephone call, or the urgent need to set his papers in order, or some other kind of imaginary bureaucratic nuisance). The happiest interludes were the visits he paid with Silva to Greenwich Park, where she used to ride a horse she hired on the cheap through her mysterious émigré connections.

Until recently they had both enjoyed the rides. Although Felix did not dare mount a full-sized horse, he always rented a tiny pony, for a joke. Silva, dressed in riding boots and a hard riding hat, would ride up to the ring on her thoroughbred and laugh at the spectacle of Felix bouncing up and down on his mount, looking like a Mullah on a donkey. She would laugh her fill and then ride off to a distant corner of the park, while Felix, well satisfied, would betake himself to a pub called the White Horse, where he would sit on a bench by the pond with a mug of beer, observing from afar how expertly Silva sat her horse and rose to the trot, criss-crossing the huge meadow with its groups of oak trees that stood at a distance from one another, as if on parade, waiting for her to gallop past on a tour of inspection. Like all great horsewomen she was also a fabulous mount in bed, although as is always the case on such occasions she never deferred to the rider, but set off at a gallop from a standing start. However, Felix did not get the chance to repeat that Moscow experience. 'Don't, stay away,' she said, firmly rejecting his obstinate yet tentative attempts to renew their joint riding lessons. 'Not everything in life has to be repeated; the times were different and so were we.' When he heard this polite sentence of death passed on their former relationship, Felix accepted the situation for what it was. But it became clear, with respect to the impending advent of Victor, that his bad temper and touchiness were manifestations of a common or garden jealousy. For some weeks now the rides had been taking place without him.

Riding had gone hand in hand with jealous scenes from the day they met. When Felix first met Silva almost two decades ago at one of Avestin's Thursdays (Migulin had brought Felix there) he recognized her at once. And she recognized him. They recognized one another when he mentioned the indoor ring and riding school located in dark back streets behind the nearby railway station. Despite the stunningly thuggish, criminal and felonious character of that part of Moscow, Felix observed, it also contained elements of semi-underground chic and privileged pockets of Moscow civilization. In return for a handful of pennies artfully removed from parental pockets, you would be given a placid mare which you could ride around the indoor ring for half a day. Sometimes the resident instructor would come out. He would stand in the centre of the ring and, rocking slightly on his heels, possibly under the influence of alcohol, in his tightly fitting nankeen breeches and his beautifully polished riding boots, he would let out a stream of sarcastic and accurate comments on the riding skills of the timid dollies with perms riding gingerly round the ring and the teenage boys who had played truant for a day in the saddle. No one asked unnecessary questions here about where you were from and why you were not at school. The instructor sometimes brandished a whip which he cracked with a perfect sense of rhythm, as he hoarsely shouted 'Trot on!' or 'Gallop on!' – at which point you had to raise yourself in the saddle at the right moment (when the horse's hindquarters were lowered under you) if you were to avoid doing serious damage to your pelvis.

That evening at Avestin's, Silva was the first to admit that she remembered Felix perfectly, remembered his face with the hair that had been red in those days, and she voiced an ironic doubt as to whether Felix remembered what she, Silva, used to look like. As if she didn't realize that you never forgot a face like hers. Could anyone forget the way that the curve of the eyebrows echoed the lips, forget the line of her thigh echoing the line of her chin? Everything about her was in harmony: her past even harmonized with her future. In retrospect, either remembering or embroidering, he mentally retraced her flaw-less seat as she bobbed up and down to her horse's trot (needless

73

to say, she had managed to win over the instructor so she got to ride the best mount in the stable) as he trailed behind her round the ring riding an ancient mare. Even in London, years later, she would sometimes turn her head in his direction and smile that same sly smile she had used when flirting with all and sundry. He remembered its immodesty, and the way his balls felt girded tight in his breeches, and how long it took them to start to talk to one another. After her ride she always met a bunch of street smart kids, all mini-skirts and tight trousers, and would go off with her arm round the most obnoxious one, enthusiastically licking the ice-cream cone that her admirer had bought her. There was no point in Felix – with the corduroy breeches he was too old to be wearing (his parents were saving money) – even trying to compete with that crowd. Who would ever have thought that one day it would be he who would saddle that horse, while her dandy-admirers would continue to turn circles behind the station obedient to the rhythmic whip-cracking of the chief instructor of the Politburo.

As a matter of fact, wasn't it Victor who went out of the riding school with her, patting Silva's behind in the stretch breeches, as Felix marked time some way off pretending that he was reaching for something in his school satchel – to avoid leaving with them and witnessing his own disgrace, the disgrace of the loser. And wasn't Victor the one who challenged Felix by handing him the reins of his fiery mount that was champing at the bit, as Silva, smiling her sly smile, with turned head to see if Felix would dare accept the ride. He well remembered the faces of her grinning gang of admirers. He remembered the horse suddenly rearing up on its hind legs as it moved round the ring, suddenly coming to a halt, kicking, and trying to throw Felix. He had forgotten all about the reins, and was hanging on to the horse's mane in mortal terror. He remembered the instructor swearing as he ran into the ring cracking his whip, a blur of faces, screams, horses' hindquarters shying away from him – and then flying through the air, upside down, wondering whether the sawdust would save him and whether it would be harder or softer than a snowdrift.

After a week in hospital, some stitches in his head and a back-brace because of serious bruising of the spine (none of which, incidentally, did anything to save him from a serious black mark for playing truant) he turned up at the riding school again. The instructor swore at him roundly, cracked his whip and told him never to show his face there again. But Felix had no intention of going near the horses and damaging the instructor's reputation. Felix hoped to see Silva, her sly smile, her riding breeches, her lips and the ice-cream cone. And she came out to greet him, as imperial personages greet the casualties of war. She permitted him to take her arm and they went to the shooting gallery in the Children's Park. Felix hit a patridge, a hare and a pheasant. He told her how they used to kill cats and stray dogs in backyard rubbish dumps because cats and dogs were carriers of rabies. With the ignorance of adolescents they took the name of the disease literally; it actually sent you mad. On a street corner he bought ice-cream cones for them both; they went into an alley and Felix, switching his cone from his right hand to his left, put an arm round her shoulders and tried to press his lips to hers. 'Just because you've bought me ice-cream, does that make me your whore?' She pushed him sharply away. 'Let's get one thing perfectly clear. I'm not to be had for one ice-cream cone, sonny!'

It was being called sonny that got to him, not the idea of her being for sale. He was just a sonny to her, although he knew perfectly well that Victor was in the sixth grade, and was no more than thirteen at the most, while Felix was finishing the eighth grade and was two years older than Victor, and at that age two years was as good as twenty. All his life Victor contrived to act as if he were older, wiser and more experienced, and over the years Felix came to refer to this superior maturity as competence. 'Victor really is so on the ball and competent,' Felix would observe whenever he got wind of another of Victor's innumerable and sensational exploits – under interrogation, in letters to the leadership, or conversations with foreign journalists; people seemed to forget that his witty jousts with the Soviet authorities cost Victor years in prison. What made Felix so boyishly immature and so dull in those riding-school days of his happy Soviet childhood? Why was he always put with the younger ones in any age group? What was the real explanation? Was it the hateful corduroy breeches his parents made him wear, like the knickerbockers he had to wear in kindergarten? Victor had them too, but he managed to look English in them. What made Felix get childishly upset and back down from his own threats while rehearsing *The Two Gentlemen of Verona* when, as a second-year university student, he ran the amateur theatricals at the school where Victor was in his last year? Why was it that Felix, playing the part of a sick and bitter old man, moving with a grunt and a curse from one chair to another, still could not help seeming the carefree though admittedly ageing student, while Victor – who with his smiling enthusiasm, his readiness to take off in any direction in search of an exciting adventure, his physical and mental agility, might have seemed the incarnation of the eternal adolescent – was always taken for the elder of the two? What was the cause of this illusory seniority? Was it the experience of prison that had left its indelible mark? But a lot of people tell you that prison keeps you young. Even emigration proved unable to give Felix a head start, although any experienced exile, émigré, expatriate will tell you that anyone who leaves his country begins life over again, from zero, and hence is older, by the number of years he has lived abroad, than those who arrive after him. All the same, when Victor finally made his appearance in the British Isles the age gap, the competence gap, reappeared in the course of their very first conversation.

'What are you up to?' asked Victor when they finally got a chance to be alone in the midst of one of the numerous trendy parties thrown in Victor's honour.

'I'm translating Pushkin,' Felix muttered.

'Pushkin? From what into what?' And on learning that it was into English he expressed surprise at Felix's knowledge of that language.

'For the moment I am just using a dictionary to do a literal translation,' Felix explained diffidently.

'And you're not afraid?' Victor asked after a moment's pause.

'Why should I be?'

'Well, if you don't see, then you're not afraid.' Victor gave him a patronizing pat on the shoulder. And Felix, red with anger, recalled that they had once had a conversation like that in Moscow, (most probably at one of those farewell parties in honour of those departing for the West) even though, of course, nothing in this world repeats itself.

The so-called 'third-wave' of emigration had long since ceased to be a mighty comber, and had degenerated into a line of dirty spindrift. Victor emerged from this spindrift, from the

76

stale sound of the émigré surf breaking on a Western shore, like an exotic apparition. Snatched from the underground world of eternal permafrost, a Soviet aircraft brought him across the Iron Curtain and dumped him unceremoniously in Vienna. From that moment he was permanently surrounded by a throng of journalists, which is not to say that Felix and, more especially, Silva went completely unnoticed. Far from it. Their photographs appeared regularly in the newspapers, always in the company of a haggard Victor. They were part of the immediate entourage permanently accompanying the heroic dissident; they attended dinners at the Polish Club, where they were served bortsch and vodka, on behalf of starving fellow Slav dissidents, and took exotic cocktails at the Reform Club with the leading reactionaries of the day. Nevertheless, it soon became clear that the intensity of their friendship, and their sense of the vast significance of their situation, could only thrive on distance and absence. After the initial hugs and toasts and mutual interruptions, it became clear that Victor had little time for them; he was entirely absorbed in a headlong plunge towards a turbulent and radiant future – which is how he saw his own heroic past. He was convinced that all England, nay the great world itself, was totally absorbed by the prospect of an impending Russian revolution – which is how he saw his own present. In those days Victor saw Silva and Felix's refusal to participate in the circus of émigré politics as evidence of their moral decay occasioned by emigration. Like every true Russian idealist, he was convinced that the world rotated around the axis of his own particular convictions.

When talking with Felix or Silva, Felix more particularly, Victor always seemed to be in a hurry to be off somewhere, would turn away as they spoke, looking for someone else, was always itching to move on to the next group at receptions. He was always terrified that he might be missing out on someone or something. At these fashionable gatherings, Felix and Silva soon discovered that, after accepting a drink or two, there was absolutely no point in staying. After the first lunch they had with him just after Victor arrived in London, they never again had a chance to be alone with him. He was staying at a smart hotel in Belgravia from which you could walk to Buckingham Palace. All paid for by charities and conservative organizations, Amnesty International and, as everybody supposed, Lord

Edward, who had failed to appear in London personally to greet his protégé in the struggle for human rights. He was travelling somewhere between Malta and the Sinai Desert, in connection with some other no doubt charitable undertaking.

Felix sat up, threw back the blanket and glanced out of the window, but failed to feel the usual chill of a London morning. Through the window he could see a hot blue sky looking like the satin lining of a quilt. The view from the window looked like a faded transfer, and the cedar of Lebanon in the garden next door, where the grass shone in the sunlight as it did on the hillsides of Jerusalem, looked like a mosque, and reminded him of the day he arrived in Israel. He'd hurt his bad thumb throwing back the blanket (beneath the splintered growth a soft new nail was forming, and growing harder, it seemed, by the hour) and the pain made his temples throb. Then his headache returned to remind him of the cold he'd caught despite the extraordinary heat. It was just another of those epidemics of African flu or Siberian fever – one of those strange infections that nobody could trace. His legs felt like cotton wool, which reminded him of the transport strike, on the very day that he had to drag himself to the far side of Greater London to the Home Office, for yet another meeting to discuss his émigré status. Once the signalmen went back to work, the traindrivers went on strike, to be followed by the conductors and ticket sellers. Every now and again trains would run, but not as they should, as if to remind their passengers that they could act and function as they pleased, because power was in the hands of those who transported others, and they, the passengers, had no choice but to remain seated, if they could get a seat, or stand in the corridor, or, when there was no standing room either, wait on the platform for another train.

'Because beauty is eternity, that is to say repose, repose and eternity create virtue. Evil, as the antithesis of good, is inconstancy, change, movement. Anyone who is constantly on the move, rushing about, agitated, is a monster,' the loquacious Dr Genoni used to say when they were in Italy. 'Emigration, like every change of residence and ways of thought, is monstrous and lacking in goodness. As in Pirandello, your body and your soul separate; your body's here, but the soul is still flitting around elsewhere: in Russia.'

'If my soul's in Russia, where's my heart? In Jerusalem?'

'Or has all this wandering over the face of the earth made your heart sink into your boots? In that case your heart's all covered in corns and calluses,' Felix remembered Dr Genoni replying, demonstrating his Shakespearian wit.

The grassy expanses of Blackheath, on the way to the station, looked like the Nile Valley at the time when the Jews of ancient times were building the Pyramids; in place of Egyptian Pyramids, the grass, burnt yellow as sand by the heat, was adorned with pyramidal piles of black plastic garbage bags. In addition to the transport strike, the dustmen were also out. Actually, even when they were working, the street still looked like a rubbish tip that had been scattered by a hurricane. It was as if the inhabitants of Lewisham had grown so fed up with their grey and ugly streets that they spontaneously decided to decorate them as each thought best; it was as if the brightest, most colourful and cheerful substance that the outskirts of London had to offer was garbage. The locals, wandering to and fro between supermarkets, crowded fancy goods stores and piles of rotting refuse, also looked like garbage to Felix – garbage that had been left scattered over the face of the earth because the Great Dustmen of the Universe had gone on strike.

Felix didn't see any point to the strike; the street was never cleared as it was, strike or no strike. The road sweeper who put in an appearance once or twice a week, wandered up the hill of a morning looking more like a down-and-out who just happened to be there than a road sweeper. He was a black, and he wore a scruffy old orange overall which he'd pulled on over various sweaters and cardigans, like a leper's skin. The lower half of his face was covered by an old rag and wrapped in a scarf, and he wore a knitted wool hat pulled down over his forehead. He dragged a filthy old cart behind him, which seemed to contain, not rubbish, but rather all his worldly wealth. His approach to rubbish collection was highly selective, as if he only bothered to pick up things that might come in useful some day, such as a piece of cloth or a cardboard box. He speared his booty with a long metal pole, turning it over and gathering up articles deemed suitable for collection, with the help of a metal hook. When he got to the bend on the top of the hill, he usually stopped to say hello to his pal, the black rag-and-bone man with a rickety horse-drawn cart who would call out for 'any old iron' with an extraordinary sort of a shout.

Lewisham, the capital of South East London, combined all the shortcomings of Western democracies with all the horrors of the Gulag. It was incredibly hard to get to, and once you got there it was even harder to leave. Even during the day, the few bridges, such as Westminster Bridge, Vauxhall Bridge, Waterloo Bridge and Blackfriars Bridge that joined the ghastly high-rise slums of South London to the elegant neighbour-hoods in the centre, were so clogged with traffic that only the most desperate drivers attempted to break through to the other side. The great majority of the population of Lewisham had long since grown reconciled to their role as the pariahs of the metropolis, and with that typically English readiness to make a virtue of necessity they elevated their condition of remote isolation from the civilized parts of London into a source of pride and self-congratulation, thought of themselves as country squires, and when travelling to the city centre referred to the twenty-minute train journey, with its four stops to Charing Cross, as 'going to London'. Like a jailor, London the aristocrat keeps its plebs in confinement, just as the plague-stricken are placed in quarantine barracks where even the windows are boarded up.

Even an everyday journey on the suburban train reminded Felix of the refugees' last escape. When the board unexpectedly showed a train departing the crazy business of getting on it would begin. Latecomers squeezed through the iron gates to get on to the platform. The way they clanged shut no longer reminded Felix of the Iron Curtain, as it had a year ago; it now made him think of a medieval city with a wall to defend it against enemies, against the plague. The whistles of the guard announcing the train's departure made his head hurt; it sounded as if someone was being arrested, or being chased, a terrorist, an illegal immigrant, or someone without the authorization to reside in this country. In the wake of the police whistles came the last deafening, panic-striken salvoes of doors slamming shut. The train seemed to contain as many doors as it did passengers, one apiece. This contributed to an illusory sense of separation, of distance between individuals; as if everyone carried their own door which they slammed to behind them, thereby shutting themselves away in their own private compartment (translated into Russian, 'compartment' comes out as 'Communist Party' – joke) or, quarantine. This phoney separation looked doubly grotesque and illusory when everyone was crushed up against everyone else in the over-full carriage, thighs, buttocks, breasts and other parts of the body all jammed together, as if locked in some orgiastic embrace. For all that, the English managed to act as if there were no one else around, as if they were sole survivors of an epidemic of the plague. The fact that it was a smoking compartment made for a doubled sense of separation; everyone was wrapped, not just in their own thoughts, but in their own cloud of cigarette smoke too. The compartment (which rocked at every joint in the rails like an elderly drunk staggering his way home), with its faded antediluvian velvet upholstery, its antique luggage racks and all its other Victorian monstrosities, had something of a time-machine about it, stuck, in the eternal quarantine of time, half-way on its journey to the present. And the passengers, whose faces were impossible to distinguish, coughing and hawking amid the thick clouds of sour smoke, looked like the inmates of a pest-house.

After his visit to the Home Office Visa Department, Felix went to bed with a temperature. Being a hypochondriac, he was almost certain that he'd contracted gangrene from the split nail on his thumb. But what connection was there between a cold and gangrene? For it had all started with a cold, and he wasn't the only one. It was as if all those around him had been taking too much snuff, and were ceaselessly sneezing, coughing, blowing their noses as if they were caught in a mass epidemic of hayfever. If all the emanations from their noses and throats had poured into the Thames, there would long since have been a catastrophic flood which would have inundated the whole of central London with phlegm and snot. But central London was saved. The colds and coughs ceased and gave way to shattering headaches, throbbing temples and giddiness. It all happened as suddenly as sun follows rain on these islands, where both the climate and the national character were 'cloudy and change-able'.

It was rumoured that the mysterious flu had been brought to England by immigrants from India or by African monkeys. 'What's so surprising?' exclaimed Mary-Louise (who'd brought Felix the latest corrected page from Wilson's *The City of the Plague*, transcribed by Felix to serve as part of his English version of Pushkin's 'Festivities at the Time of Plague').

'What's so surprising? For centuries, these islands were isolated, and now, in fact, they're blaming foreigners for all the illnesses these days. Chauvinists!' Felix agreed. Wrapped in rugs, scarves and cardigans, he sat in an armchair looking like a scarecrow, and cursed English draughts and English houses, that let the cold air in through the windows, the floorboards and even the ceiling; he cursed the English as such. Mary-Louise agreed, remarking that the upper classes went to public schools where they were raised as Spartans and stoics, and the dormitory windows stayed open even in winter, while the working classes admittedly didn't actually heat their bedrooms, but at least kept warm under eiderdowns, which is why they caught colds at the drop of a hat, because they weren't as tough as the upper classes.

Listening to this nonsense, Silva observed that all this talk of warm bedrooms and being immune to cold was neither here nor there for the moment, since the heavens looking down upon the capital of the former British Empire seemed to be overcome with nostalgia for a colonial past, and had decided to expose the green grass of Old England to an Indo-Arabian heatwave. 'Instead of giving the English shit, why don't you take some vitamin C, it's good for colds,' said Silva. But Felix categoric-ally refused to take vitamins. He said that taking vitamins for a cold was just another one of those confidence tricks that subjective-idealist English doctors like to play on you. They liked to pretend that there was no medicine to treat the flu and everyone had to manage as best they could. ('Typical Thatcherism,' said Mary-Louise.) In that sense, British doctors, according to Felix, were no better than Soviet ones, who insist on the need for various vaccinations, against rabies for example, to distract people, or else frighten them for political purposes. The number of rabid dogs on the streets of Moscow grew in proportion to the campaign against rootless cosmopolitans and doctor-poisoners. Epidemics in general regularly coincided with every wave of mass arrests. 'How does rabies occur anyway?' asked Felix, who had stolen the idea from Migulin. 'When you've got rabies, the slightest sound, the faintest knock at the door, sends you into convulsions. Every other person used to go into convulsions on hearing a knock at the door, thinking it was his turn and that they'd come for him.'

'How old were you when Stalin died?' Silva asked with an

ironic smile. 'You were small enough still to be walking around under tables and sitting on potties, rather than waiting to be arrested.'

Her words rang with a kind of aggression that Felix hadn't heard for a long time. Not since Moscow. The tone of groundless bad temper, and a groundless wish to argue, the childish desire to say something unpleasant, to disagree, to quarrel. He'd already realized that Silva went in for this kind of bad temper and argumentativeness whenever Victor was around, and she had to pretend that nothing had changed, and that her conversations with Felix were important to her regardless of whether or not Victor was there. But Victor's presence could be felt in every conversation. It could even be felt in the flat. His room was already waiting for him. It was empty, as if under seal, waiting for the return of the real master of the house. Felix felt like a usurper. 'Would you mind moving into the corner bedroom?' Silva had asked when it turned out that Victor was thinking of leaving the smart London hotel which he couldn't afford and moving in with her.

Before Silva moved into the flat a number of people had clearly been living there; it was the London version of a communal Moscow apartment, a series of furnished rooms with a basin in each. The 'corner' bedroom, which Felix was moving to, was the furthest away from the bathroom and the lavatory, and also the smallest in the flat, with no fireplace, looking more than ever like a prison cell, since its window overlooked the inner courtyard, which is why the room was so dark. Felix moved into the room with a conspicuous enthusiasm; as if he had exchanged roles with Victor, with all the discipline of Solzhenitsyn's Ivan Denisovich he started arranging his worldly goods upon the shelves: change of underwear, shirts, pyjamas, slippers, razor and shaving cream by the basin, ready to serve his term, exiled to the outer rim of communal life. But in the morning there was sunlight, reflected off the French windows of the flat on the other side of the narrow yard. No one ever came out on to the balcony, with its iron railings; the French windows were always shut, blocked with piles of junk. Obviously the balcony was being used as a kind of outdoor storage area and dump. A naked man sat on top of the junk pile, a mannequin, bald, in the sense that it had no wig, and minus an arm. Screwed together at the hip-joints, he sat, or rather half stood, leaning over the iron railing. If you were half asleep you might take it for someone wondering whether or not to commit suicide.

Felix lay on the sofa opposite the window in the classic pose of an invalid in a nineteenth-century print – all those people suffering from TB and typhoid – lying back on the pillow, a hand dangling down, nearly brushing the floor, the other brushing away a lock of sweat-soaked hair from his forehead. Just above his head was a huge, bright poster of Jerusalem, and the golden mosque on Temple Mount was reflected in Felix's eyes. He kept staring at the window through which he could see the balcony opposite. Reflected in the French windows was a view of a corner of Blackheath, with one tall pyramid-like tree which, with its dried and yellowing leaves, looked like a scruffy mosque. In the background of this 'Palestinian' view, which blended strangely with the view of the hill of the Holy Sepulchre from the poster reflected in Felix's feverish eyes, sat the crippled mannequin. When Silva, worried by the fact that he hadn't come out of his room all morning, opened the door wide, he beckoned to her, took her hand and, pointing at the French windows opposite, started to recite: 'It was the capital city of a kingdom lying unknown among unvoyaged seas, where towers and temples of an Eastern structure with airy pomp bewildered my soul. When gazing on them I was struck at once with blindness and decay of memory . . .' He looked at Silva short-sightedly, as if dazzled by footlights, with the expression of a provincial tragedian.

Except for brief moments when he half slept or half passed out, Felix had been delirious for twenty-four hours, and until he announced that he was himself again Silva couldn't tell whether he was acting, or really was raving. If his body was still in the London flat, his mind was clearly flitting over the valleys of the Holy Land. Physically he was still drawn to Silva, whom he'd made sit down next to him on the bed; clutching her hand he called her Lyudmila, Milka, Matilda, after his ex-wife, muttering in sorrowful, feverish tones that alas it was not possible to get back together again on a permanent basis. Of course he was grateful to her for extracting him from the iron grasp of the Soviet system, but where on earth had she brought him, exploiting his Philo-Semitism and sense of loyalty to those who had set him free? He gestured weakly towards the reflection in the French windows opposite, believing it to be the view through the window; the burnt grass and the tree that looked like a dilapidated mosque lay there in the bone-hard sunlight. According to Felix's nightmarish vision, while he and Lyudmila were basking in the radiant sunlight of moral righteousness and detachment, Silva, who had been left alone in Moscow (with Victor in prison and Felix in Bathsheba), was moving from one flat to another, hiding from searches and arrests, and sleeping alone between cold sheets.

The wretched picture of the abandoned and hounded Moscow woman dissident was humiliating, and profoundly unattractive, or so it seemed to Silva. Partly for that reason, and partly to distract Felix from his delirious obsession with their Moscow past, she started trying to convince him, speaking as his ex-wife Lyudmila, that she, Silva, had only slept with him that hot August night to use him like a pillow to cry into – worse, like a handkerchief to blow her nose on. Following her train of thought, Felix began to speak of the select nature of his Israeli exile, speaking of Jerusalem as a city where you could always see the horizon, because it was built on hills, and when you can see the horizon you know where you are, and when you know where you are you feel at home. Thus Jerusalem was their new home. And both he and Lyudmila were pilgrims who had finally arrived at the Holy City.

In the close sweaty twilight Felix drew closer and closer to her, to 'Lyudmila', and was getting further and further away from the Silva of Moscow. He started to undress her, and she didn't resist, although she realized that she'd played the part of her old girlfriend and Felix's wife in Jerusalem a little too well, when his hands, lips and tongue started lapping, groping and licking her body grown sweaty from the heat and the tension, with the inventiveness and tirelessness of a masturbator, not trying to possess her, or enter her, but, as it were, fettering her, so that when she tried to free herself she'd end up in a still more awkward and improbable position. He only calmed down when he'd managed to have an ejaculation somewhere in her armpit. He went over to the window like a blind man, made it to a chair and sat down, naked, his head in his hands – like a mirror image of the mannequin on the balcony opposite. He started mumbling again, and now it turned out that she, Lyudmila, had seduced him, woven a spell around him, tied him to her again, in the hope that he would forget Silva once and for all. But he hadn't forgotten Silva. He felt more passion for her than ever, fired by betrayal and by their parting. And if jealous, lustful and vindictive Lyudmila continued to try to tempt him, he'd have to kill her. It looked as if he'd have to kill her anyway, even without Silva. He couldn't kill Silva because she was a long way away, but Lyudmila was right here.

Silva decided to telephone Victor at his hotel without waiting for the morning. He answered sleepily, his voice hoarse and uncomprehending. He apologized, saying that he'd had too much to drink at the latest party given in his honour, and that they all needed to get together, talk about things and work things out. But in a minute or two he realized why Silva was calling him in the middle of the night. 'He's bluffing,' he assured her. 'The only way to deal with all these mind games is to persuade Felix that you really are Silva, and that you are not in Jerusalem, or in Moscow, but somewhere entirely different.'

'But I am somewhere entirely different, I'm in London,' said Silva.

'There you are. He has got to leave the geographical settings of his delirium, Moscow and Jerusalem, and move to the reality of London. You'll have to convince him that his presence in London is absolutely essential, that you're in deadly danger. From an epidemic, say. Convince him that the plague has broken out in London.' She heard him trying to refrain from yawning.

'He's convinced of that as it is. He was convinced when he was perfectly normal. I think that's what first drove him crazy.'

'So now he's completely out of his mind, you've got to restore him to that former craziness of his. Normality is simply the particular kind of madness that you're used to. The condition of someone mentally ill who's in a lunatic asylum is normal. And Felix is not even mentally ill,' he hastened to add reassuringly. 'He's just suffering from an émigré fever in an émigré situation.'

'When are you going to return to the land of the normal, come back to us?' asked Silva tentatively, not really expecting a reply.

'Very soon. A couple of official receptions, and I'm yours.' He told her that on the following day he finally had an invitation to the estate to meet Lord Edward, and he'd be able to raise the matter of Felix's illness. Perhaps his lordship would find room for him in some private psychiatric clinic (for Lord Edward was, after all, the prime mover behind the campaign against the abuse of psychiatry for political ends), if it really was something more than a simple case of fever and delirium. In the meantime, if she was too frightened to stay alone with Felix he would treat her to a room at the hotel. Silva bit her lip as she realized that he hadn't invited her to share his room. She looked in on Felix. He was either asleep or pretending he was. As she extracted her panties from under the blanket she found a medicine bottle under the pillow. She could make out the word 'barbiturate' on the label. It wasn't the first time that Silva had noticed Felix swallowing mysterious pills. Was his delirium that of a drug addict? She started shaking Felix hard, but he was snoring away and dead to the world.

11

Asylum

The sun eventually started to do its stuff (after all, Kent was on the same latitude as southern Russia), and at the moment they decided it was lunchtime, the haze that had lain like sweat over the warm fields started to dissipate. The green fields shone as if they'd been laundered, under the blue soap-powder sky. Here even the sky seemed to be the work of human hands, set in perfect harmony with the proportions of the surrounding hills, with their sheep and cows, their goats and chickens, their grazing horses and the dogs pursuing them – a place for everything, and everything in its place. The oak in the middle of the meadow was balanced by the scarecrow at the far end. A distant wind was making its sleeves blow about so that it appeared to be dancing under the radiant sky. It felt good to be alive. They decided to lunch al fresco in front of the house. Although the wind sometimes reached them to ruffle the tablecloth, it simply reinforced their sense of freedom and release, completeness and joy, that never left them even for an instant.

Lunch was a simple affair: roast pheasant with a nut sauce, and some claret, a Médoc. The pastoral scene was somewhat clouded by Felix and Victor having a stupid argument – not even an argument, more of a misunderstanding. Felix asked for some mustard to put on his pheasant. Silva was about to ask the servant to fetch some from the kitchen when Victor stopped her, saying that you don't put mustard on pheasant, you can eat it with cranberry sauce, but not with mustard. Felix retorted with some asperity that a pheasant is a sort of chicken, and since he was accustomed to putting mustard on chicken why couldn't he put mustard on pheasant? Whereupon Victor observed that a pheasant was a bird, whereas, of course, a chicken was not. 'In the same way as a woman isn't human?' Felix joked and Silva left the table. But Dr Genoni persuaded her to come back, and persuaded Felix to try some cranberry sauce, even though he continued to insist that pheasant tasted just like chicken, and if mustard went with chicken then why couldn't he put it on pheasant, even if a pheasant was not a chicken?

After lunch Felix went back to his notes:

'Why did Pushkin get so interested in John Wilson of all people? Why, for instance, didn't he start translating passages about the plague from a well-known poem of the time, *The Season* by James Thomson, "the king of descriptive verse" (a work that the great Turner read and reread constantly): "From stifled Cairo's filth, and foetid fields with locust armies heap'd, this great destroyer sprung. Her awful rage the brutes escape [sic!]; man is her destined prey." "Brutes" in this context means animals. Thus dogs would survive, dogs were unaffected by the plague. But Pushkin was interested in something else. It was not a poem about the plague he wanted, but a play, a little tragedy, armchair theatre . . .'

He couldn't complete his train of thought because Silva switched on the radio and started listening to the BBC's Russian Service. Their theatre reviewer, Gluzberg, was reviewing *The Two Gentlemen of Verona* performed by the Royal Shakespeare Company, emphasizing as always the political undertones of the production. (The Duke of Milan's court was treated as the symbol of a totalitarian regime, authoritarianism and male chauvinism.) The whole complicated plot and the conflict between the two heroes, Proteus and Valentine, was turned into a conflict between dissidents and conformists. And there was no doubt whatsoever that the play was dealing with exile and emigration. Judge for yourselves: Valentine flees abroad to escape the avenging hand of the Duke, and joins a band of robbers in the forest, who call themselves exiles and émigrés. The theme of emigration was brought to the fore in Proteus's very first monologue, when he was seeing off Valentine, who was leaving for Milan. Proteus was staying behind because he was in love. Love attached him to his native land. It was bizarre to hear a Russian voice talking about emigration in the midst of a typically English landscape. The voice was literally out of this world.

'The most remarkable thing about all that garbage,' said Victor, making Silva switch it off, 'is that you can really find a basis for all those pretentious speculations in the actual text. That's what makes theatre so irritating; it's like Russia, you can read whatever you want into it. A piece of painted board on a backdrop becomes the sky and the border becomes the Iron Curtain and as for plaster bread and coloured water in place of wine . . .'

'As you know, there was once someone else who did that kind of thing,' said Felix.

'How do you mean?'

'Turned water into wine,' said Felix with a knowing smile.

'And another thing, these religious associations of yours are all part of your perverse, theatrical way of thinking. Have we been viewing people from a divine standpoint for long now?' Victor asked sarcastically.

'Ever since we emigrated, because we chose to,' replied Felix with studied evasiveness.

'Some chose to, others did not,' said Victor dryly.

'Oh, come on,' said Felix dismissively. 'You went out and chose to behave in a way that got you chucked out of the country willy-nilly.'

'The dog is not responsible for its master.'

'But the master isn't responsible for his dog if it starts to stray.' Felix leant forward like someone who had at last found what he had been searching for. 'What strikes me about *The Two Gentlemen of Verona* is the way that the master and the dog are identical. Take the character of the servant-jester Launce, or rather not Launce himself, but the fact that, for whatever reason, he is constantly hanging around with his dog. As you know, the comedy is full of notorious absurdities and mistakes. But that kind of thing is forgivable and understandable in a way. But what is that idiotic servant doing there, and why does he have a dog? Do you know, it was only in England that I saw a real dog onstage for the first time. The English insist on literal interpretation, on naturalism. We're going to show you exactly what's contained in the text, and it's up to you to make what you want of it.' Felix turned to Silva. 'When Victor played Launce in my school production, of course, we had no trained dogs. We first thought of using a toy dog, something made of plaster of Paris. But then I realized that what we had to do was to pretend there was a dog on stage. So Launce sits there holding a leash, with the dog itself offstage.'

'Permit me to observe,' observed Dr Genoni, 'that your production featured a typically Russo-Soviet symbolic dog, which in England has become a real one.'

12

The Plasticine Castle

Victor Karvalanov woke up with the conviction, as unexpected as a blue sky over London, that his was a unique destiny. He had felt something like that twice before: at the time of his first arrest, and when he learnt of his father's death. On this August morning in 1984 he finally realized that he was free once and for all. Not even the knock at the door announcing breakfast made him start out of his bed – with the panic of someone hearing the camp reveille, or the fear that he was about to be searched. Even when he was still half asleep and had not yet woken up properly he knew for sure that he was not in a cot in the camp, that he was lying under a magnificent eiderdown, that his past was another country now. He'd become part of the local exotica, where the early morning shadows on the wall turned the clusters of leaves in the window into a gigantic leopard, prowling the cage made of patterned wallpaper in the old-fashioned hotel room, with its gilt taps in the bathroom, where the lamplight, shining through painted waxed paper shades, gave his haggard face a healthy-looking tan in the shaving mirror. Scraping away the luxurious expanse of foam with his double-edged Gillette, he smiled yet again as he recalled his one moment of panic, when they took the handcuffs off him and kicked him out of the Soviet aircraft on to the tarmac of Vienna airport; what was he going to do without the razor-blade which he'd so cleverly sewn into the lining of his prison jacket? He'd had to exchange it for a suit, a magnificent example of the Soviet tailor's art, before boarding the aircraft, and idiotically he'd forgotten about the razor, which would have come in handy, if not for him, then at least for his mates in the camp!

At breakfast the starched napkin was eager to leave its tight-fitting silver ring to take its place upon his knees. The triangles of toast looked eagerly out of the silver toast-rack like certificates of good conduct, while the fried egg's yellow eye stared at him unthinkingly. Even when it was captured by this shiny distorting mirror, his reflection looked as if it were being observed through the peephole in the door of a prison cell; looking back from now to then, that's what he used to be like: an animal hounded into a corner, with a face rendered shapeless and swollen from innumerable beatings and hunger-strikes.

'*The Times*, sir?' the waiter asked confidingly, but without a trace of familiarity, as he bent over a table with a selection of the morning papers.

'Umph.' Karvalanov nodded like a guest of long standing, and was given a copy of *The Times*, warm as new-baked bread and smelling of printers' ink. Sipping a cup of colonial Earl Grey, and smoking a Senior Service – he still refused to smoke filter-tips – he scanned the headlines. Trade unions, the price of oil, nuclear disarmament. I wish I had your worries. He corrected himself – they were his worries now. Take rabies shots, for instance. A column at the bottom of the third page informed the readers of *The Times* of a terrible danger threatening Albion. For centuries this country had naively regarded the fact that it was an island as a form of quarantine that served to protect it against the epidemics that devastated other nations and peoples. But it would only need one rabid rat to reach these shores, slipping past Passport Control and Customs in the bilges of some foreign ship, and the last vestiges of the British Empire, the United Kingdom, would be destroyed by hydrophobia. In no time at all this island would become a pen full of rabid dogs – with the insouciance of islanders, the authorities had never required pets to be given rabies shots or set up vaccination stations. Just a month ago Karvalanov, a Soviet political prisoner, couldn't have cared less about the danger of such an epidemic. But now, here, a British citizen by virtue of the law pertaining to political refugees, he was no different from any other stray British dog.

Suddenly he got the shakes and spilt his tea on the tablecloth. He looked at the sunbeams dancing on the busy waiter's silver tray, at the spectacles and distinguished bald patches of the scattered guests, and his stomach gave a painful flip – it was either his old camp ulcer acting up, or the long-forgotten fear of a schoolboy before his final examinations. Soon the charitable organizations would stop paying for his hotel room. He was no longer a political refugee, no longer a privileged martyr, just one of the country's three million unemployed citizens, in the same boat as the local inhabitants, and no dissident past was going to help. Maybe it wouldn't, but then again may be it would. His plain old Soviet past. Because, like the majority of Pioneers of his generation, he had been vaccinated against rabies – everyone used to get bitten by stray dogs in the post-war years. He absolutely must use this in his next interview or lecture. Look how the Soviet regime prepared me, from childhood on, to be an émigré in England, with its national obsession with disease, TB and rabies. The only thing is, was the Soviet vaccination a short-term affair, or was it good for the rest of my life?

Instinctively he slid a hand under his jacket, to his heart, checking that it was still there, and, in his inside pocket, feeling the telegram from Lord Edward, inviting him down. The prospect of the visit seemed to him at that moment to contain the promise of a radiant future in this unfamiliar exile of his. Karvalanov felt like the consul of an empire that didn't quite exist yet. In this empire – or, as they'd say in the camps, mafia – Lord Edward was going to be the Godfather. With his contacts in Parliament and the Cabinet, all he'd need would be a shove in the right direction to get him going, once Karvalanov had won him away from other émigré factions defending human rights, from monarchists to social democrats. None of that activist riffraff realized that all those political slogans, professions of faith and legal issues mattered not one iota, the only thing that mattered was power; only force could topple the Soviet colossus with feet of clay behind the Iron Curtain. And let no one talk of the disappearance of the aristocracy as a ruling class; everybody in this country still took their lead from this moribund class, from its manners and its way of life. And in this country it was manners, and not fundamentals, that were decisive.

He asked for more tea, spread the marmalade thickly on another piece of toast and devoted himself to a page of *The Times*, adorned with his photograph, with the gates of Buckingham Palace in the background, in place of prison bars. The journalist had exaggerated here and there, and some of the piece was pure invention, but on the whole the interview had turned out rather well. It was snappy, full of jokes, spiced with the odd touch of realism, and had none of those religious and rhetorical exclamation marks which they just loved the

Russians for over here; and, the main thing, there was no sentimentality. The lone hero driven into a corner by a pack of thugs and torturers – that's the sort of thing the English like. Back to the wall, alone against the mob, with no one else to count on. That's when you can tell what someone is made of. If you can keep your head when all about you are losing theirs.

When you're dealing with the Bolsheviks you have to fight fire with fire. That's the lesson to be learnt from the most successful political strategists in human history – the Bolsheviks themselves. They used the State Duma's parliamentary forum to preach revolutionary terror; in order to preach anti-Soviet dissent in England it is obvious that we need to use the House of Lords, which is so proud of its spirit of open-mindedness. Clearly he'd have to work on Lord Edward, get rid of all that rubbish about universal human rights regardless of time and place, all those apartheids and Sandinistas. He'd have to drum in the uniqueness of the Soviet situation, its monstrous originality, its pathological singularity, and then the philosophical confrontation of Marxism and democracy would turn into the most basic of all emotions, hatred of the enemy. That would soon put a stop to revisionist statements about the CIA being no better than the KGB. It wasn't a question of which security service was better, it was a question of which side you were on. Because there was a holy war going on, or, if you like, a duel, and whose second are you? The image of the duel was actually more appropriate. Duels implied rapiers, swords, Cossack sabres, Caucasian daggers, English crossbows, the fateful barrels of Lepage's pistols, in short they implied weapons, and aristocrats love to collect antique weaponry. Karvalanov pictured an aristocratic estate, a house with fireplaces and rugs, the walls adorned with crossbows, suits of armour, muskets. He was convinced he'd get on with Lord Edward. The hall porter gave him a friendly salute, and politely opened the heavy oak door with the bronze handle – exposing him to the welcome of a sunny London street.

Belgravia that morning was getting ready for the coming day as if it too were going out. Even the caretakers and porters at work outside the snow-white houses looked like busy errand boys. Stopping on a corner, Karvalanov smiled to himself as he observed a black man in a uniform cap, polishing the marble steps of a three-storey house as if they were his master's boots.

That is just how he'd imagined London: squares with green trees, houses with white columns, like rows of imperial sentries, standing at attention guarding streets in which the red of revolution was reserved exclusively for buses and pillar-boxes.

The heels of his excellent leather shoes tapping as he walked, he gloried in every new sign attesting to the enduring nature of this hierarchical society, the aloof aristocratic mansions with their columns, and the democratic raffishness of the grass in the squares open to the public, the stiff-necked stuffiness of smart grocery stores and the vulgar jostle of the supermarkets, the discreet diligence of the sales assistants in their striped jackets, and the slow-paced hauteur of women in sable coats emerging from Rolls-Royces. He delighted in the elegant discretion, the carefree and haphazard nature of London churches, which lacked the stridency of the phallic domes of Orthodox churches; he enjoyed the cosiness of the low London sky, with the breathtaking expanse of London's huge parks – in short he delighted in the existence of ranks and barriers, in both the metaphoric and the literal sense; like the smoking and non-smoking sections of buses, and the distinction between the public bar and the saloon bar in pubs. It wasn't like Moscow, where poets, informers, dissidents and the grandchildren of distinguished Bolsheviks, Zionists and computer programmers were all lumped together. Here, however vague and diffuse things might appear, you could always find a contour, a clear dividing line, a barrier, a yellow line where you could park – after six o'clock.

At about this time in the morning, a month ago, they were taking him out of the camp's residential area to be searched before the start of work; and it had occurred to him that the camps, prison, were the only place in the Soviet Union which had anything approaching a civilization, with its careful attention to detail, to established order and routine, its hierarchical division of inmates into aristocrats and plebs according to unwritten 'class' principles. And he, Karvalanov, was undoubtedly one of the aristocrats of this prison society; he was always treated with a special respect by the prisoners and by the guards, by the interrogators and by foreign correspondents. His accusers hadn't been able to frighten him, not because he didn't know the meaning of fear, but because they didn't understand what made him afraid; they didn't realize that his fear was the fear that he would repudiate certain mysterious convictions; it was essentially a fear not of this world, a fear of renouncing the right to be called the chosen one, which was not given him by this world, and which this world could not take away. Anyone else who had done what he'd done, would have been broken by the camps or emerged from the prison psychiatric ward as a drivelling wreck, but here he was strolling through London; all he needed was some leather gloves and a cane. No wonder an English lord had headed the campaign for his release. No wonder he'd invited him down to his place. An aristocrat of camp civilization remained an aristocrat in the civilized West. 'Aristocrats of the world unite!' was the slogan his heels were tapping out as he walked beneath the echoing arches of Charing Cross.

The suburban countryside slipped past the train window, looking so deserted it seemed unreal. There was something dream-like about the tree-crowned hills, the tiny houses, and the sheep scattered around the sparse thickets, like bread-crumbs in the beard of a lunatic. It is only in your dreams that you're one with the landscape, as if it's not over hills and vales that your eyes are moving but rather over the bumps and crannies of your own brain. He'd been travelling for an hour now, and hadn't seen a single soul gracing the pastoral scene. The local station was just as empty, with the fretwork fringe of its roof looking like the giant porch of a vanished country house, its cast-iron columns adorned with the coat of arms of the royal railway line, clumsily picked out with childish tawdriness. It was a masterpiece of Victorian architecture, renovated every five years by the brush of a lowly house-painter, chief engineer of this time-machine named England.

The person in charge of this entire architectural mirage was a kind old stationmaster standing at the exit, in a black uniform with shoulder-straps, wearing a cap with a railwayman's badge. His chubby cheeks were made up, Dickensian fashion, with rouge and grey sideburns. The gentle smile on Karvalanov's face suddenly turned into a panic-stricken grimace when the rustic stationmaster, who looked like a portrait of an Academician of Pushkin's time, stopped him quite sharply at the barrier.

'Your ticket, sir?'

Like any ticketless passenger caught red-handed, Karvalanov started rummaging in his pockets, sorting through his wallet and shaking various papers, zipping and unzipping the numerous fasteners on the bag which contained a present for Lord Edward. He even dug down into the hole in the lining of his jacket pocket, although in fact he knew perfectly well that he had no ticket. He'd thrown it out of the window as they approached the station, on the Soviet assumption that it had been inspected as he got on the train, which of course it had not, although the fact had escaped his attention, and he did not realize that in England tickets are inspected as you leave the platform, not when you board. Which is what he tried to explain to the stationmaster: in the Soviet Union it's all the other way round, and tickets are inspected at the departure point not at the destination, when you get on the train not on the way out, since, he tried to joke, making brave use of his English, there was no way out anyway – 'it's the only line we've got, with Communism at the end of it'.

'Isn't it true that public transport is free in the Soviet Union?' inquired the stationmaster, who clearly had not grasped the anti-Soviet thrust of Karvalanov's joke. 'You speak excellent English, sir. Isn't it true that education is free in the Soviet Union?'

'I paid for my education with a prison term. I learnt English in a Soviet jail,' Karvalanov answered sombrely. But in fact he was enjoying his conversation with a representative of the common people in a country where even a railwayman spoke better English than the Professor of English at Moscow University. Karvalanov apologized for his accent. He'd only been in England a month. But he had a decent vocabulary. He'd done his time in a prison which had already been famous for its library before the Revolution; its collections were the product of nearly two centuries of Russian dissent with its attendant confiscations, searches and arrests: 'tens of thousands of volumes, all the English classics, and you even find semi-banned contemporary authors that you can't get hold of on the outside. You can say that prison did me proud as far as my English was concerned.'

'A decent education costs a fortune in England.' The stationmaster was pleased for him. 'How did you manage to get into such a good prison, sir?'

'It was easy.' Karvalanov enjoyed enlightening the foreigner. 'They transferred me from the psychiatric clinic to prison after the psychiatrists' forcible treatment failed to persuade me that I was mad.'

'I've heard that all medical treatment is free in the Soviet Union.' The stationmaster nodded like someone in the know. 'But here you can be blind, with a cataract, and your turn for an operation will never come. So why did you refuse treatment if it was free?'

'Whether or not I was actually sick in the head wasn't the point. It was a question of who told me I was mad,' Karvalonov replied rather shrilly. 'According to Soviet psychiatrists a mentally healthy person has no need to prove it. If a patient needs that kind of proof, it automatically means he's crazy. In order to be discharged from the hospital I had to prove that I was perfectly normal. From the psychiatrist's point of view that meant proving I was crazy! Don't you see, it's a vicious circle.'

'It works the other way around here,' the stationmaster grunted. 'They've started discharging psychopaths from mental hospitals, because they say they can't afford to keep them. If you're not violent, then be off with you and do as you please. So there are loonies wherever you look, there's no getting away from them. Who got you admitted to hospital?'

'The KGB. The security services think anyone opposing them must be mad. Which is why I told you that it's not a question of whether or not we're crazy, the point is who thinks we are.'

'We read a lot about the KGB in our papers. I'd have thought, sir, that if someone is right in the head he's not going to fight that lot,' the stationmaster observed sagely.

'In a way you're quite right.' Karvalanov nodded sombrely.

'So you're not fighting the KGB any more, seeing as how they discharged you from hospital?' the railwayman asked slyly.

'They didn't discharge me, they exchanged me.'

'So you're one of those dissident fellows, are you? I thought I recognized you. You were on the telly. Swapped you for an Argie spy, didn't they?'

'For a Chilean one,' Karvalanov corrected him. 'He wasn't a spy, just a Communist in prison over there.'

'He refused treatment too, did he?' asked the stationmaster, pointing to his head to signify mental disorder. 'And what brings you to these parts?'

98

'I'm visiting Lord Edward.' Karvalanov cleared his throat. His conspicuous dignity of manner was intended to impress upon the over-familiar stationmaster that he'd been invited down as a guest and wasn't just some foreigner come to gawp.

'Lord Edward?' the stationmaster repeated in genuine amazement. 'But isn't he abroad? I loaded his trunk myself. You haven't come to shoot pheasants have you? His lordship doesn't care for that. I've been through three wars – people or pheasants, it's all the same to me. Anyway the season hasn't started yet, sir.'

'I don't know. I've been invited. I expect there's a taxi waiting for me outside the station.' Karvalanov made an impatient move to get through the barrier.

'What about that ticket, sir?' The stationmaster straightened his cap.

'But I just explained to you.' Karvalanov was stunned.

'Thank you for the stories, but the fare's got to be paid,' said the stationmaster in a surprisingly curt official tone as he barred the way. By Soviet standards it was a huge sum of money; compared to English prices, Soviet public transport is practically free – the stationmaster knew what he was talking about there. Karvalanov had to consult him again when it transpired that there was no taxi waiting for him outside the station. He had to go back to the barrier to ask the way to the estate. The guardian of the barrier was once more transformed into a jovial Dickensian squire, and started reeling off a series of crossings, turnings and junctions at a dizzy rate: you went from the Horse and Coaches to the graveyard gates, from the cricket field to the church, behind which there was a juniper hedge, stables and a gamekeeper's hut. Thanks to the powers of recall he had developed in the camps, Karvalanov reckoned he'd find the way blindfold. Setting off along a shady gravel path that seemed to lead through a park, he turned left at the first crossroads as instructed, then right and then left again, but for some reason failed to come upon the graveyard, the pub or the stables – just a solid expanse of woodland stretching away unbroken before him.

It was an ordinary sort of wood, mixed, with a narrow path that wound between oaks and chestnuts, ash and hazel trees politely inviting one to step into their glades, where the light shone down through the billowing leaves above, and gleamed in the tangle of young grasses, mixed with last year's leaves, shot through with lilies of the valley, looking like beads amidst the acorns and the horse chestnuts. But this seemingly ordinary English wood had something strangely foreign and exotic about it, as subtle and as imperceptible as the glide into a more intimate mode of address in English. On its outskirts there grew a gigantic rhododendron bush that properly belonged in a botanical garden hothouse, and two intertwined wild magnolia trees barred the way – clearly the Gulf Stream provided the island with a form of central heating. What's more, there were disturbing rustling sounds. The bushes along the path, the treetops, the brambles and the mulberry trees, the heather and the gorse all seemed to be alive, emitting a ceaseless twittering, the rapid fire of bird calls, and the squeaks and squeals of other kinds of wildlife. Despite an apparent resemblance to the woodlands outside Moscow, the nameless wood was strange and so exotic it seemed almost like a jungle with boa constrictors and alligators round every corner. It was the jungle of the Western world.

The meadow that suddenly materialized before him, as if from behind a curtain, helped to convince him that the place was under a spell. It looked like an illustration to a children's fairy tale in an expensive presentation edition. Never before in real life had he beheld such lush grass, rippling in the breeze, and in turn the grass tantalized the shadows cast by the passing clouds above the treetops, as if the clouds were holding back, and the trees themselves mutely muttering, not daring to enter into the dance of wind and shade upon the grass of this magic circle. A magic circle, because in its midst stood a magus making mysterious passes with his hands. He didn't wear a nightclub conjurer's coat and top hat, or even the robes and turban of a dervish, but nevertheless he had the appearance of somebody not of this world, or not, at any event of the world of an erstwhile Soviet Pioneer, who was kicked out of the Young Communists' League for attacking the one-party system which in due course sent him into exile. The magus seemed to have stepped out of a nineteenth-century print depicting a royal shooting party, or else to have fallen straight out of Turgenev's nest of gentlefolk.

The trees and sky were reflected in his highly polished boots, and his deerstalker gave him the perspicacity of two-faced

Janus. He seemed to hold the whole meadow in his quiet thrall. It was in response to the commands of his all-seeing hypnotic eye that the treetops swayed, that the clouds sailed across the sky, and the grass modestly rippled. Suddenly the hypnotist became a mysterious shaman. Squatting down, the sorcerer started emitting a series of trills, chirps, clicks and whistles. He was holding a tin, and on it he started to knock out strange spellbinding rhythms, as if he were accompanying his whistling. In answer to the bird-catcher's calls, from all over the meadow there tripped towards him peculiar creatures with feathers the colour of ripe chestnuts and with sharp darting heads adorned with Asiatic topknots. Emerging from nowhere, the birds advanced deliberately on their frail legs, their heads nodding in unison, never averting their gaze from the hypnotic magus. In their wake, equally under the spell of his wand, Karvalanov moved towards the centre of the meadow. Which was a mistake. A twig snapped under his foot and the meadow's spell was broken in a trice: he jumped at the hysterical screeching, the squawk of collective indignation uttered in unison by scores of birds. The squawk had none of the grace of the creatures that had just been moving across the lush grass like a troupe of dancers; flapping their wings inelegantly, like gigantic moths fluttering about the lamplight on a terrace by a country house, the exotic creatures rushed towards the meadow's edge. A moment later they had vanished without a trace, leaving not a feather behind. Karvalanov was alone with the master of this woodland life. The sun, as if in panic, tucked its head beneath the pillow of an especially fat cloud, and a gust of cold wind finally dissipated what was left of the enchantment.

It was no mysterious magus that turned towards Karvalanov; instead what he saw was the face of a farm manager. A face of someone who specialized in fattening battery chickens, it had no place in a magic world of sunbeams and birdcalls. Red and wind-blown, it looked like a worn leather book-binding with two metal clasps for eyes. Retrieving his shotgun from the grass, he raised himself to his full sturdy height. It was only the extraordinary noises emerging from the mouth of this enraged rustic, his face distorted by fury, that indicated his exotic and mysterious racial origins. He sounded like a howling Chinaman who had retrained as a muezzin. The meadow was filled with a cacophony intolerable to a Russian ear, consisting of a kind of nasal and gutteral quacking, invertebrate and quite lacking in consonants – none of which would have come as any surprise to a linguist studying provincial variants of Cockney. But Karvalanov, backing away into the bushes, could, with the utmost difficulty, make out just two words, 'bloody' and 'bastard'. But these first faint glimmers of mutual understanding developed no further. The bird-catcher in the deerstalker put his shotgun to his shoulder in a single flowing action and, as in a conjuring trick, his face vanished in a puff of smoke. A moment later, Karvalanov heard the echo of something crack overhead; either a branch had snapped off or a piece of shot had whistled past his ear.

Karvalanov fell backwards into the bushes, his fall precipitated not by the shotgun's deadly aim, but by someone's arm that had jerked him back and yanked him down. He heard an urgent whisper: 'Keep down! Over here! Follow me!' Had it not been for the fact that the instruction had been conveyed in impeccable upper-class English, he would have assumed he was being kidnapped by Soviet agents. He couldn't see his rescuer's face, but of the two evils confronting him – the shotgun in the meadow or a Soviet jail – he chose the one he knew, jail, and set off behind the back he could still glimpse moving off through the undergrowth. Practically on all fours they moved down a shallow gully; they were scratched by dog roses, stung by nettles, and the strap of his bag kept getting caught in the magnolia branches, but none of it mattered. The main thing was that the menacing cacophony of curses and gunshots faded gradually, to be replaced by that of two sets of lungs breathing heavily. At last they came to a gap in the bushes and found themselves on the edge of the wood.

'I hope you realize, my dear Karvalanov, that he was ready to gun you down like a stray dog?' His rescuer spoke to him like a schoolmaster chiding an errant pupil as they sat down together on a tree-trunk to catch their breath.

'I'm not a stray dog,' muttered Karvalanov, gingerly feeling the back of his sweat-soaked head; he rather thought that the shot had singed his hair and that he was feeling blood, not sweat.

'To a certain extent, my dear Karvalanov, all of us are strays,' his companion replied in melancholy tones that brooked no contradiction.

'Some stray dogs quickly retrain as guard dogs,' Karvalanov countered. 'By the way, how d'you know my name? Have you been following me?'

'We really must have a talk about guard dogs,' said the Englishman, ignoring his question. 'You really don't look like a stray. But he could have shot you anyway as an incompetent poacher. There's nothing like the excitement of being allowed to kill. Pheasants, stray dogs, poachers – what's the difference? Besides which, he was obviously all worked up after his ululation.'

'What ululation?' Karvalanov couldn't see what this mysterious inhabitant of that mysterious spot was getting at.

'Any calling. Doesn't matter. You can make any kind of noise – here's a call I learnt as a child,' and his companion put his hand to his mouth and started to drum on his lower lip with his forefinger. Guttural cries answered him from the bushes. Karvalanov was in no doubt: they were pheasants. 'You call when you're about to feed them – sounds like Red Indians whooping, doesn't it? Or a bunch of Zulus. The main thing is that the pheasant gets used to the call. I can only say that for him the call is the voice of brute instinct. He's quite incapable of human speech.'

'Who, the pheasant?'

'What've pheasants got to do with it? I mean that murderer.'

'What murderer? Who's a murderer?' Karvalanov asked nervously.

'Can't you see who? The dictator of this estate, my estate. My gamekeeper.' Stunned by his companion's glaring obtuseness, the Englishman, smiling in embarrassment, gestured awkwardly.

Karvalanov leapt to his feet and made a clumsy attempt at a bow. He didn't know what to do: should he stretch his hand out, give a careless nod of the head or bow his knee reverently? He should have guessed a long time ago; everything about the fellow's appearance betrayed the aristocrat. In fact that was just how he had imagined an English lord: suede shoes with leggings and silver buckles glistening through the dirt that had stuck to them; the cloak that looked as if it was on loan from the Middle Ages, tied at his throat with a silk cord, and under it he was probably wearing a lace collar. As for the head, with its jutting chin, bright blue eyes and high forehead, it was the spitting image of Prince Myshkin. The comparison had struck him long ago, in the camp, when he first saw a photograph of Lord Edward on a much-crumpled page of the *Morning Star* which had miraculously got past the censor to find its way into the camp along with an English grammar. That, of course, was some years ago; his lordship had aged since then, and there was no saying how old the photograph had been in the first place. All the same, Karvalanov felt awful; he should instantly have recognized the man to whom he owed his freedom. For years he'd been hearing the echoes of voices from abroad, their broadcasts describing Lord Edward's struggle to have Karvalanov set free. And here they were face to face, and again there were enemies around them, again they were conspiring together, hiding, this time, from the ubiquitous gamekeeper.

'I knew you'd get lost, did the right thing to come to meet you. Karvalanov, I was waiting for you.' And Lord Edward took Karvalanov's hand between both his, almost in supplication. His aristocratic haughtiness, his carelessly offhand manner, gave way to something close to servile deference. He'd made no preparations for his visit, he muttered apologetically, he'd been prevented by the highly constricted nature of his current circumstances. 'It's almost like being in prison,' as he put it. He stared up at Karvalanov, who was standing over him, and this made his plaintive look almost hangdog. Karvalanov tried to sit down beside him, expecting a long explanation, but Lord Edward drew him back into the woods, along a path that was all but invisible to the naked eye. He started to move off so briskly through the trees that Karvalanov could scarcely keep up, let alone follow Lord Edward's haphazard comments on forest life, woodland lore, mysterious ululations and bloody rituals, which he described as they went along, as if he were talking about the authoritarian ceremonials of ancient despotisms.

'And all this, mind you, is part of my estate.' Lord Edward gestured towards the wings, arches, balustrades and pediments of his woodland castle. 'D'you like it?' he asked Karvalanov. 'Would you like to live here?'

'I would,' Karvalanov nodded an obedient head.

'So would I,' Lord Edward concurred in mysterious irony. 'Careful, don't touch!' He stopped Karvalanov from reaching a curious hand out to the kind of wire mesh, stretching from tree to tree, that he had suddenly come upon. It looked like an enormous volleyball net, with the sun like a ball that had got caught up there in the foliage. 'Actually you're in no danger. You're not a stray dog, are you, just an incompetent poacher.' Lord Edward explained that the net was electrified. Low voltage, though, enough to make you uncomfortable, but not enough to kill you. They kept young pheasants inside it – it was the pheasant pen.

'Looks like a concentration camp,' muttered Karvalanov as he whipped his hand back from the wire. But Lord Edward pointed out that it was glib and indeed wrong to compare his pheasants to the victims of Nazi persecution, when the wood's wild population – hares, squirrels, foxes, stray dogs and cats – were killed on the slightest contact with the electric fence that enclosed these pompous feathered creatures of foreign origin.

'And don't you accuse me of being a chauvinist and xenophobe,' he added quickly, on noticing Karvalanov's amazement at this anti-pheasant diatribe. 'Everybody knows that pheasants were introduced into this country from Thailand or Ceylon or God knows where – anyway, one of those pseudo-republics run on principles of the cruellest Asiatic tyranny. The pheasant, by nature, is an obedient slave. Just take a look.' Lord Edward bent down and showed Karvalanov a neat little opening in the wire. All the keeper had to do was call and all the pheasants, in single file, would troop to be fed, through the hole, which was too narrow to admit any of the free inhabitants of the wood. 'When I was just a boy I used to bury the innocent victims of this electrification of the coverts. I'd dig graves with my toy spade for stray dogs, cats, hares. I could hear the groans of the dying through my bedroom window at night. It's covered in graves here, we're walking over the bones of the innocent victims of a good day's sport – do you understand, Karvalanov?'

It wasn't hard to understand Lord Edward's English. But Karvalanov didn't know how to react to this English concern with the plight of animals. He wasn't prepared for the way things were turning out, especially since he had done in his fair share of stray cats in his youth, chasing them through rubbish dumps with his mates. 'What a lot of fences.' He cursed as, under Lord Edward's guidance, he climbed over yet another barrier.

'All my land is rented out for the pheasant shooting,' Lord Edward said in gloomy anger. 'Every gun has a number; they wait their turn to take a hand in the killing. To begin with, everything is so quiet, then over there, behind the coppice, that noise begins like an evil whisper.' Lord Edward leant against a tree and clutched his head.

'Are you all right?' Karvalanov didn't know what to do; his companion was clearly overwrought.

'The beaters move forward in a semi-circle. It's like a pogrom, like the forced deportation of a nation. The beaters wave rattles and noise-makers and stamp their feet, they shake every bush. No wonder they're called beaters, they beat and beat and beat!'

'Beat who?' asked Karvalanov, who was also getting excited.

'They beat the pheasants out of the covers. And these idiot birds, these Asiatic pheasants, fly up in a panic, beating their stupid wings, they shoot out of the woods and stagger over the meadow, halfwits on their clipped wings.'

'I don't blame them,' Karvalanov chuckled. 'Where else are they to go? Where else can these Thai refugees head?'

'Where? They should scatter through the woods, hide in the fields, fly off to another country – anywhere! But they just sit here, let the gamekeeper feed them, and wait till the beaters drive them out of the covers over the guns. There's a sound of cocking, a quick report and feathers fly through the air. Then a dog brings back the bloody carcase of a pheasant. Dogs! The keeper knows how to sick brother on to brother, how to divide and how to conquer. He keeps a whole pack, they obediently herd the pheasants, they retrieve their blood-stained corpses at the snap of the keeper's fingers. They don't understand that the whole enterprise results in the genocide of their own kind; stray dogs by the dozen die on the wire of the pheasant pens so that disgusting nouveau-riche foreigners, full of nostalgia for the good old days, can imitate the bloody habits of the English aristocracy.' Until recently it was mostly Germans who rented the shoot. But recently they'd had quite a few Japanese, with cameras. He wouldn't be at all surprised to see the estate occupied by Chinese Communists one of these fine days. 'What on earth would my father, my ancestors have said?'

'My great-grandfather was a tenant.' Karvalanov brought in his ancestors somewhat *mal à propos*. It wasn't just their class origins that made them different from Lord Edward's. 'My great-grandfather was a Jew. Jews weren't allowed to own land, so he had to rent his country place from a Russian landowner.'

He said this as if he didn't quite believe it, which always happens when your own past suddenly turns into someone else's present; just as Karvalanov's father, an engineer and Party member, didn't quite believe his mother; even now Karvalanov could remember her long stories about his great-grandfather's huge country house, in the midst of the Byelorussian forests, with its marble staircases, its family silver and a real carriage drawn by four horses.

'Did he have a pheasant shoot?' asked Lord Edward with ill-concealed suspicion.

'He was a timber merchant. He sold wood wholesale. Ruined a lot of forest land, I suppose,' Karvalanov answered, the subject of his ancestors and the massacred forests of Russia eliciting a note of sadistic pride. It occurred to him that he was an accomplice of the Russian Revolution, if only because he had left a land where the revolution was already victorious, to come to one where the revolution was as yet no more than a remote threat, some time in the future. He was marked, excluded and saved as if by the scar of a childhood vaccination. The scar was an invisible one, but it freed him from the nightmarish delusion that a time-machine had carried him back across the Iron Curtain to a time before the Revolution which he only knew from Soviet school books.

'What happened to your great-grandfather's place?'

'Haven't you heard? Russia had a revolution.' Karvalanov was amazed at his companion's naivety. 'They chopped down the cherry orchard.' But literary allusions were lost on Lord Edward.

'I'd happily chop the whole wood down if only I could get rid of these damn pheasants. But I'm sorry for the other poor animals. They'd be left without a home, like lost souls. Like me, ever since I was a boy.'

'You're a lost and homeless soul? On your own estate?' Karvalanov finally plucked up the courage to ask. But Lord Edward said nothing. Taking Karvalanov by the arm, he led him to the edge of the wood. Below them, as if set in an elaborate picture frame of beeches, was a lake with swans on it, overgrown with weeds and looking like the work of a nine-teenth-century Russian landscape painter. As if growing out of its own reflection, a creeper-clad mansion loomed above the lake.

'Is that your castle?' Karvalanov could scarcely repress a gasp on seeing this original of all the cheap portrayals of grand country life.

'My father's place,' Lord Edward replied reverently, as if referring at the very least to the Holy Sepulchre. 'But now it's a hostelry for nouveaux-riches and gamekeepers, to which I'm denied entrance.' He took Karvalanov's arm again – making him flinch a little: it felt too like a turnkey's hand guiding him down the corridor for interrogation. When they got to the lawn in front of the house Karvalanov moved towards the gravel path that led to the steps of the main entrance with its portico and columns. However, Lord Edward nudged him in the direction of the rhododendron bushes, surrounded by darkened peeling statues, at the side of the house. Dragging Karvalanov in his wake, he started to move round the mansion left-handed, along a narrow winding path, darting forward a short distance at a time and looking warily around him. Karvalanov saw a woman dressed in starched apron and mobcap and carrying some crockery appear briefly in a doorway – obviously a servant. She might have stepped out of a nineteenth-century painting portraying the life of the gentry. She started to cross the yard and suddenly stopped, as if rooted to the spot, when she saw Karvalanov and Lord Edward. He made a point of drawing himself upright and giving her a curt bow. She shook her head in evident reproach and quickly went back inside.

'She'll tell on us, she's bound to tell,' Lord Edward muttered, and cursed in most unaristocratic language. With his arm round Karvalanov's shoulders, as if trying to shield him under his cloak from prying eyes, he shoved him towards some huge French windows at the back of the house, where the roses were not so well cared for, and the paint on the trellises was peeling and looked like burst soap bubbles in a dirty bath. Taking another look around him, Lord Edward peered through the window, shading his eyes, and then drew Karvalanov closer.

'Look,' he whispered. Karvalanov pressed his nose to the pane, and stared in at the darkness with the hungry curiosity of a street urchin who hadn't been invited to a classmate's grand birthday party. Out of the blackness of the glass, as out of a dense fog, the outlines of massive leather began to appear, grouped around the black lake of a lacquered table. A shadow flitted over the lake – either Hamlet's ghost or the two conspirators, caught in the window-frame like exhibits in a glass case.

'This is where my father used to smoke cigars and drink whisky with the guests after the day's bag of dead pheasants had been distributed. Murder leads to murder – between the birds and the guns there's only room for a beater,' and as he turned away from the window Lord Edward rounded off his peculiar maxim with a question: 'Is your father still alive?'

'He died of a heart attack. The third. He had the first when they searched my place, the second when I was arrested. And the third, which proved lethal, as they told me, when they kicked me out of the country. So one way or another we both ended up in another world,' Karvalanov said with a wry laugh.

'So you were the cause of his death?'

'The thing is that mine is a generation that swapped roles with their fathers, playing out the legend of Pavlik Morozov. Pavlik Morozov died trying to make his father the kulak into a good Soviet citizen. My father died trying to make a good Soviet citizen out of his dissident son.' Judging by his expression, this excursion into the history of the Soviet version of the Oedipus complex was lost on Lord Edward. 'So you don't want to go into the house because you're on bad terms with your father?'

'Bad terms, with my father!' Lord Edward shrugged. 'There's the only place I can meet my father.' He pointed upwards. 'Up there. My father died up there. Enemy anti-aircraft fire brought him down over the Channel. A quick report, some smoke, and the aircraft's wings flutter down like feathers. No dogs found my father's remains. Shsh!!' He grabbed Karvalanov's arm again and put a finger to his lips. They could hear footsteps on the gravel round the corner, slow and measured, the deliberate tread of a man full of self-confidence. With a dexterity that any turnkey would have envied, Lord Edward directed Karvalanov to a niche in the wall, shoving him and his bag into a narrow space behind a plaster vase, while he set off, seemingly insouciant, towards the footsteps that were growing louder every moment. Karvalanov stood motionless, his back against the rough texture of the wall. It felt as if some disgusting insect was crawling down his neck; perhaps it was just the shivers, anyway he didn't dare move a finger. The footsteps stopped at the corner, and Karvalanov could hear scraps of a seemingly trivial conversation.

'How do you feel, My Lord?'

'Perfectly fine, thank you, I feel perfectly fine.'

'A little overexcited perhaps?' Karvalanov could hear the speaker rocking back and forth on his heels.

'Overexcited? Not a bit of it. It's just the fresh air, the oxygen, don't you know. Wonderful day, isn't it?'

'Proper summer's day, eh? I don't like the look of you. I'll look in after lunch.'

'Quite unnecessary. Goin' to work. Do Not Disturb.'

'Saving animals are we? Fine, fine, it's a good cause. But don't overdo it, eh?'

The deliberate, self-confident footsteps crunched away over the gravel. Peering out of his niche, Karvalanov caught a glimpse of the mysterious speaker as he moved off towards the park; built like a heavyweight boxer in a well-cut pin-striped suit and shiny shoes, with a large bumpy bald spot, he sported a bulldog jaw that jutted over his bow-tie. He was the personification of determination and good sense, and for a moment it occurred to a craven Karvalanov that this was his last chance to escape from this evidently disturbed lord pheasant-hater, with his keepers and beaters.

Back to the underworld. It would seem his interrogator was not far wrong when he pigeonholed Karvalanov as basically a criminal type. Crime was like a drug for him, he suggested. Karvalanov was the kind of person who was simply incapable of leading an ordinary life with its daily routines. If he hadn't had the regime to fight, he'd have found another reason to go underground, but underground he would most certainly have gone. He hung out with others like him, who were disturbed, not quite all there, people who couldn't settle into the collective, who dropped out, who were always looking for something they couldn't have. In that sense there wasn't much to choose between lunatics, Utopian thinkers, dissidents – and common criminals ready to do anything for 'a bit of high life'. Did Karvalanov have any friends who were completely adequate psychologically? And now it looked as if it was going to be the picture as before. And small wonder. Only someone who feels inadequate in the midst of his fellow-countrymen would be ready to set off to the end of the world in quest of justice. Take Karvalanov.

Or take Lord Edward, who reappeared at the far end of the

lawn as soon as the pin-striped back of his authoritarian companion had vanished down one of the walks. Karvalanov felt bad about his secret act of mental betrayal as he saw Lord Edward beckon to him, announcing that the coast was clear. With his ragged beard, his waving velvet cloak and his clownesque striped leggings, he looked so awkward, so pitiful, and yet, paradoxically, he made you want to smile. Karvalanov smiled, waved in reply, and slinging his bag over his shoulder he set off again along the gravel path.

'As you may have gathered, not only am I forbidden to try and save the keeper's four-legged victims, I am not even permitted to receive members of the human race that I have contrived to save,' Lord Edward muttered with bitter irony as he moved through the thickets, parting the branches before him. 'Welcome to my modest abode. My HQ or, if you like, the British version of your prison,' and he pointed to a cottage on the far side of a small expanse of grass. Instead of having the short-back-and-sides appearance of an English lawn, it looked like a blasted heath overgrown with docks and nettles. 'The only way they humour me. I told them not to cut the grass, my dependants feel easier in the midst of these modest but to my mind delightful growths. And here they are.' Lord Edward held out his arms as if to embrace the pack of dogs running to greet him. They threw themselves at him with barks of unsolicited goodwill, placed their forepaws on his chest, executing complicated pirouettes, licked his face, threw up clouds of dust with their tails and busily investigated Karvalanov.

'Recognize anyone?' Lord Edward asked with a sly smile. Karvalanov looked about him blankly, pushing back the dogs, expecting to be surprised by old friends who happened to be staying with his host. But the lord was referring to dogs, not people. He bent down, patted their necks and scratched their ears. Most of his dependants looked like mongrels, ill-groomed, clumsy and lop-eared. 'I find them all over the place, on the road, in ditches. A lot of them would have died ages ago, and not because the keeper would have shot or trapped them, or because of the electric fence, but quite simply of starvation. Their owners just left them to their fate,' he said sadly, looking at Karvalanov, and started to distribute sugar lumps which he extracted from his numerous pockets. Watching the dogs cluster round their benefactor, Karvalanov noticed that they were all damaged: one had a limp, others lacked an ear, or an eye, or in one instance a tail. The psychological cripple seeks out physical ones.

'They look like Moscow yard dogs,' said Karvalanov.

'Are you surprised?'

Lord Edward burst out laughing and, slapping Karvalanov on the shoulder, he opened the door. 'Welcome to my political asylum.' This was the fourth name he'd given to a residence which at first glance could be taken for the Leninist propaganda office at a regional Party headquarters. Karvalanov had heard and read a lot about the eccentricities of the British aristocracy. But that room was something he could never have imagined as part of the home of his aristocratic liberator. Every square inch of wall was covered with posters, defending animal rights in general and opposing pheasant shooting in particular, portraying a pheasant looking rather like Dracula, pecking away at a dead dog, its head sporting a halo, entangled in the barbed wire of the pheasant pen. But Karvalanov gave a start when he saw a photograph of something completely different. The Cathedral of St Basil on Red Square was thrusting its garish domes up into the Moscow sky, and before it, on the Place of Execution, stood none other than Lord Edward. But even here his love of strays had a place. He was holding a bitch of uncertain pedigree that was obviously trying to get free and relieve herself upon the cobblestones of Red Square.

'Czeslaw, Lazio, Taras, Vova!' Through the open door Lord Edward called out a series of names that sounded familiar to a Russian ear. The dog-pack tore into the room and swirled, fawning, round their master, who'd started opening tins of dog food. 'And now let's see what the maid's done about our lunch,' said Lord Edward, who was delighted to observe that his dogs were duly chewing and chomping in close harmony. Leaving them to their bowls, he moved to a polished table with a dish under a silver cover in the middle, along with a water jug and an elegantly folded napkin. He lifted the cover, narrowed his eyes and made a face. 'They're out to get me, they are obviously out to get me. Just take a look.'

Karvalanov took a sniff and lifted the lid. Some kind of game, little wings and all, was sitting there steaming in a brown sauce. 'It may be a provocation, but it certainly looks delicious.' Karvalanov's mouth began to water. 'Looks like some delicious kind of game.'

'Game?' Lord Edward exclaimed. 'That's just the point. Game! Lunacy! They had the nerve to serve me pheasant – pheasant to me! Shove it at me. Unbelievable!' He chased round the table like a dog on a chain.

'But I thought the pheasant season was over, so what are these birds doing here?' Karvalanov recalled the information he had gleaned from the stationmaster; far from questioning Lord Edward's ability to identify the birds correctly, he was endeavouring to provide a measure of reassurance.

'My dear Karvalanov, you've come from a country where they don't know the first thing about pheasants. Do you seriously think that they clean the birds and stick them in the oven the moment they've been shot? The carcase has to hang for at least a week, to go bad, to get good and rotten, before those corpse-eating greedy-guts are prepared to indulge themselves by consuming that garbage. Try for yourself. Take a fork. Try some – you're not a vegetarian, are you?'

'Tastes very like chicken to me,' Karvalanov observed with a small sigh of relief as he chewed tentatively on a piece of the mysterious fowl. 'It's chicken, I'm absolutely certain of it. Not rotten at all. Delicious chicken!' he said and started chewing on a leg with gusto. He suddenly realized that he was incredibly hungry. All that chasing across the meadows and through the trees had done wonders for his appetite. 'Only thing missing is mustard. Do you happen to have any?' he asked, tucking into the chicken and fastening the napkin round his neck in a businesslike manner.

'You don't put mustard on pheasant,' said Lord Edward stonily. He had not joined Karvalanov at table.

'What do you mean, you don't? What's wrong with mustard?'

'There is nothing wrong with mustard. But mustard is for ham. Pheasant, if you want, you can eat with cranberry sauce.'

'Never tried it. Anyway I'm used to mustard. I'm talking about chicken and mustard, and clearly this is a chicken, not pheasant at all.' Karvalanov ventured to take a firm line on the issue. Just because Lord Edward had got him out of a Soviet labour camp, it didn't mean he was going to call a chicken a pheasant just to please him. His Soviet interrogators couldn't make him call white black, and an English lord wasn't about to make him call a chicken a bird. Karvalanov recalled a Russian proverb, 'A chicken isn't a bird, and a woman isn't human,' and, unfortunately, laughed out loud.

'I would be obliged if you would refrain from arguing!' Lord Edward was clearly upset by the laugh, reacting like a pheasant hearing the beater's rattle; his chin gave a jerk and his lips began to tremble. Seizing the dish from an astounded Karvalanov, he emptied its contents into the rubbish bin. 'Leave it alone!' he shouted, growled almost, and Karvalanov froze. But he wasn't shouting at him. The dogs that had rushed towards the scraps in the rubbish bin stopped instantly and, wagging their tails sheepishly, clustered round the table, expectantly staring at Karvalanov and Lord Edward.

'I absolutely forbid them to eat game.' Lord Edward spoke in a schoolmasterly tone intended to calm things down. He started to go into a detailed explanation. 'First of all, they could choke on a bone. Secondly, the more game a dog eats, the more it chases pheasants, and thereby lands in the moral trap the keeper obligingly sets it and falls victim to canine genocide. But let's dispel the English spirit of pheasant shooting with some Irish moonshine.' It transpired that Irish moonshine was known as potheen, which Lord Edward obtained from a friendly Irish neighbour who was in favour of the withdrawal of British troops from Northern Ireland, and therefore fiercely opposed to pheasant shooting, which he considered a way of training people to shoot at Irish targets. Karvalanov, delighted at the chance to make a joke, translated Irish potheen into the Soviet 'mighty potential' – a joke that seemed to fall pretty flat, judging by Lord Edward's bewildered expression. He got it though. Taking a massive Bible off the bookshelf, he reached behind it and extracted a bottle with an illegible label. 'Religion is the secret repository of all potency,' he joked in his turn, pouring out two glasses of the fragrant liquid. 'To the potential success of our forlorn hope' – wittily transposing the words of a toast that had been very popular among Soviet dissidents ten years before. They clinked glasses.

Karvalanov couldn't believe his ears. The story of Lord Edward's confinement in the wretched cottage where he was treated like a jailbird, sounded like something out of a Gothic novel, with the villainous role of the usurper played by the vindictive gamekeeper who had caused his own father's death during a shoot. His father, as might be expected, had also been a keeper, at the time that Lord Edward's father had been a lord, which is why they were facing one another on the occasion of the shoot. Lord Edward's father and his guests were up on a hill, and his keeper was in charge of the beaters down in the covers. Edward was only four at the time, but he remembered the shooting accident with astounding clarity, although it wasn't clear where exactly he was standing when the keeper's son, Edmund, who was crawling round the legs of the guns, accidentally knocked into Lord Edward's father as he was taking a shot. He stumbled and shot low, and instead of aiming at the soaring cluster of birds coming over he fired into the line of beaters.

'I saw it all happen at once, saw the keeper's son playfully knock into my father, who stumbled and seemed to bow to the keeper, who was walking up the hill towards him. A puff of smoke and a dry report, the keeper's thick spectacles flashed in the sunlight, and I could see a bloody flower growing on his white shirt before my very eyes,' Lord Edward whispered angrily. Obviously he wasn't telling his story for the first time; it was as polished, as bookish almost, as a part well rehearsed. 'The keeper kept coming towards us – or rather his body did, but the face was already a death mask. Just a moment before, he was shouting encouragement to the beaters, cursing, yelling, and suddenly there he was, stretched out on the grass, powerless, harmless, helpless. Only his lips were moving – 'below the belt, he shot too low, below the belt . . .' – his spectacles lay beside him. They carried him into the keeper's hut and laid him on the floor in the midst of piles of dead pheasants, bedraggled and bleeding, with broken wings – and his body seemed to shrink, become insignificant and uninteresting, like a ragged dead pheasant, with a bloody bruise on the chest. I still remember my father, pale and worried, anxiously asking the guests to take their pick of the dead birds, muttering various saws and sayings that the keeper used to use to encourage them. But my father lacked the keeper's touch and, with an awkward insistence, thrust dead birds at the guests who were trying to back away and leave, as the birds fell to the ground with a thud. Someone muttered something about 'Wonderful shoot, fine day,' and it was obvious that they all wanted to get away from the estate as quickly as possible. Soon afterwards the place was full of police, doctors . . . The next morning my father went off to the war.'

Lord Edward fell silent, then got up heavily, leant across the table and half whispered, half hissed at Karvalanov: 'Now do you understand why the keeper's son hates me? He wants revenge for his father's death. The shooting accidents of the fathers are visited upon the heads of their children. My father should have bagged the keeper's son too and made a clean sweep of it.' Edward got up and started walking round the room. The dogs looked up, thinking it was walk time. But he had just gone to look out of the window to make sure they were not being spied upon. 'They keep me here as if I were in exile. I'm an internal emigrant. I'm a foreigner in my own country, an enemy of the people almost. I imagine you are familiar with that sense of duality, Karvalanov?'

'Duality?' Karvalanov's forehead was furrowed in an ironic frown. 'These last years I felt absolutely nothing. I just wanted one thing: not to be part of anything, not to participate. That's how you become whole. Prison makes it possible. You're cut off from the regime by barbed wire – which incidentally is electrified. There's no feeling of duality. And the Iron Curtain has the same effect. That's why I'm so pleased to be here. It's hard to understand.' Karvalanov looked round the peculiar abode where he had ended up after so many strange renunciations, refusals to give evidence, stormy separations, bouts of solitary confinement, interrogations and all the rest. He was not reassured by what he saw. On the contrary, it all looked as if nothing had changed; he'd just turned up on the other side of the Iron Curtain, the other side of the prison wall, which was now behind and not in front of him. You used to lean your face not your back against it, but it was still a prison wall. And along with the wall, the itch for freedom was still there. Only the language had changed, with foreign English replacing odious Soviet Russian. He spoke them both fluently and entertained little affection for either. In prison, he studied English from dictionaries to the constant sound of broadcast Soviet-speak, and got hold of English newspapers by hook or by crook. Here no doubt he would devote as much energy to obtaining *Pravda* and *Izvestiya* in order to discover what was going on back there, inside, just as he used to try to discover what was going on over there, on the outside. Here and there had changed places, but that hadn't made anything any easier; he'd just exchanged one form of alien existence, one which he would steadily forget, in favour of another.

'Aren't we all servants here below, if only servants of the Lord?' The mysterious lord echoed his thoughts. 'I tried to go away and disappear, not to relate to anything, to play no part in this bloody slaughter. Don't you think, Karvalanov, that I tried to forget? Forget that keeper and the stupid way he died, and my father and the family house, and the horrors of the pheasant shoot. I tried to think of nothing but blades of grass and the roots of trees, of the way the corn ripens and worms work their way up through the soil. I spent hours in the stables, breathing in the smell of horses till it made my head spin. I even tried milking the cows and cleaning their stalls out.'

The mission to the people. A movement that brought forth small deeds and great vileness. Karvalanov felt the time-machine had transported him back to a Chekhovian hunting party. He wanted to get out, to get to the big house on the spring lawn he could see through the window, away from this wretched cottage with its atmosphere of small-time conspiracy, its crippled dogs constantly growling and barking. Just to get out to the edge of the wood, wearing a decent shooting jacket trimmed with fur, and stout leather boots; to look up at the sky and spy a pheasant, or a partridge, even a crow would do, swing the double-barrelled shotgun to your shoulder in one smooth movement and let fly, killing two birds with one stone, and sit down and relax between the horns of the dilemma, between dog and pheasant, gamekeeper and lord.

'Has it ever occurred to you that you even have to call a child who's killed his own parents an orphan?' Karvalanov gave a nervous laugh. 'What happened to the luckless orphan – the keeper's son, that is?'

'The parricide really was an orphan, because his mother left them when he was still a baby. My mother died giving birth to me, and my father was killed in the war. So you see, he and I are alike.' Lord Edward continued drawing his Gothic parallels.

'All enemies are alike, and every friend becomes an enemy after his own fashion, or maybe it's the other way around,' Karvalanov muttered, striking a Tolstoyan note of reassurance. Everything was confusion in the household, Russian literature mixed with English civilization, a keeper's privileges confused with the obligations of a lord. Karvalanov attended to Lord Edward's family chronicle like an analyst, recognizing that every madness had its own logic; he'd abandoned notions of objectivity and accuracy long ago – in the interrogation rooms of the Lubyanka.

If Lord Edward was to be believed, he and the keeper's son were raised together as equals, since Edward's father, and later his guardians, tried to do all they could to cover up the scandalous shooting accident. His guardians practically kow-towed to the keeper's son; it was he who got the best cricket bat, the best pony, while Edward gradually turned into his errand boy. He was shown where to set the traps for the foxes, where to put up the electric wire round the pheasant pens, how and when to feed the birds. What at first seemed like a children's game, a 'cultural exhange' between an aristocrat and a worker, gradually became an elaborate conspiracy on the part of the keeper's son and Edward's guardians. The point was, the upkeep of an estate like Edward's cost thousands of pounds; ever since the turn of the century the family had been living with the constant threat of bankruptcy. Edmund, the keeper's son, who had won the confidence of the guardians, managed to convince them that the only way out of the financial crisis was to let part of the estate for pheasant shooting, to anyone, nouveaux-riches and foreigners mostly, who might wish for an aristocratic form of amusement with its accompanying pomp and ceremony. Not long ago, the estate contained orchards, and fields growing crops such as peas, and various cottage industries flourished; now all that had been abandoned, shut down, nailed up. Acre by acre, the whole estate had been turned into one gigantic pheasant factory; the shoot had absorbed everything. And of course the person in charge of this sporting kingdom was none other than the keeper's son. He'd become irreplaceable; nothing could be done without his participation; the guardians by now were just another part of the administration, rubber-stamping the decisions made by the gamekeeper's offspring. The lord's son, the legitimate heir, did all the keeper's dirty work.

'Why didn't you lodge a protest with the House of Lords?!' Karvalanov's dissident nature began to stir. It was as if he'd been deprived of the right to administer all this land and real estate, which reminded him so strongly of his great-grand-father's estate in Byelorussia.

'My protests to the House of Lords ended a long time ago with electro-shock therapy in a psychiatric hospital,' was Lord Edward's laconic reply, and noticing the change in Karvalanov's expression he began to explain that his protests against the keeper's plans in general and pheasant shooting in particular provoked the British people's deep-rooted love of what they described as field sports – shedding blood and pretending that they were doing it for sport. At first his anti-pheasant shooting behaviour was taken by his guardians as a sign of shocking left-wing eccentricity, a degenerate letting down the family name. But there was something else at stake beyond the clash between a black sheep and the family pheasants: the family fortune – and the fact that the game-keeper did as he pleased with it.

'You ain't my master no longer, says he, and I am no longer your servant, sir. Times, he says, 'ave changed, sir. Your papa passed on long ago, and meanwhile we 'ave to make ends meet.' Lord Edward was apparently mimicking the keeper's accent and manner, and doing it so well that the dogs all got up, clustered together and started snarling and barking at the lord in the guise of the keeper. 'It's me what's keeping you, sir, and not the other way around. The estate rests on my shoulders, sir. It's me the Germans pay. Good money for good birds, sir, and the birds ain't exactly yours, sir. I rear them, sir – on German Deutschmarks, as a matter of fact. And I would ask you, sir, not to try to go knocking my business with your claptrap in public. I won't 'ave scroungers! Sir!'

'I'd have gone on hunger strike!'

'And given up the last of my strength – much to the delight of that parricide! One time when the usurper started making speeches about Germans, who shot down pheasants as once they'd shot down my father's plane, I lost control, jumped on the swine and tried to strangle him. And that, sir, is how I ended up in a straitjacket. They re-educated me with electro-shock therapy, Karvalanov. The psychiatrists said that it was a wonderful way to acquire mental equilibrium – shocking off a shock. This strange rattling sound I keep hearing in my head – like the sound of beaters waving their rattles during a drive – it seems to be stopping.' Lord Edward started to rub his temples nervously, frowning as if in pain. 'But I'm grateful to them, to my torturers.'

'English sado-masochism,' snapped Karvalanov.

'You don't understand. I'm grateful because I personally experienced the suffering endured by the victims of the barbaric traditions of the English aristocracy – all those hapless dwellers of the woods and fields that die on the electrified wires of the pheasant pens. Electro-shock therapy connected me to the victims of the keeper's persecution, connected me literally. When I came back from the clinic I was told that I and my bunch of strays were to be permanently resettled in the cottage.'

'I said they'd steal the estate from you,' Karvalanov exclaimed bitterly, as if it was his estate that had been stolen.

'The keeper has turned my ancestoral home into a hotel for visiting barbarians equipped with firearms. It's a real military invasion or, if you like, a revolutionary coup. Karvalanov, they've kicked me out of the family seat. My clients, sir, cannot be expected to sleep under the same roof as a pack of stray dogs.' Lord Edward again imitated the keeper's accent. There was a pained silence. Even the clinking of the bottle of potheen against the glasses came as a welcome interruption.

'And here I was, expecting to cross the drawbridge of your castle,' Karvalanov sighed. 'The bridge is let down to greet us, we go over the moat, and drive into a paved courtyard, where servants meet us by oaken wickets and iron gates. The passages are lit by smoking torches. We pass upstairs, through state rooms, watch the sun going down over the lake, inspect the stables, sit in the garden, go back to the candle-lit library. The carpet rustles beneath our feet. We sit in leather armchairs in front of the fire, the logs crackle, the candles sputter, the carpet rustles, the torches smoke, the chairs creak, there's a sound of horses' hooves and the sun goes down. Wait, I forgot!' said Karvalanov as he jumped up and got his bag from under the table. Unzipping it he removed a cardboard box tied with string. Bits of cotton wool went flying with the string, and finally Karvalanov produced his present, wrapped in a copy of *The Times*. This too was tossed aside to reveal a plasticine model of a medieval castle, mounted on plywood. 'My present. Your castle.' Karvalanov pushed the plasticine castle down the table.

'Mine?' asked Lord Edward in touching confusion, quietly fingering the plasticine towers.

'Yours,' nodded Karvalanov. 'Or anyway that's how I imagined it, in solitary confinement in Vladimir Prison. It's as if

I've lived in that castle for a hundred years, and shaped every stone with my own hands – from the foundations and secret passages to its steep roofs and high towers. This imaginary castle saved my life. My interrogators never knew that I'd return from one of their sessions to an interrupted fireside conversation. How were they to know that I was talking down to them from my castle walls? What could they and their stupid questions do to its thick stone walls, its towers and loopholes? When that pack of wild animals known as the collective has put you away behind barbed wire in its own defence, the only thing left for you to do is to put an imaginary wall between you and the collective – a castle wall, your castle, where you are the boss, you are the lord. I knew of the existence of castles, and of lords, of watchtowers of a different sort, with moats and drawbridges, and this "castle of the mind" helped me stay sane, stay myself, when there was nothing around me but barbed wire and barking dogs.'

'What kind of dogs?' Lord Edward interrupted.

'Barking Alsatians. The usual kind of escort and guard dogs. They're kept behind barbed wire too – only on the other side.'

'Let me ask a silly question, Karvalanov. In this country we don't know anything about the situation of Soviet guard dogs. How does the camp management treat them? How do they fit into the penal system? You wouldn't have any photographs, would you?' The more excited Lord Edward became about dogs, the more confused Karvalanov felt.

'What photographs, what for? They treat dogs there like they treat all the inmates. I'll tell you how. They're underfed, they're kept chained up. No wonder they're ready to fly at your throat the first chance they get. But even the most savage dog can be fooled. Actually those are the stupidest. In one camp we managed to smuggle two cats into the living quarters. We tied their tails together. Ha! So what happened was the cats started squealing, meowing and kicking up a hell of a row, staggering all over the camp, being cursed by the guards and unable to get free. Something incredible happened to the Alsations. They broke their chains and started to jump the barrier; the guards lost their head and started shooting.'

'And those innocent animals were gunned down.' Lord Edward, horror-struck, buried his face in his hands.

'But whoever wanted to, escaped – the guards had their hands too full to watch the prisoners.'

'Did you escape?'

'Me? If all the prisoners in Siberia, every one, were to escape en masse, I'd stay behind. Just in protest. To prove that there were still political prisoners in the Soviet Union. Anyway you don't get far when you escape,' he added after a moment's pause. 'Some are betrayed by civilians, some come back of their own accord, with frostbite, and some just die in the snowy forests.'

'Perhaps you can understand now why I won't leave my estate or, to be precise, the estate that used to be mine.' Lord Edward waved a helpless hand around him. 'Even if no one were keeping me here by force, I'd stay anyway. What was it you said? In protest. As the last witness to what bloodthirsty gamekeepers have done to these unfortunate creatures. But who's going to listen to a lord who's been certified insane, on the subject of pheasant shooting? Who – the RSPCA? The Greens? They're just a tiny handful of dissidents in English society!'

'In Russia there were even fewer people like me. But that didn't mean that the Western press didn't write about us.' Like a good dissident Karvalanov couldn't help arguing, although he could see that Lord Edward was talking real sense for the first time in the course of their whole conversation.

'They write about you because it's Russia. You know, the Tsars, the revolution, Stalin, anti-Semitism, *Doctor Zhivago*, the Gulag. Major historical shifts going on all the time, social transformations, cataclysms. And always the devil operated on a scale that shook the world. We all know that everyone's mad about Russia. But what are we to do here, where the devil, and evil, break down and disperse into tiny splinters, lodged in everybody's heart? And there are no "foreign correspondents" to let the free world know all about it; there is no "free world beyond the Iron Curtain" to run to and escape the tyranny of routine, there is no "abroad" at all – just the petty, isolated, insular habit-driven sense of law and order. There's nowhere else to go to. Who am I going to protest to, and what about? And this is all there is, this is it, for keeps. This liberated slavery is for ever, do you understand, Karvalanov? Do you know what that means, for ever?'

'Careful,' Karvalanov just had time to yell as he watched Lord Edward nervously fingering the castle's plasticine towers. But he was too late. One of the corner towers started to lean to one side and broke off at the base, as if it had been felled by an earthquake. 'Look, the watchtower's collapsed again,' he muttered grumpily as he tried to restore the ruin.

'It must have been damaged already, shaken up when we were being chased. Look, it's that damned keeper's fault again,' said Lord Edward.

'It's not the keeper, it's your English plasticine. It won't stick, it won't stick and that's all there is to it. The moment I get the drawbridge fixed the watchtower falls over. When I get the watchtower back in place the wall collapses. These islanders can't even produce decent plasticine; it just won't stick.'

'What islanders?'

'The English, who else? Everyone goes on about English tradition, about the present enshrined in its past, but the plasticine lasts about as long as a mayfly, by evening it's nothing but a handful of dust.'

'I expect you bought the cheap stuff. You can find dozens of different kinds here, for children or grown-ups, as you wish.'

'I don't need a dozen different kinds. I don't want any odd kind. Give me the plasticine they gave us in the recreation area in Vladimir Prison. That was plasticine for you. It was soft when you wanted it to be and set hard as concrete. Democracy's no help here, and in that sense Soviet prison was more harmonious than British democracy; the castles, the locks and the plasticine are all better there. And its smell reminded me of my childhood. I could carry the castles I modelled in jail undamaged from camp to camp. But here, time and again I try to recall and recreate my plasticine prison dream, but by evening invariably it starts to fall apart.'

'Your plasticine castle in the air comes apart before your very eyes, and in the meantime my own stone castle is turning into a plasticine dream even as I speak.' Lord Edward gave a philosophic sigh. 'The plasticine may be different here, but you can't recreate your castle in the air either. The soil is different, the clay is different, the water's different. Because you're right, England is an island. Did you know that any Englishman travelling abroad in the last century would take a bottle of fresh English spring water with him?'

'I'd heard about that kind of xenophobia,' said Karvalanov, smoothing out the page of *The Times* he'd used to wrap the castle in. 'It's an illness known as hydrophobia, or rabies. Look what it says here: it would just take a single infected rat to get here and the whole population will die of rabies.'

'It sounds strange, but if it hadn't been for the rabies problem you, my dear Karvalanov, wouldn't be here at all,' said Lord Edward, smiling *à la* Myshkin. Prince Myshkin ('Mouse-kin' in Russian) as the Pied Piper of Hamelin. Ha.

'I don't get it. What connection could you possibly make between what happened to me and rabies?'

'Same as with anybody else. Through dogs. The point is that it was only in Russia that I got to know of the problem of rabies and dogs,' explained Lord Edward with unshakeable aplomb.

'I thought it was your struggle for human rights that sent you to Russia,' said Karvalanov.

'I'm terribly ashamed to say that before I went to Moscow I hadn't even heard of Soviet dissidents – or of dogs with rabies, for that matter. All I knew about Russia was that it had had a revolution of the proletariat. That gave me some grounds for hope,' said Lord Edward.

'I don't see why,' said Karvalanov.

'Because there was no more gentry – which meant no more gamekeepers. And no more gamekeepers meant no more pheasant shoots. D'you see?'

'Just because there's no gentry any more? Do you seriously believe that all the pheasants were shot, like they shot all the bourgeois and the aristocrats during the Revolution? So what about Stalin's keepers on government-owned estates? The whole Politburo used to go shooting,' Karvalanov exclaimed heatedly.

'In those days I knew nothing about corruption in the Party. I went to Russia feeling I was returning to a spiritual homeland, one free of keepers and pheasants. I'd even wondered whether there was any point in getting a return ticket.' According to Lord Edward, his guardians were delighted to see the back of him. They started to spread the rumour that not only was he of unsound mind, he was also an agent of the Communist International. He was obliged to issue a press statement to the effect that he was visiting the Soviet Union, not because he was pro-Communist, but because of his love for hunted animals. He was immediately contacted by one of the innumerable charities concerned with human rights in the Soviet Union. Its representative held forth to him at length about 'the necessity of displaying moral support for Soviet citizens who dare to offer open opposition to the totalitarian regime'. Lord Edward didn't really understand what could be wrong with a totalitarian regime where they didn't shoot pheasants, but he took some addresses with him anyway, just to be polite to the representative of the anti-totalitarian organization.

'What was it called?' inquired Karvalanov.

'Ammmm. Amnesia, Amnesia International?' suggested Lord Edward.

'Not Amnesia, Amnesty! Amnesty International. Not amnesia, that mean's loss of memory. Even though Amnesty International does sometimes contract amnesia. It forgets all about the political idealogy of some governments that infringe human rights.' Karvalanov nearly launched into a tirade of the differences between the totalitarian governments of the Soviet bloc and authoritarian South American dictatorships.

'Quite agree,' Lord Edward interrupted the tirade, nodding. In his opinion Amnesty International forgot about the issue of animal rights in totalitarian countries, where they used dogs to guard their frontiers, and required them to attack people, as if the dogs were rabid. Whatever direction the conversation between Lord Edward and Karvalanov might take, it always ended in the kennels. It started off human and ended up a dog's dinner. Anyway, much to Karvalanov's delight, soon afer Lord Edward's arrival in Moscow he was given to understand, in no uncertain terms, that his interest in Soviet fauna could not be permitted to extend beyond the area open to foreigners, that is to say beyond the Moscow city limits. Since he had nothing else to do, he called on one of the addresses provided by Amnesty International.

'Bes . . . bes.' Edward tried to remember the four-syllable Moscow address. 'Pis . . . Pissdummkopf?' he finally ventured.

'Beskudnikovo!' Karvalanov deduced. 'I used to live there, in between arrests.'

'The bus queues there!' Lord Edward shook his head in sympathy. But Karvalanov started to stick up for the queues, maintaining that queues in the Soviet Union were a form of parliament, or national assembly, that they created one big family.

'Of course, they'll shout at you, and even give you an elbow jab or two, but there's such a sense of unity there. Just what's lacking in the West.' With that kind of remark Karvalanov really astounded Lord Edward, though less than he astounded himself. He'd always insisted on his right to live and act as an individual, far from the crowd, but on coming to England, where every man was an island, he'd started to miss the feeling of being at one with the masses.

'Do you know, people in the queues seemed to think I was a spy,' said Lord Edward. 'But in the actual buses I really did feel a sense of oneness. A genuine oneness of body and soul. They all smell there, Karvalanov!' he said with an apologetic smile. Outside the bus, according to Lord Edward, everything seemed part of a mirage. An empty snowy desert. Antarctica. With whitish apartment blocks like icebergs, no house numbers, no street names. Just a mirage.

'I know those buildings,' said Karvalanov. 'There are no streets there and the numbers go by blocks, like prisons. What number were you looking for?' he inquired, like a well-informed local, as if they were both standing on a corner of his neighbourhood in Beskudnikovo. Lord Edward leafed through his notebook. When Karvalanov heard the number of the house, the block and the flat he exclaimed: 'But that's where I live. Lived,' he corrected himself.

'What other address would Amnesia International have given me?' Lord Edward persisted in getting the name wrong. However, when it came to finding him, the fact that Karvalanov was so well known to international organizations with exotic names was no help at all in his own country. Anyway there was nowhere to inquire, no one to ask. There was nothing but snow, frost and the howling of freezing dogs. A whole pack of strays surrounded him, as if they wanted to talk to him. Lord Edward could still recollect one of them; it had a huge black burn like a bruise under one eye.

'Round the right eye?' asked Karvalanov.

'He seemed the most miserable of them all,' Lord Edward nodded. 'I tried to make contact, stretched out a hand, the hand of friendship to pet him, and do you know what happened? He bit me in the leg. A pool of blood on the snow. I started to yell from pain and desperation. They write a lot these days about the compassionate nature of the Russian soul, but do you know, not one of those dogs displayed an ounce of compassion.'

Leaving a trail of blood over the snow, Lord Edward managed to get to the bus-stop. It's hard to say how he got to the treatment centre; a policeman brought him there half-unconscious. Instead of treating the nasty bleeding bite-wound immediately, they started to make conversation, as if they were at some small London party, about where he was from, when and where he was born, what was he doing in such a remote part of Moscow and why he'd tried to play games with the local strays. Then all of a sudden they informed him that he would not be released until he had undergone a course of forty anti-rabies injections, one a day. Lord Edward's return flight left in a week's time and he had already confirmed his seat, but the doctor said that only a lunatic would release a rabies suspect, and that far from being a lunatic he was a responsible Soviet doctor, and determined not to let Soviet medicine down in the eyes of the West. Lord Edward asked to put in touch with the Embassy immediately, but he was told that 'the Embassy could wait' and that 'no one wanted rabid foreigners, not even the West'.

'It's one of Stalin's old tricks. The struggle against cosmopolitanism, the doctors' plot to poison the Politburo, foreign attitudes corrupting the Soviet way of life.' Karvalanov got a little carried away by a development in the conversation that had, if only for a moment, taken them away from the tedious subject of pheasant shooting. 'Surrounded by enemies within and without, and here you have a rabies epidemic into the bargain. Everyone is scared of injections. The doctor from the clinic was obviously in with the KGB. He'd set up the whole business about rabies and a foreigner. No wonder a policeman was there during the interrogation.'

'What interrogation?' Lord Edward was clearly mystified.

'At the treatment centre. You told me they asked you questions: names, addresses, telephone numbers. Did they ask you for my address? And by the way, did they confiscate your address book?'

Edward couldn't say for sure. The point was that the first injection had made him pass out, and when he came to he was in his hotel room. He had all his possessions about him, including the address book, but not his wits. He almost convinced himself that it was all because of the business in 'Bes . . . Piss . . . whatever the place was', and the next day he set off, as instructed, to the treatment centre in the clinic for his next shot; after which he felt so incredibly faint that he could scarcely stand. On the way back the doorman stopped him at the hotel entrance. With a bandaged leg, unshaven and unwashed – he'd decided not to bathe because of the bandages – he did not look at all like a foreigner to the doorman. Moreover his dizzy spells had caused him to leave behind all his documents, from his passport to the pass admitting him to the Intourist hotel. The police had to be called, and the questions and interrogations began all over again: who was he, where was he from, why was he in Moscow? From that moment on, Lord Edward realized that he was under constant surveillance.

'Quite close by, across the street from the hotel, I began to notice KGB men, usually three of them together. When there were only two they'd gesture to me to join them, and suggest that I partake of some poisonous drug that came in a clear bottle, obviously designed to stupefy naive foreigners like me. They took it in turns to drink the mixture in the bottle, and can you imagine the effect it would have had on foreigners, if every gulp of the stuff those chaps took put such a funny look on their faces?'

'Not unlike the effect your Irish potheen has on me.' Karvalanov was amused by the foreigner's reaction to the Moscow practice of drinking in threes, sharing the expenses. Swigging down the last of the Irish moonshine from the bottle, he shook his head. 'It makes you see treble.'

'Look at the fix I was in. Three security men outside the hotel, the walls and towers of the Kremlin opposite me – I felt I'd been shut up in some prison fortress,' Lord Edward continued with his sorry tale. The Embassy told him in no uncertain terms that they couldn't help him: rabies injections were a matter of Soviet internal policy, and since the regime was a totalitarian one, a British subject, respectful of the laws of a sovereign nation and believed to have contracted rabies, must patiently submit himself to totalitarian methods of treating this internal affliction. The consul then offered him a glass of whisky and a cigar as the best way to deal with dizzy spells. He was quite astounded to learn from Lord Edward that he was forbidden to drink while undergoing the course of shots. The Embassy immediately got in touch with the health centre to ask what right they had to order a British gentleman to forgo the pleasure of partaking of good British whisky. The consul reminded them that the gentleman in question had declared himself perfectly willing to offer up his behind to the totalitarian needle, but that was not to say that anyone was going to gag him and thereby prevent him from taking his daily dose of Scotch whisky in the wake of his daily cup of Indian tea. To which the clinic replied that milord could drink all the whisky he pleased if he was happy to die of convulsions at the sight of a glass of water. How, asked the bewildered consul, did they know that this particular British subject was indeed infected with rabies, otherwise known as hydrophobia? Because, replied the doctor, he had been bitten by a stray dog. But not all strays were rabid, replied the consul. Certainly, agreed the doctor; if it were possible to locate the actual dog that had bitten Lord Edward, and establish that ten days after the incident the dog in question was still alive and biting people, it would mean that the dog was not rabid. But the dog that had bitten Lord Edward had been a stray; it was hence not possible to locate him, check his condition and determine whether or not he was still biting people. Until such time that the dog was found, said the doctor, they had no alternative but to consider the wounded English lord as rabid. 'It was a madhouse,' Lord Edward concluded, drawing breath.

'Now do you see why they wouldn't let me out of the psychiatric clinic?'

Karvalanov nearly jumped out of his chair, detecting the presence of a familiar kind of vicious circle in Lord Edward's story. The dogs got excited too and gathered growling at Karvalanov, urging him to sit down again.

'Have you been bitten by a mad dog?!' Lord Edward exclaimed. 'But you told me that you'd been vaccinated against rabies as a boy.'

'What've dogs got to do with it?! Sorry, as a matter of fact that's where the dog lies buried,' said Karvalanov, allowing himself to transpose a familiar Russian saying into English. 'What was it your doctor said? If you've been admitted to our clinic under suspicion of having been bitten by a rabid dog, we consider you to be rabid, regardless of whether the dog that bit you was rabid or not. An ordinary medical precaution, wouldn't you say? In my version the dog was the KGB. It didn't matter whether the KGB was actually rabid or not. If you think the KGB is after you, it automatically follows that you are of unsound mind.'

'But is the KGB dog actually rabid or not?' Lord Edward enthusiastically picked up Karvalanov's train of thought. 'If the dog is still alive ten days after biting you, it means, the doctor told me, that it was not rabid. Since the KGB are as active now as they were ten years ago, they could not possibly have rabies. In which case there can be no question of your being of somewhat unsound mind?' Lord Edward looked at Karvalanov with an unusually penetrating stare.

'Exactly.' Karvalanov prepared to launch into paradox. 'If you want people in the Soviet Union to think you're sane, you have to regard the KGB not as a rabid dog, but as your own father almost. But considered from any sane viewpoint the KGB is a rabid dog. But if you insist on the fact, the psychiatrists have every right to consider you to be rabid and put you in hospital. In other words, if you stay sane you will automatically be considered insane by a Soviet system that derives its criteria from Soviet psychiatry. Do you see? I insisted that I was sane and that the KGB was a rabid dog. From the standpoint of Soviet psychiatry that was illogical and irrational and proved that I was suffering from split personality. You cannot, at one and the same time, say that you've been bitten by a mad dog and that you're not infected with rabies.'

'Couldn't agree more,' nodded Lord Edward. 'So what's to be done? What are we to do?' He emphasized the word 'we'.

'I don't know what you would have done in my place, but in Moscow I was left with only one logical way out. I started to insist that it was not I but my psychiatrists who had been bitten by the rabid dogs of the KGB. Sent completely mad, they kept the only sane people in the country, that is to say the dissidents, in mental asylums run by psychiatrists of unsound mind. That is to say by psychiatrists whose minds had been infected by the rabid dogs of the KGB. A phenomenon known according to my now famous formula as "political abuse of psychiatry". My revelations got me transferred from the psychiatric hospital to prison – the only place for a sane man to be, since the rest of the country was one big asylum. Becoming a prisoner of the Soviet Union is like getting a certificate of sanity. That's what I said to your ticket collector: it's not a question of whether or not you're crazy, it's a question of who thinks you are.'

'Shouldn't have done that,' muttered Lord Edward sombrely.

'Why shouldn't I? It was a point of principle for me.'

'Shouldn't have talked to the ticket collector. He's a friend of the keeper's. And they're both in it together with my guardians. The stationmaster receives and sees off the nouveau-riche Germans, he's practically one of the servants, and in return he gets pheasants, and of course tips. You've no idea what the corruption is like on my estate. He's bound to have let them know that you were coming to see me. I've felt they've been watching me closely ever since this morning,' and Lord Edward went to the window and cautiously moved aside the curtain.

'Who did he let know? Who's watching you? Do you mean to say that my being here is a secret?' Karvalanov couldn't help asking directly.

'Of course it's a secret, and I'm here incognito too. I have high hopes of you. Together we're going to thwart the keeper's plot. Karvalanov, you just opened my eyes to the link between the KGB and rabies. Until now I was naive enough to think that my guardians and the gamekeeper were just after the money. I paid no attention to the fact that it was when I got back from the Soviet Union that they begn to treat me like a real prisoner, from the moment I began the campaign to get you out of prison. And, as you can see, I am in jail myself.' Lord Edward gestured at his surroundings in ironic welcome. 'Naively I'd supposed that my jailers were being so hostile and suspicious because they thought I'd caught the Communist infection and was out to put an end to the feudal traditions of the shoot. But now I realize that they and the KGB were blowing the same horn. The KGB regard all dissidents as rabid stray dogs; my guardians, the masters of the pheasant shoot, regard all champions of stray dogs, including myself, as dissidents who need to be treated for rabies. D'you see the connection? My guardians had me certified insane, and now they're cutting me off from the world with the help of the KGB – just because I decided to save and liberate yet another Soviet stray.'

'What stray?' Karvalanov protested. 'I thought it was my release you were talking about.'

'You only think of yourself,' said Lord Edward peevishly. 'To be able to work on your release the first thing I had to do was to get out of the clutches of those sadistic poisoners in the vaccination clinic.' And he reminded Karvalanov that to do so he had to track down the stray dog that had bitten him in

Beskudnikovo. So he spent his last ten days in the birthplace of proletarian revolution looking for the mangy hound. Day and night he crawled over rubbish dumps, investigated doorways and froze in frost and snow around apartment blocks on the outskirts of Moscow. 'But the harder and more unpleasant the search became,' said Lord Edward, 'the more I began to identify with its fate, with the fate of the stray dog. We were both straying through the bitter cold, thrown out by our owner to fend for ourselves, both orphans, forsaken by God, howling in the darkness in a language no man could understand.' Lord Edward addressed the infrequent passers-by in broken Russian, with an incomprehensible question he had cobbled together with the help of a phrase book; something about a dog who 'has a sharp tooth and bites'. Finally, having virtually given up, he found some kind of old lady in one of the innumerable frosty courtyards he visited; she was so bundled up in old coats and scarves that you couldn't see her eyes, and was throwing some scraps of potato peel to a pack of dogs; the hungry dogs were pulling the scraps right out of her hand. She looked quite as peculiar as Lord Edward; which is no doubt why they struck up a conversation. At the same time she vented her displeasure on a gang of children throwing snowballs at her. They called her 'Bitch's Guts'. Lord Edward could clearly remember the albeit incomprehensible insult.

'That must have been Aunt Manya – Bitch's Guts, our janitor.' Karvalanov gave a nostalgic start. 'She never stopped informing on me to the police.'

'Strange,' reflected Lord Edward. 'It's denunciations like that which end up with dogs losing their masters. Yet that woman "Bitch's Guts" seemed to me to be the only person in the whole of Moscow who really cared about dogs left to fend for themselves and condemned to be strays after the arrest of their owners. The Russian soul really is a mystery.'

'How did you know that the owners of that pack of dogs in the yard had been arrested?' Karvalanov ignored the reflection upon the mysterious nature of the Russian soul.

'Not all the owners, of all the dogs,' Lord Edward corrected himself. But the moment he asked the janitor about the dog with the sharp tooth 'who bites' she immediately told him that of course she knew it! If people fight with one another, of course the dogs are going to join in. And she showed Lord Edward the fiercest dog in the pack, with a burn under its right eye. She was certain that was the one. 'Following in its master's footsteps,' she said. 'He's in jail, and this one will end up the same way. Mark my words. If it keeps on attacking people they'll arrest it and send it off to join its master in Vladimir Prison.'

'Vladimir!' Karvalanov pricked up his ears. 'What was his name?'

'I didn't get his real name. I hope you'll be able to help. I decided to call it Vova.'

'I'm not interested in underground nicknames. I want to know what his surname was,' repeated Karvalanov.

'We're used to calling dogs by their nicknames in England. Without surnames. I never realized that every dog in the Soviet Union had a surname.'

'A passport too.' Karvalanov was getting angry. 'But I wasn't asking you the dog's name, I meant his master's name, the one in Vladimir Prison!'

'Vladimir?' Lord Edward seemed startled. 'But he's not in Vladimir any more. He's here in England. Don't you understand: Vova's master is in England. I called him Vova because it was a diminutive of Vladimir, where his master used to be – which means you!'

Getting up triumphantly, Lord Edward proceeded towards the canine parliamentary opposition which was all piled up together in a corner of the room. The dogs got up, wagged their tails and started to bark excitedly, in the expectation if not of food then at least of a walk. Karvalanov sat rooted to the spot. He didn't budge when Lord Edward introduced him to a degenerate specimen of the canine race with the ineradicable characteristics of a Russian yard dog. It had crooked legs, a short tail, a torn ear, and indeed a dark mark like a bruise all across the right-hand side of its muzzle.

'Get acquainted.' Lord Edward dragged the dog on to Karvalanov's lap. 'A British citizen of Soviet origins. A stray. Don't you recognize him?'

The rootless cosmopolitan, political refugee and passportless dissident parasite Karvalanov automatically fondled the ear of the meritorious canine émigré. It was not so much the sentiments of an erstwhile owner that moved him, as a kind of morbid curiosity with regard to a relic of his own past. It was a past that he had believed to be closed to him, once and for all, by a kind of impenetrable iron curtain. And suddenly there it was, standing in front of him, bristling, on four legs. His past had been dragged into the present on a dog's leash. The dog, incidentally, had no collar.

'Where's the collar?' Karvalanov inquired mechanically.

'I left it in the Soviet Union. My protégés don't wear collars, it's a stray's privilege,' Lord Edward observed proudly. It was a privilege that Karvalanov had to pay dearly for. No sooner had his hand touched the bitch's ear than she gave a growl. The past bristled, snarled and sank her teeth into her old master. Karvalanov gave a yelp and started leaping round the room, blowing on his bleeding finger. Lord Edward pursued him with a paper napkin and the rest of the potheen as a disinfectant.

'I'm incredibly surprised, upset and shocked, Karvalanov, that Vova didn't recognize you.' An embarrassed Lord Edward hovered round the snarling dog. 'But you must make allowances, it's been so long since he last saw you. I expect you've changed a lot. They say prison alters you terribly.'

'They're lying dogs!' Karvalanov yelled, in pain or rage. 'What do you know about prison? Prison doesn't age you. It keeps you the same age. A kid who's done twenty-five years comes out and behaves like the same young kid. Fifty years old and he behaves like an ageing, childish, mental deficient like you!'

'But during his time as a stray, Vova became much wiser than he was when you last saw him in Moscow as an angry adolescent.' Lord Edward ignored the insult in his haste to reassure Karvalanov, who thought he could detect a fair measure of spite in his voice. 'You didn't recognize him, Karvalanov, and he took it badly. He's upset with you. Or else he didn't recognize you and is feeling bad about it. He's not used to you. But you'll grow used to one another again, really, won't you, Vova, won't you?' Lord Edward intoned, scratching the dog behind its ear. Vova was growling or muttering away, its eyes on Karvalanov. The latter sat in a huddle, groaning with pain.

'Why in God's name did you bring it back from Moscow? So that it can attack people here too?'

'Where's your public spirit, Karvalanov? Do you mean to say that, in my place, you'd have left this four-legged friend to its fate?' exclaimed Lord Edward.

'Evidently I left my public spirit in my cell, along with my personal effects, when they took me straight from prison to the aircraft and sent me across the Iron Curtain,' Karvalanov brought himself to say.

'But you're here. You're here because I managed to track down your dog in Moscow. In fact, if it hadn't been for him I wouldn't be here either. If I hadn't produced your dog, alive and kicking, the crazy doctor at the clinic would never have let me leave the Soviet Union. They'd have kept me there on a trumped-up charge of rabies.'

'I'm beginning to think that the Soviet doctors made a terrible mistake when they let you out.' Karvalanov was beginning to behave badly. 'Anyway, how did you manage to convince them that this really was the dog that bit you? Very trusting of them, I'm sure.'

'But I had witnesses – the janitor, as you call her. She told them your dog attacked everybody because you were in prison. Actually that made it much harder for your dog to leave. I expect the KGB had something to do with it. The authorities refused to give permission for it to leave, although no dog had needed permission before. They were obviously afraid to let the dog of a famous dissident go abroad.'

'They were afraid it would start barking anti-Soviet slogans,' sneered Karvalanov.

'In a sense they were quite right. What happened to the dog changed my political views and I started to agitate for your release. But don't think the English behaved any better than the Soviets. My fellow-countrymen categorically refused to let a stray Soviet dog into this country. A typically chauvinistic British attitude to refugees. The pretext for their refusal was the same old excuse – suspected rabies. Have you noticed how the British establishment, hounding me here, in my own country, is so like the Soviet security organs that used to hound you in yours? In some ways it was easier to get you into the country than it was your dog. I mean, both sides suspected him of having rabies. But as you can see, my years of struggle ended in a victory; at least one Soviet dog, reduced to being a stray by a totalitarian regime, could be reunited with his imprisoned owner.' Lord Edward gave Karvalanov a friendly pat on the shoulder.

'I'll let you play the part of the imprisoned owner,' stated

Karvalanov, starting away from Lord Edward's touch as if he'd had an electric shock. 'I can see that you two have grown very close – no collar, no chain or handcuffs. By the way, it's not a dog, it's a bitch, and she's called Kashtanka.'

'Isn't Vova a girl's name, like all those Russian names, Masha, Vera, Vova? I trust you don't discriminate against women when it comes to civil rights? I hold that any dog, regardless of sex and nationality, has the right to an owner of its own. People get thrown into jail and as a result innumerable domestic animals are turned into strays. With their owners behind bars, they're deprived of their civil rights and their means of support.'

'Who are?'

'The dogs, of course. Humans have fun struggling for power and shooting pheasants, and who has to pay for it? Dogs, that's who. Left-wingers are stupid enough to believe that the October Revolution brought freedom. The story of your imprisonment shows us that, in fact, it did the opposite; hundreds, thousands of political dissidents are arrested without warning, and their four-legged companions are left to fend for themselves. They perish before our very eyes, hungry and homeless, and we say nothing. People like my guardians deliberately draw a veil over the atrocities taking place in the Soviet Union. And no one knows anything about the plight of dogs in the corrective labour camps. Today, Karvalanov, you opened my eyes, I had no idea that they kept dogs chained up, behind barbed wire, that they sick them on to one another and on to their feline brethren. Karvalanov, you absolutely have to make a public statement about the sadistic way that dogs are treated in the camps at the meeting of the RSPCD. I can't wait for the lecture you're giving tomorrow.'

'At a session of the RSPCD? A royal society. About dogs?!'

'RSPCD, yes, the organization has been deemed worthy of a royal charter.'

'You expect me, at a meeting of the RSPCD, the Royal Society for the Prevention of Cruelty to Dissidents, you seriously expect me to talk about the plight of guard dogs? You are joking, aren't you?' Karvalanov laughed hysterically.

'There's been a misunderstanding.' Lord Edward shifted awkwardly in his chair. 'Someone's misinformed you. RSPCD is a royal society all right, but the D stands for "Dogs". The

Royal Society for the Prevention of Cruelty to Dogs. Dogs, not Dissidents. I speak as an active member of long standing, and there is no need to make a face like that. The society has a considerable number of distinguished members and they are all opposed to pheasant shooting. Don't be in such a hurry to sneer. It was their attention that I drew to your plight, and the plight of your comrades in prisons and labour camps. Russian dissidents received letters and all kinds of support from this organization because so many of you left dogs behind when you were arrested – dogs that their tragic circumstances turned into homeless dissidents.'

Karvalanov listened to all this stony-faced. The most remarkable thing was that he should have carried on listening at all – stony-faced or otherwise; with the face of a stone guest, perhaps? Had he heard anything so totally ridiculous, such doggone rubbish at home in Moscow, he would long since have started yelling and being obnoxious, would have delivered a slap to the face and walked out, slamming the door behind him. But he was hypnotized by the sound of English. His status as a foreigner, a stranger, a newcomer, required him to be excessively polite, constantly to convey a sense of mutual sympathy and understanding. Newcomers suffer from a misdirected sense of subtlety that has them eager to find shades of meaning that simply aren't there. At the same time they are unable to spot the all-important point where foreign irony and humour end and give way to a threat or, on the contrary, to a cry for help. And it would go on like that for the rest of his life, because there was no prospect of going home again. The foreigner has to make a joke of everything and approach every situation ironically – just in case he may have missed the point of some rapid-fire conversation. You can't take anything seriously, not even when the local keepers are baiting the trap, leading you by the nose and trying to ensnare you.

Karvalanov finally admitted to himself that the only reason he insisted on continuing to take his companion for an eccentric or a psychopath was that the assumption preserved his conception of English exile as a kind of rural idyll, and posed no threat to his sense of wellbeing in emigration. It would, for instance, have been most unpleasant, indeed humiliating, to discover that he was in fact being made a fool of. There was another, much more disturbing alternative. Suppose he'd been

lured here by you know who, and they were making fun of him
before disposing of him once and for all? There was a method
throughout all the crazy lord's madness. What if it had all been
a put-up job from the very beginning, from the telegram right
up to the encounter with the keeper? And suppose this lunatic
were an imposter? Karvalanov would soon be provoked into
losing his grip and would end up in a mental asylum, thereby
discrediting his whole campaign against the political abuse of
psychiatry. Which was precisely what was being done to him at
that moment.

'Why did you drag me down here? Who are you? Would you
be kind enough to show some proof of your identity, sir?'
Karvalanov adopted the familiar tone of a Soviet dissident
exchanging words with a policeman. He got up from the table
and moved towards Lord Edward, but was instantly obliged to
take a step back because Lord Edward swept him aside with a
peremptory wave, as if drawing a curtain, and now he too rose,
and drew himself up to his full height. Karvalanov scarcely
reached his shoulder.

'I would not advise you to follow the example of my keeper
and question my titles, charters and prerogatives,' he said,
lifting his chin so high that Karvalanov could only see the tip of
his nose. 'And first of all allow me, sir, to set you the same kind
of question. What about you? How can you prove your
identity? And don't start showing me your refugee papers,
documents and certificates. All that can easily be faked. Is there
anyone in England who can confirm that you really are
Karvalanov, and not some KGB agent sent here to recruit me,
and, incidentally, discredit Karvalanov? Which of your crowd
of so-called friends can really swear that you are you – after so
many years of prison and exile? Plastic surgeons can work
wonders these days. What if you're wearing Karvalanov's face
like a mask, but behind it you have long since become one of
their gamekeepers?'

Picking up on Lord Edward's threatening tone, the pack of
dogs began to close in around the table, growling quietly at first,
their growls becoming louder and more insistent and turning
into a chorus of furious barking. Lord Edward turned towards
them. 'I can tell you who can really establish your identity.
Your dog, that's who can confirm that you really are
Karvalanov. A dog cannot fail to recognize his former owner,

his eternal master. Vova, come here!' Lord Edward slapped his knee and summoned the dog to the table. He was about to get up, wagging his tail, but stopped in his tracks when he heard Karvalanov's sudden cry:

'What Vova, damn it! I told you the bitch's name is Kashtanka. Kashtanka! Stay! Jump! Here!' Kashtanka writhed about nervously, sniffing the air.

'Vova, here!' commanded Lord Edward hypnotically.

'Kashtanka, stay!' Karvalanov ordered in a voice grown hoarse with shouting.

Kashtanka, in her misery, pointed her muzzle at the ceiling and began to howl, like a child that sees its parents quarrelling. The louder the shouts of the dissident and the lord, the louder the dog howled. The barking of the dogs became a chorus, with a solo part performed by Kashtanka, who, in England, went by the pseudonym Vova.

To start with, the knocking was circumspect and polite. However, it quickly changed to a frenzied drumming, as if a sentry were warning a garrison of approaching enemy forces. 'Shhhhhh!' Lord Edward froze, stunned, when he finally heard the knocking at the door over the barking of his four-footed friends and the sounds of the raging quarrel. His eyes bulging with alarm, he put a finger to his lips and leant across to Karvalanov in search of support. 'Do you hear it?'

'Someone seems to be at the door.' Karvalanov made a move to open it, but Lord Edward took his arm in an iron grip. The drumming ceased for a moment, they could hear low voices on the other side of the door, and the drumming gave way to a series of measured blows. The dogs started to give tongue with a renewed vigour. Lord Edward ran around the room, biting his nails. As if forgetting that a moment before he and Karvalanov were ready to fly at one another's throats, he took the Russian's hand between his own, in an imploring gesture that verged upon a prayer; he seemed ready to go down on his knees before him.

'Karvalanov, you hear that noise, those voices, getting the dogs all worked up?' he whispered, pointing to the door. 'Do you realize who they are? They're beaters. It's the gamekeeper and his henchmen. They want to trap me, put me behind barbed wire, and drive me towards the guns during a shoot.

You alone can protect me from this gang. We've got to stick together, we stray dogs and dissidents. I saved you from prison, now it's up to you to keep me out of the clutches of these rabid keepers. You are proof that I am sane, do you see? You're a witness. And this country's Conservative government is on your side. We'll fight the keepers together; because they're working for the KGB. So my enemies are your enemies, even if you don't give a damn about dogs and pheasants. Can you hear, they've surrounded us, you and me? The beaters have surrounded us.'

The steady blows had given way to spasmodic rattling. They were doing all they could to break down the heavy oak door. Another second and it would fly open. It was only now that Karvalanov noticed that the door had neither lock nor key, just an iron bolt, a strong one doubtless. With a flash of iron will Karvalanov regained his almost forgotten instinctive response to dawn searches and arrests. Like Lord Edward he felt trapped. He went quickly to the window, pulled aside the curtain and looked for the catch. There wasn't one. It was a sash window; you didn't open it, you raised it. Lord Edward guessed his plan, rushed across and threw it up. His action revealed something that had been there all the time, to which Karvalanov had hitherto paid no attention: the window was covered with an iron grille, which he had hitherto taken for a set of harmless shutters. In one second, Karvalanov seemed to be transported from a gentleman's residence to an oh so familiar prison cell. He turned round in panic.

The bolt fell to the floor. The door opened with a sigh. On the threshold stood that self-same gentleman that Karvalanov had had to hide from in the park by the big house. There he had strolled along the path, mystically crunching gravel to punctuate his careful questions. Here he was the chief administrator, a man of few words. A tall fellow in an immaculate three-piece suit, with a bulldog jaw and gaze under a furrowed brow and balding head, holding a shiny leather Gladstone bag. He took a step towards the master of the house, and two orderlies rushed after him as if they'd been let off a leash. They twisted Lord Edward's arms behind him and put a gag in his mouth, as two farm labourers, who clearly had helped break down the door, drove the growling, snarling, barking, yelping and totally helpless dogs out of the cottage.

'What are you doing? What's going on?' stammered an astounded Karvalanov. He hadn't been able to run. The only thing left was to try to act a bit simple.

'Sister, prepare the vaccine,' the bulldog-like gentleman ordered briskly, opening his bag. It was only then that Karvalanov noticed, in the midst of all the confusion, the serving woman in the starched apron whom he had glimpsed in the yard behind the big house. In the meantime Dr Bulldog picked up the empty bottle of potheen, took it to the light, tut-tutted and tossed it into the rubbish bin. 'Don't you know that he is absolutely forbidden to drink?' he said as he bent over the sink, carefully soaping and rinsing his snow-white hands. Karvalanov only realized that he was talking to him when the doctor half-turned and indicated Lord Edward. He was sitting on the floor, all hunched up in a corner, whimpering quietly. Karvalanov tried to joke his way out of it, suggesting it wasn't Lord Edward who needed vaccine, he did, and that he shouldn't be drinking since he had just been bitten by a mad dog from Russia. But suddenly his English started to sound exceptionally awkward, halting and obscure. The doctor cut short his mumbling.

'How did you get here? Who, may I ask, invited you, my good sir?'

Actually no one had invited him here. They'd kicked him out of 'there' and dumped him 'here'. Here he was, without an invitation, on an uninhabited island; because, for an émigré, natives don't count, the life of the natives is obscure and incomprehensible, like the obscurity beyond an open door. Saying nothing, Karvalanov moved in that direction, from one obscurity to another, to the literal obscurity of the darkened garden outside, where the path marked his every step with an exasperated crunch of gravel, and the bushes along the side of the path, wrapped from head to toe in the evening mist, turned their inhospitable backs to him.

He started when he heard an echo following him; heard gravel crunch beneath polished footwear. He had no doubt that the masterful doctor and his henchmen were trying to catch up. It cost him a tremendous effort to slow his walk to a stroll, put his hands in his pockets and prepare to be questioned. The doctor joined him at the entrance to the big house, and his bulldog profile, back-lit by the light from the windows, looked like a huge black cut-out. He'd left behind both his henchmen and his hectoring tone as he addressed Karvalanov.

'I do most humbly beg your pardon. I didn't recognize you. All that fuss, and I didn't recognize you at first sight,' he began, talking fast like a family doctor. 'I should have known – your Russian accent, the way you use your hands when you talk. You must be Karvalanov. You are, aren't you? Allow me to introduce myself. Genoni. Dr Genoni.' Karvalanov tried to make his way out to the front drive, but his pursuer literally blocked his way. 'Please, Lord Edward will never forgive me if I leave you here like this, at nightfall, and look, it's starting to rain.' Dr Genoni stretched out a hand and waggled his fingers in the air in an effort either to ascertain whether or not it was indeed raining, or to feel out Karvalanov's intentions. 'Please don't be too hard on us. Lord Edward is away, he just happened to read of your sudden release in the papers. He'll be back from his tour of Third World countries in a month. He's really excited about meeting you. I hope you got his telegram? We certainly were not expecting you today.' The doctor cum major-domo put his heavy head on one side in an almost dog-like quest for approval.

What forthcoming meeting was he on about? Had Karvalanov really muddled up the day, the city and the century? As the estate manager continued his stream of polite exclamations, Karvalanov was fumbling through his pockets in search of the crumpled telegram. He'd probably thrown it out with his ticket, it was too late to have it checked, he'd have to pay all over again, everything in life had to be paid for twice, it was all symbolic. Symbolism begins when life gets muddled. Life gets muddled when you have to put an end to the way you live now. The way you live now comes to an end when you emigrate.

'I wonder on what days your charge is entirely himself? What kind of insulin dose, may I ask, does he need for his tour of the Third World?' Karvalanov struck a note of spiteful sarcasm to make up for his own confusion.

'Insulin? Do you mean for Edmund?' The doctor shrugged sceptically. 'I'm afraid it's too late for insulin by now.'

'Is he on insulin too? He nearly killed me in the meadow this morning. I startled his pheasants when he was feeding them.' Karvalanov gave a short sombre laugh as he remembered the keeper's son's furious leathery face.

'Unhappy young man!' The doctor nodded his agreement. But obviously he meant someone quite different from Karvalanov. 'Mixed identity. A classic case – in an aggravated form. One personality is driven out by the other – substitution of the self for the victim; the sense of guilt compels the memory to give up its own past entirely. Just imagine, as a child, by dint of a tragic accident, you shoot your own father the keeper. Incidentally, about that shot. Our patient is obviously confused. With a shoot going on a keeper would never put himself within range of the guns, not unless something extraordinary had happened. I think it must all have been a great deal simpler or a great deal more complicated than our charge would have it. But at any rate, the shot was an aristocratic one, from Lord Edward's father's gun. Hence the hatred of pheasants – a repressed form of hatred of the aristocracy. Lord Edward's death in the war – both a kind of revenge and release of a sort – unhinged him completely. Of course, there was already a predisposition. Hereditary alcoholism. Of course. But, do you know, I'm a psychiatrist of the old school. I've never been one for egalitarianism. I warned his lordship's family that they were ruining the child; you see, they tried to bring Edmund up with Edward, as an equal, as brothers almost. Now, every third generation of this family produces, shall we say, to put it gently, an eccentric. You can see what came of it. These endless trips abroad to countries with peculiar habits. The young Lord Edward dragged Edmund along with him everywhere, he even took him on his luckless trip to the Soviet Union. I can only tell you all this human rights stuff, it disturbs the balance of the mind. In Moscow Edmund went completely out of control, used to drink himself senseless, and went wandering around dubious parts of town, on the outskirts, where one day he was bitten by a stray dog. It's a long story. He had to be given injections, you know, rabies shots. And he started imagining things. I expect he told you quite enough about it himself. Of course he couldn't resist enticing the famous Karvalanov to his place while Lord Edward was away. Actually I'd like to have a chat with you about this and that myself. I am, let us say, especially interested in the phenomenon of bestiality, which you encounter among schizophrenics of the upper classes. Did you come across anything of the kind in Soviet prisons? Perhaps you'd care to drop by the clinic. I've got a bottle of Jameson's, the finest Irish whiskey, in my office. What do you say?'

'Do you mean this is a psychiatric hospital?' Karvalanov exclaimed, coming to a standstill outside the building that, not long ago, had seemed to him to be an aristocrat's ancestral castle, his hearth and home.

'The best private clinic in England. You can't say that Lord Edward's family lacks generosity in matters of medicine or human rights. This is the main building, but there are cottages too, like Edmund's, when a patient needs special treatment or privacy. Come, let me persuade you to take a glass by the fire, and eventually you will meet Lord Edward. Please say yes! Where can you go now, it's almost night time. I wouldn't go wandering around the estate. The new keeper is very strict and suspects everyone of being a poacher!'

But Karvalanov wasn't listening. Nothing was what it seemed, neither the plasticine, nor the castle; the lord, the psychiatrist, the gamekeeper, they were all fakes. He turned and dashed straight into the bushes, running towards where headlights and the sound of engines indicated the existence of a road and twentieth-century civilization, in place of this time-machine which had set him down in a Gothic novel of émigré horrors. Desperate cries pursued him, pheasants maybe? Or was the man in the cottage calling 'I'm a lord, I'm the Lord'? Another lunatic. Here in the West about as many lunatics had associated themselves with him and his accomplishments as there'd been Old Bolsheviks who'd joined Lenin to carry that timber beam on the first Saturday of voluntary Communist labour. But none of this comforting self-mockery could eradicate the image of that hunched and hunted creature trying to protect itself from the needle. His hand ached where the émigré dog had bitten it. He'd scared off someone else's pheasants. He was a poacher. A dog had bitten him. It ought to be shot. He needed a rabies shot. And a tetanus shot too. Of course, a tetanus shot. Tetanus. Lockjaw.

13

Asylum

'The scale kept getting smaller,' Felix read from his notebook. 'To reach the tiny village of Denholm, you had, according to Mary-Louise's instructions, first to take the train to Glasgow, then a bus to a nearby town, and from there all you could do was take a taxi – which required courage and decisiveness to overcome your fear that the driver's Scots accent would compound your lack of ability to enunciate the improbably Scots name of the tiny village. The taxi couldn't take him all the way to the house of Jennifer Wilson – Mary-Louise's Scottish aunt. At high tide the road connecting two parts of the hill was underwater, so you had to cross a bridge on foot. It seemed that it wasn't enough for the island culture to be a distance away from the continent. Within that culture everyone kept their distance from everybody else, every man being an island. It was just that the scale of the distance kept growing smaller. Even the aunt's house had been shrunk to the size of the tiniest miniature island, to the point that it could scarcely be termed a house. It was a remodelled tower that had once been part of the local lighthouse, which overlooked an inlet of the modest local loch: in those bygone days people actually used to fish in it for profit, not just for pleasure, so the fishermen built themselves a lighthouse. Now there was nobody to buy the fish, the level of the loch had gone down, and no one went fishing at night any more except for the occasional tourist. The tower was given to the local priest, Jennifer Wilson's father. He'd gone out of his way to get it, for symbolic reasons; religion being after all a bearer of light, a lighthouse for lost souls; besides, was not the Saviour a fisher of men?

'The seventy-year-old Jennifer Wilson explained all this, quickly, concisely and not always comprehensibly as she hurried up and down the house trying to get her guest, that is me, a cup of tea. The tea things were on the second floor, the stove was on the first (the bedroom on the third). But the word "floor" is something of an exaggeration, because like all light houses the building consisted primarily of stairs. Really the living space was constituted by a series of landings, and the lady of the house moved up and down between them tirelessly. In appearance she resembled a good-hearted, bustling cleaning woman, with steel-rimmed spectacles and clad in a washed-out old blue skirt and a much-patched homespun wool cardigan. She had, indeed, been a cleaning woman all her life – had washed floors in other people's houses, run errands for everyone and looked after her father all her life until he grew senile, and then she nursed him till he died.

'At the age of sixty-six, she said, her spectacles flashing, he abandoned the affairs of his flock and started to prepare himself for a pilgrimage to Jerusalem. However, the doctors forbade him – a bad heart – from going on such a dangerous and exhausting journey. But Reverend Wilson was adamant. Since, he said, the whole point of a pilgrimage resided in the spiritual ordeal imposed by the distance you had to travel to reach the Holy Places, he was prepared to make the journey from Denholm to celestial Jerusalem by dint of walking round and round his house and praying whenever he took a break. Every morning he went out with staff and scrip, and started his daily peregrination around his tower, always moving in an easterly direction, towards Jerusalem – that is to say counter-clockwise. It is worth recalling incidentally that our Russian patriarch Nikon, of schism fame, introduced the practice, on the occasion of marriages and christenings, of proceeding round the lectern counter-clockwise, where previously the ceremonial required a clockwise procession, and Nikon's opponents considered this break with tradition to be the consequence of the devil destroying his reason. Every day old Rev. Wilson walked a set number of miles, with a short break for lunch. He was always accompanied on the pilgrimage by his loyal daughter Jennifer, with some medicine ready in case of a heart attack. The worst thing about this religious ordeal was the open-air break for lunch. Like most Scots families of the period the Wilsons ran a very unpampered household. They only put in running water the previous year, Jennifer said, and there was still no question of a water-heater. The house was heated by one wretched little stove. Nonetheless, in view of the vagaries of the

Scottish weather, an autumn day's picnic with haggis and boiled turnips on the banks of a loch lacked appeal even to the least-pampered Scots stoic – such as Jennifer Wilson.

'Every pilgrimage comes to an end eventually – if only geographically speaking. One fine day Reverend Wilson made some calculations and solemnly announced to his daughter: 'Here we are in Jerusalem.' Jennifer's joy knew no bounds. But it was premature. 'I don't know about you, my daughter,' added the minister, 'but I am resolved to remain here and pass the rest of my days in the Holy Land. You, however, must return to Scotland.' He went inside and spent the remaining four years of his life in his room, believing himself to be in Zion, by the walls of the Holy City. Apart from the prayer book, he would, for relaxation, read the only work of literature he considered to have any merit – a drama in verse written by his great-uncle, John Wilson, named *The City of the Plague*.

'You could only wonder at the encyclopaedic knowledge of this Scottish aunt with the face of a cleaning woman, living in a freezing tower with an earth floor and a smoking, sooty stove. She even knew of Pushkin, her knowledge having nothing to do with her great-grand-uncle ("Push-kin, eh? Near kin to us because of John Wilson?"). Her father the vicar had a considerable library, and a considerable collection of family records. How deceptively simple foreigners can seem, and how geography distorts literary reputations. In Russian literature, John Wilson is no more than a footnote to Pushkin's "Festivities at the Time of Plague". But in Pushkin's time, or more exactly the time of Walter Scott, in the literary circles of London and Edinburgh, John Wilson, as his great-grand-niece made clear, was number one. He was editor of the most important literary periodical of the age, *Blackwood's Magazine*. He held the chair of Moral Philosophy at Edinburgh University. He could make or break a literary reputation. It was he who had woven myth and legend about his friend Thomas De Quincey (the author of the notorious *Confessions of an English Opium Eater*). He was a fanatical admirer and friend of Wordsworth – who had introduced him to De Quincey. His series of imaginary conversations with distinguished contemporaries (James Hogg, Lockhart, *et al.*), "Noctes Ambrosianae", signed with the parodic pseudonym Christopher North and published in *Blackwood*'s, were read all over Scotland. They contain some interesting reflections upon "voluntary and involuntary exile". It was obvious that John Wilson (Christopher North) had no love of émigrés.

'As she explained all this the seventy-year old Jennifer Wilson kept bustling up and down stairs looking for the collected works of John Wilson, the author of the narrative poem we only remember today thanks to Pushkin:

> . . . I hae witness'd
> A sight more hideous still. The Plague broke out
> Like a raging fire within the darksome heart
> Of a huge mad-house; and one stormy night
> As I was passing by its iron gates
> With loud crash they burst open, and a troop
> Of beings all unconscious of this world,
> Possess'd by their own fearful phantasies,
> Did clank their chains unto the troubled moon
> Fast rolling through the clouds. Away they went
> Across the glimmering square! some hurriedly
> As by a whirlwind driven, and others moving
> Slow – step by step – with melancholy mien,
> And faces pale in idiot-vacancy.
> For days those wild-eyed visitors were seen
> Shrieking – or sitting in a woeful silence,
> With wither'd hands, and heaps of matted hair!
> And they all died in ignorance of the Plague
> That freed them from their cells.
> ....
> Yet two such wretches have I chanced to see,
> And they are living still – far better dead!
> For they have lost all memory of the past,
> All feeling of the future.

'Pushkin doesn't translate this passage. Strange, because the theme of madness in his version of the festivities at the time of plague is most certainly there (take the President: "Quite mad he raves about the wife he has buried"). Moreover, a series of Pushkin's most telling lines are devoted to having to choose – between madness and the plague. "Lord, do not let me lose my mind, I'd lief the beggar's bag and staff, I'd rather plague and famine." Maybe Pushkin just didn't get that far; after all, it is on page 127. Only Pushkin scholars would have the requisite stamina.

Before I fell into this dream, I saw
A most magnificent and princely square
Of some great city. Sure it was not London
No – no – the form and colour of those clouds
So grim and dismal never horrified
The beautiful skies of England, no such thunder
Ever so growl'd throughout my native clime.
It was the capital city of a kingdom
Lying unknown amid unvoyag'd seas,
Where towers and temples all of eastern structure
With airy pomp bewildered all my soul.
When gazing on them I was struck at once
With blindness and decay of memory,
And a heart-sickness almost like to death.
A deep remorse of some unacted crime
Fell on me. There in dizziness I stood,
Contrite in conscious innocence – repentant
Of some impossible nameless wickedness
That bore a dread relation to me.

'Of course, Pushkin didn't, couldn't have written lines like that. If he'd even taken a look at them, yawning over the English version of the play at Boldino, he'd have forgotten them, thrown them out at once. His generous poet's hand swept themes like these ("a deep remorse for some unacted crime", "repentant of some impossible nameless wickedness") to one side and left them for Dostoevsky to eat up. For instance:

A ghastly old man – and a noble youth,
Yet with fierce eyes that smiled with cruelty,
Came up to me all lost in wonderment
What spots of blood might mean beneath my feet
All over a bed of flowers. The old man cried,
Where is thy mother impious parricide?!
....
Until I wept in utter agony,
And all the while I saw my mother's corpse
Lying in peace before her frantic son,
And knew that I in wrath had murder'd her.

'Of course, Pushkin's Boris Godunov has his vision of "blood-stained boys" and so on but that's all motivated by the theme of regicide and the impostor – by the theme of the father. When, I wonder, did the theme of parricide begin to be replaced by the loss of the mother, parentlessness by the loss of maternal affection (there's not even a separate word for it)? Probably when the theme of the tragedy of the revolution stopped being topical and was replaced by the tragedy of emigration (all revolutions lead to emigration), since revolution, like all victories over power and authority, is a form of parricide, while emigration means breaking with the homeland, and in Russian at least the homeland is the mother, the motherland. How little Pushkin writes about his parents. Of course, "My Family-tree" deals with his ancestors and so on. But there is very little about the parents as such. "My mama", "my papa", and that's it? I must ask a Pushkin scholar.'

Felix laid his notes aside.

14

Zero Meridian

'Now move your foot a bit to the right – no, not your right foot, the left foot to the right,' said Silva, and Felix elaborated: 'Not the right foot of human rights, the left foot of Communist left deviations,' and he laughed with a laugh that turned into a bronchitic cough, which sounded absurd in the heat of the afternoon. 'Now d'you understand? You've got one foot in the West, the other in the East,' laughed Silva.

They were standing, not entirely steadily, since they were not entirely sober, in the mossy courtyard of Greenwich Observatory, above a strip of brass rail which consituted the zero, or prime, meridian. Trying to keep his balance on it with a splay-footed stance was the dissident Karvalanov, hero, martyr, prophet and comic spectacle.

Karvalanov only turned up in Silva's flat after his misadventure. His mumbled and confused account of the meeting with the lord and the keeper made him look a little sad and pathetic. While they were wandering through Greenwich towards Lewisham Felix kept his distance, staying back and playing the part of a deposed ruler.

'And what are these?' asked Victor, pointing to some metal bars on the way out of the Observatory. Silva embarked on an explanation about world standards of weights and measures, yards and feet, and their connection with the zero meridian, but Felix interrupted her, saying that émigrés don't measure distance by yards and feet.

'We measure distance by how far away the flats of our friends are. Our émigré geography is quite as ideological as, say, Soviet geography is political – with its distinctions between socialist and capitalist countries. For émigrés can think of no place on earth they couldn't, in theory, emigrate to where they would not or could not find friends and acquaintances.' He started coughing again as he pointed down the slope to the Thames.

'There, do you see those high-rises over there, that's Deptford. Another maniac, and a despot too actually, used to live there. One of ours. Peter the Great.' Listening to Felix acting the guide, holding forth about Peter the Great, his play regiments, about pretenders and false Tsars at the court of Ivan the Terrible and Peter the Great, Silva began to recall another court but the same conversation, in the stifling Moscow night, and she began to fidget and yawn (which she always did when she was nervous or embarrassed – I don't know, I'm tired, I need to sleep, what was that you said?), for that idiot Felix was capable of anything; perhaps he was going to tell Victor what had been going on in the next room the time Victor's room was searched and he was arrested on the night of August 6 (old style)? Her blouse stuck to her sweating back. The air over Greenwich hill had grown sultry and heavy, hard almost, like a wall, a wall she was once leaning hard against, in an attempt to become invisible, as she tried to make out the murmuring voices of the police and security men in the next room. With some difficulty Silva made out the words 'As Migulin used to say about psychiatric hospitals . . .' but then the danger faded.

'The damage was terrible. It was one of the finest old mansions on the south bank of the Thames. You get the feeling that they had to cover Deptford with concrete high-rises simply because of the damage Peter did in the seventeenth century. I've read a description of the damaged property.' Felix fell silent and then added, as a kind of moral: 'And that's what happens when you invite Russians to stay.'

'You obviously know your local history,' remarked Victor with icy politeness. 'Because there's nothing else to do,' Felix snorted. 'You know that in every country, each historic spot is much written about, so every famous site becomes wrapped in a kind of cloud of words. Well, I can only tell you, when it comes to the number of words per square inch, England leads the world. With every step you take, you find yourself trampling on the private life of someone who lived three hundred years ago; you can't strike a match to light the fire without setting someone's manuscript alight.'

'How d'you know all this?'

'Who better than the translator of Pushkin's "Festivities at the Time of Plague"? Who better than Pushkin? Besides I've been here a year. You have to find something to keep you amused. You can't spend all day and night wringing your hands about the way you were victimized by the Soviet penal system. By the way, don't forget that today is the day that all those people, who did spend their time wringing their hands, are coming here to welcome you; the ones who spent all day and all night thinking about how much you were suffering.'

The latter part of the day saw Silva's party. The assortment of guests who had come to get a glimpse of the great Karvalanov was, to put it mildly, a motley one. Silva had, shall we say, invited all and sundry, on the pretext that Victor had appeared so suddenly that a fair measure of improvisation must needs determine the nature of the party she was giving in his honour. The immediate effect of these arrangements was felt right on the doorstep. The party was already honoured by the appearance of yet another prominent personality with various credentials.

'All this travelling, do you know, I keep falling asleep on my feet!' burbled Kupernik, a visiting poet and translator, aged about fifty, quite short and wearing dark glasses. He stepped out of the hall to greet them like a host woken up by old friends. Felix and Victor both sensed a dangerous intruder: he was clearly the sort who after being around for a few minutes starts behaving like an old hand. Still trying to make out how and why this man had turned up at Silva's house, Felix was weighing up the intruder's appearance. Since he was plumpish, the glasses made him look like a low-ranking Mafioso, or rather like the hero of a Polish film of the Sixties, in turn imitating a Hollywood version of California fashions. He was wearing a black leather jacket that was much too young for him, which seemed to have been taken off the back of a pretty boy from one of the pages of a Christopher Street male porno magazine, who had got the idea from a Puerto-Rican lover, who, in turn had appropriated the macho style from the Chicago Police Department. Kupernik was obviously a Soviet tourist. Because Soviets loved leather (after all, so many Soviet citizens had been tanned alive) and hated spending money (accustomed to living meagrely, but free of charge), Kupernik's jacket was made of imitation leather, man-made like everything else he wore, from the polyester tie to the plastic shoes (his love of man-made substitutes deriving from his veneration of technology). It was all some second- if not third-hand, nostalgic reworking, Soviet-style, of the fashions of an earlier age; add a pair of jeans and, over here, the low-ranking Mafioso bore a distinct resemblance to an out-of-work Liverpudlian, although back in Moscow these garments testified to his enviable ability to travel abroad.

Victor exchanged glances with Felix. It was the first time that they felt the need to gang up against the common enemy. Whereas his appearance inspired in Silva a scornful sympathy, there was something else about Kupernik that clearly irritated Victor; was it his bald patch, his little tummy, which testified less to his active sex life and his greed than it did to his membership of that tribe of balding and owlishly foolish workers on the intellectual front, who were wined and dined, as if they were in a heavenly psychiatric ward, a form of confinement for the blest, to prevent them from getting under the feet of the proletariat nation in its steady historic march towards the future? They celebrated the beauty 'that would save the world' and 'inner liberty', despising dissidents for their 'obsession with petty political squabbles with authority'. In other words, the touring Soviet poet-translator represented everything that Karvalanov and his kind most hated. Currently he was holding centre-stage, addressing his audience with the quick-fire speech of a traveller in transit.

One might ask who was not a traveller in transit in this room. Perching on the books piled up in the corners, occupying the shaky chairs and shabby sofa (from the second-hand furniture shop round the corner), leaning against the walls or simply standing in the middle of the sitting room as if lost in the wilderness, the crowd of guests consisted of every imaginable type of the uprooted. There were the usual academics from Slavonic departments – those vegetable-looking chaps whose cannibalistic cravings for the big Russian heart, soul and liver transformed them into freaks in the eyes of their own tribe. There was also an assortment of BBC Russian Service and Radio Liberty contributors who, used to going on the air every day, regarded themselves as being somewhere in the sky above the ordinary, definitely not in an émigré quarantine. There were also those, like the émigré essayist Gluzberg, with no patriotic heart whatsoever, who simply covered with their British passports a big emotional hole in their breasts.

Regardless of their status in this world, all of them looked in the presence of a full-blooded Soviet citizen like a bunch of displaced apparitions. The only person who could claim to be alive and kicking and drunk was Mary-Louise, who was here not in her capacity as Felix's assistant translator but, seemingly, as an interpreter for Kupernik. His Russian, however, was obviously too quick for her.

'All these trips and excursions have worn me out,' he complained coyly. 'You know how it is, I grabbed a couple of drinkies, as you say, and just crashed. Had a bit of a snooze next door' (he pointed to the bedroom) 'came to, and what do I see? Jerusalem! Out of the blue, as the English say. Before my very eyes, as if it had dropped out of heaven, as we say back home. Jerusalem the golden. Dear Lord, I think and with good reason; it is Jerusalem, after all. But then I got it. It was a poster, right over the bed. But right now, you know, I'm up to here with my translation of the Psalms. I go to sleep dreaming of Jerusalem, wake up and there it is in front of me. You've got a good set-up here, Felix. A walking dream, or daydream as the English put it.'

Mary-Louise, stammering and, like every novice at simultaneous translation, afraid she might drop a word and miss the point, began to turn this drivel into an improbable kind of English.

'Mary-Louise, do you really think there is anyone here who doesn't speak Russian? Is this a press conference or something?' Silva interrupted, ostentatiously covering her ears.

'Who is that young lady?' asked Victor, who was standing next to Silva at one end of the room.

'Mary-Louise – she's helping Felix with his Pushkin translation, but now she is working as a guide and interpreter for our poet-translator, on behalf of the Anglo-Soviet Love and Friendship Society.'

'I don't understand at all. If he's a poet-translator, why does he need an interpreter? What do they translate into and from, and what kind of love and friendship do they have going?' Whatever kind of love and friendship they had going, Victor was left out of it, judging by the fact that the crowd of guests was gradually gravitating towards Kupernik rather than Victor in his corner.

'Day-dreaming, as the English say.' Kupernik continued to

hold forth in his corner. 'Felix, you're from Jerusalem, aren't you? Do you know that in the city itself you have absolutely no sense that there's a war. Open a paper here and you'd think there are all kinds of horrors and holocausts going on. But when you're there – I was at a poetry translating conference – it's, well, like a Black Sea resort, well armed of course, but still, a Black Sea resort. The food's all right too. I stayed with Petya – if you remember he was' – turning to Silva – 'Lela's lover, Lela the secretary of the literary translation section of the Soviet Writers' Union, and incidentally she remembers you well, and your spectacular typing when you worked there after the Pushkin Museum sacked you. Anyway, he introduced me, as the Israelis would say, to the renowned Israeli pitta. It's cheap and cheerful, as we'd say. Besides, you can eat and go sightseeing at the same time, because with pitta you don't need a plate.'

'You don't need a plate when you eat a sandwich. How is it different, I'd like to know? You can eat sandwiches and sightsee at the same time,' said Felix. Kupernik's drivel irritated as much as it fascinated him – it was a parody of a fool's account of life in another country, forgiven only because the narrator of this drivel came from the Soviet Union. He blushed at the thought that his own first impressions of his travels abroad were not unlike Kupernik's.

'How right you are! Israel's got it all. If it's pitta you want, there's pitta; if you want a sandwich, you can have a sandwich too. It's all there. The variety, as the English would say, of food, and particularly vegetables, in the West is amazing. On the other hand, there are problems with the traffic, which is particularly bad in this country. Too many cars, that's the trouble. In general, psychologically speaking, you Westerners lack (as the English would put it) the fear of death. People are prepared to risk their lives without a moment's hesitation. Because they have no experience of danger. They are constantly prepared to change their style and way of life, their place in society, don't you know. Yesterday he was writing poetry, now he's a stoker, and he'll be a carpenter tomorrow, and the day after he'll open a bakery and sell bread.'

'That's because there's such terrible unemployment. People can't find skilled jobs, so they end up cleaning public lavatories,' Mary-Louise interrupted.

'I am not sure that that is entirely factually correct,' Kupernik carried on, unperturbed by her Trotskyist remark. 'It seems to me that a significant role is played by the difference between the Eastern and Western character. Consider our dearly beloved Maya, from the Bolshoi. Could anyone think that our little Maya would give up the ballet, to become a nurse somewhere in, forgive me, starving, stinking Ethiopia? Of course not; she'll go on dancing the part of the deranged Giselle until she reaches a ripe old age, until she falls into the swan lake of total senility. But your Lynn Seymour fell in love with a jazz musician, and what happens? Yesterday she was the star of the English ballet, and now she's playing trombone in her lover's band. People do whatever they want. Whatever comes into their head. Because they don't know fear. Here today, and tomorrow at the end of the world. That's what I sensed in the West. You know I can travel as much as I please these days. But you know that's really not the same. I just love London – do you know, even the water tastes better. I swear to God. When I was staying with Sashka in Chicago – you know Sashka, don't you? He was an errand boy for *Izvestiya*, and is now the senior leader writer for the weekly *Chicago Pravda*. Anyway, when Sashka, the great tea-making expert, brewed me up a pot in Chicago, I immediately realized the water was just not the same. I have a sensitive stomach, it can tell. And in London it's never upset. Or take the milk now, the milk here is absolutely superb. Just now in the kitchen I put milk in my tea – like an Englishman, you might say (I'm not that keen on the hard stuff, just on special occasions, or, like now, at journey's end) – and I must say that English milk is as thick as cream. And no wonder, the grass is so rich here.'

'It was cream – cream for the strawberries and cream, the dessert. If you've left any,' remarked Silva.

Kupernik blushed slightly, but soon recovered. 'Actually, after the facelessness of Moscow, everything seems so rich, so thick, you even mistake the cream for milk. Actually coffee is best in Italy. Have you been to Italy? I can't speak a word of Italian, but you find our émigrés everywhere. I met John there, quite well known actually. You know, the John who used to hang around in Gena's flat in Moscow. I didn't actually know him in Moscow, but there was this Irish girl there I had a one-night stand with, as they say over here, she was divorced from a

Muscovite who was a friend of Gena's, and she'd met John at Gena's place. What I'm getting at is, all I had to do was mention her name to John, and he immediately got Evgenii to arrange for me to have an audience with the Pope.'

'Are you a Catholic into the bargain?' muttered Mary-Louise. She would have been pleased in fact if Kupernik had turned out to be a Catholic too. A Communist, a Jew and a Catholic to boot – who in his left mind in this country could ask for more? It was clear that the blatherer was becoming the life and soul of the party. 'Are you?' Mary-Louise repeated her question on Kupernik's Catholicism.

'Umph. Let's just say that poetry is my religion. I'm a Jew by birth. I'm a Jew, the Pope's a Pole, so you might say that we have Russia in common. And imagine the coincidence, Evgenii is attached to the Vatican now. He's Orthodox, but they took him on for ecumenical reasons. You know, it's a great advantage to be Russian these days. You've heard of Evgenii, haven't you? If not, you must have heard him. He used to work as an announcer on Soviet radio. Anyway they hired him as an announcer for Radio Vatican. The foreign news service. He's got a fantastic set-up, I must say. The radio's got its own store there, you can get cigarettes, salami, rolls, brandy, tinned food, and all at cut price, subsidized and tax free. In fact the more I look around the more it seems to me that you émigrés are doing fine over here. Our people – hee! hee! – turn up everywhere. It's a real émigré empire. Is there a country we haven't occupied? Our people are in Australia even – and I don't mean the Russian Chinese, who've been there for ages. I have a friend there who wrote and told me he goes to work on a kangaroo.'

'Not on a kangaroo, I think you mean he drives a Jaguar. That's a kind of car,' Mary-Louise corrected him.

'Well; live and learn – and discover the ways of the West. Anyway, there I was at St Peter's Square, struggling to get as close as possible to the Pope. Evgenii got me a pass. But it was so crowded, it was like being at a Mayday parade on Red Square, except that on St Peter's Square, in front of the reviewing stands, as it were, there are nothing but cripples, in wheelchairs, on stretchers and crutches, awaiting the papal blessing. I shoved my way between the crutches, and when the Pope turned in our direction I just couldn't help it, I yelled out: "I'm Russian, I'm Russian." And let me tell you, I really saw his face change. It was as if his antennae had picked up familiar sounds coming from somewhere. He turned in our direction, took one look and came straight towards me. The cripples moved aside to let me through, right up to the barrier. I stood there weak at the knees. The Pope approached, and can you believe it, a Catholic Pole with a Russian Jew, he took my hand in his, in a trusting sort of way. Do you know what his hands were like? They were like a sculptor's who works with clay the whole time.'

'The only sculptor here is Karvalanov,' said Felix. 'Or was. He built a plasticine castle in prison. Silva, what are his hands like, are they rough?' With ill-concealed aggression he turned to Silva, who was sitting on the sofa holding Victor's hand in both of hers.

'Rough – rough is precisely what they were not!' Kupernik exclaimed. 'They were not rough at all; on the contrary, the palms felt amazingly smooth. People who work with clay develop strong but gentle hands; it's as if their skin had been ironed smooth by the action of the clay.' Taking Mary-Louise's hand between his, Kupernik assumed an unctuous, almost tearful expression and continued: 'The Pope shook my hand, like this, leant closer, and quietly asked me: "Are you Russian?" He spoke English, but in that question you could hear his understanding of the whole Soviet situation. His voice was full of pity, sympathy and concern for the fate of Russia beneath the Communist yoke. He looked into my eyes and started speaking very quickly, talking to me and to no one else. I just stood there, stunned, not knowing how to act, I even forgot to kiss his hand, I forgot to kiss the holiest hand in the world – and all around me cameras were snapping away, recording this extraordinary encounter.'

'So what did he say? What did he ask you? About Soviet tanks in Europe?' Mary-Louise was anxious to know every bit of news from this first-hand source.

'That's what's so awful. I have no idea what he said. The point is that he only spoke to me in Polish. And all I know is the Polish for "Thank you, sir" and "Dogshit".' Kupernik spread his hands despairingly at his shocking ignorance of the Polish language. 'So to this very day I have absolutely no idea what he said to me, what great words of wisdom and consolation he uttered. Maybe he even asked me to take some message to the

Russian people, some great speech to see me on my way, a fateful warning, words of comfort or a blessing. It's awful. The Pope of Rome made a historic speech for my benefit alone, and I can't tell you a word he said.'

'So ever since then you've done nothing but translate psalms?' asked Silva. But Kupernik did not notice the irony in her voice.

'The other way round really. It was my translation of the Psalms that brought about this historic encounter. I always believed Oscar Wilde's axiom that nature imitates art and not the other way around. By the way, did someone say they wanted to hear my translations of the Psalms?' And as befits a poet confronting his audience, he looked nervously around the noisy gathering.

People standing in the same group as Kupernik couldn't help glancing to one side and sidling surreptitiously away to the other end of the room, in an attempt to avoid his invitation politely. No one was especially sober any more, and the prospect of listening to psalms was not appealing. A knock at the front door saved the situation. It was Sorokopyatov, once a Moscow philosophy professor, a man of enormous size, distinguished by the directness of his gaze and the ambiguity of his views (*Duality as Ambiguity*, Moscow State University, Moscow, 1968), a condition attributed to the fact that he was obliged to wear bifocals.

'Do you mean to say you don't like my beret?' he asked Silva, using the beret in question to wipe his brow.

'I don't,' the art historian Braverman answered in her place. He used to be Silva and Lyudmila's boss at the museum. 'I wouldn't say that the beret is bad in itself. I assure you I've nothing against the beret. What I don't like is the fact that you, Sorokopyatov, stuck it on your head and are such a jerk that you're proud of the fact. I don't like the fact that it makes you look like a clown.'

'I am not offended, my dear Braverman, by your referring to me as a jerk. A philospher is able to learn a useful lesson from any aspersions cast upon his philosophic talent. But, my dear Braverman, philosophy is nothing but a form of clowning. And I, in an ambivalent sense, and by your gracious leave, am myself a clown. Hence the clown's beret.'

'Perhaps real philosophy is a form of clowning. But allow me, as an art historian, to tell you, Sorokopyatov, how to tell the difference between a clown and a phoney jerk. A real clown never wears a beret that makes him look like a clown except when he's in a ring. A real clown knows the difference between the circus ring and real life. I assure you a beret like that doesn't suit a clown in real life. But you it suits – which is why you are not a real clown.'

For every word of Sorokopyatov's, Braverman immediately had ten rejoinders, or else a single all-embracing one for every ten words of Sorokopyatov's. The reason for their antagonism was mysterious, yet very simple, like every émigré myth. The years each of them had spent away from their old country had moved them away from their old selves, had changed them; but each could only see this change in the other person, and each thought of himself as remaining true to his old values, let down by an erstwhile close friend who had become a sworn enemy. The presence of Karvalanov, appearing from the other world, the place where, for all of them, time had stopped, obliged them all to behave in front of one another as if they were being examined. Everyone there was a close friend, or a friend of a friend, except, of course, for the unavoidable presence of Slavists and advocates of human rights for members of both sexes. Karvalanov remembered his old acquaintances as nimble, bold, self-confident regulars at parties, late-night conversations and discussions, in which each one had their own unique, allotted part. Here, without the protective colouring of their own tight little circle, people seemed turned inside out, like an old coat brought out of the attic, taking on a new appearance, and they seemed eager to reveal those aspects of their nature which they used to be obliged, as they thought, to keep hidden, to keep silent about, to keep tucked away, in the old country. So instead of being the theatre for a single noisy but chaotically coherent ongoing conversation, the party's rhythm was set by a series of excited cries and squeals interrupted by long silences.

Those Russian guests who had discovered, once they were abroad, that they were Slavophiles managed to grab a few chairs, and barricaded the table by sitting round it in a tight circle with their backs to the rest of the guests. The hors d'oeuvres varied (as the poet-translator Kupernik might have observed) in the same degree as the national and ethnic origins of the guests, ranging from Russian salt herring, of Dutch origin, to rolls of Parma ham with pasta filling, to Boursin with grated avocado from the Italian deli. Exhausted by the Russian exchanges between Sorokopyatov and Braverman, a number of the Slavists had switched to English, and to add to the confusion Mary-Louise, who was bored, turned the stereo up to full volume. Although the amplifier was ten years old and looked unimpressive, it was quite powerful enough to cause the downstairs neighbours to lodge a complaint.

Mr Mackerel was wearing a dressing-gown and long johns. It was hard to make out Mrs Mackerel at all under her massive battery of rollers which dangled from her head like a swarm of parasitic insects. Each of the four or so times that they put in an appearance that evening, threatening to call the police, they had to explain who they were all over again, because each time they'd speak to a different 'Russian', who would be slightly drunker and more familiar than the one before. When Victor heard that they lived downstairs he said: 'Do you mean to say that you are beneath us?' Sorokopyatov expressed surprise that only the downstairs neighbours saw fit to complain while the ones upstairs did not, to which the Mackerels sensibly replied that this was because there were no upstairs neighbours, nor could there be, since they were on the top floor and above them was 'only the sky and nothing else', which provoked Sorokopyatov into asking them, quite truculently, whether this meant that they denied the existence of God and His angels. Braverman, who happened to be nearby, started arguing immediately. 'So, Sorokopyatov, it would seem that you feel obliged to populate the heavens themselves with your friends and acquaintances, so that you have a place to run to if things don't work out?' Mr and Mrs Mackerel's bedroom was directly under Ms Silva Lermontov's sitting room, said the Mackerels, and all that dancing and arguing about the existence of God had been keeping them awake for hours. Felix cast doubt upon the location of the matrimonial bed, since he had never heard it give a single creak – or perhaps Mr and Mrs Mackerel didn't go in for that sort of thing? To which Mr Mackerel replied that it was none of his, Felix's, damned business what the English did at night; their bed had been where it was for ten years, and a bunch of foreigners were not going to make him change his habits and move their bed. Mary-Louise proposed that Felix move his bed into the sitting room and engage in sex, Russian-style, upon it, so that the house would know no peace twenty-four hours a day, which would make the Mackerels think back to all that dancing and talk about God as if it had been the music of the spheres.

In order to provide a living example, Mary-Louise grabbed Victor and they started dancing, holding on to each other tightly and gyrating on the spot. 'Mackerels and sex don't belong together; fishes don't fuck. It's obvious. In point of fact, it's not surprising, living in England. Karvalanov, you should know that here they've reached the point where no one these days looks a woman in the eye. And if he doesn't look at me how can I tell if a man, in point of fact, wants me to look at him? And if, in point of fact, no one grabs me, how can I want to be grabbed? If you don't lie under a brick, the water won't flow, am I right?'

'What water, what brick?'

'It's a Russian saying,' said Mary-Louise.

'Water doesn't flow from under a well-laid stone,' prompted Felix, the folklore expert, who had grown used to Mary-Louise's idiomatic distortions.

'There you go, well-laid. But first you have to lie down, right? And who with, you might ask? English men are so scared of losing their purity and innocence that in point of fact they'd rather fuck themselves. As a dissident, Victor, you know what I mean, right.'

'What's being a dissident got to do with it?'

'What do you mean, what? What's the life of a Russian dissident like, in point of fact? When you're abroad you spend all your time with lords, and when you're at home you spend all your time in prison. And we all know what people get up to in prison. Soviet prisons are breeding grounds for traditional English male chauvinism; buggery and masturbation – what else is there to do in prison? And as a result, just look around, nothing but pederasts and wankers. The only reason I'm against the Soviet political system is because it turns people into perverts.'

'Speaking of sex in the two systems' – the poet-translator Kupernik literally thrust himself between them – 'I have, as it were, one buttock in the West and the other in the East, if you see what I mean. What amazes me about sex in the West is how incredibly well-mannered it is. I've noticed that everyone here has good manners, just take restaurants and supermarkets. But to get back to our discussion about sex, the other day I found a sex shop in the heart of your fair capital, in Soho. In this Aladdin's cave of sexual curios, sons of Albion and citizens of other Western parts, imbued with the characteristic British sense of parliamentary tolerance and calm curiosity, were inspecting various creations of local and foreign manufacture, cunningly devised to satisfy sundry erotic fantasies, and to drive various libidinous desires out of the subconscious in order that they should play their part in the sexual revolution. In other words, rubber cocks of various sizes, inflatable rubber cunts in various shapes and colours, and splayed rubber bottoms. And the magazines, well, they bring a blush to the cheeks. Everyone stripped right down to their genitals, to their balls and labia.' He stopped to get his breath back. 'But here's the strange thing: behaviourism, that is to say the behaviour of the customers inspecting these objects of sexual gratification. Someone simply has to jog someone else's elbow, while leaning intently over a display case full of female pudenda and penises, for both parties to turn to one another with impertubable expressions saying: "Excuse me, sir," or "Pardon, monsieur" or "Entschuldigen Sie" or some other form of well-mannered apology. And those manners are an expression of people's respect for others' privacy, of a sense of that parliamentary democracy rooted deep in their hearts and sexual organs, which, let's face it, we so sorely lack in Russia.'

'Because sex means death, sex in Russia is linked, excuse me, to the KGB. No wonder they're called the security organs,' remarked Sorokopyatov with a giggle.

'How right you are, Professor, how right!' Kupernik exclaimed enthusiastically. 'I had a session with a psycho-analyst here – pure curiosity, you understand, please don't think there is anything the matter with my perversions. But psychoanalysis is nothing but the hypothesis that we all have sexual organs in our heads – a Western concept, as you so rightly pointed out, Professor, that would seem to be nothing to do with us. But since, as you pointed out, the KGB are also organs, sex, for us, is bound up with the KGB, which we all have in our heads, right? In mine at any rate. I was twenty years old when I was summoned by the KGB. In '52, was it not? Just before Stalin died. I still don't know what they were after. Maybe it's because my name was Kupernik, a member of the Shchepkin family – you know, the woman who translated Shakespeare? So it may have had something to do with the fight against cosmopolitanism, translations from the English? But Pasternak translated Shakespeare, and no one summoned him to the Lubyanka.'

'No need to summon him, Stalin telephoned him in person,' said Felix.

'I am sorry to say that Stalin did not telephone me. So off I go to the Lubyanka, Felix Dzerzhinsky Square. The statue of Iron Felix is motionless to windward. There's a frost. Usually people pass that building as fast as their legs can carry them; but suddenly I notice that passers-by are as still as frozen cod. I get closer and see that even the guards that march to and fro outside the entrance seem to be seizing up, are slowing down, coming to a stop. I pushed through the crowd and there I saw him – a walking personification of the problems of sex, politics and the punitive organs. A citizen was pacing slowly along the pavement. Un citoyen de l'Union Soviétique, as a Frenchman would say. A solemn upright stance, and his bearded head held high. But the main thing was that this citoyen was stark naked. With every step he took, his genitals, which were of imposing proportions, swung between his legs. I still, to this day, cannot conceive of a more shockingly anti-Soviet gesture, a more provocative performance, as a young English artist would say, than those swinging genitals. And the face was worse. A beard, moustache, and the way he parted his hair all made him a spitting image, a Xerox, of bronze Dzerzhinsky on his pedestal in the middle of the square. It was as if the statue had removed his bronze trousers and taken a stroll along the pavement, with, forgive me, his sexual organ swinging from side to side. The guard was paralysed, hypnotized you might say, by this act of sacrilege. And he displayed his non-Party member as if to say: you can all do you know what – if the ladies will excuse me, "go and fuck yourself". That was my natural sexual revolution. Looking at this naked citizen standing in front of the stunned guards, in their caps and greatcoats, I decided not to visit the KGB that day. I felt just as naked as that nude gentleman, who by now was blue with cold. And I decided to keep that nakedness to myself.'

'And what happened to him, to the nude Dzerzhinsky?' asked Mary-Louise.

'I don't remember exactly who but someone in authority came to his senses, rushed up and covered the naked scoundrel with a coat. But they didn't realize that with a coat on he looked more like the bronze statue of Dzerzhinsky than ever; the only difference was that he was barefoot. But, do you know, once he was no longer naked the charisma vanished. He became just another ordinary Soviet there on the pavement. Just another Dzerzhinsky, if you like. The security guards and police came to, rose as one man in defence of their motherland, grabbed him and dragged him along the pavement, leaving a trail of blood from under the overcoat.'

Complete silence followed his words, as if the whole room was in mourning for the murdered madman in the story. Most of the guests gathered round Kupernik in an attentive circle. All this time Victor had said nothing, though he was following the story with close attention. Now his voice was heard from the far corner of the room, as if from another planet. 'So what happened to you, did they send for you again?' he asked.

'They did, but then Stalin died. And they stopped sending for me. So that I missed my shot at martyrdom.' The poet-translator smiled ironically, and turned his attention to the food, like an artist who had earned his bread or a lecturer who had finished answering questions from the ignorant audience. For him Victor was just one of the crowd.

Clearly irritated by Kupernik's unconsciously haughty and disdainful manner, Victor took Felix and Silva on one side, turning his back on the party and making a space. 'Who is this man, where did he come from?' he asked in a whisper. It felt as if the three of them were under siege, surrounded by the enemy, or were spies in a foreign land.

'How should I know?' Felix shrugged. 'He's to do with that Society for British-anti-Soviet Friendship or something. I thought he was a friend of yours. You were so pally with him.'

'I was? Only after you started slapping him on the back, giving him the big hello and introducing him to everybody.'

'What do you mean, the big hello? If you mean was I friendly, the answer is yes. And why not? He knows all my closest friends in Moscow, and told a whole batch of the latest Moscow jokes. So why not?'

'What jokes, why Moscow jokes? He's not from Moscow, is he?' Silva chimed in.

'That's what he says anyway,' Felix nodded his head. 'To begin with, I thought he was from Jerusalem. He told masses of Jerusalem stories. What kind of cream do you ask for in Jerusalem chemist shops if you've caught something like crab-lice on the Tel-Aviv beaches. I thought that's where he was from.'

Silva was puzzled. 'But just a moment, he talked to me about Paris, and I was convinced that he lived there. He's a friend of Kesha and Vika and knows all about the local émigré quarrels.'

'He just travels a lot,' said Felix. 'While we sit here rotting,' he added bitterly.

Silva hastened to demonstrate her impartial generosity. 'All right, so they let him travel abroad a lot – what's so strange about that? He's a Soviet poet, a translator, who's allowed to travel.'

'And?'

'And what?'

'And what was it you wanted to say about our spite and paranoia?' asked Felix, poised for a verbal strike.

'I don't want to say anything. All I want to say is that he is a pleasant older man, and that's enough for me. Besides, he came recommended by Pasha. A nice guy. He just talks too much. He talks and talks.'

'Who's Pasha?' asked Victor, bewildered by this avalanche of names.

'You know, Lika's brother, sort of.'

'What Lika?'

'You know, I don't quite remember.' Silva hesitated before answering. 'When he mentioned Lika I thought I knew who he meant. She was an old Moscow lover of Sorokopyatov's. That's what Roman said. I don't actually remember her myself. Most probably that's the way of it. I never kept track of Sorokopyatov's lovers.'

'And what does Sorokopyatov say?' inquired Felix.

'Do me a favour, what could he say, "by your gracious leave", if he insists on calling Roman Shchepkin.'

'All right, I agree Sorokopyatov is hopeless, but who's Roman?'

'What do you mean, who? That's him: the poet-translator

Roman Kupernik.' Silva was starting to show signs of impatience. She felt she was being made responsible for something that was entirely beyond her control. Typical of Felix and Victor.

'Roman translates poetry. Stylish,' sneered Felix.

'And what does he translate?' added Victor, joining in the questions.

'Basically he drives the stray sheep of national minorities back into the fold of the great and mighty Russian language,' Silva explained ironically. 'He told me himself that he makes his money working from cribs of various Tamurlaines and Genghis Khans.'

'But at night his conscience troubles him. If he were to die and God were to ask him, and what did you, Kupernik, you Jewish soul, do all your life? Translate May Day poems from the Uzbeki? And then he puts his hand in his pocket and takes out his translation of the Jewish psalms.' Felix started to elaborate this explanation sneeringly.

'All you want to do is air your opinion, or rather your prejudices about the man, but you're not the least bit interested in finding out about his life,' said Silva.

'What's there to find out, when his life is written all over his face?' asked Victor.

'You could be wrong.'

'I'd rather be wrong and keep my distance just in case,' said Victor.

'Naturally. You've all managed to get set up in your political sanctuaries, and everybody else is a spy, an agent, a snitch. Do you realize what courage it took to smuggle out his translations of those biblical psalms? He could have been charged with Zionism, with carrying coded messages. You seem to have forgotten what it's like.' Silva frowned indignantly.

'I trust he's not going to ask for political asylum?' Felix inquired.

'He was told he could spend the night at my place,' said Silva.

'Naturally.' Felix gave a jocular wave of the hand. 'No one has been turned away from your place, as far as I can tell. He's already started getting kissy. Slapped you on the bottom of course – like an old pal and a good comrade. In short, I have the feeling that he's been well informed about the local amenities.'

Silva took a swing and slapped Felix's face. The sound of a

slap, like a shot or the popping of a champagne cork, always makes a crowd fall silent. A huge gap suddenly opened up between the trio of bosom friends and all the rest of the guests. Mary-Louise was the first to take matters in hand. She was the only one who finally remembered who was the real reason they had gathered in Silva's flat.

'We haven't drunk Karvalanov's health yet, in point of fact. What about a toast of welcome?' she exclaimed in too loud a voice, speaking with a South London accent, and everyone started to reach for bottles and glasses. The bottles were empty, every one, from the French Mouton-Cadet and the Italian grappa to the English Vladivar and the Irish Jamesons.

'Why don't I nip down to the store?' said Victor.

'The noble action of a great man,' said Felix, 'but a totally pointless one. You can't buy spirits after eleven o'clock.'

'Well, let's go to a pub then, shall we?' Victor suggested tentatively.

'Pub derives from the word "public". You will not get served in a pub after eleven o'clock at night. It's against the law.'

'What law? We're adults living in a free society. Why?'

'Why ask? Every nation has its dietary laws. Jews don't eat pork, and the English don't drink in public after eleven o'clock at night. It's regarded as sacrilege. It's not kosher. Here kosher is a matter of the time of day. There's no point in looking for any logic here. There is no logic to religious proscriptions, else they wouldn't be religious.'

'Call a taxi,' said Victor.

'Why, where to?'

'The taxi driver will find us a bottle.'

'This isn't Moscow. Taxi drivers don't sell vodka.'

'Who said anything about vodka? Whisky will do. If the taxi driver doesn't sell it, he's going to know who does. There are certain professions that do their stuff regardless of the regime.' Victor was clearly back in charge. 'You lot have all lost your touch with your hypocritical observation of local customs. You've turned into conformists who blindly obey the licensing laws. Silva, call a taxi!'

15

Asylum

'Who would have supposed that Pushkin's text is a word-for-word version of Wilson's? Pushkin's "Festivities at the Time of Plague" is a wonderfully faithful rendering of act I scene 4 of Wilson's verse tragedy *The City of the Plague* – 166 pages long (of which Pushkin translated six at the most). Nothing much happens in the extract. There's a bunch of revellers, with two loose women, Mary and Louisa, and a young man, Walsingham, who presides over the revels. They drink a toast to an old friend and drinking companion, the previous "President", who has just passed on to the next world. Walsingham asks Mary to sing a Scottish song, then a negro drives by on a cart filled with plague-stricken corpses and Louisa faints. Then Walsingham sings his "In praise of plague". A priest appears who speaks harshly to Walsingham and tries to persuade him to follow him, but he refuses. He is condemned by fate to continue his celebrations. "I may not, must not go! Here am I held by hopelessness, in dark futurity, by dire remembrance of the past, – by hatred and deep contempt of my own worthless self, – by fear and horror of lifelessness that reigns throughout my dwelling." In his delirium he thinks he sees his recently buried wife, Matilda, and that's all there is.

'It's unclear why he picked the Walsingham scene out of all the various interwoven episodes and themes; perhaps it was by chance, perhaps he couldn't be bothered to read on? It's a pity that he didn't translate the exposition, when London appears to the principal characters like a strange Oriental city in a mirage, or the lines about the doors of Bedlam's dungeons being opened, setting lunatics wandering about the city not knowing whether they were alive or dead. But the section that Pushkin selected is translated with a refined accuracy, if you make allowances for some completely justified trivial alterations.

However, in most cases Pushkin's translation doesn't alter Wilson's version so much as improve its style.

'Besides, as always happens with translations, Pushkin attaches particular weight and significance to certain details, which may well have found their way into the original by the purest chance. For example, Louisa faints when she sees the cart full of corpses driven by a negro. The Young Man comforts her. "Did you not know that that black cart may travel where it pleases? We have no right to bar its way." Thus the cart driven by a negro becomes the black cart, where "dying men lie and mumble their mad and horrifying words". Wasn't Pushkin's mind's eye identifying the black cart with the black wagon of the police, with the Black Maria?! When they arrest someone at dawn after a search. And is it really accidental that Louisa should hate Mary. "We thank you, pensive Mary . . ." Mary – Maria. Though with respect to the Black Maria, I'm not actually sure that they used that piece of prison slang in Russia in the early nineteenth century.

'Wilson's play is essentially the epic of London during the Great Plague, with absolutely realistic place-names and heroes. The principal character in Pushkin's extract, the mystic president of the festivities, Walsingham, is described by Wilson as a captain in the Royal Navy, and a friend of the two principal characters in the play, Frankfort and Wilmont, who are also sailors. The play begins with them coming ashore in London, it would seem at Greenwich. They have returned from a long voyage to the West Indies, or possibly Palestine, and Wilmont accompanies Frankfort through the City to Aldgate, where his old mother lives – actually it is unclear whether she is still alive or whether she has died of the plague. (It turns out in due course that she is indeed already dead.) On the way to Aldgate the sombre canvas of life in London during the time of the plague unfolds before their eyes. In particular, they find themselves at the festivities presided over by Walsingham, close by Aldgate parish church; its vicar being the priest who appears at the festivities and seeks to shame the dissolute Walsingham with the memory of his dead mother and wife. It is clear that he had heard their deathbed confession. Moreover the Young Man, who exasperated Walsingham with his vulgar witticisms, turned out, in the original, to be Irish. He constantly made fun of the priest, and of religion in general. These attacks by a militant atheist on "clerical charlatans", "mountebanks", "hypocrites" and "idle gossipers in surplices" is either a reflection of the author's Reformed Church hatred of Catholicism, or of his distaste for the original of his character, the Irishman. "Had yon old dotard staid but a little, I had read him a lecture on the Christian's outworn creed." "Thou in thy heart hast said there is no God, yet knowest thyself – a liar." In the wake of this exchange, the President of the festivities, Edward Walsingham, challenges the lout to a duel and kills him. (Pushkin killing d'Anthès?) Before the duel scene, he seeks consolation with Mary, conversing with her along these approximate lines: "I swear to love thee . . . as a man sunk in utter wretchedness may cherish for a daughter of despair . . . in the breast even of this prostitute (why should I fear that word of three unmeaning syllables?)" Mary replies: "All names are one for me. I often love the imprecation of brutality, because, with vain contrition for my sins, I feel that I deserve them all." And on they go, wading through that Dostoevskian morass, a predictable sado-masochistic blend of blood, religion and prostitution, straight out of *Crime and Punishment* or *The Idiot*. This all emerges in the fourth part of the fourth scene of the first act. Pushkin leaves it out. He had no interest in religion as such. God exists, but that doesn't make dying any easier. Pushkin is more interested in the aesthetics of mastery over the fear of death.'

16

At the Court of Her Majesty

The drastic change in the course of their relationships since Victor had joined them in London, took place during that party in his honour when it was decided, at Victor's prompting, to hire a taxi to get a bottle. That night in August, London, cooling down after the day's fierce heat, with its lights and smells coming in through the taxi window, was absolutely magnificent. From upper Greenwich you could see the high-rise council blocks all ablaze, like gigantic fading bonfires. There was something alarming about the way their lights flared; it was as if fire brigade and police sirens were going to sound the alarm at any minute. In fact there were sirens to be heard, but they were not announcing an impending catastrophe, plague, pestilence or famine; they were just trying to sort out the ordinary human tangles that had come about on that sweaty, luxurious Indian night. A slightly sickly aroma emanated from piles of uncollected rubbish, mingled with the scent of late roses and warm dust – and over it all the odour of burnt grass, hay, haymaking. The London taxi, black and roomy as a royal carriage, didn't purr along on hissing tyres, like a modern car; the diesel engine chattered away in an old-fashioned Dorset-shire accent. Between the masses of high-rise buildings there flared up, with all the suddenness of a flashbulb going off, an illuminated pub sign – with the crest of its brewery, swaying in the wind like the flag of a foreign embassy.

'The main thing is not to end up back in Greenwich,' said Karvalanov, who was becoming well versed in the local geography. 'Or else we Western folk will end up in the East again.'

'End up in the Soviet Union if he keeps on driving this fast,' Felix warned him.

'The main thing is to find a liquor-store, isn't it,' Silva reminded them.

'If we end up in the East, smoking tobacco will be our only consolation,' said Felix.

'And why's that?'

'Because in the East they smoke tobacco; alcohol is drunk in the West. In the East the Koran forbids alcohol,' said Felix.

'In that case I don't see why people in the East are so keen on the idea of inner freedom,' said Victor.

'Where's the contradiction? I don't get it.' The logic of their dialogue was deteriorating too quickly or getting too complicated for Felix's brain, befuddled with alcohol.

'Smoking is the exhalation of smoke, that is to say an outwardly directed activity.' Victor was pursuing his own logic. 'Alcohol on the other hand is imbibed, it addresses the stomach, is concerned with, if you like, inner freedom. So there's something Eastern about it, since people in the West regard freedom as something absolutely manifest, to be experienced on the outside, like smoking.'

'It's because the Arab East is not the real East,' explained Felix, the greatest Russian specialist in things Oriental. 'Russia is the real East, because it's surrounded by the West. And in Russia, of course, people prefer to seek the inner, Eastern kind of stimulus, with the help of vodka. While in the West they don't use alcohol, instead they shoot up heroin, snort cocaine and smoke marijuana.'

At this intriguing point in their discourse the black cab came to a jolting halt and the driver, winking in complicity, indicated a small pool of light dancing on the pavement, cast by a naked bulb over the entrance to a shop. He promised to wait. They slammed the door shut and landed in a place of pure delirium; everybody there was a stranger, so you, a stranger here yourself, felt as if you'd come home. Crowding around, waiting for the door to open, were faces of many different hues, bums, drunks, and ordinary lonely people. A bunch of Rastas, in knitted wool caps of extraplanetary proportion, were shuffling to an imaginary reggae beat. Sometimes they mingled with the crowd, and then a ripple went through it, part whisper, part laughter, part talk – people would laugh quietly and move from one spot to another, form a group and wander off again. 'What's happening?' Felix shifted to a whisper too. 'Nothing's happening, I expect they're dealing hash,' said Victor authoritatively. All this shuffling and whispering was like life backstage before the curtain went up. Our trio approached the entrance as the last stroke of midnight chimed out from a neighbouring church and the shop door opened wide.

The press of customers surging towards the counter was a source of nostalgic pleasure, recalling food shortages and restrictions on the sale of alcohol. It was ages since Felix had witnessed that kind of turmoil in an English shop. People were grabbing cartons of canned beer, bottles of cider and vodka. When it was their turn the colossal black woman behind the counter barked: 'We're out of vodka. Only got gin. All right?' and without waiting for an answer she pulled two bottles of Beefeater from under the counter. They took the two bottles without protest, scarcely believing their luck and stunned by how well Karvalanov the newcomer had done. The black lady was even obliging enough to find them three paper cups – there's civilization for you! They left the shop like conquerors, looking for the taxi that was still waiting for them with its motor running. But suddenly the triumphant expression on Victor's face gave way to confusion, panic almost, when he noticed a miserable-looking dog with a floppy ear and a burn mark under one eye sitting on the pavement by the entrance to the shop.

Karvalanov paused, and the dog got up, came towards him as if he belonged to him, started to wag his tail and licked his hand. Karvalanov backed away towards the taxi, urging Felix and Silva on. Looking around him, he managed to shut the taxi door in the very face of the stray. 'Let's go,' he ordered the driver, as if they were being chased. 'Home?' asked Silva. 'To the river, you always cross the river to throw a dog off the scent.' Clearly it wasn't just megalomania that his years in prison had instilled in Victor; he had also developed a persecution complex, which, in point of fact, is the same thing as megalomania.

'Can you see a dog?' He tugged Felix by the arm as he looked out of the taxi's rear window.

'Of course I can see a dog. There are dogs on every corner. They're all over the place.'

'Do you see anyone by the dog?' Victor persisted. Felix turned to look through the darkened window again, squinting like a marksman, his drunken gaze trying to pierce the darkness.

'I can see another dog. Let's have a drink, shall we?' and he started pouring the gin into the paper cups, spilling some of it on the seat.

'There was only one dog on the corner. You're seeing double,' said Victor, taking the paper cup from Felix. 'I wouldn't be surprised if you see treble. You spent a third of your life in Moscow, a third in Jerusalem and a third in London. And, you have forgotten how to drink, oh venerable voyager.'

That was the night they resurrected their ancient custom of consuming quantities of disgusting alcohol (gin without ice, lemon or tonic) in the most disgusting places; the most disgusting and exotic of them all being the banks of the Thames. Not the Embankment, but the actual river bank. They reached it by climbing down a slimy stone stairway covered with moss and weed. The river was very low indeed, and shone with oil and garbage, while the banks and its exposed bed were polluted with civilization's refuse; but the gin triumphed over all of life's miasmas, and the lights on the far side of the river, either Big Ben or the City, began to seem like the lights on the east side of the Moscow River, and the Thames was no longer the Thames, but some Rubicon or Jordan. Bayonets of the enemies of the Revolution flashed by the river's edge, and to the accompaniment of songs of the civil war and the age of Stalin they climbed back up the stairs and started to make their way to the other side of the river, over an utterly deserted bridge – Waterloo Bridge perhaps – leaving behind them a trail of clay and ancient silt from the riverbed – which may be how the keeper-lord tracked them down.

They wandered into a park in search of a lavatory, passing an arch and column which were obviously not the Place Vendôme, although the arch could have been an Arc de Triomphe. But in any event the park was not in Paris, let alone Moscow. It was in London, in England, in the sense that nature here had been ordered by the hand of man. They started wandering through the night-time, pre-dawn Turneresque fog, that had wrapped itself around the trees in the aftermath of the heat of the day, spreading across the grass and the surface of the lakes, and catching the light, in such a way that you couldn't tell whether the swans were sleeping on grass or water, or whether they really were swans or simply wisps of fog shaped like swans' necks, hanging motionless in the still night air. You couldn't help feeling that this was all a long familiar illustration from some children's book. And as they caught a waft of something dear and familiar, they were overcome with the overwhelming urge to pee and mark the spot; it was a purely canine reflex. All three of them felt it at the same time, and without a word they moved off in different directions. Felix and Victor disposed themselves by the trees, and Silva squatted down behind some bushes in the middle of the park.

'Amazing how men need some kind of cover when they're taking a pee, a cosy little spot, but a woman will just squat straight down and do her stuff,' said Felix.

'That's because men need an obstacle, like a wall or a tree-trunk to demonstrate their strength; pissing, for them, is like target practice. Besides, men are always trying to erect a monument to themselves; by leaving their mark on the snow, on a tree or a fence,' they heard Silva say from behind the bushes.

'As if a woman doesn't leave her own mark on the snow!' Victor answered them both. 'A man hides himself away because he really has something to hide. Unlike a woman, all his tackle sticks out, and if he's not careful he'll be caught red-handed. A peeing man is defenceless.'

As usual Karvalanov was right. Suddenly their half-visible figures among the trees were snatched from the darkness and fog by the searchlights jumping all around the place. When the brakes of the police cars squealed to a halt on the cinder paths Felix and Victor didn't have time to zip up their flies, but Silva just got up off the grass as if she'd been sitting there waiting for the sunrise. The policemen came rapidly up, asked them who they were and what they were doing in the park at that hour. Karvalanov answered quickly and clearly. He was a tourist, from Vienna, he loved England, the Queen and English parks. Which was all true; from the very moment they took the cuffs off him and threw him out of a Soviet aircraft on to the runway of Vienna airport, the Viennese had given him honorary Austrian citizenship, while he had nothing personal against the Queen of England, and adored English parks and, as we know, castles too. He told the police just enough for them to feel that they had done their duty, and quite enough for them to begin to get bored.

The officers of the law were quite ready to leave, assuming that they were dealing with three half-crazed Austrians, when Felix started to shove his laissez-passer at the policeman who had been interrogating him. In confused detail he started to explain that he was an Israeli citizen, of Soviet origin, but was actually living in the United Kingdom, where he was doing an

English translation of a Russian poem based on an original written by a Scottish poet. 'My heart speaks Russian, my lips speak English, and I think in Hebrew. Pure bloody Nabokov, eh? This urge to be original. Nothing good comes of it.' Victor cursed aloud in Russian. And he was right again: no good did come of it.

'Do you speak Russian?' asked one of the policemen, speaking Russian slowly and with visible effort – he had clearly never completed his Russian classes. 'Do they speak Russian in Austria, then? And is that dog of yours Austrian, Israeli or Russian?' he continued in English, as if he were making a bad joke, which he was not.

'I told you we were being followed,' whispered Victor furiously. Felix and Silva followed his angry look. Sitting there in front of the bushes, as if it had come out of nowhere, was a flop-eared yard dog with a burn under one eye. Equally suddenly, a figure emerged from the bushes and advanced towards them. From Victor's lugubrious account of his visit to the estate, Felix immediately recognized the keeper-lord, now a trifle the worse for wear. The suede shoes and leggings, with their silver buckles shining dully beneath layers of dirt, the cloak, its hood thrown back, seemingly borrowed from a museum devoted to medieval mystery plays, tied by a cord knotted at the neck, with a lace collar visible underneath it, the jutting chin, the lock of red hair across the high pale forehead shining in the lamplight. Dostoevsky's Idiot personified, or Dr Who. In an evident state of inebriation.

'Do you speak Russian?' repeated the policeman. And what else should a famous Russian dissident, tossed up with his dog by an evil empire upon Albion's fair shores, be speaking, pray? And was it really the case that he, Lord Edward, an English aristocrat, had no right to take a stroll with that dog, the dissident and his friends through the royal parks? Was Her Majesty truly so inhospitable that she sicked the police on to subjects of hers that had happened to wander into one of her parks? An eccentric gentleman with a dog was bombarding the policeman with his questions in a haughty and persistent manner reminiscent of that of an ombudsman or a prominent parliamentarian. Total amazement was written not only on the policeman's face but on the Russian faces too. 'I hope everything turned out all right at the Palace yesterday?' But now Edward-Edmund was talking to Victor. 'I shall be absolutely delighted if this dog, with its tragic fate, finally finds a home beneath its master's roof.' The dog rubbed up against Karvalanov, wagging its tail, and a second later turned and started snarling at the policemen. After a moment of confusion, the policemen recovered from the hypnotic trance they had been placed in by the appearance of the aristrocratic scarecrow and his dog, and silently invited the detainees to accompany them to the neighbouring station for further explanation.

They were only released after forms had been filled in, telephone calls made and consultations had taken place. It was still night time on the stiflingly hot streets, but the sky was beginning to pale in the gaps between the buildings and the trees. Using the trees for cover, as if they were frightened of the dawn, they worked their way round the edge of the park and ended up by a semi-circular open space. 'You know the Palace, of course, but allow me to draw your attention to the statue on the other side.' Edward-Edmund pointed towards a huge, brilliantly lit edifice behind a wrought-iron gate, and started to cross the road. There was indeed something very familiar, touristy about the building behind the railings, that was somehow reminiscent of a picture postcard. But for the moment the somewhat intoxicated Felix couldn't recollect its caption. A façade with pillars seen through the cast-iron work, two guardsmen behind the great gates, wearing busbies with cockades – bayonets flashed in the darkness; who could they be guarding? A hint, like a prompter's whisper, came from the empty balcony over the main entrance, from the balcony which doubtless afforded a splendid view of the square, where enthusiastic crowds shout hurrah, toss their hats in the air and wave flags on high days and holidays. Who would appear on the balcony? Whose empty square was being so zealously guarded on that stifling night? Who was going to command the parade? The Queen, my God, of course, the Queen!

'Karvalanov, do you realize we're standing in front of Buckingham Palace? That we tried to have a pee in front of the royal palace in St James's Park?' Felix was visibly flabbergasted and his voice displayed amazement mingled with genuine shock.

'Let us for the moment leave the Queen to her rest. Let us continue our argument, my dear Karvalanov,' said Edward-Edmund. 'Allow me to offer you a glaring example of the conspiracy between the British aristocracy and the Soviet propaganda machine. Please take a careful look at that man and that woman.' He didn't mean Felix and Silva, who were standing a little way behind. He pointed to the statuary in the centre of the square. The central figure sat there holding a sceptre and wearing a crown, surrounded by baroque extravagances including decorative streams of water emanating from a fountain; she was flanked by four other sculptures at the four corners of the monument. Two faced the palace. Executed in a pseudo-Roman heroic style, in which Victorian zeal strove to emulate the ancient Empire's pseudo-Roman canons of beauty (which was to save the world) and majesty, indecent in their homosexual musculature and state of semi-undress, as if they had recently emerged from a bath, with their stone garments suspended from the most unsuitable parts of their body, two figures directed a fixed, almost hostile gaze at the palace before them. Stone lions lay at their feet. 'Forget the lions,' said Edward-Edmund. 'Just look at what the man and woman are holding.'

'Impossible,' whispered Felix, who could not believe his eyes. The woman held a sickle and the man had a gigantic hammer in his massive grasp. 'And who's in the middle? Who is she whom these two workers are holding in their proletarian thrall?'

'Queen Victoria,' their guide hastened to add. 'You might just as well put our Victor here in her place. They both have the same attitude towards working-class culture. So the symbolic significance would be the same, only it would be expressed in a different language, with different names, translated, as it were, from the Russian into the English. And how, dear Felix, is your translation coming along?' Felix realized that, although they might be dealing with a madman, the madman knew absolutely everything about them, and contained in his madness there was a method.

'Isn't it time we got back to our guests? I expect they're all asleep by now,' said Silva and took Edward-Edmund's arm, ignoring Victor's furious glances. She yawned, pretending to be tired, and from a fleeting, scarcely perceptible glimpse of compliance in her glance (she'd suddenly stopped looking them in the eye as if she was afraid she'd let something out) Felix understood, with the infallibility of an experienced lover, that in future his rivalry with Victor would degenerate to the level of an act. A third party had appeared in Silva's life. Breathing a sigh of relief, Felix gave a gesture of dismissal and hailed a passing cab.

17

Asylum

Everything glowed in the light of the westering sun: the meadow, the tree and the glassed-in verandah where they had settled to have tea. Silva dismounted from a glowing horse and appeared on the verandah in glowing silhouette.

'Tea?' Dr Genoni rose to greet her. 'Earl Grey or Lapsang Suchong?'

'I don't feel like lapping,' said Silva. 'Let's have some Earl Grey.' She felt that she was disturbing some intimate 'boys'' conversation. Dr Genoni was too caring, almost brotherly, and hastened to serve her, abandoning his pose as a cool analyst of the medical profession. Victor too was unusually forthcoming and attentive. He made room for her, brushing some crumbs off his knees. They drank their tea, eating scones spread with strawberry jam and thick Cornish cream.

'I think I'll take a stroll,' said Victor, getting up and stretching. He moved off in the direction of the lilac-coloured meadow with a glowing horse by a dark blue oak tree.

'Don't wander off too far,' warned a fatherly Dr Genoni. 'Or else you'll run into that keeper again.' But Victor gave a careless wave and went off in the direction of the violet-coloured wood.

'Like every Englishman, Edmund had hoped that in the company of you carefree foreigners he would find the peace that comes from . . .' Dr Genoni hesitated, trying to recollect his train of thought. 'From being fatherless. But not in a negative sense. Like a cosy nursery, with your brothers and sisters, without any grown-ups, nannies, parents, keepers, or God to supervise, watch and judge you. A kind of paradise lost, a world of children without adults.' He introduced the subject of Edmund's preoccupations with due caution as a kind of philosophical dilemma, very much hoping that Felix and Silva would pick up and develop the theme in a more concrete and detailed way. But Silva had something else on her mind.

'Having read more than enough Hemingway, we used to regard ourselves as the lost generation, the fatherless generation. Our fathers, you might say, betrayed us. So we are orphans, kind of. But actually it wasn't like that at all.' Silva carefully put the fragile teacup back on its saucer. 'We're a lost generation, not because we're fatherless children, but because we're childless, never had children, never became parents. We're a generation of lost fathers, nonexistent fathers, and mothers that never were.'

'What's the matter, are you crying?' Felix noticed Silva's trembling lips. That sudden show of emotion on Silva's part was quite a surprise. Felix got used to the feeling that however sharp the exchange of ideas between them might become, their dialogue was conducted in a Socratic spirit, on the abstract level.

'All I can add is that we're an aborted generation, and that I've done my fare share to earn us the reputation.' Silva's tone reverted to the matter-of-fact.

'Whose was the last one? Not the lord's? How did you find the time?'

'You just can't help being sordid, can you? But if you really want to appear smart and on the ball, you shouldn't ask who, you should ask when and where.'

'All right, when and where?' Felix asked like an obedient schoolboy.

'Not in London, anyway. The only place in Europe that you have to get an abortion after casual sex is of course Moscow.'

'If you count Moscow as Europe,' Felix began ironically as usual but then, with a glance at Silva's face, he cut himself short. 'You mean you had an abortion in Moscow? Who was it? I hope you don't look on our Moscow relationship as casual sex,' he muttered.

'Could be. But the nights I spent with Victor were more like casual sex. You never knew when and how long he was out for. And when he used to come back, that made our relationship, yours and mine, into casual sex, did it not?'

'But surely you remember dates, and your period and things? Women always know who the father is.' Felix was trying to look like an old hand.

'My dear Feliciano. You may have studied the subject of pregnancy in the Talmud, but let me assure you that there are occasions when Solomon himself would not be able to tell what's happening in the womb of a woman who is opening up her frontiers to two diasporas at the same time.'

'You mean to a diaspora and an exile. That night I was diaspora, Victor was exile.'

'That is just the kind of remark that explains why I had an abortion. Because we're incapable of being parents; for us, children are just a proof of something or other, a debating point in an argument about something else.'

'Or someone else,' interrupted Dr Genoni, who had been listening carefully and making notes. 'Why don't you admit that you have something else on your mind when talking about that sordid business of casual sex? You want to prove something to Felix, to prove that he is not omnipresent and omniscient, don't you? If you are really going to lay out the whole truth,' he said, paying no attention to Silva, who was looking surprised, and not best pleased, 'why don't you go all the way, and tell us who, apart from Victor, was actually involved in this business of casual sex and dubious paternity?'

'You mean was there a third? What's he mean, Silva?' Felix sneered.

'People fail to notice the obvious. Our eyes don't take in whatever is there for all to see. The obvious and the banal are alien to us, we're more at home with complexity. And so on. Remember? After all, it was you who told me all about it during the last session,' prompted Dr Genoni, as if he were dealing with a less than gifted pupil.

'You mean the story about Avestin, and the way he hid the matches from the nurse in the psychiatric ward? By putting it on the most obvious and visible spot?' Felix was slowly getting worked up.

'And who told that story?'

'Migulin. It was an absolutely brilliant story about Avestin putting on Pirandello in the psychiatric hospital, where all the actors turned out to be fathers who had killed their children. But wait a minute. It was – what? – ten years ago, or more? How do you know about that night? Did I tell you? Or Victor?' Felix passed his hand across his forehead as if wiping out invisible sweat. 'It was unbearably hot and there was too much talking and drinking, and I went off to get some more vodka – we'd run out – I went down to the store. Migulin's tales of the psychiatric hospital were, if you like, a classic part of our set's folklore, I knew them by heart, which is why I went out to get the vodka, leaving Silva to listen . . . Actually she knew them by heart too; I mean, she's known Migulin longer than she's known me almost . . . What are you trying to say? Silva, what's he trying to say?'

'All right, all right. I did sleep with him then.' A feeble apologetic smile appeared on her face. 'I felt sorry for him. I knew he needed it. To me he was already an old man. He went out so rarely. For Migulin it was just physical, a bodily necessity, like a medicine, a pain reliever, and I gave it to him. What's so terrible about that?'

'Nothing terrible, I suppose, not really,' muttered Felix, wiping his forehead again. 'It's just that you started talking about abortions, and whose child it might have been, mine or Victor's. How could you have forgotten Migulin? How could I have forgotten Migulin? So for all these years you kept up this – this casual relationship?'

'Amazing how people don't notice the obvious.' Dr Genoni returned to his topic. 'The most amazing thing is that you all knew it, and chose to ignore it. For some reason it never occurred to you that there could be anything more between Silva and Migulin than friendship and gossip. For you, he was too Olympian a figure, he was a guru, a teacher, a father. That's it, a father. You know that for us the strongest of all taboos is the nakedness, the nudity of the father. Do you know why Jung broke with Freud? Because they'd promised to tell one another all their dreams, and one day Freud refused to tell Jung his. He'd dreamt about his father, naked. And Jung realized that, for Freud, respect for his elders was more important than the truth. He just couldn't trust him any more. You could not face up to the fact that, besides you, besides you and Victor, there was a third character, so mighty that you couldn't imagine him doing what you were doing. That's it, isn't it? Instead you subconsciously brought in Victor, the inevitable participant in your inseparable ménage à trois, although on that occasion, Silva, he couldn't have featured in your calculations. If you remember, he was arrested that night, and you looked out at him being taken away from Felix's room.' Felix sat there, very pale, saying nothing. Silva covered her face with her hands.

'But let me remind you why have I prompted you to this

conversation on the subject of parenthood and childlessness, forgetfulness and sense of guilt,' said Dr Genoni after a pause required by politeness and to show his sensitivity. 'Let me remind you that you've been brought here on condition that through an attempt to sort out and clarify your own past you'd help me to resolve the enigma of your liberator. Or is he your jailor? Let's not forget that we are here to find out who is our lord, and who is our keeper.'

18

The Opium Eater

'Pardon, in point of fact I thought it was that couple from downstairs that can't get it up, right?' Mary-Louise greeted the late-night alcohol hunters. She herself had had one too many and experienced some difficulty in getting her body from the reclining position and standing on her feet. She was leaning on the wall in the dimly lit entrance hall. They'd had to bang on the door for a good quarter of an hour. Clearly endeavouring to increase the neighbours' creative potential, the record player was still at full volume. The music, however, could not entirely drown the sound of various guests slumped snoring in corners, the sudden surges of ideological dispute between old foes still not asleep, and the indefatigable poet-translator reciting his renderings. 'The Mackerels are still threatening to call the police,' said Mary-Louise, eyeing the trio as if wondering how the police would react to the less than reputable appearance they had assumed after their nocturnal adventures. Not to mention the dog. She clearly wanted to ask them also about the identity of the strange apparition accompanying them with his cloak, ribbons and breeches. But thanks to their rotten Russian manners, they didn't bother to introduce Edward-Edmund to the rest of the guests. Kashtanka, confused, gave a snarl, and Edward-Edmund, followed by Silva, took the dog into the kitchen for some food. 'The first thing you do is feed your horse its oats,' said Victor with sombre irony. As she left the room, Silva turned off the record player with a snap. In the ensuing silence, a few guests that had not departed or fallen asleep made a circle around Felix and Victor, as if anticipating some news from the outside world, or rather like a theatre audience waiting for two actors to start the performance.

'Typical English hypocrisy,' muttered Felix as he sprawled on the sitting room sofa. 'They claim that everything is for the benefit of the people. Walk where you want. There are parks and benches galore. But all you have to do is unzip your fly and a whole posse of police comes flying at you out of the bushes. Just like the Soviet Union.'

'I wonder how many policemen would have jumped you if you'd unzipped in the middle of Red Square, up against the Mausoleum?' Victor answered Felix with a snort. The short honeymoon period of their relationship was drawing to an end. Hours spent at the police station did not improve the chances of reviving the atmosphere of camaraderie. Victor was obviously looking for a scapegoat. 'The KGB has at least one good lesson to teach: never answer a question until you receive it in writing. But you've taken to answering questions that exist only in your imagination. And do you know why? Because you're far too enamoured of your complicated past and your unique personality, and the complex process of its development. But I'd even have got out of that mess had it not been for our keeper friend.'

Mary-Louise started at his words, as did all the other guests who had sat back and enjoyed the performance. Both speakers were also somewhat uplifted by the turn their dialogue had taken, as if they had both accidently stumbled upon the real author of their current troubles.

'Lord or keeper, he was the only Englishman in the party. They believed him, so you could say that he sprang us from a police cell,' said Felix.

'Not us, you.' By now Victor was almost shouting. 'I'd have managed perfectly well if that lunatic hadn't intervened.'

'But if it hadn't been for you, he wouldn't have been there.'

'How did he know that I'd wander off to Buckingham Palace in my cups?' demanded Victor.

'Maybe he didn't, but the dog, your dog, led him there, following your scent.'

'It does smell funny in here,' said Braverman, sniffing.

'Could it, by your gracious leave, be dog shit?' inquired Sorokopyatov.

The answer came from the other end of the room. 'It's the bones,' said Silva, coming out of the kitchen. She pronounced the word 'bones' as some new converts would repeat a sacred blessing. She had definitely had a profound conversation back in the kitchen with 'His Gameship Lordkeeper' – as she put it. She was also quite tipsy. Her reappearance drew the whole company closer together, and with the word 'bones' everyone seemed to be stirred from their drunken torpor.

'What bones, whose bones?' the murmur went round the room.

'Dog bones, boiled dog bones,' said Silva. 'He said the dog needs bones to practise its biting.'

'Its biting? I can well believe it, its biting!' Victor muttered angrily, looking at his hand that was still bandaged where the dog had bitten him in the country.

'But, do you know, I sort of like the smell. In a way it smells like our Russian meat in aspic.' Kupernik rubbed his hands. He was looming somewhere in the background, anxious to enlighten the audience with yet another piece of wisdom from the mouth of an international voyager. Until this moment, however, the details of getting a bottle of gin in London after midnight were outside even Kupernik's vast experience. But the memory of the delightful meat in aspic was too irresistible to keep silent about. 'For you will be pleased to recall that they use bones in its preparation, is that not so? We eat the stock, and the bones go to the dogs. To help them bite.' Kupernik licked his lips greedily.

'I say, there's an international congress of bone specialists taking place in this flat,' said Victor. 'Mary-Louise says that we're living on top of a pile of human bones here, are treading on the remnants of three-hundred-year-old plague victims. Am I right, Felix? Felix has crawled through every sewer in the district looking for metaphors for his translation of "Festivities at the Time of Plague". I haven't been here a day yet, properly speaking, but everywhere I look I find plague-stricken metonymies; from the heat and the boiling bones to a bunch of books and poetic quotations.'

'The first part of the translation has already been published in the *Scottish Review*, and the *Times Literary Supplement* has already described the extracts as the unprecedented discovery of a link between Pushkin and the poets of the Lake District,' said Mary-Louise proudly, who had managed totally to avoid using the expression 'in point of fact'.

'Not without your help, Mary-Louise,' said Felix, who would rather she shut up.

'All I did was alter a couple of commas, and the odd definite article,' said Mary-Louise, blushing.

'I really must take a look at the translation,' said Kupernik. He had suddenly become agitated again, and at the same time unusually attentive to every word and gesture around him. He sidled up to Felix and touched his elbow. 'You know I'm an expert on Scottish poetry. False modesty aside, do you know, I got a better reception in Scotland than I did in Georgia. Do you know, I spent the night in Robbie Burns's bed? You'll be interested to hear that I met a descendant of the John Wilson who wrote the poem that Pushkin borrowed from. Do you catch my drift? We really need to talk about this, OK?' He gave Felix a pat on the shoulder.

'I'm a bit tired of exhuming literary corpses.' Felix backed away from him, smiling a little tensely. 'Are we going to get anything to drink at these festivities in the time of plague? We should have the best part of a whole bottle of gin left. Gin overcomes all bad smells, even the smell of your Kashtanka's bones,' said Felix, getting away from Kupernik and joining Victor on the sofa again as he watched Mary-Louise pouring drinks from the bottle that survived their adventures.

'There you go again: *your* dog, *your* Kashtanka. She is no more mine than she is yours. You know a dog forgets its master completely after being apart for nine months?' said Victor.

'The cycle of some women's loyalty doesn't last longer than nine months of pregnancy, either. I think that we are witnessing the birth of a new pretender to the throne of Her Majesty Silva,' said Felix. 'And it's scarcely surprising – after all, there are more Russian Jews and dissidents per head of population than there are English lords. And our Silva was always an elitist, and unlikely to pass up anything exclusive, as our poet-translator would put it.'

'But you know he's no more a lord than I am – just a stray dog,' said Victor.

'That won't stop Silva. She has always wanted to nurse distinguished lunatics. I say this taking account of the fate of previous pretenders to the throne.'

'If you're referring to the time I spent in a psychiatric hospital, I can assure you I got there thanks to a very different kind of diagnosis,' Victor replied curtly. 'I never thought I was somebody I wasn't.'

'You're still suffering from that very illusion. You believe you know who you're not,' said Felix.

'It seems to me that it's a great deal worse to be like you and convince yourself that you really know who you are, and then accuse everybody else of getting you wrong. We had someone like that in our ward. He thought he was Jesus Christ. He stole an icon portraying Our Lord from the Tretyakovsky Gallery, spent a week contemplating it and then went off to the local police station. He complained that the artist was a lousy painter, since the icon was such a poor likeness of him.'

'That's not your story,' said Felix. 'It's taken from the annals of the pyschiatric hospital in the Fifties. You stole the story from Migulin. He told it that evening . . .' Felix stammered, 'that Moscow evening when you turned up late for your birthday, when the place was searched and you were arrested, the year of the drought and the cholera, like this year, remember?'

But Victor didn't have time to reply. Edward-Edmund, 'Prince Myshkin', came into the room accompanied by Kashtanka. It was a stately entrance. He stopped in the middle of the room and glanced around as a slightly short-sighted monarch would observe and assess his cabinet ministers at a time of crisis. Everyone forgot Victor's quarrel with Felix, including them, and turned their heads to that part of the stage where the new protagonist of the same drama was preparing himself for action. While Kashtanka was wagging her tail and sniffing out the corners, the prince, disregarding the guests, opened a closet where the coats were hanging and started to go through the pockets of various jackets and overcoats with the deliberate thoroughness of a policeman conducting a search. After he'd been through the summer clothes in the closet, he started shaking and inspecting the coats and summer jackets that the guests had left in a heap in the passage. There was the sound of money rolling on the floor. He looked like a rag-and-bone man, a junk dealer, a fanatical collector of curios. The guests all fell silent as they watched him move through the flat. Suddenly he halted in the middle of the sitting room, smacked his forehead and smiled a smile of relief. He turned and went to where Karvalanov was sitting and, without saying a word, started rummaging in the pockets of Karvalanov's summer windcheater, which was hanging over the back of the chair. It was not easy to rummage because Karvalanov was sitting in the chair, which is doubtless why Edward-Edmund decided to put the windcheater on, and continued to go through the pockets with ever greater care.

'Give me back my windcheater,' Karvalanov jumped up.

'You'll get your dissident's hide back in just a moment, my dear Karvalanov,' said Edward-Edmund, turning the pockets of Karvalanov's summer windcheater inside out. 'To begin with, I thought I'd hidden my piece of heaven on earth in the Jerusalemic raiment of our dear Felix: the Middle East is the motherland of hashish. Zionism, like all religions, is the opium of the people.' As he spoke he put his fingers in an inside pocket and smiled triumphantly. 'But then I realized that the police would hold to the same opinion, which is why I decided to place this piece of terrestrial bliss in the coat of a dissident – the symbol of moral rigour, refusal to compromise and spotless virtue. How could I have forgotten?!'

'What did you put in my pocket?' Victor could hardly believe his ears. 'Are you saying that all this time I carried that stuff in my pocket?' He jumped from the sofa and started pacing up and down the room. 'I think it's time I looked for political asylum a little further away from these parts.' But his words were ignored not only by Edward-Edmund – everyone was watching the results of his search.

With a boyish half sigh and half whoop of joy, his shaking fingers removed a small packet from an inside pocket. He unwrapped it to reveal a piece of dark resin. Establishing himself in a corner, like a Siberian shaman, Edward-Edmund started to work his magic with the substance. He scorched it with burning matches and cut it into small pieces with his penknife. Then he mixed them with some aromatic tobacco which he carried in a tin box, and extracted a long-stemmed pipe from an inside pocket. Carefully filling it with the mixture of tobacco and hashish, he leant over it with a lighted match as if he were cutting himself off from the whole world, sucking and puffing, lighting and relighting it with match after match. Finally it caught. Edward-Edmund drew on it and, no longer taking short sharp puffs, settled into a long steady pull. It was as if he were putting on a circus act that made pipe smoking as long, slow and drawn-out a process as a bad novel. He drew in air with a whistle and frowned in concentration as his jaws clamped on the pipe with a mighty effort, and his brow furrowed in the effort to find his way to a radiant future through the opium dream. At last he leant against the wall with a relaxed expression while his eyes, clouded over, had at last lost their feverish glow. The sweetish reeking smell of hashish filled the room and for a moment made everyone feel and behave as if they too were under the influence of it.

'Decadent aristocracy, in point of fact?' said Mary-Louise, who sat herself down on the floor next to Edward-Edmund. 'Won't you let me have a puff, My Lord?' Smiling blissfully, Edward-Edmund handed the pipe to her. 'Mary, Mary-Juana,' he murmured. Mary-Louise emulated his inhalations, and soon she too began to seem at peace with the world. 'This pipe, My Lord, makes me somewhat keener on the British aristocracy. But in point of fact, I never could understand why we need a House of Lords.'

'It is a tricky question,' agreed Edward-Edmund. 'Since the Lords don't actually decide anything, the house's function, or so it appears to me, is to confuse and make trouble for the government. By virtue of their continual debates and amendments, they add a measure of confusion to the whole business and keep the government in a state of continuous uncertainty, thus ensuring that it does not feel able to do as it pleases.' His observation contained so much unexpected political good sense and logical elegance that even Victor started to lend an attentive ear.

'You personally, it seems, did a great deal to confuse the government in the House of Lords,' said a curious Kupernik.

'I made a speech about the problem of the rabies infecting dogs in Russia that had been turned into strays by the arrest of their dissident owners.'

'And what were you doing near Buckingham Palace anyway? Were you following me?' Victor interrupted him.

'My dear Karvalanov, you are suffering from *folie de grandeur*. You think the whole world's following you.' His eccentric and neurotic mannerisms gave way to the benevolence and irony of a clear-minded, though slightly quaint, political thinker. 'I was trying to get into the Palace for reasons of my own. The Palace security is so rotten that I was trying to break in to get a personal audience with the Queen, following the directions of a friend, a dyed-in-the-wool supporter of the monarchy, though a hopeless drunk, who turned up in Her Majesty's bedroom one evening, very much the worse for wear, in order to raise a glass in her honour and wish her a pleasant night. My ambition, as you know' – he took another puff, for courage as it were – 'is to make Her Majesty aware of the existence, in this country, of a conspiracy between great landowners and the KGB; the KGB regards dissidents as mad dogs, while anyone who protects stray dogs from the wrath of gamekeepers is here presumed to be a dangerous dissident. People like me live under perpetual threat of involuntary confinement in a psychiatric ward. As you all know, the Queen always surrounds herself with corgis, so I'd hoped that she would understand. Who would have thought that you and your friends were also going to the Palace for the same reason?'

'Who told you that we were having an audience with the Queen? We'd wandered off into St James's Park for a very different purpose,' said Silva.

'What purpose?' Edward-Edmund turned to Victor. 'Are you perhaps one of those who win the Queen's confidence and then fill her head with all sorts of rubbish, under orders from the gamekeeper fascists?' Edward-Edmund rose unsteadily. Victor got up to meet him. Both almost bumped into Kupernik, who happened to be standing between them like an umpire.

'Did you know that it seems the Bolsheviks never did shoot the Tsar's spaniel?' Kupernik's timing was excellent. 'It seems that the spaniel left Russia with the family's English tutor, who, if I remember, was called Gibbs. They managed to save the Tsar's dog. Everyone thought it was sharing the Tsar's grave, but all that time it was in England, scampering about Hyde Park. Thanks to the English monarchy, by the way.' Kupernik held forth nervously, looking at Victor's and Edward-Edmund's furious expressions. They might well have come to blows had it not been for Silva. Stepping between them, she told Edward-Edmund that the police didn't let Victor into the Palace because his knowledge of etiquette was less than rudimentary. He had no idea of how and when to bow, when to kiss Her Majesty's hand and so on.

'Her hand?' Edward-Edmund was surprised. 'It's absolutely forbidden to kiss her hand. The Queen may not be touched. Moreover the first time you address her, you must call her "Your Majesty", after which you must use the form "Ma'am". Moreover . . .'

'Continue, continue,' said Silva in a haughty, grating

assumed voice. After a moment's deliberation, she clambered on to a chair, arrayed in a costume she had cobbled together, with an old white tablecloth serving as an imperial toga, and a plastic bag on her head – looking like the combination of a papal crown and a dunce's cap. She extended a gloved hand, scouring the room with her bright eyes in search of a volunteer. Everyone apart from Victor was drawn into a circle around the chair, attracted by her circus routine. But to everyone's surprise, Edward-Edmund was the quickest to join in the game. With an agility and deftness unexpected in a person whose mind was clouded with hashish, he gave a solemn bow and kissed her hand. Silva immediately assumed an expression of mock indignation, playing up to her partner as if she had rehearsed this two-hander in advance. She gave a friendly slap to the 'lord's' dutifully bowed head. 'You, sir, appear to have lost your senses,' she said in a high-pitched, authoritative voice. 'How dare you kiss my hand? There can be no kind of physical contact with Her Majesty. Nor is one permitted to smoke hashish mixed with tobacco. I would recommend that you recall the labour camp punishment cells. Now, let us become acquainted. I am Her Majesty.'

'And I am Victor, which in Latin means "the Conqueror".'

'Is it in your honour that the defenders of human rights founded the Victoria and Albert Museum?'

'Victoria, Your Majesty, was the name of your grandma. My name is Victor, not to be confused with Victoria. My friends call me Vova.'

'Vo-va – it sounds like a girl's name in English.'

'It's a diminutive of Vladimir. Which is the name of the most terrifying prison in Russia, where, incidentally, I spent the best years of my life. We use diminutives to diminish our own fear. Vo-Va is somewhat reminiscent of Frou-Frou, a mare owned by Vronsky, Anna Karenina's lover.'

'Do you mean to say that Anna Karenina slept with mares?'

'No, she hung on Vronsky's neck, an Anna round the neck.'

'Hung? I thought she threw herself under a train. Did you take her death badly?'

'Instead of a woman, I got myself a dog, and moved from Vladimir to that Be . . . Bloody hell, what was it?'

'Beskudnikovo!' the Russian guests prompted Edward-Edmund in chorus, laughing at the improvised piece of theatre.

Hearing the naming of familiar names was more entertaining than any kind of political or personal squabbling. Felix threw a quick glance at Victor sitting on his own on the sofa. He was staring past the guests at the wall in front of him, 'held here', as John Wilson had put it, 'by hopelessness, in dark futurity, by dire remembrance of the past, by hatred and deep contempt of his own worthless self'. Felix heard Mary-Louise giggle and watched in amazement the miraculous ease with which Edward-Edmund was shedding the Edmund of his game-keeper's self and becoming more and more 'Edwardian' in his aristocratic manners, his quickness of mind, his knowledge of things Russian and of Victor's past and present. Silva was clearly no less surprised than the others by this transformation.

'I hear that you built yourself a castle in Beskudnikovo.'

'Oh yes, there's a whole neighbourhood of high-rise castles in Pisskudnikovo, and none of them have numbers on the doors – to confuse spies and anti-Soviet agitators. During my regular absences in Vladimir, the castle was guarded by a fierce dog called Kashtanka. One day she sank her teeth into the leg of an excessively tiresome foreigner.'

'The left leg or the right one?'

'The right, of course. The foreigner was in the right, he was a human rights activist.'

'Why didn't he defend his human rights from her with his left hand?'

'Because the trouble with these foreign visitors is that their left hand never knows what their right foot is doing.'

'So that, the next morning, this soldier of righteousness got up on the left foot?'

'The main thing was that once she had tasted the hard currency of a foreigner's blood, Kashtanka went totally crazy; her head became infected by foreign ideas, and her loyalty to her own blood and soil was totally destroyed by the taste of that foreign lymphatic liquid, which made her emigrate to the New Jerusalem, England's green and pleasant land.'

'Where the sheep shall lie down between the dog and the wolf.'

'The dog barks and the caravan moves on, but the man remains silent.'

'Why does he?'

'I suppose because he's in prison, and in prison there's no freedom of speech.'

'So Soviets go to prison to get away from barking dogs?'

'As you know, they go to prison to get away from Stalin.'

'Do you mean to say he's still alive?'

'For us Soviets he is, alive and well.'

'How nice to stay alive, if only in the eyes of others. I regret not being a Russian empress. You are so zealous in your concern with the longevity of your monarchs. Does Stalin seek to prolong his life by jogging?'

'Of course. He does it to keep warm. Nikita Khrushchev threw him out of the Mausoleum, and Stalin, without a roof over his head, began jogging round it to keep warm. He gradually got into shape and started to run further, describing larger and larger circles, stretching out his hands further and further; perpetually vigilant, he covers every square inch of his native soil, patrolling the frontiers of our motherland, grabbing hold of anyone who tries to cross the frontier and escape to the West to get away from his imploring cries to return him to the Mausoleum.'

'Yes, I had heard that they jam the BBC Russian Service; so those are the luckless Joseph's lamentations?'

'Absolutely. Since Stalin is just a ghost, his lamentations are only to be heard in people's minds, like the fear in their hearts. No tablets, pills or medicines were of any help, nothing could shut people's minds to the sound of Stalin's growls. But Russians are wise, they invented vodka, the Sputnik, the samovar. And once again their skills didn't let them down. They converted Stalin's old prisons into soundproof isolation cells. The walls were so thick that not a sound could get through them.'

'Either incoming or outgoing. I see. But anyway you managed to escape, abandoning your dog to its fate? And your family?'

'Managed to escape? That's a good one. They threw me out – for bad behaviour. Your Majesty has no idea of the effort required to get there. It is necessary seriously to antagonize the authorities, in order to provoke them into arresting you and confining you to a soundproof isolation cell. This requires immense suffering. Being sentenced to prison is not nearly as easy and simple as English parliamentarians suppose. You have to earn the nation's respect. You have to become a hero to your fellow countrymen. Of course, if you've got friends and connections who can fix things for you, getting to prison's easier. Especially if you've already got friends inside, better still relations. Then you can demand to be sent to prison because, according to the Geneva Convention, families have a right to be reunited.'

'I was told that you had a lady with a little dog. I was told that you swore you would be faithful to her unto the grave. What became of her when you managed to get into your privileged isolation cell? Did she and the dog have to stay and wait for you, to the tune of Joseph's dreadful howls?'

Everyone instinctively fell silent. Their not entirely sober pantomime had suddenly taken a serious turn, and their speeches were beginning to get hurtful. Up to that moment Victor had pretended that he wasn't paying attention to their clowning. But now he raised his head and looked around, like an ageing father irritated by the turmoil some out-of-control children were causing round the house.

'In the matter of faithfulness to maidens, Your Majesty' – he joined in the charade with the crooked smile of a Dostoevsky character – 'maidens of that ilk only await the advent of some visiting foreigner before biting his whole hand off – just let them get a glimpse of the fingers and the hand is history. Take, for example, the case of my own dog, who came to New Jerusalem because she got a foreigner in the leg.'

'What a curious sense of logic you Russians have, comparing women to dogs.' Silva tried to keep on with her earlier stagey voice but then broke down. 'You began by denying your complicity in a crime, and will end by renouncing any kind of association with women or with dogs. That idiotic castle of yours. And what about our castle in Moscow, what about our life together? I was your queen, remember? I'd have given you any castle in the world. But you preferred a version built of plasticine in solitary confinement.' Her voice started to tremble. 'So where does the lady of your heart dwell now? In some Palestine or other?'

'Who are you talking to?' muttered Victor.

'We are not talking to anybody. We are giving you a lesson in manners in the presence of Her Majesty.' She spoke matter-of-factly, and there was tiredness in her voice. Everyone suddenly looked exhausted. Clearly the pantomime was over. It was time for Victor to step in.

'When we were in front of the Palace tonight,' he said hesitantly, as if he were trying to grope his way out of a tight spot blindfold, 'you started to inspect that man and woman worker with the hammer and sickle. But I couldn't take my eyes off the dark Palace windows. It was as if I could see a polished floor, with the candlelight reflected in it, heavy curtains hanging over the doors, and leather armchairs around a fireplace with crackling logs, and gleaming crystal glasses full of port. As I stood there watching, a light came on in an upper-storey window, then another, illuminating the cornice and the capital, the towers and the roof line. In one window, people started moving about, joining others in another window, behaving in a highly businesslike manner, preparing and organizing something. It was probably the servants, getting up before dawn, to get everything ready for the next day in good time. In other words those shadows in the window were living a life of their own, and even though it might have seemed like a mirage, it was a mirage that had nothing to do with me. Through the wrought-iron railings, the Palace looked like an alien Kremlin seen through the bars of a prison cell. It had nothing to do with my prison life; nothing to do with the plasticine castle of my prison mirages, with the models I'd made of my dreams during my Soviet years. There in the Palace, in the royal castle, were real people, servants and their masters, living their own lives, without any relation to how we imagine them to be living, without any relation to our crazy conception of our own lives. I had no power whatsoever over them, not even the power of imagination, to make them into what I wanted them to be. They were too preoccupied with their own affairs, and viewed in the light of their absorption in their concerns that clay castle of mine seemed like a vulgar and ugly nightmare. What had seemed, in the Siberian frosts, to be a castle in the air, became a chunk of plasticine that melted away in the heat of the night, to become a grey formless blob. And the time has come to get rid of it as quickly as possible, to throw it down the drain and get the sticky remnants off my fingers.'

19

Asylum

'In other words, Pushkin's translation followed Wilson's original so closely that all I had to do was copy out six of the 166 pages (*The City of the Plague and other Poems*, by John Wilson, second edition, printed by James Ballantyne & Co., Edinburgh, 1817) and the translation Lord Edward had commissioned of Pushkin's short tragedy would be done in a trice. True, there were problems with two of the "songs" in the poem, Mary's Scottish song and Walsingham's song. Mary's song was about life in the village before and after the plague. Dostoevsky, who only had a vague inkling of the existence of an original version of Pushkin's "translation", is full of praise for this song in his commemorative Pushkin speech, as an example of the way that Pushkin was able to get into the very spirit of another nation: "this English song, this melancholy British genius". But in fact there is nothing, in the whole of Pushkin's translation of Wilson's piece, more abstract, more smacking of German Romanticism, than Mary's song. The song is almost entirely his own invention. But the second song, the hymn in praise of the plague sung by Edward Walsingham, though not invented by Pushkin, has been totally changed in translation. In Wilson's version the President compares the fate of those who fall in battle on land and sea to those who die of the plague, and tries to convince his audience that the latter suffer less. He compares the plague to fever, tuberculosis and paralysis, endeavouring to prove that it is nobler than any of those afflictions. He praises the plague for tearing away the mask of hypocrisy and disposing of those who seek to stop others from enjoying their lives, for revealing the falsehood of judges and priests, for returning the miser's gold to its rightful owner, and granting lovers their freedom. On the other hand Wilson is constantly seeking to dethrone "the deadly King". And he declares that the enemy he has to struggle against (the fear of death) simply does not exist. Pushkin has no interest in all this teleology. Pushkin praises the act of triumphing over the fear of death, by means of taking pleasure in fear. Sensual pleasures – the maiden-roses – are rendered more acute by the awareness that "perhaps" they are fatal (breath, exhalations, "rotten with the plague"), become the pleasure taken in destruction itself, spiced with the thought that such pleasures "may be" a pledge, omens of everlasting life.

'"Whoever conquers pain and fear himself becomes a God; God is the pain of the fear of death," says one of Dostoevsky's "Devils". "All his life he sought out danger, grew drunk on it, so that his nature came to crave it. A constant exultation in victory and the knowledge that you could not be vanquished, that is what intoxicated them." There's nothing like that in Wilson, or if there is it's only hinted at. Reading Wilson, Pushkin unearthed the future outlines of Dostoevsky: the deceptive appearance of logic, with an undercurrent of madness. Dostoevsky, for whom the originality of Pushkin's rendering was in no sense suspect, begins the dramatic elaboration of lines of play, contained in Wilson's tragedy, that Pushkin's translation bypassed. Thus Dostoevsky's heroes are so spellbound, so hypnotized, by the nightmare in which they find themselves, that they are prepared to renounce their liberty and all earthly joys, simply to be able to contemplate and get their fill of this sinful and turbulent chaos, in the midst of the insulted and the injured. It is there that they begin to glimpse the uncreated light. You believe that we are insulted and injured, but in fact our weakness is our strength. You think that we are slaves, but in fact we are emperors.

'This is an ideological crossroads from which emerges Dostoevsky's main concept of the "socialism" of Aleko and Evgenii Onegin, and all who run away from the confusion and wretchedness of everyday life – to the gypsies, the people, to Utopias or foreign parts. "The truth, he believes, is elsewhere," Dostoevsky observes in his speech; "it may be somewhere in another country, a European one, for example, with a sense of order founded in history, the source of a stable social and political life." Walsingham has no time for such Utopias; he will remain where he is. "I cannot, must not follow you." Follow whom? The priests! Priests are persons of ideas, doctrines, concepts. Walsingham (and Dostoevsky with him) rejects orthodox religion and moralizing ideology, substituting for it a mystical "inner freedom", albeit one which admits sin and terror, but – once the fear of death has been conquered – one which also hopes that "beauty will save the world". It is a militant kind of mysticism; otherwise it would be impossible to understand Walsingham's last lines, which he directs at the priest: "Go in peace, but a curse on whoso'er goes with you." That is to say, a curse on whoever is led, not by their inner self, but by the authority of an idea. Or, in Dostoevsky's terms, "The truth is not outside you, it is in you; find yourself in your self, grow obedient to your self, win mastery over your self and you shall see the truth." To put it more succinctly: "Humble yourself, proud man!"'

Felix closed his notebook and reached for the sherry decanter. He downed the contents of his glass in one gulp, wiped his brow and leant back in his chair triumphantly, like an actor after a particularly brilliant performance.

'Well, well, well.' Dr Genoni clapped his hands in a token gesture of appreciation. 'Do you mean to say that Dostoevsky wouldn't have approved of your emigration away from your "inner self"? Amazing how they believed in that "inner self". And they also believed in a "world" that had to be saved. It's become clear to us that if anyone does go out and save some world or other, it won't be the world that I, or you, or even they, had in mind. Why didn't you tell Victor you were pregnant?' he asked, pouring Silva a glass of sherry. The question was so unexpected and was put in such a shamelessly direct way that at first Silva could not believe her ears and sat there speechless. The golden liquid in her glass glowed from within, in the light of the setting sun, and the glow was reflected on the plasticine castle on the cottage windowsill seen from afar.

'Because Victor would simply have taken it as a cry for help and nothing more. And I'd promised myself I'd give up going to him for help,' she said at last in a quiet voice, clasping her hands in her lap.

'Wasn't it because you once did something that would make any cry for help seem like an admission of guilt and a plea for forgiveness?' asked the doctor, pressing his point.

'What happened was no betrayal, but Victor might have taken it for one,' she said after a slight hesitation.

'You mean that business about his father's country villa

being searched?' Dr Genoni made it clear that he was by no means ill-informed.

'So Victor has already told you his version? And did he mention the typist too?'

'Victor said that you were so crazy with jealousy that you were taken in by a bunch of letters the security services had forged, love letters between the typist and him.' Dr Genoni deliberately let drop another bit of information.

'Forged, is that what he said? Forged by the security services? What other good things did he have to say about me?' A bitter smile twisted her lips.

'He said that in a fit of jealous rage you told them they used to meet at his father's villa. The KGB searched it immediately, found copies of Solzhenitsyn, and this all led to arrests, interrogations, trials and so on. Did you really tell them about the villa?'

'Did he say that I did?'

'All he said was that you knew about it,' Felix chimed in. He felt rather uncomfortable. He did not like this conversation, did not like it at all. Of course they were here to rake over their past for the clues to the present disaster – but not to scratch the sore wounds over and over again. 'He said that you knew he used that dacha as a samizdat hiding place.'

'And that he used to meet the typist there? He really said that the KGB showed me forged letters?' Silva continued her counter-interrogation.

'Forgeries, and the fact that you gave them the address, and even the typist's name.'

'I didn't give them one single name, or any address for that matter. And the letters were not forgeries. The only people involved in their writing were the signatories.' Now Silva was clearly waiting for the next question, well prepared.

'How can you be certain? Can you tell forged handwriting from an original?' asked Dr Genoni. It was as if the two of them, Silva and Genoni, had rehearsed the whole conversation in advance, for Felix's delectation.

'No, but I saw the original,' Silva replied promptly. 'I saw one of those letters before they started shoving them under my nose during my interrogation. Before going to the Lubyanka, in a state of panic, just before we were about to be searched after Victor's latest arrest, I was trying to get rid of the files and was shoving papers away in various hiding places. That's when I found Victor's unfinished letter to her. Later the KGB men showed it to me together with some others they'd taken from her when she was being searched. I couldn't possibly read the letter. I felt sick. With despair and hopelessness. If someone close to me could write a letter like that, what might not others be capable of?' Silva's lips began to tremble, and she started to straighten her hair, in order to brush her eyes with the back of her hand. 'Why can't one forget rubbish like that? It was so banal. The letters of a shifty, vulgar bigamist.'

Something clicked in Felix's mind as if he had cracked the secret code of this conversation. Dr Genoni was trying to expose Victor to Felix as yet another treacherous slave of the Soviet system. And Silva, for all her trembling lips and wet eyes, was helping the doctor willingly. The awful thing was that Felix was anxious to find out something nasty about Victor's past in order to be able to demolish the hero, to debunk him as yet another Soviet hypocrite. Still, parodoxically, he wanted to keep that nasty secret to himself, between himself and Victor. He did not want it to be done in front of Dr Genoni, or even Silva. How dare she?

'And you officially confirmed that they were his letters, his handwriting?' asked Felix. Silva nodded. 'But that meant that their relationship was confirmed and, as it were, officially registered. And they could have issued a warrant in her name.'

'In the first place, they knew perfectly well who the letters belonged to: the "My dearest, sweetest, gentlest Julia" of the correspondence was well known to every man in the street as the best underground typist in Moscow. Besides, she was stupid enough to make copies of her correspondence with Victor (for posterity?), on her own typewriter. And the KGB could recognize it from a mile off. So my identification of their handwriting made no difference whatsoever.' She sighed. 'I know it's disgraceful all the same, and it would have been better if I hadn't. But I really was mad with rage.'

'What happened to Julia, the typist?' asked Felix.

'She . . .' Silva hesitated. 'She tried to hang herself. Later she tried to kill herself again, under a train. Since then she's been in a psychiatric ward.'

'Incredible. Anna Karenina all over again!' Dr Genoni got up from his garden chair and started walking excitedly round the table. 'What an amazing country! Amazing! Russians behave with such a bookish passion.'

'After the suicide bid, I decided to emigrate. I thought: enough of all this literature.'

'You mean to say that it wasn't you, it was her who broke under pressure, told them the address of the villa and what was hidden there and so on, and then couldn't forgive herself?' asked Felix after some calculations.

'Quite possibly. Probably, even. She told them about the hiding place and the manuscripts. But I'm absolutely convinced that they knew all about it anyway, without her. That's their favourite sport, their idea of a good time: to draw everybody in and make them feel guilty. To burden us all with the sense of our own guilt. In the meantime our friends all started to hound me. Victor'd done a magnificent job. It's stupid to try to prove that you were innocent, not involved, especially to someone who believes that no one can ever be innocent, or uninvolved.'

'So is that why you decided, that evening, when he was so slow in coming, that hot August evening, that you decided . . . to be with me?' Felix tried to avoid looking at her.

Silva could scarcely conceal her smile. 'It's so easy to make men feel guilty: they're so egocentric. They always think everything revolves round them – which is why they feel responsible for everything, and guilty about everything.'

'But this time you have no one to share the guilt with. The Soviet regime is the last effective cure for loneliness.' Dr Genoni rubbed his hands in satisfaction.

'Now I know what I don't like about our conversation,' Felix exploded under the astonished stares of Silva and the doctor. 'Don't you see that we are doing exactly the same now, trying out again and again this Soviet recipe for collective paradise by proving to each other that we are all shit, that we are all guilty and accomplices and no better than the KGB itself. A perfectly organized piece of mutual blackmail. After spending quite a few years abroad, I am inclined to call this uniquely servile form of mutual dependence "friendship Russian-style". It's amazing – if that crazy lord hadn't turned up in our émigré world I would never have given all this a moment's thought.'

'Don't get carried away by all this intellectual breast-beating.' Dr Genoni gave Felix a friendly pat on the shoulder.

'Your tragically complicated and amoral relationship is not as unusual as you suppose. Your triangle, and in particular the relationship between Victor, Silva and Julia, is straight out of *The Two Gentlemen of Verona*. Don't forget that Russia got everything from the West, good, bad and ugly. What seems to you a Dostoevskian tragedy is actually no more than a Shakespearian comedy; so carry on as you began. Carry on.' Dr Genoni gesticulated at them like a director asking his players to continue their performance.

20

By the Waters of Babylon

The Soviet poet-translator had got his own way. He had captured the attention if not of the whole audience then at least of one important listener. The keeper-lord Edward-Edmund was sitting, glassy-eyed, as if he had been nailed to the chair in the corner, the irrepressible Kupernik hovering over him like a lugubrious owl, bending and straightening to the resounding beat of his biblical verses. In the midst of the sound of petty quarrelling and the settling of old scores he had managed to corner Edward-Edmund, and now his vocal chords were doing their utmost finally to drown out the last futile attempts at conversation. He read in the traditional Russian manner – with a kind of sobbing howl, so that every over-insistent sonorous rhyme came out sounding like a slowly executed slap in the face. It made you want to look away, cover your face with your hands, protect yourself. But having smoked his fill of hashish, Edward-Edmund sat there absolutely expressionless, as if he were quite deaf to the sound of rhymed lamentation, and the molten flow of the waters of Babylon rushing through Kupernik's doggerel. Which was scarcely surprising; he had only managed to learn two phrases of Russian: 'Let's have a drink' and 'Beware of the Dog.' When Kupernik had read himself to a standstill, all that could be heard in the embarrassing silence was his panting, the wheeze of an out-of-breath speaker. Then a short snort from one of the guests broke the silence, bringing to an end the serene snooze which most of the audience had fallen into. That rousing sound proved to Kupernik that the guests slumped on the chairs and the sofa among the debris of the party were not dead bodies, victims of his recital. Edward-Edmund was the first to clap.

'Jolly interesting sound,' he said, an expression of mild curiosity on his face. 'You could use a sound like that to call pheasants at feeding time.'

'It was a translation of the Psalms,' Kupernik informed him with polite scorn, somewhat on his high horse.

'Which psalms?' asked Silva in a hostess's attempt to divert attention from the absence of enthusiasm in the audience.

'What do you mean, which psalms?' Kupernik was bewildered. 'The Psalms of King David. Haven't you read them? It's a wonderful book, the Bible, an excellent read. Though I'm afraid the translation's no good.'

'Did you study classical Hebrew?' asked Felix, his voice tinged with envy.

'No I didn't. Why should I?' Kupernik gave a dismissive shrug.

'So what language did you translate from?' asked Felix.

'I used a crib. That's what I always work from,' replied Kupernik, quite unperturbed.

'What crib? What part of the Bible is a crib?' Felix couldn't understand what Kupernik meant.

'The whole thing is a disgraceful mess,' Kupernik started to elaborate in the tone of a high school teacher. 'You can't possibly call it a professional translation. It's a crib, and the work of an amateur at that. You know perfectly well what the interpreters and translators of Ancient Greek were like in old Russia. They got everything mixed up, used appalling archaisms. It's all pointless, all a handicap as the English say. They obscure the absolutely modern significance of the biblical Psalms.'

'Appalling archaisms? Obscure?' Felix looked stunned. 'Do you realize what kind of rubbish you're talking? Don't you realize that the Russian Bible, whether or not it was a bad translation from the Greek, or whether even it was just plain wrong from start to finish, is the Russian language. Take it or leave it. Are you proposing to translate Russian into Russian?'

'But unlike some others, I'm not blindly following the original. I'm using rhyme,' said Kupernik partly defensive and partly proud of himself.

'Rhyme?!' Felix couldn't believe his ears. 'Are you going to put the whole Russian language into rhyme? Aren't King David's *vers libres* good enough for you?'

'You don't look like King David. You look more like a pheasant,' Edward-Edmund remarked, joining in this linguistic discussion from his corner. His logic was clearly breaking down. 'Yes, I think you are King David's pheasant. But I am not your keeper.'

'But you are our Lord,' a stoned Mary-Louise continued in the same vein.

'Here I am held by the soft balmy kisses of this lost creature, lost, but beautiful, even in her sin,' mumbled Edward-Edmund. He sounded like a perfect Walsingham from John Wilson's tragedy.

'And we will build Jerusalem, on England's green and pleasant land,' Mary-Louise sang to him softly.

'You're already unpleasantly green,' Silva told her, irritated by their cryptic exchange.

Kupernik moved closer to their side, glad to get away from that impertinent Felix and seize another opportunity to continue his recital.

'Jerusalem. Yes, yes. Oh Jerusalem! Down by the waters of Babylon-Assyria, your people in exile can only grow sillier,' he declaimed. 'An original assonance, don't you think, Assyria – sillier? With sort of a Yevtushenko – Voznesensky rhythm, you know, to give it all a contemporary feel. Babylon-Assyria, of course, is Soviet Russia (there's even a visual echo between "Assyria" and "Russia") where Jewish refuseniks dream of repatriation to Israel. There was a guitar player in the Zionist movement who even wanted to set my translation of the psalm to music. It would have made for, you know, a kind of March of the Refuseniks: "Beneath the tyrant's iron heel, We dream of thee O Zion, Jerusalem you make us feel, That we have wings to fly on." And then the chorus: "Oh Jerusalem! Down by the waters of Babylon-Assyria, your people in exile can only grow sillier." He did a magnificent job with the arrangement and everything. But then the guitarist emigrated to Israel to the delights of pitta and falafel, and left us weeping down by the waters of Babylon-Assyria.'

'Yes, of course, you're all so spiritual over there. And we're all flesh. Physical and base. And you lot are pure spirit. Meat we've got, but we have no spirituality,' remarked Braverman sarcastically, coming up behind Kupernik. He joined in, together with Sorokopyatov. They both woke up at the first sound of an argument about emigration and spirituality.

'In spirit we are with you,' Sorokopyatov gave Kupernik a pat on the shoulder. 'Our bodies are here, but our spirit, if you permit me to say so, is with you. We have, as it were, rented our bodies out. So what should we be called? Zombies? The living dead? The material envelope is here, but the spiritual contents, our souls, if you like, are behind the Iron Curtain, in a place not of this world.'

'Since all of us here, with the exception of Comrade Kupernik, are living corpses, I suggest we all move to the Kidron Valley in Jerusalem – the most holy Jewish cemetery in the world; and the place where the resurrection of the dead will begin.' Felix couldn't pass up an opportunity of teasing poor Kupernik. He poured the remnants of gin from the bottle into the glasses and clinked his with Kupernik's. 'Next Year in Jerusalem?'

'Jerusalem? Israel?' The stoned Edward-Edmund resurfaced. 'They should be sending pheasants there, not Russian Jews. Let them kill the pheasants instead of killing one another. I prefer another Jerusalem, the one in the heavens, or even the one in the picture. I saw Jerusalem somewhere in this flat.' He got up off the floor unsteadily. Everyone stood back, afraid of this tall figure that swayed ominously, ready to fall and crush everything in its path. Silva and Mary-Louise stepped in like two nurses, took him by the arms and led him into Felix's room. Kupernik heaved a sigh of relief. He obviously didn't know how to react to that strange individual of mysterious origin.

'I don't understand what pheasants have to do with it? Jerusalem and pheasants, what's the link?' He gave an exasperated shrug as Edward-Edmund was being escorted from the room.

'Simple really, our lord exchanges pheasants for dissidents,' replied Felix.

'Crazy birds for crazy dissidents. In order to keep the distribution of loonies throughout the world in proper equilibrium.'

'And in the course of the exchange you can get bitten by a mad dog,' added Karvalanov, with a conspiratorial wink at Felix. Without exchanging a word, in a strange twist of emotions they suddenly felt united behind Edward-Edmund against the insolent intruder Kupernik. They were teasing him and enjoying it.

'You, Felix, called him a lord, but Karvalanov, I believe, referred to him as a gamekeeper. What a peculiar title, Lord Gamekeeper!' Kupernik blinked and smiled ingratiatingly, failing to appreciate Felix and Karvalanov's dark exchange.

'I don't see anything peculiar about it,' said Felix with

feigned indifference. 'There are all sorts of lords, Lord Privy Seal, Lord Gamekeeper. A lord in charge of the royal keepers.'

'Like the Lord Hofmeister?' Kupernik demonstrated the extent of his knowledge.

'Hofmeister? What is this, German beer or something?' frowned Felix.

'That is the Russian term with which the most recent edition of the *Geographic Encyclopaedia* translated the title Lord Chamberlain,' announced Kupernik diffidently.

'Let me assure you that the Lord Chamberlain should be Lord Kammerherr, and not a Hofmeister at all.'

'There are various fashions in translation,' a somewhat embarrassed Kupernik continued to insist. 'You know I'm not bothered by all these titles you have over here. If it's Chamberlain, then it's Chamberlain, if it's Keeper, well and good, let it be Keeper.' He hastened to pour oil on the waters. 'It's just that it's not every day that you meet an English lord. You like to know what sort of lord and what you should call him. That's obvious. Do you know, I agree with our Fedor Mikhailovich. What Russia needs is a dozen noble men, those aristocrats of the spirit that Russia was created for.'

'What Fedor Mikhailovich?'

'Dostoevsky of course. And how, may I ask, is your Lord Gamekeeper known?'

'As Edward, Lord Edward,' replied Karvalanov with a straight face.

'Edward, Lord Edward? Your benefactor, your saviour?'

'The same. He exchanged Karvalanov's dog for a Chilean pheasant,' said Felix.

'But I met him last year in Rome – has he really changed as much as that?' Kupernik was genuinely puzzled. 'Or was it in Missolonghi, where, as you may know, Byron died, and I attended a conference on Scottish literature, if my memory serves me right. Do you know, in Scotland they welcomed me as one of their own. I even spent the night in Robert Burns's bed. Perhaps it was in Scotland that I ran into Lord Edward. I wonder why he didn't recognize me?'

'These things happen. It's like the joke about the Jew,' said Felix, imitating a Jewish accent: '"How you've changed, Rabinovich." "But I'm not Rabinovich!" "There you are! Not even Rabinovich any more!"' No one laughed. Everyone in the room was silently following this bizarre conversation about the lord's identity.

'Perhaps there are two Lord Edwards in England?' suggested Kupernik on his own initiative. 'Two lords with one and the same name. Namesakes.'

'It could well be,' said Karvalanov, welcoming this strange suggestion. 'Namesakes. The more so since our Lord Gamekeeper is clearly suffering from a split personality.'

'But excuse me, in this case one personality seems to have split into two lords,' observed Kupernik dubiously.

'Two lords are better than one,' said Felix. 'Contacts, contacts, contacts.'

'But that means that one of the lords is pretending to be someone he's not.' Kupernik ignored Felix's jocular tone. 'I can see Lord Edward's face in Rome as clear as today. It was in Rome, Rome, absolutely, after my meeting with the Pope. He gave me his phone number.'

'Who, the Pope?' Karvalanov queried.

'Lord Edward. Gave me his phone number and invited me to come and stay. I always wanted to stay with a real English lord. I even remember the address: Gamekeeper's Cottage, Thanksgiving Lane,' Kupernik announced. Victor and Felix exchanged glances as Kupernik leafed through his address book. 'All we have to do is telephone and the whole mess will sort itself out, and we'll discover which is the real lord and which one is the phoney pretender. Where's the telephone?' he asked, trying to get into Silva's room, but Victor and Felix barred the way.

'Look, in London the telephone is an expensive luxury. This isn't Moscow, where people can jabber for hours,' Felix started to explain to Kupernik, with bureaucratic insistence, fiddling with the lapel of his leather jacket. 'They charge by the minute here, and the rate depends on the distance. If we were to let anyone who comes here make calls all over the place, all the translations in the world couldn't pay for it. So only the residents get to use the telephone.' Just then Silva entered the room and, feeling the highly charged atmosphere, stared at Felix inquisitively. 'Comrade Kupernik wants to telephone Lord Edward in Rome,' Felix explained to Silva.

'Not Rome, his estate in Kent,' Kupernik hastened to correct him.

'But Lord Edward is in the next room,' said Silva.

'Imagine, Comrade Kupernik is of the opinion that it is not Lord Edward. He doesn't look the same as he did in Rome. In Rome he looked like a different person.'

'We'll have to wait for him to wake up to ask him why he's changed,' said Silva.

'A displaced person, displaced by alcohol and hash,' said Karvalanov.

'As far as I could tell, Lord Edward didn't recognize Kupernik either,' said Felix. 'It would seem that Kupernik too is not the same person. He was different in Rome and Lord Edward did not recognize him. Perhaps it's a different Kupernik? Perhaps there are two of them? And one is a fraud and a pretender.' With every word his voice was becoming less and less jocular, and more and more aggressive, even malicious. 'I cannot believe that a poet-translator of Kupernik's stature could produce such a talentless translation of the Psalms. The great Kupernik would never have used a crib.'

'What on earth are you talking about?' said Kupernik indignantly. 'I can confirm my identity. I've got a passport, a Soviet passport.'

'Exactly. How do you manage to travel about so freely with a Soviet passport?' asked Karvalanov.

'And another thing, what were you doing in Rome? Who invited you, the Pope?' Silva joined in the interrogation. The room fell quiet. Even Sorokopyatov and Braverman stopped quarrelling, and Mary-Louise had obviously sobered up. Kupernik stepped back as if being physically threatened.

'My ticket to Rome was paid for by Lord Edward.' He spoke more rapidly. 'You know how keen he is on developing East–West relations. I was there to attend a conference on Pirandello translation,' Kupernik observed somewhat self-importantly. 'Have you heard of Pirandello? He used to live in Rome.'

'Lived a double life.' Felix nodded his head.

'I am the main Russian-language translator of Pirandello, as you may know,' Kupernik informed Felix proudly.

'That's where I'd heard the name before.' Felix snapped his fingers. 'I thought it was Shchepkin-Kupernik and Shakespeare, or Copernicus and his solar system, but the answer was Pirandello!' he went on excitedly. 'You're the one who gave me all that trouble in Verona. It's a grotesque translation! Do you know what it's like to use your translation for a students' play-reading? You can't say a single line aloud, it all sounds horrible and the syntax is a total mess. How could you ever turn that melodious Italian into such an unspeakable Russian?'

'I didn't translate from the Italian,' Kupernik blushed and smiled feebly as if asking forgiveness.

'Another crib? Do you know, I'd rather have any crib than this thing of yours,' Felix replied to Kupernik's sad little nod. 'I wonder who did the literal version this time?'

'You wouldn't know him.' Kupernik waved dismissively. 'No one's heard of him. He used to teach Italian theatre. He's called Avestin. An intellectual drop-out. He's a sick old man, and not quite all there. He spent some time in hospital.' Kupernik tapped his temple, and then stopped dead in his tracks as he saw the three of them staring at him. He couldn't understand why these words had such a cataclysmic effect on the trio. Victor, jumped up and started walking round Kupernik, drawing menacingly close. Felix made a noise somewhere between a cough and a belch, and started cracking his finger joints in a kind of frenzy. Silva went across to the table and started collecting the dirty glasses. She dropped one on the floor.

'Not quite all there, is that it, not quite? And so you're a shrink too?' Karvalanov drew closer, biting his nails. 'So we wouldn't have heard of Avestin? He's a sick old man, is he? And who made him old and sick? I suppose you know who's normal and who isn't, who's the lord and who's the keeper, which is the original and which is the crib? Do you know that it was because of that translation of Pirandello that he went hungry, supported himself, earning God knows how little, by giving private lessons, and through your grace and favour spent time in a prison psychiatric hospital?'

'That's simply not true,' protested Kupernik. 'I used his translation after he'd been discharged. I helped him financially by commissioning a literal translation. He thanked me in writing,' he added desperately.

'And what else was he to do? Unlike you, as I understand it, he had not earned the gratitude of the Party and the Government, the Motherland and its People.' With every word from the Soviet patriotic vocabulary, Karvalanov was driven back into the frenzy of his Soviet past filled with venom and vengeance. 'Perhaps you'd like to tell us what you did to earn the confidence of these organs of government? Which brilliant translation did they mark down as a crib in order to present its distorted version as an academic masterpiece? Is that why they started to let you travel abroad so freely? And now perhaps they want another favour? Perhaps a short poetic account of the way that émigrés and ex-dissidents live in London?'

The suggestion was so appalling and unjustified that Kupernik, disbelief written all over his face, gave up the struggle. The dawn was about to break, and the electric bulb had become superfluous in the dim morning light.

'Shame on you, Victor.' He sighed in distress and made a dismissive gesture. 'A Soviet intellectual only has to get permission to take a couple of trips to the West, and immediately you suspect him of being an informer. After all the humiliations that getting this visa cost me! So what makes you so different from the KGB? You think the same way!'

'I'm just using that way of thinking as a crib. Felix, shouldn't we telephone Moscow and ask our friends who the poet-translator Kupernik really is?' said Karvalanov, moving towards the telephone. Kupernik thrust himself in his way and grabbed him imploringly by the hand.

'Please, no phone calls!' He wiped the sweat off his forehead and looked around him with the eyes of a hunted man begging for mercy. 'All right. I may have exaggerated a little about Lika and Vika, and all the others. I only know them by sight. But I so wanted to get to know Silva and you, Karvalanov. You know, in Moscow you're a legend. They tell stories about this house. You know, the émigré Bohemia, the hothouse of anti-Soviet propaganda. I just dreamt of seeing the legend. Can you imagine what'll happen to me if they, you know who, know I've been to Silva's flat? One call to Moscow and – they listen to all of them you know – and you can put a cross on my grave, or a yellow star for that matter. Have you really forgotten what it's like for us in Moscow? Of course I have to go to Party meetings and all that stuff. Party meetings or meetings of the union or something else of the sort. Everyone has to make do as best they can; we all lead this wretched double life. If they ever find out who I stayed with here they'll never let me out again.'

'So what are you doing criticizing others for leading a double life?' asked Silva.

'I thought that over here everything was different, that you'd

214

got away from the double life. Unlike some others, you didn't leave Russia for, as one might say, material advantage, you didn't desert like, you know, like . . .'

'Like rats from a sinking ship?' Felix prompted. 'But my dear Kupernik, besides the rats that abandon the sinking ship, there are the rats who remain behind in its dark corners.'

This classifying of rats according to their moral attitude to the question of emigration broke the vicious circle of personal innuendos and drew others into the argument.

'It was such a warm winter this year that it made all the rats of Blackheath come out,' interjected Mary-Louise, who was having some difficulty speaking clearly. 'They used to winter in the chalk pits and caves under the common here. But now they've all come out. Every morning we find a dead rat in our back garden. They put down arsenic to poison them and the Heath is covered with dead rats.' She hiccuped. 'If things carry on like this there's bound to be some kind of epidemic. What does the government think it's doing?'

'We've already got an epidemic, have had for some time; just look at the way everyone's coughing and sneezing,' said Braverman.

'It's the influence of art upon nature. It's doubtless all because of Felix's brilliant translation of Pushkin's "Festivities at the Time of Plague",' said Sorokopyatov.

This nonsensical exchange had given Kupernik a necessary respite from verbal humiliation. With every second he was regaining his composure and his ability to fight back. Miserable and full of self-pity when threatened, he was someone who became insolent and intolerant when he felt his power and strength.

'You've been after me like a rat all evening.' Kupernik turned to Felix and stuck his chin out truculently. 'You came at me for being a Party man, and for using cribs. But unlike you I never made a secret of either fact.'

'What have I made a secret of? Pushkin, perhaps?' quipped Felix with a shrug.

'No, in your case Pushkin was not the crib. But you made a secret of the fact that Pushkin's text is a translation from the English. You concealed its original, you made a secret of John Wilson.'

'I didn't make a secret of anybody.' Felix stopped in his

tracks. 'It's there in Pushkin, in black and white: "From the tragedy by Wilson".'

'If you'd been translating Wilson into Russian, Pushkin would have provided the crib. But you're proposing the original English text as your translation of Pushkin. It's no longer just a case of using a crib, or imitating original material, this is plagiarism pure and simple!' Now Kupernik was holding the stage. He was standing in the middle of the room, clearly rising on his toes with every word, as if stretching himself after a long sleep. 'All evening I have been trying to avoid the subject. But I cannot remain silent any longer. It's the kind of thing you can only get away with abroad. You émigrés have severed your ties with Russia and so you think that this sort of literary crime will go unpunished. You don't suppose anyone will notice? You're relying on the fact that no one's heard of John Wilson? But some people have. I'm a professional poet-translator, and I've done a bit of reading in my time; such as the articles Yakovlev wrote in the Twenties about Pushkin and Wilson. It's all laid out there. When I was in Scotland – where, did you know, I was offered Robert Burns's bed for the night (actually I think I already mentioned that, and anyway it's beside the point) – when I was in Scotland, I took the trouble to track down a distant relative of John Wilson, a most remarkable old lady named Jennifer Wilson. She recalls things that happened a hundred years ago as if it was yesterday. And she keeps in touch with literature. How do you suppose she felt when she saw the words of her distinguished ancestor described as a brilliant translation from the Russian done by some Soviet émigré with an unpronounceable name? I've compared your so-called translation to Wilson's original; you've changed absolutely nothing except for a comma or two. And now the *Times Literary Supplement* goes and praises you to the skies! This isn't even plagiarism, it's highway robbery!'

Kupernik's lips trembled; he was shaking all over, yet he continued to yell out his humiliating charges at Felix, like a screaming, scratching adolescent cornered by a crowd of his contemporaries. But then a deathly silence fell. Kupernik was breathing heavily and spasmodically. Trying not to notice the stares, and without saying a word, Felix continued to back away, looking for the exit, trod on something, slipped and fell to the floor, with his back against the wall. He groped around and much to his disgust came across a bone, which he picked up and threw into the opposite corner.

'Fuck that bitch,' he growled. 'Bones all over the place, just like a cemetery. I hope they're dog bones, bones to practise biting on. At least there are no human victims so far. Where is the bitch anyway? Where's Kashtanka, who started this whole sorry business?'

Everyone looked round. In the doorway, holding the dog on a leash, stood Dr Genoni.

21

Asylum

'In his shocking essay "Murder as one of the Fine Arts", De Quincey describes the murder of an old woman who, it was alleged, had some two thousand dollars in coin concealed somewhere in her residence. She was killed in the bedroom, and the body of her maidservant was found upon the stairs. Suspicion fell upon a local baker and upon a chimney-sweep. The crime had been committed at noon. The incident was described in the papers, where it was said that the murderer, who had shut himself in the bedroom with the dead woman, heard a knock at the door. De Quincey was much struck by the situation of a killer caught in the act by an innocent girl knocking at the door. "One night in high summer, when I lay tossing and sleepless for want of opium— I amused myself with composing the imaginary *Confessions of a Murderer*: which, I think, might be made a true German bit of horror, the subject being exquisitely diabolical; and, if I do not flatter myself, some few dozens of useless old women I could frighten out of their wits." Three amazing words stand out from this curious conception: "useless old women". A similar killing of "a useless old witch" deadened the imagination of Dostoevsky's Raskolnikov, who hacked an innocent maidservant to death after killing the old female money-lender. The ideas outlined by De Quincey in his essay ("Works of art could attain power and grandeur by evoking sensations of terror in their audience"), and his notion that everything is permitted only to persons of genius ("It only shows the danger that dunces run into, when they imitate men of genius"), are Raskolnikov's ideas in *Crime and Punishment*.

'Dostoevsky was greatly taken with Thomas De Quincey, and even planned to translate his *Confessions of an English Opium Eater*. But Dostoevsky had no idea that De Quincey's *Confessions* and his essay about murder as one of the fine arts were much touted by Wilson both in his journal and in his parodic records of conversations held by the regulars of Ambrose's Tavern, his "Noctes Ambrosianae". When Dostoevsky considers "Festivities at the Time of Plague", he doesn't realize that Wilson and De Quincey were good friends, or, the most important point, that those bits of Pushkin that were important to Dostoevsky found their way into Wilson's drama thanks to Thomas De Quincey.

'"They met in the breakfast room at Allan Bank," writes Grevel Lindop, a chronicler of the Lake District, ". . . De Quincey, failing to find in Wordsworth the father-figure he had sought, was ready to accept Wilson as a protective 'elder brother' . . . Both men loved walking and thought nothing of a brisk sixteen-mile hike. Wilson was also interested in cock-fighting. He kept his own birds [*sic!*] and bred them with meticulous care, matching them against neighbours' birds at 'mains' which attracted crowds of spectators. Once a main of cocks was actually fought in the drawing-room at Elleray (Wilson's house), the unfinished flooring being covered with turf for the occasion." But one should not suppose that Wilson preferred cocks and pheasants to the trusty hound. He was fond of dogs too. To the point that when he held the chair of Moral Philosophy at Edinburgh University, he was an object of mirth to the students specifically because of "his habit of keeping his dogs under the lectern, absent-mindedly treading on them as he talked and eliciting yelps of pain."

'The parodic nature of Wilson's professorial persona (his ludicrous habit of rubbing his forefinger against his nose at the end of every paragraph) was compounded by his total ignorance in matters philosophical. "What constitutes moral obligation? What should be read on the Stoics and Epicureans? He asked De Quincey to send him some long letters on such points, adopting 'some ingenious disguise as to your object in writing' –so that no one would guess that De Quincey was writing his lectures for him." The question of who was borrowing from whom pursued De Quincey all his life, partly because he wrote slowly, with great difficulty, and used constantly to air his every idea out loud, during after-dinner conversations with friends; the friends would listen attentively then go home and carefully write down everything they had heard. Thus De Quincey's paranoia is totally justified when, for example, he starts accusing Coleridge himself of borrowing from second-rate

German authors. (I wonder what he would have said about the translatory nature of the poetry of Zhukovsky, Pushkin's mentor?)'

He was plundered, in a literary sense, in precisely the way that Coleridge had plundered the German Romantics. The similarity to Coleridge was compounded by externals – they were both drug addicts. "Hang you!" exclaimed Wilson one evening, "can't you take your whisky toddy like a Christian man, and leave your damned opium slops to infidel Turks, Persians and China men?"

'Amongst the "dark reflections" De Quincey called up from his own dreams were three women whom he named "Our Ladies of Sorrow". He associated the Ladies with the three Fates, the three Furies and the three Graces.

'Three women feature in Pushkin-Wilson's "Festivities at the Time of Plague". One of them is Jenny, from the song Mary sings to the President of the festivities, that selfsame dead Jenny that Edmund will only rejoin in a better place. On earth, at the plague-stricken feast, he is in the thrall of Mary, "a fallen creature though a dear one", and in the President's delirious ravings there recurs, as if in a reprise of the song Mary sang at the beginning of the piece, the image of his dead wife Matilda, the third of Our Ladies of Sorrow.

'Wilson's repertoire had included rather a good impersonation of De Quincey. When Wilson died, De Quincey, perhaps with a feeling of having the last laugh, repaid the compliment and treated mutual friends to impressions of Wilson lecturing:

> I rise to give, most noble President,
> The memory of a man well known to all,
> Who by keen jest and merry anecdote . . .
>
> Much cheer'd our out-door table, and dispell'd
> The fogs with this rude visitor the Plague
> Oft breathed across the brightest intellect.
> But two days passed, and it cannot be
> That we have in our gamesome revelries
> Forgotten Harry Wentworth. His chair stands
> Empty at your right hand – as if expecting
> That jovial wassailer – but he is gone
> Into cold narrow quarters.

Harry Wentworth's chair has been taken by Edward Walsingham, the new President. In place of jokes and bitter witticisms, we hear hymns to the plague. Was it perhaps De Quincey himself that Wilson had placed in the President's chair? And who is Harry Wentworth? Wordsworth? Or Coleridge? Or, as if the poem were a kind of prophecy, was it a posthumous self-portrait on the part of Wilson? In Pushkin's translation Wentworth has become Jackson. So did Pushkin's translation evict Wilson from the chair of literary history? Besides, as regards the passage we best remember in Pushkin's translation, the hymn to the plague, surely Pushkin stole it, not from Wilson, but from the future Dostoevsky, who was so steeped in the works of De Quincey?'

22

The dress rehearsal

'Had it not been for Kashtanka, my dear Russian friends, I would never have found my way here,' said Dr Genoni, giving the dog a friendly pat. 'She led me to this political asylum. Nothing in foreign parts is as complicated and confusing as the side streets of South London. All you have to do is cross the river, and it's as if you've gone abroad – which makes the sight of old familiar faces doubly agreeable.' His suave manner, like that of a doctor at the deathbed of a rich patient, could not conceal the way his stern eyes scrutinized the room as if assessing the damage caused by naughty children. In the hazy morning light, his tall bulky figure looked like a mighty apparition who had come to warn the earth dwellers of their imminent comeuppance. Everyone in the room felt as if they had been caught in the act of indecency. With a half-smile Genoni watched Felix rising from the floor, a bone in his hand, and then turned to Victor. 'So was it you, Victor, who showed what was once your own dog the door because you'd started to identify it with the keeper? Or did Felix banish it into exile because he began to associate it with the concept of plagiarism? I've been standing here and listening for quite some time. What an admirable series of reappraisals. But isn't it strange that however much someone reappraises his position, he stays basically the same? It's like a signature; you can alter it any way you like and still the scrawl is recognizable as yours. Even if you can't see it, others will. You can forget somebody's name, and associate it with someone else's face, associate that face with someone entirely different, but you won't forget the actual face, the person! Let's ask Mr Kupernik. He certainly remembers my face, but doesn't know who I am, do you?'

'Of course I know who you are. On the contrary, we were just talking about your "identification", so to speak.' Kupernik ran forward, enthusiastic about the new visitor. In fact, he was not absolutely sure where they had met before, but the gentleman would no doubt protect him from this kangaroo court of anti-Soviet conspirators. He remembered the aristocratic figure very clearly. 'We met in Rome,' he guessed. 'Moreover it was you, and not Evgenii from Radio Vatican, who got me the pass that enabled me to meet the Pope. I've just remembered that Evgenii had already been dismissed for ecumenical tendencies. So that you alone, Lord Edward, could have got me that pass.'

'None of us, my dear Kupernik, has ever seen Lord Edward,' said Dr Genoni, settling into an armchair and lighting a cigar. Kupernik, fidgeting, raised his bushy brows and opened his mouth in surprise, about to say something. 'No, you heard me perfectly. Let me tell you a secret. Even I, the famous Genoni, his personal doctor, advisor and private secretary for charitable affairs, have never, ever encountered Lord Edward face to face. I have spoken to him on the telephone, we have communicated by letter. But during the two years I have worked for him, whenever I've been on the estate, working in the clinic, he's been abroad; whenever he returns I've been travelling abroad on his orders.' He studied the ash forming on the tip of his cigar. 'To tell you the truth, I got here as soon as I could in the hope that I would finally have the opportunity to meet him face to face. Scotland Yard telephoned to say that Lord Edward had been detained in St James's Park under mysterious circumstances in the company of the dissident Karvalanov. I concluded either that Lord Edward had slipped into the country to meet Victor incognitio, or that his alter ego, Edmund the keeper, had got him mixed up in his idiotic canine conspiracy again. When I was greeted by a barking Kashtanka I realized that, once again, I should not be seeing Lord Edward.'

'So my doubts as to identity are not, as the English would say, entirely groundless? So this Lord Edward of yours is not Lord Edward?' Kupernik turned triumphantly towards Victor and Felix.

'In the same sense, shall we say, that the present Pope, John Paul, is a Pole named Wojtyla,' Dr Genoni replied on behalf of the two friends. Kupernik noticed with alarm that, contrary to his expectations, Genoni was not entirely on his side. 'Pope John Paul is an idea, a symbol, a profession of faith, and the Pole Wojtyla is a real person. Remember your own meeting with the Pope. You didn't understand a single word of your audience with the Pole Wojtyla, and yet every moment of your encounter, every word he said, is precious to you. Because you saw, in the Pole Wojtyla, the Pope John Paul VI. A noble fiction means more to us than mundane facts. Our keeper is the hypostasis of our lord.'

'Maybe, but pardon, as the French say, I haven't yet reached the mental condition of the Pirandello hero who saw in every servant the hypostasis of Pope Gregory VII. Pardon, but none of my screws are loose. So don't try to confuse me.' At this point he lifted his chin defiantly and his whole posture acquired a defensive and absurd aloofness. 'A Pole can be a pope, but a gamekeeper can never be a lord. If a gamekeeper thinks he's a lord he needs treatment.'

'A gamekeeper can't be a lord. But a lord can become a gamekeeper. And that is the foundation on which I am going to base Edmund's treatment, and I think we all want to see him get well again,' said Dr Genoni, looking enigmatically at everyone in the room. 'That's why you were all brought here,' he added, smiling like an omniscient dictator.

'Who brought us?' Karvalanov frowned. 'I don't like the sound of this. Do you mean someone lured us all here? Who did?'

'Let's say I did, pursuant, of course, to Lord Edward's instructions, in so far as I could divine his intentions.' Dr Genoni sat up in his chair like a lecturer coming to the most important part of his discourse. 'Let's start with pheasants. I mean the estate's financial affairs. Because of the notorious tragic accident that took place nearly fifty years ago, pheasant shooting has ceased entirely ever since Lord Edward took over the running of the estate. Since there could be no question of getting rid of the keepers and farm workers involved in pheasant rearing – that would never do – the pheasants are quite simply sold, as I told you before, to zoos and to shoots in countries where it is necessary to prevent the genocide of the local fauna. Of course, such *Geschäft*, as Felix would put it, is not all that profitable. It's charity, not business. The estate is on the verge of bankruptcy, and until Edmund has recovered, Lord Edward will not permit shooting to start again. The situation drives the keeper mad.'

'What keeper? D'you mean the son of that dead keeper? Our Edmund, the parricide?' asked Karvalanov.

'So the impostor is a parricide too?' Kupernik spread his hands in a despairing gesture.

'Let me say it again.' Dr Genoni gave a tired sigh, as if he were addressing a particularly dense fifth form. 'Edmund is the son of a former keeper. When Lord Edward is away he believes that he is Lord Edward – the son of the lord who accidentally killed his keeper during a shoot. Edmund-Edward is convinced that the estate's present keeper is Edmund, son of the former keeper, who is out to avenge himself on Lord Edward, that's to say on him, Edmund.' The furrowed brows of all those present were proof of how hard his listeners were trying to follow Dr Genoni's logic.

'In point of fact they're actually second cousins, Edmund and the current keeper, right? Old Charlie from the White Horse told us,' Mary-Louise declared confidently. 'Because the keeper who got shot was Charlie's brother, or a cousin maybe? I don't remember, but anyway they were related, right, and this keeper is a nephew of his.' She rounded off the sentence with less certainty in her voice than she started with.

'Charlie didn't say anything about this keeper.' Felix corrected her with a certain relish, rescuing from oblivion an episode from his London past that now seemed as remote in his memory as Moscow was geographically. 'He actually said that he and the former keeper were brothers or cousins, so that Edmund is his nephew. That's all he said. This keeper is someone completely unrelated.'

'Mary-Louise, you will be rendering a serious service to psychiatric science if you can draw up the family tree of Lord Edward's keeper,' said Dr Genoni. 'The present keeper, the last scion of the line, is due for a breakdown. Like any self-respecting keeper he can't see the point of rearing pheasants that no one shoots. Currently, in protest at Lord Edward's humanitarian attitude to pheasants, he's in East Berlin at the annual conference of gamekeepers. He'll soon have to be hospitalized as a political dissident.'

'I think that soon we'll all have to be hospitalized,' said Silva, breaking her self-imposed vow of silence.

'I can't wait!' cried Genoni with uncharacteristic enthusiasm. 'Especially if, Silva, I get you and Victor and Felix. The three of you together, what a treasure trove for us psychiatrists.' His face lit up at the thought. 'Although I am in charge of one of the most exclusive psychiatric hospitals in the world, I don't have the right to admit new patients. It is Lord Edward's wish that the clinic remain empty until its only inmate, Edmund, is well again. It is to that end that I brought you all to England.'

'So I can finally stop torturing myself with the question: why on earth did I emigrate?' said Felix with grave irony.

'Do you recall our Italian conversations, my dear Felix?' Dr Genoni turned to him. 'About the two techniques of acting, and the two ways of treating mental illnesses? A return to the original place and time. For Pirandello it was time that mattered the most.' He turned in his chair to face the rest of the guests, anxious to be understood by everyone in the room. 'In his play about Henry IV, the doctor-psychiatrist tries to take his deranged patient back to the very moment when he lost his reason and a new time began – the time of insanity. By bringing him mentally back to that crossroads, they hope to give him a jolt and, this time, make him tread the road of reason, as opposed to the road of madness. However much of a petty-bourgeois relativist Pirandello might have been, he believed in the march of time. What an amazingly confident time it was anyway, one that believed in itself, and in the existence of time itself, in a past, present and a future. They believed that you could take a look into the past and make corrections in the present to live the right sort of new and progressive life in the future. However, now that I study you émigrés from over there, I can see that, in actual fact, there is no time.'

'Of course no one has any time,' grunted Braverman. 'Like you, everybody these days is too busy.'

'By dint of studying your biographies, my dear Russian friends, and analysing your case histories, I came upon a remarkable fact. In the case of Soviet émigrés, the past is identified not with time, but with space, geography. A return to the past is a return to your home town. You can't go back again, not becaue time-travel is impossible, but because your home town is behind the Iron Curtain. Back in the USSR, time has come to a stop; you can enter and leave the past whenever you want. All you have to do is get back to where you used to be. There's no time, there's only space.'

'No space either,' said Sorokopyatov. 'Take a look, this émigré communal flat is so jam-packed you can't move.'

'For our purposes we need to move to new accommodation, to the open space of woods and fields. But your experiences, Karvalanov, show us that the concept of prison is a relative one, while you, Felix, have cast doubt upon the originality of the original. My idea is a simple one.' He rose from his chair impatiently and started pacing up and down the room in front of his listeners. 'Aren't we all, in one way or another, émigrés and dissidents in this world? All cut off from our pasts by an "iron curtain" of things done that cannot be undone. In order to restore an émigré to reason you have to break that taboo, enter the forbidden zone, cross the iron curtain and get back into the past. Our patient must regain his psychological past, not in time, but in space, by getting back to the situation in which the keeper first supposed himself to be a lord.' He stopped abruptly and looked over the heads of his audience towards the door.

'Especially since, unless I am much mistaken, the chief protagonist has already worked his way into the part. The dress rehearsal can begin.'

Dr Genoni stepped back furtively into the corner near the bookshelves as if trying to make himself invisible. Everyone turned and followed his glance towards the door. There stood the aristocratic keeper, leaning against the door-frame for support. Edmund looked frightful, with a midnight stubble, a velvet bow-tie dangling round his neck like a hangman's noose, a dazed expression and drug-crazed eyes shining with the mad stare of a fanatic from under red and swollen lids. He looked like a tramp. He was carrying some scraps of torn-up newspaper.

'Who wants a number?' He surveyed the assembled company in the businesslike manner of a maniac. 'Anyone who wants to join the pheasant shoot must take a number, a badge, a yellow star,' he repeated and started going from guest to guest, presenting each of them with a scrap of newspaper with a number on it. 'Everyone participating in the shooting must affix the number to their chest. If we had sticks, as the ritual requires, you could have put the numbers on them, but there aren't any. There's just one mop to go round all the guns. Let me explain the ritual of the shoot to you ignorant foreigners. Gather round.' He bustled about like a kindergarten teacher, taking Silva, Victor and Felix by the hand. 'Number one, a thirty-yard gap, then number two, another thirty yards, then number three . . .' Smiling sheepishly, they all three took a number, muttered their thanks and continued to listen atten-tively to Edmund's instructions.

'On your marks,' Edmund ordered sharply. 'As soon as the

pheasants start to fly I'll call out a number – and you'll have a chance to settle accounts with the past. All these notions of treachery, jealousy and disappointment, all these stupid imaginary pheasants with their wings clipped – isn't it wonderful to let loose with both barrels and see their feathers fly? Victor, you shoot first. The truth does not come from fighting your father, and it's not concealed within castle walls. What appears to be a castle in the distance turns out to be a prison when you come close.' Victor was visibly startled as Edmund's delivery became more and more like that of a preacher. 'Felix, you no longer have to pretend to be someone you were not – take careful aim at your original self. It's the surest way to stop plagiarizing. And finally Silva. Your lovers disappoint you because they're obsessed with false ideals. But without that falsity you would never have loved them. Aim for sincerity, aim for the heart.'

'What's he doing, reading poetry?' The solemnity of this madness was already beyond Kupernik's comprehension 'Excusez-moi, but I find the English hard to understand.' Kupernik, naive as ever, and somewhat bemused by events, broke the deadly silence. Edmund turned towards the mysterious sound of Russian.

'And just what do you think you're doing here?' he asked Kupernik menacingly.

'I am a poet-translator, from Moscow,' he replied and all but showed him his passport in confirmation of his identity. He turned his eyes imploringly towards the rest of the company seeking support, but they all shrugged their shoulders helplessly, secretly relieved that Edmund's attention was directed at someone else.

'You don't look like a poet to me. Poets don't look so romantic. You're a poacher.' Edmund was closing in on him, ignoring Kupernik's protestations. 'Don't argue. To punish you I'm going to appoint you head beater. Ex-poachers make the best assistants, and some actually turn into gamekeepers. You have to make unpoetic sounds. Take this can and fork.' Edmund grabbed an empty beer can and, seizing a fork, began to drum deafeningly upon it. Then he took the other guests, starting with Mary-Louise and Sorokopyatov, by the hand, and woke the dozing Braverman with a shove. He handed each of them plates, cans, knives and forks. 'You're all beaters – go and stand in the corners, and drive the pheasants from under the sofas, from behind the cupboards and off the shelves. Are the guns ready? I can hear the beaters closing in, I can hear the dry leaves rustling under their feet; twigs snap, the noise-makers are rattling, there's shouting, there's a whirr of wings, prrrr, prrr, prrrr, and, snap, snap, snap, the guns are cocked. Bang, bang, bang, can you hear that deafening noise?'

'I think someone's knocking at the door.' Mary-Louise was the first to understand what Edmund was babbling about. 'I expect it's those damned Mackerels again!'

'What mackerels? Are we playing a fishing game? I don't understand. It's a pheasant shoot, isn't it?' A confused Kupernik obediently continued to beat the beer can with his fork. Edmund raised his hand abruptly and the room fell quiet.

'I knew he was here. The head keeper. Gamekeeper. It's all a game for him,' Edmund said, his voice sinking almost to a whisper. Taller than anyone else in the room, he was the first to notice when Dr Genoni, carrying his bag, left his corner and emerged from behind the backs of the guests. Everyone stepped aside, letting him through. Edmund walked towards him, a sacrificial smile on his lips. 'The hour has come, the circle has drawn tight.' He was almost chanting. 'The victim is ready. The gun's loaded. I'm waiting for the shot. That dastardly shot. That shot below the belt.' He sat down obediently. The doctor went up to him, opened his bag and took out a syringe and some ampoules.

'Please don't do it, please,' came the voice of Silva. She made a dash forward but was stopped by Felix and Victor holding her on either side.

'So now we have our main protagonist,' Dr Genoni said as he gave Edmund his injection. He turned to the guests and announced like a master of ceremonies: 'Now we need a change of scenery. How many characters in this shooting psychodrama? one, two three, four . . . and the beaters.' He counted those present on his fingers. 'I think three taxis should do it. We'll be at the estate in an hour, by which time the injection will have worn off and the play can begin.' Everyone exchanged glances and started to move about as if coming back to life after a temporary paralysis.

'I believe I'm right in saying that once he is restored to reason Pirandello's hero realizes that the only way to stay sane in a crazy world is to continue to pretend to be mad,' said Felix after some deliberation, still keeping away from the rest of the company. He was sitting on the windowsill, setting light, one by one, to the scraps of newspaper with numbers on them, and dropping the smouldering remnants into the ashtray. A sudden puff of wind set them aglow. A distant clap of thunder rang out like a shot. Suddenly the heat broke and collapsed as if felled by a stray bullet. A storm was coming. There was a gust of humid wind which made the smoking black scraps of burnt paper start to soar out of the window. From the outside it looked as if the flat were on fire.

23

Asylum

They discussed the menu for their modest dinner. They decided to have the remains of the pheasant as an hors d'oeuvre. Then fresh Scotch salmon baked in foil. For dessert Dr Genoni had brought up some chocolate, nuts and a bottle of vintage port from Lord Edward's cellars. Victor went outside for a breath of air, and through the windows he could be seen leaning on the fence watching the clouds that formed castles in the sky lit up by the setting sun.

'The conversation about his father and about fatherhood began when Edward-Edmund was already half delirious,' said Felix, 'after he'd finished the best part of a bottle of whisky and had moved on to the hash. He sat there on the floor in my room under the poster of Jerusalem, leaning against the wall, with his hash-pipe. The door was open, and in the sitting room Sorokopyatov could be heard holding forth about the fact that the proletariat was sex-drive incarnate, the libido of a class-structured society like England (Mary-Louise had started the conversation with her complaints about the sexual inadequacies of the English ruling classes), and during revolutions it attempted to kill its father the intellect that had given birth to it, i.e. the bourgeoisie. Thus the proletariat was as traumatized by an Oedipus complex as the rest of us; and revolution was quite literally a form of parricide. And so on, and so forth. Edward-Edmund commented on the assertion from his corner, observing that his father died in a very different manner. To which I replied that not every father owes his death to an Oedipus complex. Then he called us émigrés "children of the revolution". He was happy to be among us, because the post-revolutionary world was a world without fathers, lords or keepers. But we were not without maternal feelings, I said. Silva felt for him like a mother, and their relationship bordered on incest. If Silva was his mother, said Edward-Edmund, I

must be his eldest sister. We should call one another sisters.'
Silva smiled. 'I had no objections, since my own father won't
even acknowledge me as his prodigal son.'

'Is your father still alive?' asked Genoni, who'd been
listening to these reminiscences rather earnestly.

'I think so.' Felix shrugged. 'The only piece of news that's
bound to reach me would be the news of my father's death.
Since I've had no news from Russia I assume he's still alive.'

'You sound as if you're waiting for him to die,' said Genoni.

'All I mean is that I've absolutely no contacts in Russia any
more. I don't write to anyone, and unlike Silva I don't
telephone anyone, I don't keep in touch with anyone, especially
my family. In that kind of situation you only hear about your
family when someone's born or someone dies. Since my mother
died a long time ago, and there is no chance of my father being
born again, the only news I can look forward to is news of his
death. Of course, it's hard to say which of us is dead and which
alive, since the moment I emigrated they regarded me as having
passed on. But anyway, as far as my family's concerned I died a
long time ago, I died when they started to regard me as a Jew.'

'What do you mean, "regard as"? Aren't you Jewish, isn't
your family Jewish?' Genoni raised his eyebrows and checked
his notes.

'Who said so? Why so certain? Because my ex-wife's Jewish?
Or because I've got Israeli papers? Amazing, it's just like
Russia: once someone somewhere has taken you for a Jew it's
absolutely pointless to try to convince people otherwise.
Everyone's convinced you're just trying to get out of it, deny
your Jewishness,' he concluded on a note of exasperation,
meeting Silva's look of disbelief.

'Deny your Jewishness, you? As far as I can tell, you try and
ram it down everybody's throats!' exclaimed Dr Genoni.

'Up to a point. Because for someone like me, who was born in
the back of beyond, Jewishness meant life in the capital, the
chance to escape the provinces, get to Moscow, get abroad, and
so on,' and Felix waved his hand as if greeting the bright future.

'And where is "so on"? The beyond? Listen to me, dear boy,'
said Dr Genoni, giving Felix a slap on the shoulder. Felix's
identity twists were clearly too much even for Genoni's
psychodramatic method. 'Having heard in the course of our
conversation of so many cases of duplicity, aren't you simply a

232

bit envious, my dear Felix, of other people's doubleness? If you're not a Jew you're suffering from a dissimulation complex. Do you know what that is? It's when a madman, in order to conceal his genuine psychic sickness, pretends he's suffering from another psychosis, lunacy, form of craziness, which is more respectable, romantic, emotionally correct than his actual affliction. Do you see, he uses one sickness to conceal another?'

'As if someone stricken with the plague explained his loathing of the human race by the fact that he'd contracted rabies?' Curious, Felix helped his own psychiatrist with a sophisticated example to clarify the point. Too sophisticated, in fact.

'Not bad, not bad at all.' Dr Genoni nodded rather doubtfully. 'If only because your dissimulation is just as idiotic. So you tried to get rid of your provincial inferiority complex by trying to pass as a Jew?'

'In the first place, I didn't try to pass as a Jew.' Felix was visibly irritated by the suggestion. 'I simply discovered Jewish connections, to get me from the provinces to Moscow, and then abroad. In the second place, I can only tell you that in the Soviet Union it's better to be born a Jew than to remain a provincial. Have you any idea what a Soviet small town is like? A street, a street-lamp, a pharmacy. A pharmacy, a street, a street-lamp. The street-lamp is smashed, the pharmacy is shut and the street so dirty it's impassable. The master who teaches Marxism at the local school is killing flies in the empty café. In the administration building the Party boss is bawling out a cleaning woman. And everyone guzzles down the vodka. Ask Silva, ask Victor. There was a time in Moscow when the names of cities like London, New York and Paris sounded as if they were part of a spell, magical place-names from another world, from abroad, from beyond the limits of Soviet comprehension. But names like that didn't even register with us. In our hole in the provinces, Moscow itself seemed like another country, even Moscow Radio sounded like science fiction. That was a time when for a provincial to dream of getting to Moscow was the equivalent of a Muscovite dreaming of getting to London. The stamp in your passport, your residence requirement, meant a lifetime's sentence to the place of your birth – which would also be the place of your death. A living death as well. Prison and exile were better because all such sentences were for a limited time. But your residence requirement was for ever. And if you lost it that was for ever too. And when you don't have one and are living with your wife in Moscow illegally – it's still worse. Yes, of course I knew that no one would put me in prison or send me to the Gulag for signing some kind of protest letter; times had changed, and besides I wasn't that important. But they'd kick me out of Moscow. That was all there was to it, and no radio stations, no foreign intellectuals, no all-Russian patriarchs of the dissident movement, would be there to intervene. Because there would be nothing illegal about it there'd be no grounds for complaint. Infringement of the residence requirement. After university I'd lived in Moscow illegally, and the law would send me away. To my home town. It's not big and it's not small, and it's got one street full of potholes as if it had just been bombed.' Felix paused and tried to compose himself as he noticed the look of commiseration on Silva's face. 'Anyway I told all that to Victor that night and asked him to remove my signature from the protest letter.'

'What protest letter, what night?' Silva frowned, as if caught unawares and awaking from a dream.

'That famous letter protesting about the use of psychiatry for political purposes. Of course, it was Victor who distributed it. When they sent Avestin off to the psychiatric hospital, allegedly to have a medical commission review his case. But in fact' – he turned to Genoni in explanation – 'they'd been wanting to get him for ages for his underground essay on Pirandello, which treats the history of the KGB and the trials as another play by Pirandello – you know the kind of thing: all life is an interrogation and we're all under arrest.'

'The whole set of our current conversations is conducted along the lives of Pirandello. We have already discussed this point. What about signing the letter?' Dr Genoni pressed on.

'What could I do?' Felix sighed. 'Of course, to begin with, I more or less agreed to sign the letter in defence of Avestin. Together with Migulin he'd been my mentor, my maestro, and even though it had been some time ago, he was much more to me than just a name . . . It was one of those noisy farewell parties for my ex-wife at Transfiguration Square where there's a huge crowd, and everyone's convinced that the vodka is about to run out, so they all drink twice as much as they should, just in case. One of those dissident activists came up to me with a sheet of paper and said that they were collecting signatures to a protest letter, and explained about Avestin. Would I sign? Of course I would. A huge sheet of paper was shoved at me which already had masses of signatures on it. I asked where the letter was; presumably the signatures should be at the foot of the letter? I was told that they wouldn't actually be at the foot of the letter; the letter would be on one sheet of paper, the signatures on another – to preserve a separate record for the benefit of posterity. So there would just be a list of names at the foot of the letter. I wondered if I could read the letter. But I was told there was no point, Victor had been working on it, and he was to be trusted, and was currently putting the finishing touches to it in exile in Tula, while they were collecting signatures in Moscow. Fictional signatures to a fictional letter. I refused to sign. And that evening the letter was already being read on the BBC, and my name went out over the air-waves to two hundred million potential listeners. It turned out that Victor was not the least bit interested in what I thought about the letter; he was so convinced that I would sign that he included my name on the list without consulting me, and dictated the whole list over the telephone to some foreign correspondents. I felt terrible. It was obvious that the authorities were not going to let things slide, that I would come to their attention, and that they'd sling me out of Moscow in a heartbeat. And for what? In order to give Victor the chance to indulge his anti-Soviet eloquence I was going to have to spend the rest of my life in the town library of a provincial dung-heap! Besides which, according to Avestin's Pirandellistic view of the Soviet regime, it was not as if any kind of protest letter was about to change anything – it was simply a part of the KGB scenario. So basically that night, that plague-stricken night, I set it all before Victor and asked him to remove my name from the list.'

'So that's what you were talking about in the kitchen that night!' said Silva, clutching her temples like a schoolgirl taking an exam. 'Now I see why he never sent you his regards from the camps. Especially since the letter did have an effect: Avestin was released.'

'That's just another part of the Pirandello scenario: the principal director orders an actor to become a spectator for a time.' Dr Genoni inserted a stage direction.

'Yes, of course, everything is relative, but nevertheless they 'didn't actually kick you out of Moscow and you were perfectly safe,' Silva told Felix scornfully, as if reprimanding him for not having suffered enough.

'What can I tell you? Instead of going back to the provinces I cleared off to Israel,' Felix retorted brusquely.

'And Victor cleared off to the Gulag,' she reminded him harshly. 'But I must say you've got guts. It takes far more courage to remove your signature than it does to refuse to sign.'

'It seems to me that there's an important something about that night that you've forgotten.' He paused before raising his eyes to meet hers. 'It was precisely at the height of our argument about his letter that they arrested him. They took him away before your very eyes.'

'Why did you have to remind me?' asked Silva.

'All I meant was that, because of his arrest, he didn't have time to remove my signature. The letter appeared with my signature on it.'

24

A Bad Heart

The next day they were awakened a little after noon in the big house on the estate by the sound of shouting. The storm had lasted the rest of the night and all morning. Branches creaked and the wind howled, as if it were blowing the infected heat of the past month back into an earlier age of the history of mankind. Which is why the panic-stricken shouts coming from the ground floor at first seemed like geese or chickens, or a neighing horse, that the storm had caught out in the open. It was doubly wonderful to wake up and look through the window at a landscape that the storm had polished until it shone as if it were enamelled. Nature emerged from its bath-house quarantine disinfected from head to toe. Clouds scudded across the blue sky like snow-white washing in the wind. The sky was cured of a whitish ulcer of the sun. Now it looked down with a friendly wink as it played hide and seek with the clouds, sending mile-long shadows racing across the ground that momentarily transformed the outline of the hills, shifted clumps of trees and splashed colour on the tiled cottage roofs and the grasses growing in the fields.

'Edmund's run away. Into the woods. About a quarter of an hour ago.' Dr Genoni's booming voice and the clatter of his leather shoes were heard in the hall and then upstairs in the bedrooms. The household was awakening to the news. He was ordering people around. 'We'll have to start the shoot immediately. Get dressed.' He shook the sleepy participants in the shooting drama awake. Downstairs they found a complete selection of fancy dress: caps, shooting jackets, boots with gaiters and cartridge bags.

Washed clean by the dawn, after sobbing all night, the rustling woods greeted them warmly, as if they were glad to see the tardy guests. The thickets of hazel and holly, heather and gorse, overgrown with brambles and wild flowers, seemed alive, with fluttering birds calling to one another and other creatures moving through the undergrowth. Along the edge of the path, like servants in livery, grew lilac bushes and late rhododendrons that had got the time of year wrong, barring the way out to the meadow that sloped down to the far side of the wood, where the birds were due to fly from, driven out by the beaters. Sorokopyatov and Diana Myers, Golomstock, Liz Winter and Bukovsky were on one end of the line, with Braverman, Vera Chalidze, Gluzberg and Masha Slonim on the other, while Kupernik, Bernard Meares, Pyatigorsky and Mary-Louise made up the middle. They advanced in line up the sloping meadow, forming a tightening ring under the direction of Charlie, who had forgotten his cataract, two world wars, his arthritis and his corns. He darted from one subordinate to the next, up and down the line of beaters, egging them on with shouts, helping them rattle their noise-makers, beating the bushes and calling to drive the lazy pheasants out from their cover. The beaters, however, had to devote most of their energies to staying upright as they stumbled and picked their way through the undergrowth. Kupernik's cheek already bore the mark of a branch that had whipped back at him, Mary-Louise had a bleeding scratch on her elbow, while Sorokopyatov and Braverman continued to snarl at each other about which direction to take. Theoretically they were supposed to form a tightening ring around the pheasants that had taken cover in the wood, in the hope that they in turn would frighten and flush out Edmund, who was hiding somewhere in the thickets. The pheasants and Edmund would then be driven out of the wood up the slope and under the guns.

Up there Dr Genoni was in charge. He had placed Silva, Felix and Victor along the edge of the wood in a semi-circle. Each of them had a numbered stand (Karvalanov, of course, was number one), while the doctor himself got ready to act as their loader in the shoot, hefting their guns and making sure that they were loaded. All they could do now was wait. The very cries of the beaters below served to emphasize the magical silence, the enchantment of this spot, where it seemed that for a moment all movement had ceased. The sunlight shone in the clearings, picking out the swirling leaves in the treetops and the bracken down below. The lush grasses that had come alive again after the heat, swayed in the wind, and the shadows of the clouds were running away above the treetops as if they were ashamed of the naked blue sky, while the trees, embarrassed, muttered among themselves as if they hesitated to join in the dance of wind and shade in the magic semi-circle formed by the edge of the wood. Karvalanov tried to remember whether this was the meadow where he'd had his encounter with the terrifying keeper. How long ago was it? Eternity! His sense of déjà-vu increased as he heard a dog bark. Karvalanov froze and looked down the hill towards the shouts of the beaters and the guttural clucking of frightened pheasants.

And then they saw him. Standing very tall, with one shoulder thrust a trifle forward, the chief protagonist in the drama was walking through an overgrown thicket, towards some specific objective. He carried a switch of hazel in his hand, waving it as if he were the conductor of a huge invisible orchestra – up and down, right, left and across, more like a fanatical Muslim flagellating himself in a frenzy. With every step he took, with every blow of the switch to the surrounding bushes he let out a hoarse cry, and every time he did so a pheasant would fly out of the undergrowth as if from a conjurer's hat, and with every step more and more of the birds swarmed into the air. He felt hot; the heat that had blazed down on the grass yesterday was now blazing in his head. He threw aside his silk scarf, which was followed by his bow-tie and velvet jacket. He carried on now stripped to the waist, in his breeches. Kupernik, who was leading the beaters in hot pursuit, nearly fell as he stumbled over first one and then Edmund's other shoe. Mary-Louise, who had lost touch with the others, came across his white underpants hanging from a bough. She emerged on to the meadow brandishing them, as if she were calling for an armistice.

Up above, Karvalanov could see a scarecrow waving to her in panic-stricken response from the high field to the left with the dark woods behind it. And Karvalanov himself felt like a scarecrow in his shooting get-up, with the shiny leather boots that reflected the sky, a naked Edmund on his way up the hill, and dark clusters of pheasants flying through the air. His deerstalker made him look like two-headed Janus, but he lost track of any kind of foresight, or ability to look two ways at once. He could not tear his eyes away from the hypnotic nakedness of Edmund's body. His beard *à la* Prince Myshkin waving in the wind, he was smiling and flourishing his switch in time to an inaudible drumbeat. With every step his genitals swayed to the same martial rhythm. The inappropriateness of this total nudity against a background of fully clothed woods and meadows was so striking that it was this, and not the cloud of pheasants above Edmund's head, that compelled Karvalanov to bring his gun up to his shoulder.

At that moment Felix, who had completely forgotten that he was playing a part in a psychodrama, and that the guns were loaded with blanks, momentarily believed that his friend was really out to get his revenge. He threw himself at Karvalanov and managed to grab the gun and pull it down as he fired. Edmund checked, froze and sank slowly to his knees with an imploring outstretched arm, still holding the green switch. Ignoring the rituals of the shoot all the participants rushed up and surrounded Edmund, who was flat on his back. Dr Genoni approached, broke the circle with his hand in a typical gesture of authority, and knelt down and put his head to Edmund's chest. Beads of sweat appeared on his massive brow when he started to take his pulse.

'Who would have thought,' he muttered in evident confusion, 'who would have thought he had such a weak heart? I never anticipated a bad heart.'

'My plans were in the best traditions of shock therapy. Victor was dressed as Lord Edward's father, and Edmund had taken the place of his father the keeper, who was killed during a pheasant shoot through Edmund's fault when he was a child. Are you following?' asked Dr Genoni, trying to avoid the eyes of his listerners staring at him in shock and bewilderment. He clearly needed to convince himself as much as the others. 'The executioner takes the place of the victim, and thus becomes his own victim. His guilt is purged by the punishment and in consequence he regains his sanity. Elementary, is it not?' Judging by the sweat on his brow and his rapid-fire speech Dr Genoni was having trouble concealing his own state of shock, his sense of embarrassment, even of fear. He could be sure of nothing and was unwilling to make any kind of psychiatric diagnosis until Edmund came to. Bearing in mind that the massive psychic shock induced by the blank round had caused a serious heart attack, it would, he suggested, be a matter of some weeks before he fully regained consciousness. Dr Genoni accompanied his explanation with professional pats on the shoulder, shakings of the head and buttonholings. Taking each one of them by the elbow in turn, one by one, he moved the guests out of the huge room on the first floor of the big house, where Edmund was lying in bed near the window. Nurses were clustered round him, busy with hypodermics and oxygen. Despite the reigning chaos and confusion, Dr Genoni ensured that all the guests except for Silva, Felix and Victor were packed off to London in taxis after they had had some tea and sandwiches – it should be said that nobody touched the sandwiches. Genoni only put a foot wrong when suggesting that each of the departing guests take the customary brace of pheasants with them – as he suddenly remembered that the shoot had all been a piece of fiction.

All this time Karvalanov never let go of the whisky bottle. But it wasn't making him drunk, he simply had red eyes as if he hadn't slept. He too was unable to recover from a kind of state of shock, his hands shook and now and again tears would roll down his cheek, which he was unable or unwilling to stop. Genoni suggested he give him a tranquillizing shot, but Victor waved him angrily away. Felix appeared to have survived the shooting incident better than anyone, silently pacing from one corner of the room to the other, but then he suddenly started to utter heart-rending screams to the effect that he hadn't left Russia to get involved in hysterical scenes about guilt and complicity. Silva was sitting with her legs drawn up in a huge armchair, her head on her knees, staring motionless out of the window.

'Did you notice that one of the pheasants dropped dead out of the sky?' she asked suddenly without turning her head.

'Isn't that the point of a pheasant shoot?' Karvalanov replied hoarsely.

'You've forgotten, the guns were all loaded with blanks,' Dr Genoni was anxious to remind them.

'Which means that the pheasant had a heart attack too.' Felix couldn't resist the black humour. 'Besides, what makes you so sure that all the guns were loaded with blanks?'

'Good old Charlie took care of all the fitting out,' said Dr Genoni in a voice that lacked conviction. 'We have no reason not to believe him. Besides, in a sense he's your oldest friend. An old soldier, fought in three wars.'

'It seems as if he's been concussed once too often. He gets everything muddled up, and besides he's got that cataract in one eye,' said Felix. 'For example, he declared that Edmund wasn't his nephew at all.'

'What made him say that all of a sudden?' asked Victor.

'It seems that he lacks some kind of a birthmark under his right nipple, or a scar on his left ear . . . the usual kind of thing. He hadn't seen that nephew of his for twenty years, although he lived just round the corner, but that's the way they are in this country. I wouldn't trust the senile old fool,' said Felix.

'Did Charlie ever say that Edmund was his nephew?' asked Silva, slowly getting drawn into a game of detective work. It definitely helped clear the atmosphere of gloomy hysteria.

'Certainly. He said that the dead keeper's son was his nephew. He must have meant Edmund, who else?' asked Felix.

'What do you mean? What about the present keeper, who is at the gamekeepers' conference in East Berlin?' said Karvalanov. All three of them suddenly got very interested in the keepers' nephews and their origins.

'We can't ask him, he won't be back for three more weeks: annual holidays, the unions!' said Dr Genoni.

'But if Edmund isn't his nephew that means he's not the keeper's son, so who is he?' Silva turned to the doctor.

'I know what you want, you want Edmund the keeper to be Lord Edward,' said Felix with a sarcastic grin.

'If Charlie hasn't seen his nephew for twenty years, we have to wonder how much he knows about his brother's family affairs,' said Karvalanov, whose sense of logic had been honed by years of expert interrogation.

'Perhaps Edmund is just another son of the gamekeeper, Charlie's brother, a son that Charlie never knew about, from another marriage perhaps?'

'And this keeper may be Charlie's nephew, but he's the son of another of Charlie's brothers, not the dead keeper. Because all the time Charlie was talking about his nephew as such, not about the actual son of his actual brother the keeper.' Dr Genoni was glad to try out any kind of explanation for this identity mix-up.

'My head's spinning,' said Silva.

'But the idea of Edward pretending to be Edmund is an interesting one,' went on Dr Genoni, rubbing his chin.

242

'Actually Edmund is not so much suffering from paranoia as from schizophrenia, a split personality. This wouldn't mean that his other self would be incapable of writing business letters, giving orders, doing charitable work and travelling all over the world. It's possible, it's perfectly possible, that we're dealing here with a very curious form of dissimulation.'

'Who's dissimulating and why?' asked Silva. She turned her gaze back from the window, where the sun was winking at her between the scudding clouds.

'Edward pretending to be Edmund,' Dr Genoni replied. He was standing in the middle of the room, his hands in his pockets, his lower lip jutting out thoughtfully. 'Let me repeat that dissimulation is an attempt to conceal one's actual illness by pretending you are afflicted by a different and psycholigically more acceptable condition which removes the sense of guilt and shame. The sick man knows that we know him to be disturbed, and tries to convince us to accept his version of his disturbance. If he really is the son of a lord, he finds it more acceptable to pretend to be the son of a keeper who believes himself to be the son of a lord, than to have to admit he really is the son of a lord pretending to be the son of a keeper.'

'But why should a mentally disturbed lord feel more comfortable imagining that he is a mentally disturbed keeper?' asked Victor.

'I'll try to explain. Suppose the lord accidentally killed the keeper during the shoot many years ago, because it was the lord's son, not the keeper's, who was playing around his feet. That would mean that the tragic incident was no longer a case of parricide: simply a banal instance of manslaughter, where the son of an aristocrat turned out to have caused the death of a keeper, a member of the lower classes. I think that was why in that accident the keeper broke all the rules and came into range of the guns. He must have seen something that no one else had noticed, the lord's son crawling about in the long grass. He decided to try to get him away from there, out of danger.' Genoni gave his brow a weary and profound professorial rub. 'If our principal character is a lord and not a keeper, it means that he, our lord, is prepared to assume the sin of parricide, and present the affair in such a way that it appears that the lower classes are killing one another simply to keep his aristocratic caste out of the whole sorry business.'

'So that means that Edmund is Edward, who thinks he's an Edmund who thinks he's Edward?' Silva repeated, like a schoolgirl trying to take in a lesson.

'We'll just have to ask Edward-Edmund,' shrugged Dr Genoni. 'But we won't know the answer until our hero comes to. Why don't the three of you move into my clinic?' His bulldog features were imploring. 'We'll try and cure your syndrome of Oedipal dissimulation, Victor. We'll try and get rid of your duality complex, Felix, and as for you, Silva, if things work out well and you play your cards right you have a chance of becoming the First Lady of the Third Wave.' He winked at all three of them. 'Besides I should tell you that there was a fire in Silva's flat, caused either by the hash-pipe or some paper burning in an ashtray, although some say that neighbours set fire to it because they couldn't take the noise any more. So you've nowhere to go back to. Besides, we could have an interesting discussion about the practice of bestiality – occurring between prisoners and guard dogs in corrective labour camps. What about it?'

25

Asylum

They sat down to dinner at sunset. The day was almost over, and although it was still light outside, as twilight often is under a clear sky, the chickens and geese had fallen silent, and had obviously gone to bed, while the horses had been stabled. The dogs lay down by the fireguard, determined, like the humans, not to tear their eyes away from the blazing logs. The flames reflected in the windowpane blended with the golden rays of the setting sun that broke through the clouds shooting off in various directions like broken columns in the ruins of an ancient temple. An impression of stage lighting distorted the view, and created a state of geographical confusion which made the hills of Kent seem more like the hills of Jerusalem or the dales of Verona.

'How's the nail'? Victor inquired of Felix, watching him cracking nuts with gusto. There were hazelnuts, Greek nuts, pecans with their deceptively fragile looking pink shell, and warty Brazils in their triangular armour. Having tested his strength and skill on one of each, Felix put down the nutcrackers and looked carefully at the thumbnail that had once been split in two. The nail looked as whole and complete in its roundness and the quality of its finish as the nutshell that once upon a time had been the cause of its splitting.

'Since I split the nail in Italy, I think we can use it to round off the subject of Pirandellism – that is to say split personality,' said Felix, waving his new nail at Victor.

'In Italy?' asked Victor. 'I thought you did it in Moscow, when you were cracking nuts on my birthday.' He looked straight into Felix's eyes. Felix almost choked on a mouthful of nuts.

'How do you know I cracked nuts in Moscow on your birthday?' he asked when he got his breath back after much slapping on the back and coughing. 'You weren't there. You were late.'

'You told me so yourself, told me about the birthday parcel

from Lord Edward. It had nuts in it. I'm sure that you and Silva cracked them that night I got arrested again,' said Victor ingenuously.

'So you knew that I . . . was with Silva that night?' mumbled Felix.

'Of course I did, you told me all about it,' answered a smiling Victor as he observed the way that Felix, looking miserably guilty and shifty, was trying not to catch his eye. 'It's much easier to catch out someone telling half-truths than it is to nail a barefaced liar,' he said after a moment. 'Because when you tell half-truths you have to remember which half you've kept quiet about. It's better to tell whoppers. That night you told me that Silva had come for the birthday, but you kept quiet about the fact that she had stayed, and was still there in the next room when they arrested me. When I talked about your half-truth you presumed that I knew about the semi-lie. But actually I knew the whole truth all along. When they were taking me away I turned round for a last look and saw her standing by the window. But she was behind glass and it looked like a mirage, a ghost I'd conjured up, a half-truth.'

'I knew you'd seen me,' said Silva after a moment of deathly silence, biting her lip.

'And I knew that you knew.' Victor shrugged it off. 'But up to now none of us has ventured to refute the oh so convenient illusion that what I saw was an illusion.'

'You didn't ask for refutations, or for justifications. Never, ever. Why?' asked Silva with mounting anger.

'Because, as we all do, he prefers to play the part of the persecuted martyr, and the third that makes it a crowd. And all around the guilty parties go wringing their hands. And he is – the Saviour,' said Felix, reverting to his customary irony and sarcasm to hide his embarrassment.

'I'm afraid that in Russia everyone believes himself to be the Saviour,' said Dr Genoni. 'There are more than enough Saviours to go round the population, but nobody seems to want to be saved.'

'One day I escaped from a camp,' said Victor, ignoring the blasphemous rejoinder. 'Not a corrective labour camp, a Pioneers' camp, although it was scarcely any better. The instructors were sadists, we were fed rotten meat, we spent all day doing drill and singing patriotic songs in unison. I stole some rusks from the dining room and ran away to Moscow, on

246

the electric train, without a ticket. I knew that my father was away on official business, that the housekeeper was staying with her relatives in the country and that the key was under the mat. The empty summery flat, a wooden floor warmed by the sun, white covers on the furniture, the smell of dust, of no one living there, of freedom, and I was all alone there! I remember how feverishly I wondered whether to start with the cans of jam in the locked cupboard, or to try the bottle of foreign liqueur in the glass-fronted sideboard. And then came the sound of a key turning in the front door. I just had time to hide behind my bedroom cupboard. There were two of them, my father and the house-keeper, Klava. I recognized her voice, or rather her laughter. They'd obviously been away together somewhere, were stamping about in the corridor rattling china, and I could smell food. I wanted to sneak out of the front door, but I was afraid I'd run into them in the corridor. They finally went into the sitting room and sat down on the sofa, which was set against the wall that I was hiding behind. Through the wall I could hear Klava's laughter, which turned into a kind of crazed giggling and squealing. My father was grunting and groaning, but then they started making such extraordinary noises and using such incredible words that even I, a ten-year-old with only the vaguest ideas of what grown-ups did in bed, couldn't hear it all without blushing. I covered my ears. My father couldn't say things like that. Someone had taken his place. I ran down the corridor, slammed the door and tore downstairs. Running out and across the yard I gave a frightened look at our windows. My father was standing there naked, his face glued to the glass. I'm sure he saw me look round. I'm sure that he knew I'd seen him. He stepped back and vanished into the depths of the room.'

'Where did you go?' asked Dr Genoni, a pained expression on his face. It was all too real for his taste.

'Nowhere. That is to say I went back to camp. I got back at night. No one even realized that I'd run away. They all thought I'd got lost when they were out hiking. They were about to start a search when I got back.'

'A biblical sense of guilt at one's father's nakedness is sublimated into a hatred of the system that forced you to witness it.' Dr Genoni drummed his fingers on the table. 'But rejected by your father, and once more feeling defenceless, naked, before the system, you started to identify it with your father. There's an interesting mutual relationship here between your sense of guilt as witness to your father's nakedness, and the sense of shame you experience when you stand ideologically naked before your teacher (or the political system). Guilt leads to shame, and hence to rebellion. And don't forget the curious parallel between the Judaic sense of guilt and the sense of shame in Islam, which is a pupil's continuation of Judaism, if you see what I mean. In this respect, Felix, it would be interesting to recall your Jerusalemic exile as a prisoner of Zion . . .' He was starting to ramble when Victor interrupted him.

'I told my story in answer to the question why didn't I seek refutation or justification with respect to that night in Moscow with Felix and Silva in the window.' He paused. 'A week after I had decided to absent myself from camp, it was parents' day, and my father came down to visit me with some presents. He sat there silently and without looking at me. I realized that he was letting me know that he preferred not to know that I knew anything. Didn't just the same thing happen with us? Experience subsequently taught me that talking about things like that forces people into making public confessions, requires them to make a clean breast of things, and obliges them to go on record with the admission of their guilt. But we're not in the KGB or a Zinovy Zinik novel in which subtly woven plotting obliges the heroes to confess. Perhaps there's been more than enough repenting and confessing!'

He suddenly noticed that the others were looking at something over his shoulder. Through the open door a pheasant stepped majestically out of the twilight and into the room. With the bronze eye markings glowing in the candlelight, and a neck the colour of a green English meadow, he moved his head from side to side, as if he were bowing to the four of them. An extraordinary sound of knocking, clucking and whistling came from the small coppice at the far end of the field. The pheasant raised his head, listened and then turned and hurried across the meadow towards the familiar call. Was it the keeper, back again and calling his birds for a late feed?

'I fear we shall have to hear out yet another confession,' said Dr Genoni, nodding at the nurse running towards them along the gravel path. She was waving at them. 'He's come to, he's come to, he's himself again, himself!' they could hear her voice echoing.

The four of them dutifully got up, and without saying a word they all moved off in the same direction as the pheasant. A pack of dogs trotted quietly behind them.